TRANSGRESSIONS

VOLUME 3

Four brand new novellas

DONALD E. WESTLAKE
ANNE PERRY
SHARYN McCRUMB
JOHN FARRIS

Edited by Ed McBain

An Orion paperback

First published in Great Britain in 2005
by Orion
This paperback edition published in 2007
by Orion Books Ltd,
Orion House, 5 Upper St Martin's Lane,
London WC2H 9EA

1 3 5 7 9 10 8 6 4 2

A CIP catalogue record for this book
is available from the British Library.

ISBN-13: 978-0-7528-7949-9

Printed in Great Britain by Clays Ltd, St Ives plc

The Orion Publishing Group's policy is to use papers that
are natural, renewable and recyclable products and made
from wood grown in sustainable forests. The logging and
manufacturing processes are expected to conform to the
environmental regulations of the country of origin.

www.orionbooks.co.uk

Contents

Introduction

When I was writing novellas for the pulp magazines back in the 1950s, we still called them "novelettes," and all I knew about the form was that it was long and it paid half a cent a word. This meant that if I wrote 10,000 words, the average length of a novelette back then, I would sooner or later get a check for five hundred dollars. This was not bad pay for a struggling young writer.

A novella today can run anywhere from 10,000 to 40,000 words. Longer than a short story (5,000 words) but much shorter than a novel (at least 60,000 words) it combines the immediacy of the former with the depth of the latter, and it ain't easy to write. In fact, given the difficulty of the form, and the scarcity of markets for novellas, it is surprising that any writers today are writing them at all.

But here was the brilliant idea.

Round up the best writers of mystery, crime, and suspense novels, and ask them to write a brand-new novella for a collection of similarly superb novellas to be published anywhere in the world for the very first time. Does that sound keen, or what? In a perfect world, *yes*, it *is* a wonderful idea, and here is your novella, sir, thank you very much for asking me to contribute.

But many of the bestselling novelists I approached had never written a novella in their lives. (Some of them had never even written a short story!) Up went the hands in mock horror. "What! A novella? I wouldn't even know how to *begin* one." Others thought that writing a novella ("*How* long did you say it had to be?") would constitute a wonderful challenge, but bestselling novelists are busy people with publishing contracts to fulfill and deadlines to meet, and however intriguing the invitation may have seemed at first, stark reality reared its ugly head, and so . . .

"Gee, thanks for thinking of me, but I'm already three months behind deadline," or . . .

"My publisher would *kill* me if I even dreamed of writing something for another house," or . . .

"Try me again a year from now," or . . .

"Have you asked X? Or Y? Or Z?"

What it got down to in the end was a matter of timing and luck. In some cases, a writer I desperately wanted was happily between novels and just happened to have some free time on his/her hands. In other cases, a writer had an idea that was too short for a novel but too long for a short story, so yes, what a wonderful opportunity! In yet other cases, a writer wanted to introduce a new character he or she had been thinking about for some time. In each and every case, the formidable task of writing fiction that fell somewhere between 10,000 and 40,000 words seemed an exciting challenge, and the response was enthusiastic.

Except for length and a loose adherence to crime, mystery, or suspense, I placed no restrictions upon the writers who agreed to contribute. The results are as astonishing as they are brilliant. The ten novellas that follow are as varied as the men and women who concocted them, but they all exhibit the same devoted passion and the same extraordinary writing. More than that, there is an underlying sense here that the writer is attempting something new and unexpected, and willing to share his or her own surprises with us. Just as their names are in alphabetical order on the book jacket, so do their stories follow in reverse alphabetical order: I have no favorites among them. I love them all equally.

Enjoy!

ED MCBAIN
Weston, Connecticut
August 2004

TRANSGRESSIONS

VOLUME 3

DONALD E. WESTLAKE

It's an accepted fact that **Donald E. Westlake** has excelled at every single subgenre the mystery field has to offer. Humorous books such as *Sacred Monster* and the John Dortmunder series; terrifying books like *The Ax*, about a man who wants vengeance on the company that downsized him out of a job, and probably Westlake's most accomplished novel; and hard-boiled books that include the Parker series, a benchmark in the noir world of professional thieves and to which he recently returned to great acclaim; and insider books like *The Hook*, a twisty thriller about the perils and pitfalls of being a writer. One learns from his novels and short stories that he is possessed of a remarkable intelligence, and that he can translate that intelligence into plot, character, and realistic prose with what appears to be astonishing ease. He is the sort of writer other writers study endlessly; every Westlake novel has something to teach authors, no matter how long they've been at the word processor. And he seems to have been discovered—at last and long overdue—by a mass audience. His recent books include *The Road to Ruin*, the latest novel chronicling the misadventures of inept thief John Dortmunder, and *Thieves' Dozen*, a long-awaited collection of the Dortmunder short stories.

WALKING AROUND
MONEY

Donald E. Westlake

1

"Ever since I reformed," the man called Querk said, "I been havin' trouble to sleep at night."

This was a symptom Dortmunder had never heard of before; on the other hand, he didn't know that many people who'd reformed. "Huh," he said. He really didn't know this man called Querk, so he didn't have a lot to say so far.

But Querk did. "It's my nerves," he explained, and he looked as though it was his nerves. A skinny little guy, maybe fifty, with a long face, heavy black eyebrows over banana nose over thin-lipped mouth over long bony chin, he fidgeted constantly on that wire-mesh chair in Paley Park, a vest-pocket park on East 53rd Street in Manhattan, between Fifth and Madison Avenues.

It's a very nice park, Paley Park, right in the middle of midtown, just forty-two feet wide and not quite a block deep, up several steps from the level of 53rd Street. The building walls on both sides are covered in ivy, and tall honey locust trees form a kind of leafy roof in the summer, which is what at this moment it was.

But the best thing about Paley Park is the wall of water at the back, a constant flow down the rear wall, splashing into a trough to be recycled, making a very nice kind of *shooshing* sound that almost completely covers the roar of the traffic, which makes for a peaceful retreat right there in the middle of everything and also makes it possible for two or three people—John Dortmunder, say, and his friend Andy Kelp, and the man called Querk, for instance—to sit near the wall of water and have a nice conversation that nobody, no matter what kind of microphone they've got, is going to record. It's amazing, really, that every criminal enterprise in the city of New York isn't plotted in Paley Park; or maybe they are.

"You see how it is," the man called Querk said, and lifted both hands out of his lap to hold them in front of himself, where they trembled like a paint-mixing machine. "It's a good thing," he said, "I wasn't a pickpocket before I reformed."

"Huh," Dortmunder commented.

"Or a safecracker," Kelp said.

"Well, I was," Querk told him. "But I was one of your liquid nitro persuasion, you know. Drill your hole next to the combination, pour in your jelly, stuff the detonator in there, stand back. No nerves involved at all."

"Huh," Dortmunder said.

Querk frowned at him. "You got asthma?"

"No," Dortmunder said. "I was just agreeing with you."

"If you say so." Querk frowned at the curtain of water, which just kept *shooshing* down that wall in front of them, splashing in the trough, never stopping for a second. You wouldn't want to stay in Paley Park *too* long.

"The point is," Querk said, "before I reformed, I'd always get a good night's sleep, because I knew I was careful and everything was in its place, so I could relax. But then, the last time I went up, I decided I was too old for jail. You know, there comes a point, you say, jail is a job for the young." He gave a sidelong look at Dortmunder. "You gonna do that *huh* thing again?"

"Only if you want me to."

"We'll skip it, then," Querk said, and said, "This last time in, I learned another trade, you know how you always learn these trades on the inside. Air-conditioner repair, dry cleaning. This last time, I learned to be a printer."

"Huh," Dortmunder said. "I mean, that's good, you're a printer."

"Except," Querk said, "I'm not. I get out, I go to this printing plant upstate, up near where my cousin lives, I figure I'll stay with him, he's always been your straight arrow, I can get a look at an honest person up close, see how it's done, but when I go to the printer to say look at this skill the State of New York gave me, they said, we don't do it like that any more, we use computers now." Querk shook his head. "Is that the criminal justice system for you, right there?" he wanted to know. "They spend all this time and money, they teach me an obsolete trade."

Kelp said, "What you wanted to learn was computers."

"Well, what I got," Querk said, "I got a job at the printing plant, only not a printer. I'm a loader, when the different papers come in, I drive around in this forklift, put the papers where they go, different papers for different jobs. But because I'm reformed," Querk went on, "and this isn't the trade I learned, this is just going back and forth on a forklift truck, I don't ever feel like I *done* anything. No planning, no preparation, nothing to be careful about. I get uneasy, I got no structure in my life, and the result is, I sleep lousy. Then, no sleep, I'm on the forklift, half the time I almost drive it into a wall."

Dortmunder could see how that might happen. People are creatures of habit, and if you lose a habit that's important to you—being on the run, for instance—it could throw off your whatayacallit. Biorhythm. Can't sleep. Could happen.

Dortmunder and Andy Kelp and the man called Querk sat in silence (*shoosh*) a while, contemplating the position Querk found himself in, sitting here together on these nice wire-mesh chairs in the middle of New York in August, which of course meant it wasn't New York at all, not the real New York, but the other New York, the August New York.

In August, the shrinks are all out of town, so the rest of the city population looks calmer, less stressed. Also, a lot of *those* are out of town, as well, replaced by American tourists in pastel polyester and foreign tourists in vinyl and corduroy. August among the tourists is like all at once living in a big herd of cows; slow, fat, dumb, and no idea where they're going.

What Dortmunder had no idea was where *Querk* was going. All he knew was, Kelp had phoned him this morning to say there was a guy they might talk to who might have something to say and the name the guy was using as a password was Harry Matlock. Well, Harry Matlock was a guy Dortmunder had worked with in the past, with Matlock's partner Ralph Demrovsky, but it seemed to him the last time he'd seen Ralph, during a little exercise in Las Vegas, Harry wasn't there. So how good a passport *was* that, after all this time? That's why Dortmunder's part of the conversation so far, and on into the unforeseeable future, consisted primarily of *huh*.

"So finally," the man called Querk said, breaking a long *shoosh*, "I couldn't take it any more. I'm imitating my cousin, walkin the straight and narrow, and that's what it feels like, I'm *imitating* my cousin. Once a month I drive up to this town called Hudson, see my lady parole officer, I *got nothin to hide*. How can you talk to a parole officer in a circumstance like that? She keeps giving me these suspicious looks, and I know why. I got nothin' to tell her but the truth."

"Jeez, that's tough," Kelp said.

"You know it." Querk shook his head. "And all along," he said, "I've got a caper right there, right at the printing plant, staring me in the face, I don't want to see it, I don't want to know about it, I gotta act like I'm deaf and dumb and blind."

Dortmunder couldn't help himself; he said, "At the printing plant?"

"Oh, sure, I know," Querk said. "Your inside job, I'm first in line to get my old cell back. But that isn't the way it works." Querk seemed very earnest about this. "The only way this scheme works," he said, "is if the plant never knows it happened. If they find out, we don't make a thing."

Dortmunder said, "It's a heist."

"A *quiet* heist," Querk told him. "No hostages, no explosions, no standoffs. In, out, nobody ever knows it happened. Believe me, the only way this scores for us is if nobody ever knows anything went missing."

"Huh," Dortmunder said.

"You oughta try cough drops," Querk suggested. "But the point here is, this is a beautiful job, and I'm sick of getting no sleep, so maybe I'll leave reform alone for a while. But."

"Sure," Kelp said, because there was always a "but."

"I can't do it alone," Querk told them. "This is not a one-man job. So I was on the inside for six and a half years, and I'm both reformed *and* upstate for almost eighteen months, so I'm well and truly out of the picture. I try calling around, everybody's inside or dead or disappeared, and finally I reach Harry Matlock, that I knew years ago, when he first partnered up with Ralph Demrovsky, and now *Harry's* retired."

"I thought he maybe was," Dortmunder said.

Querk nodded. "He told me," he said, "*he's* not reformed, he's retired. It's a different thing. 'I didn't reform,' he told me, 'I just lost my nerve. So I retired.'"

"Pretty much the same thing," Kelp suggested.

"But with more dignity," Querk told him. "So he gave me your name, Andy Kelp, and now here we are, and we look each other over."

"Right," Kelp said. "So what next?"

"Well," Querk said, "I check you guys out, and if you seem—"

Dortmunder said, "What? *You* check *us* out?" He'd thought the interview was supposed to go in the other direction.

"Naturally," Querk said. "I don't want us goin' along and goin' along, everything's fine, and all of a sudden you yell *surprise* and pull out a badge."

"That would surprise the hell out of *me*," Dortmunder told him.

"We're strangers to each other," Querk pointed out. "I gave Kelp a few names, he could check on me, and he gave me a few names, I could check on him and you both—"

"Huh," Dortmunder said.

"So after we all meet here now," Querk said, "and we check each other out, and we think it's gonna be okay, I'll call Andy here, same as this time, and if you two are satisfied, we can make another meet."

Dortmunder said, "You didn't tell us what the heist is."

"That's right," Querk said. Looking around, he said, "Okay with you guys if I go first? You'll wanna talk about me behind my back anyway."

"Sure," Kelp agreed. "Nice to meet you, Kirby," because, Querk had said, that was his first name.

"You, too," Querk said, and nodded at Dortmunder. "I like the way you keep your own counsel."

"Uh huh," Dortmunder said.

2

If you walk far enough into the west side, even in August, you can find a bar without tourists, ferns, or menus, and where the lights won't offend your eyes. In such a place, a little later that afternoon,

Dortmunder and Kelp hunched over beers in a black Formica booth and muttered together, while the bartender behind his bar some distance away leaned his elbows on the *Daily News*, and the three other customers, here and there around the place, muttered to themselves in lieu of company.

"I'm not sure what I think about this guy," Dortmunder muttered.

"He *seems* okay." Kelp shrugged. "I mean, I could buy his story. Reforming and all."

"But he's pretty cagy," Dortmunder muttered.

"Well, sure. He don't know us."

"He doesn't tell us the caper."

"That's sensible, John."

"He's living upstate." Dortmunder spread his hands. "*Where* upstate? Where's this printing plant? All he says is he goes to some place called Hudson to see his parole officer."

Kelp nodded, being open-minded. "Look at it from his point of view," he muttered. "If things don't work out between him and us, and he's gonna go ahead with some other guys, why does he wanna have to worry we're somewhere in the background, lookin to cut in?"

"I mean, what kind of heist is this?" Dortmunder complained. "You steal something from this plant, and the plant isn't supposed to *notice*? 'Hey, didn't we use to have a whatchacallit over here?' You take something, especially you take something with some value on it, people notice."

"Well, that's an intriguing part of it," Kelp muttered.

"Intriguing."

"Also," Kelp muttered, leaning closer, "August is a good time to get out of town. Go upstate, up into the mountains, a little cool air, how bad could it be?"

"I've been upstate," Dortmunder reminded him. "I *know* how bad it could be."

"Not that bad, John. And you were up there in the winter."

"*And* the fall," Dortmunder muttered. "Two different times."

"They both worked out okay."

"Okay? Every time I leave the five boroughs," Dortmunder insisted, "I regret it."

"Still," Kelp muttered, "we shouldn't just say no to this, without giving it a chance."

Dortmunder made an irritable shrug. He'd had his say.

"I don't know about *your* finances, John," Kelp went on (although he did), "but mine are pretty shaky. A nice little upstate heist might be just the ticket."

Dortmunder frowned at his beer.

"I tell you what we should do," Kelp said. "We should find old Harry Matlock, get the skinny on this guy Querk, *then* make up our minds. Whadaya say?"

"Mutter," Dortmunder muttered.

3

Where do you find a retired guy, sometime in August? Try a golf course; a municipal golf course.

"There he is, over there," Kelp said, pointing. "Tossing the ball out of that sand trap."

Dortmunder said, "Is that in the rules?"

"Well, remember," Kelp said. "He's retired, not reformed."

This particular municipal golf course was in Brooklyn, not far enough from the Atlantic to keep you from smelling what the ocean offers for sea air these days. Duffers speckled the greensward as Dortmunder and Kelp strolled over the fairway toward where Harry Matlock, who was fatter than he used to be and who'd always been thought of by everybody who knew him as fat, was struggling out of the sand trap, looking as though he needed an assistant to toss *him* up onto the grass. He was also probably as bald as ever, but you couldn't tell because he was wearing a big pillowy maroon tam-o'-shanter with a woolly black ball on top and a little paisley spitcurl coming out the back. The rest of his garb was a pale blue polo shirt under an open white cashmere cardigan, red plaid pants very wide in the seat and leg, and bright toad-green golf shoes with little cleats like chipmunk teeth. This was a man in retirement.

"Hey, Harry!" Kelp shouted, and a guy off to his left sliced his shot then glared at Kelp, who didn't notice.

Harry looked over, recognized them, and waved with a big smile, but didn't shout. When they got closer, he said, "Hi, Andy, hi, John, you're here about Kirby Querk."

"Sure," Kelp said.

Harry waved his golf club in a direction, saying, "Walk with me, my foursome's up there somewhere, we can talk." Then, pausing to kick his golf ball toward the far-distant flag, he picked up his big bulky leather golf bag by its strap, and started to stroll, dragging the pretty full golf bag behind him, leaving a crease in the fairway.

As they walked, Dortmunder said, "These your own rules?"

"When only God can see you, John," Harry told him, "there are no rules. And when it comes to Querk, I wouldn't say I know what the rules are."

Sounding alarmed, Kelp said, "You mean, you wouldn't recommend him? But you sent him to me."

"No, that's not exactly what I— Hold on." Harry kicked the ball again, then said, "Andy, would you do me a favor? Drag this bag around for a while? This arm's gettin longer than that arm."

Kelp said, "I think you're supposed to carry it on your shoulder."

"I tried that," Harry said, "and it winds up, one shoulder lower than the other." He extended the strap toward Kelp, with a little pleading gesture. "Just till we get to the green," he said.

Kelp had not known his visit to the golf course today would end with his being a caddy, but he shrugged and said, "Okay. Till the green."

"Thanks, Andy."

Kelp hefted the bag up onto his shoulder, and he *looked* like a caddy. All he needed was the big-billed cloth cap and the tee stuck behind his ear. He did have the right put-upon expression.

Harry ambled on, in the direction he'd kicked the ball, and said, "About Querk, I don't know anything bad about the guy, it's only I don't know that much good about him either."

Dortmunder said, "You worked with him?"

"A few times. Me and Ralph— He didn't retire when I did." Harry Matlock and Ralph Demrovsky had been a burglary team so quick and so greedy they used to travel in a van, just in case they came across anything large.

Kelp said, "Ralph's still working?"

"No, he's in Sing Sing," Harry said. "He should of retired when I did. Hold on." He stopped, just behind his ball, and squinted toward the green, where three guys dressed from the same grab bag stood around waiting, all of them looking this way.

"I think I gotta hit it now," Harry said. "Stand back a ways, I'm still kinda wild at this."

They stood well back, and Harry addressed the ball. Then he addressed the ball some more. When he'd addressed the ball long enough for an entire post office, he took a whack at it and it went somewhere. Not toward the flag down there, exactly, but at least not behind them.

"Well, the point of it is the walk," Harry said. As he sauntered off in the direction the ball had gone, trailed by Dortmunder and Kelp, he said, "Ralph and me used to team up with Querk, maybe four, five times over the years. He's never the first choice, you know."

"No?"

"No. He's competent," Harry allowed, "he'll get you in where you want to get in, but there are guys that are better. Wally Whistler. Herman Jones."

"They're good," Kelp agreed.

"They are," Harry said. "But if some time the guy we wanted was sick or on the lam or put away, there was nothing wrong with Querk."

Kelp said, "Harry, you sent him to me, but you don't sound enthusiastic."

"I'm not *not* enthusiastic," Harry said. He stopped to look at his ball, sitting there in the middle of an ocean of fairway, with the green like an island some way off, ahead and to the right. Two of the guys waiting over there were now sitting down, on the ground. "I don't know about this thing," Harry said. "Let me see those other clubs."

Kelp unshouldered the bag and put it on the ground, so Harry could make his selection. While Harry frowned over his holdings in clubs, Kelp said, "What is it keeps you from being one hundred percent enthusiastic?"

Harry nodded, still looking at the clubs in the bag. Then he looked at Kelp. "I'll tell you," he said. "This is *his* heist. I never been around him when it's his own thing. Ralph and me, we'd bring him in, point to a door, a gate, a safe, whatever, say, 'Open that, Kirby,' and he'd do it. Competent. Not an artist, but competent. How is he when it's his own piece of work? I can't give you a recommendation."

"Okay," Kelp said.

Harry pointed at one of the clubs in the bag, one of the big-headed ones. "That one, you think?"

Kelp, the judicious caddy, considered the possibilities, then pointed at a different one, with an even bigger head. "That one, I think."

It didn't help.

4

New York City made Kirby Querk nervous. Well, in fact, everything made him nervous, especially the need to never let it show, never let anybody guess, that he was scared.

He'd been away too long, is what it was, away from New York and also away from the entire world, That last six and a half years inside had broken him, had made him lose the habit of running his own life to his own plans. Jail was so seductive that way, so comfortable once you gave up and stopped fighting the system. Live by the clock, their clock, their rules, their rhythms, just go along and go along. Six and a half years, and then all at once they give you a smile and a pep talk and a handshake and an open door, and there you are, you're on your own.

On his own? His two previous periods of incarceration had both been shorter, and he'd been younger, and the rhythms and routines of stir hadn't engraved themselves so deeply into his brain. This time, when he was suddenly free, loose, on his own, he'd lost his own, didn't have any own to be any more.

Which was the main reason, as soon as those prison doors had clanged shut behind him, that he'd headed for Darbyville and Cousin Claude, even though he and Cousin Claude had never been close and didn't really have that much use for one another, Claude having been a straight arrow his entire life while Querk had from the beginning been rather seriously bent.

But it was to Darbyville that Querk had gone, on a beeline, with a warning phone call ahead of time to ask Claude where he would recommend Querk find housing. The excuse was that Querk had learned the printing trade while inside (or so he'd thought), and he'd known the Sycamore Creek Printery was in the town of Sycamore, not far from Darbyville, one hundred miles north of New York City. Claude was a decent guy, married, with four kids, two out of the nest and two still in, so he'd invited Querk to move into the bedroom now vacated by the oldest, until he found a more permanent place for himself, and now, a year and a half later, Querk was still there.

He hadn't known it then, and he still didn't know it now, but the reason he'd gone to Cousin Claude in the first place was that he'd felt the need for a warden; someone to tell him when it's exercise time, when it's lights out. It hadn't worked that way exactly, since Claude and his wife Eugenia were both too gentle and amiable to play warden, and the printing trade skills that were supposed to have given him a grounding had turned out to be just one more bubble blown into the air, but that was all right. He had the job at the printery, riding the forklift truck, which put some structure into his life, and he'd found somebody else to play warden.

And it was time to phone her.

One of the many things that made Querk nervous about New York City these days was the pay phones. He was afraid to use a phone on the street, to be talking into a phone while all these hulking people went by, many of them behind him, all of them unknowable in their intentions. You had to *stop* to make a call from a pay phone, but Querk didn't want to stop on the street in New York City; he couldn't get over the feeling that, if he stopped, a whole bunch of them would jump on him, rob him, hurt him, do who knew what to him. So if he was out and about in New York City, he wanted to keep moving. But he still had to make that phone call.

Grand Central Station was not exactly a solution, but it was a compromise. It was indoors and, even though there were just as many people hurtling by as out on the street, maybe more, it was possible to talk on the phone in Grand Central with his back to a wall, all those strangers safely out in front.

So that's what he did. First he got a bunch of quarters and dimes, and then he chose a pay phone from a line of them not far from the Metro North ticket windows, where he could stand with his back mostly turned to the phone as he watched the streams of people hustle among all the entrances and all the exits, this way, that way, like protons in a cyclotron. He could watch the buttons over his shoulder when he made the call, then drop coins into the slot when the machine-voice told him how much it was.

One ring: "Seven Leagues."

"Is Frank there?"

"Wrong number," she said, and hung up, and he looked toward

the big clock in the middle of the station. Five minutes to two in the afternoon, not a particularly hot time at Grand Central but still pretty crowded. He now had five minutes to wait, while she walked down to the phone booth outside the Hess station, the number for which he had in his pocket.

He didn't like standing next to the phone when he wasn't making a call; he thought it made him conspicuous. He thought there might be people in among all these people who would notice him and think about him and maybe even make notes on his appearance and actions. So he walked purposefully across the terminal and out a door onto Lexington Avenue and around to an entrance on 42nd Street, then down to the lower level and back up to the upper level, where at last the clock said two, straight up.

Querk dialed the pay phone number up in Sycamore, and it was answered immediately: "Hello."

"It's me."

"I know. How's it going?"

"Well, I got a couple guys," Querk said. "I think they're gonna be okay."

"You tell them what we're doing?"

"Not yet. We all hadda check each other out. I'm seeing them today at four o'clock. If they say yes, if they think *I* check out, I'll tell them the story."

"Not the whole story, Kirby."

Querk laughed, feeling less nervous, because he was talking to the warden. "No, not the whole story," he said. "Just the part they'll like."

5

For this meet they would be in a car, which Kelp would promote. He picked up Querk first, at the corner of Eleventh Avenue and 57th Street, steering the very nice black Infiniti to a stop at the curb, where Querk was rubbernecking up 57th Street, eastward. Kelp thought he'd have to honk, but then Querk got in on the passenger side next to him and said, "I just saw Lesley Stahl get out of a cab up there."

"Ah," said Kelp, and drove back into traffic, uptown.

"I used to watch *60 Minutes* regular as clockwork," Querk said, "every Sunday. Even the summer reruns."

"Ah," said Kelp.

"When I was inside," Querk explained. "It was kind of a high-light."

"Ah," said Kelp.

"I don't watch it so much any more, I don't know why."

Kelp didn't say anything. Querk looked around the interior of the car and said, "I happened to notice, you got MD plates."

"I do," Kelp agreed.

"You aren't a doctor."

"I'm not even a car owner," Kelp told him.

Querk was surprised. "You boosted this?"

"From Roosevelt Hospital, just down the street. I give all my automotive trade to doctors. They're very good on the difference be-tween pleasure and pain. Also, I believe they have a clear under-standing of infinity."

"But you're driving around— You're still in the neighborhood, with a very hot car."

"The hours they make those doctors work?" Kelp shrugged. "The owner's not gonna miss this thing until Thursday. In the pri-vate lot there, I picked one without dust on it. There's John."

They were on West End Avenue now, stopped at the light at 72nd Street, and Dortmunder was visible catty-corner across the street, standing on the corner in the sunlight as though a mistake had been made here. Anybody who was that slumped and bedraggled should not be standing on a street corner in the summer in the sun-light. He had looked much more at home in the bar where he and Kelp had conferred. Out here, he looked mostly like he was waiting for the police sweep.

The green arrow lit up, and Kelp swept around to stop next to Dortmunder who, per original plan, slid into the back seat, saying, "Hello."

Querk said, "Andy boosted this car."

"He always does," Dortmunder said, and to Kelp's face in the rearview mirror as they turned northward on the West Side Highway, he said, "My compliments to the doctor."

Traffic on the highway was light; Kelp drove moderately in the right lane, and nobody said anything until Dortmunder leaned for-ward, rested his forearms on the seatback, and said to Querk, "Jump in any time."

"Oh." Querk looked out ahead of them and said, "I thought we were headed somewhere."

"We are," Kelp told him. "But you can *start*."

"Okay, fine."

As Dortmunder leaned back, seated behind Kelp, Querk half-turned in his seat so he could see both of them, and said, "One of the things the printery prints, where I work, is money."

That surprised them both. Kelp said, "I thought the mint printed the money."

"*Our* money, yes," Querk said. "But the thing is, your smaller countries, they don't have the technology and the skills and all, they farm out the money. The printing. Most of the money in Europe and Africa is printed in London. Most of the money in South America is printed in Philadelphia."

"You're not in Philadelphia," Kelp pointed out.

"No, this outfit I'm with, Sycamore, about ten years ago they decided to get some of that action. They had a big Canadian investor, they put in the machinery, hired the people, started to undercut the price of the Philadelphia people."

"Free enterprise," Kelp commented.

"Sure." Querk shrugged. "Nobody says the money they do is as up to date as the Philadelphia money, with all the holograms and anti-counterfeiting things, but you get a small enough country, poor enough, nobody *wants* to counterfeit that money, so Sycamore's got four of the most draggly-assed countries in Central and South America, and Sycamore makes their money."

Dortmunder said, "You're talking about stealing money you say isn't worth anything."

"Well, it's worth *something*," Querk said. "And I'm not talking about stealing it."

"Counterfeiting," Dortmunder suggested, as though he didn't like that idea either.

But Querk shook his head. "I'm the guy," he said, "keeps track of the paper coming in, signs off with the truck drivers, forklifts it here and there, depending what kinda paper, what's it for. Each of these countries got their own special paper, with watermarks and hidden messages and all. Not high tech, you know, pretty sopho-more, but not something you could imitate on your copier."

"You've got the paper," Dortmunder said. He still sounded skeptical.

"And I look around," Querk said. "You know, I thought I was gonna be a printer, not a forklift jockey, so I'm looking to improve myself. Get enough ahead so I can choose my own life for myself, not to have to answer every whistle. You know what I mean."

"Huh," Dortmunder said.

"That's back," Querk pointed out. "That throat thing." He looked forward as Kelp steered them off the highway at the 125th Street exit. "Isn't this Harlem?" He didn't sound as though he liked the idea.

"Not exactly," Kelp said.

Dortmunder said, "Go on with your story."

"I don't think I can yet," Querk said. He was frowning out the windshield as though rethinking some earlier decisions in his life.

"Be there in a couple minutes," Kelp assured him.

Nobody talked while Kelp stopped at the stop sign, made the left around the huge steel pillars holding up the West Side Highway, drove a block past scruffy warehouses, turned left at the light, stopped at a stop sign, then drove across, through the wide opening in a chain-link fence, and turned left into a narrow long parking lot just above the Hudson River.

Querk said, "What is this?"

"Fairway," Kelp told him, as he found a parking space on the left and drove into it, front bumper against fence. It was hot outside, so he kept the engine on and the windows shut.

Querk said, "I don't get it."

"What it is," Kelp told him, putting the Infiniti in park, "Harlem never had a big supermarket, save money on your groceries, they only had these little corner stores, not much selection on the shelves. So this Fairway comes in, that used to be a warehouse over there, see it?"

Querk nodded at the big warehouse with the supermarket entrance. "I see it."

Kelp said, "So they put in a huge supermarket, great selections, everything cheap, the locals love it. But also the commuters, it's easy on, easy off, see, there's your northbound ramp back up to the highway, so they can come here, drop in, buy everything for the weekend, then head off to their country retreat."

Querk said, "But why us? What are *we* doin' here?"

Dortmunder told him, "You look around, you'll see one, two people, even three, sitting in the cars around here. The wife—usually, it's the wife—goes in and shops, the husband and the houseguests, they stay out here, keep outa the way, sit in the car, tell each other stories."

Kelp said, "Tell us a story, Kirby."

Querk shook his head. "I been away too long," he said. "I hate to have to admit it. I don't know how to maneuver any more. That's why I need a cushion."

Dortmunder said, "Made out of South American money."

"Exactly." Querk said, "I'm pretty much on my own at the plant, and I've always been handy around machinery—starting with locks, you know, that was my specialty—and also including now the printing presses they don't use any more, and so I finally figured out the numbers."

Kelp said, "Numbers?"

"Every bill in your pocket," Querk told him, "has a number on it, and no two bills in this country have the same number. That's the same for every country's money. Everything's identical on every bill except the number changes every time, and it never goes back. That's part of the special machinery they bought, when they went into this business."

Kelp said, "Kirby, am I all of a sudden ahead of you here? You figured out how to make the numbers go back."

Querk was pleased with himself. "I know," he said, "how to tell the machine, 'That last run was a test. *This* is the real run.'" Grinning at Dortmunder, he said, "I also am the guy puts the paper here and there inside the plant, and checks it in when it's delivered, and maybe makes it disappear off the books. So you see what I got."

Kelp said, "It's the real paper, on the real machine, doing the real numbers."

"There's no record of it anywhere," Querk said. "It isn't counterfeit, it's real, and it isn't stolen because it was never there."

As they drove back down the West Side Highway toward midtown, each of them drinking a St. Pauli Girl beer Kelp had actually paid for in Fairway, Dortmunder said, "You know, it seems to me, there's gotta be more than one chapter to this story."

"You mean," Querk said, "what do we do with it, once we got it."

"We can't take it to a bank a hundred dollars a time to change it back," Dortmunder said.

"No, I know that."

Kelp said, "I suppose we could go to the country and buy a hotel or something . . ."

Dortmunder said, "With cash?"

"There's that. And then sell it again for dollars." He shook his head. "Too complicated."

"I got a guy," Querk said. His shoulders twitched.

They gave him their full attention.

"He's from that country, it's called Guerrera," Querk said. "He's a kind of a hustler down there."

Dortmunder said, "What is he up here?"

"Well, he isn't up here," Querk said. "Basically, he's down there."

Dortmunder said, "And how do you know this guy?"

"I got a friend," Querk said, "a travel agent, she goes all over, she knows the guy."

Dortmunder and Kelp exchanged a glance in the rearview mirror at that pronoun, which Querk didn't appear to see. "We run off the money," he went on, "and it comes out in cardboard boxes, already packed by the machinery, with black metal straps around it. We get it out of the plant, and I got a way to do that, too, and we turn it over to this guy, and he gives us fifty cents on the dollar."

"Half," Kelp said. "What are we talking about here?"

"The most useful currency for Rodrigo—that's my guy—is the twenty million siapa note."

Kelp said, "Twenty *million*?"

Dortmunder said, "How much is that in money?"

"A hundred dollars." Querk shrugged. "They been havin a little inflation problem down there. They think they got it under control now."

Kelp said, "So how much is this run?"

"What we'll print? A hundred billion."

Dortmunder said, "Not dollars."

"No, siapas. That's five thousand bills, all the twenty million siapa note."

Dortmunder, pretending patience, said, "And what's *that* in money?"

"Five hundred grand," Querk said.

Kelp said, "Now *I'm* getting confused. Five hundred. This is in dollars?"

"Five hundred thousand dollars," Querk said.

Dortmunder said, "And we get half. Two hundred fifty thousand. And Kelp and me?"

"Half of the half," Querk said promptly.

They were now back down in a realm where Dortmunder could do calculations in his head. "Sixty-two thousand, five hundred apiece," he said.

"And a little vacation in the mountains," Kelp said.

"Next week," Querk said.

They looked at him. Dortmunder said, "Next week?"

"Or maybe the week after that," Querk said. "Anyway, when the plant's shut down."

"We," Dortmunder decided, "are gonna have to talk more."

6

"May?" Dortmunder called, and stood in the doorway to listen. Nothing. "Not home yet," he said, and went on into the apartment, followed by Kelp and Querk.

"Nice place," Querk said.

"Thanks," Dortmunder said. "Living room's in here, on the left."

"I used to have a place in New York," Querk said. "Years ago. I don't think I'd like the pace now."

They trooped into the living room, here on East 19th Street, and Dortmunder looked around at the sagging sofa and his easy chair with the maroon hassock in front of it and May's easy chair with the cigarette burns on the arms (good thing she quit when she did) and the television set where the colors never would come right and the window with its view of a brick wall just a little too far away to touch and the coffee table with all the rings and scars on it, and he said, "I dunno, the pace don't seem to bother me that much. Take a seat. Anybody want a beer?"

Everybody wanted a beer, so Dortmunder went away to the kitchen to play host. When he was coming back down the hall toward the living room, spilling beer on his wrists because three was one more can than he could carry all at once, the apartment door at the other end of the hall opened and May came in, struggling with the key in the door and the big sack of groceries in her arm. A tall thin woman with slightly graying black hair, May worked as a cashier at Safeway until Dortmunder should score one of these times, and she felt the sack of groceries a day was a perk that went with the position, whether management thought so or not.

"*Damn*, May!" Dortmunder said, spilling more beer on his wrists. "I can't help you with that."

"That's okay, I got it," she said, letting the door close behind her as she counted his beer cans. "We've got company."

"Andy and a guy. Come in and say hello."

"Let me put this stuff away."

As May passed the living room doorway, Kelp could be heard to cry, "Hey, May!" She nodded at the doorway, she and Dortmunder slid by each other in the hall, and he went on into the living room, where the other two were both standing, like early guests at a party.

Distributing the beers, wiping his wrists on his shirt, Dortmunder said, "May'll come in in a minute, say hello."

Kelp lifted his beer. "To crime."

"Good," said Querk, and they all drank.

May came in, with a beer of her own. "Hi, Andy," she said.

Dortmunder said, "May, this is Kirby Querk." They both said hello, and he said, "Whyn't we all sit down? You two take the sofa."

Sounding surprised, Querk said, "You want me to tell this in front of, uh, the lady?"

"Aw, that's nice," May said, smiling at Querk as she settled into her chair.

Dortmunder said, "I'll just tell her anyway, after you go, so you can save me some time."

"Well, all right."

They all seated themselves, and Dortmunder said to May, "Querk has a job upstate at a printery, where one of the things they print is South American money, and he's got a way to run off a batch nobody knows about."

"Well, that's pretty good," May said.

"Only now, it turns out," Dortmunder said, "there's some kind of deadline here, so we come over to talk about it."

Kelp explained, "Up till now, we weren't sure we were all gonna team up, so we met in other places."

"Sure," May said.

"So now," Dortmunder said, "Querk's gonna explain the deadline."

They all looked at Querk, who put his beer can on the coffee table, making another mark, and said, "The plant's called Sycamore Creek, and there's this creek runs through town, with a dam where it goes under the road, and that's where the electricity comes from to run the plant. But every year in August there's two weeks when they gotta open the dam and just let the water go, because there's always a drought up there in the summer and it could get too low downstream for the fish. So the plant closes, two weeks, everybody gets a vacation, they do their annual maintenance and all, but there's no electricity to run the plant, so that's why they have to close."

Dortmunder said, "Your idea is, you do this when there's no electricity."

"We bring in our own," Querk said.

Dortmunder visualized himself walking with a double handful of electricity, lots of little blue sparks. *Zit-zit*; worse than beer cans. He said, "How do we do that?"

"With a generator," Querk told him. "See, up there, it's all volunteer fire departments and rescue squads, and my cousin, where I've been living temporarily until I find a place, he's the captain of the Combined Darby County Fire Department and Rescue Squad, and what they got, besides the ambulance and the fire engine, is a big truck with a generator on it, for emergencies."

Dortmunder said, "So first you boost this truck—"

"Which I could do with my eyes closed," Querk said. "The locks up there are a joke, believe me. And the keys to the emergency vehicles are kept right in them."

Kelp said, "Do we do it day or night?"

"Oh, night," Querk said. "I figure, we go pick up the generator truck around one in the morning, there's *nobody* awake up there at one in the morning, we take it over to the plant, hook up the stuff we need, the run'll take just about three hours for the whole thing, we take the boxes with the money, we put the generator truck back, we're done before daylight."

Dortmunder said, "You're gonna have to have some light in there. And some noise."

"Not a problem," Querk said.

Dortmunder said, "Why, is this plant out in the woods all by itself or something?"

"Not really," Querk said. "But nobody can see it."

Kelp said, "How come?"

"High walls, low buildings." Querk spread his hands. "The way I understand it, in the old days the plant used to dump all its waste straight into the creek, the people downstream used to make bets, what color's the water gonna be tomorrow. Every time the state did an inspection, somehow the plant got tipped off ahead of time, and that day the water's clean and clear, good enough to drink. But finally, about thirty years ago, they got caught. People'd been complaining about noise and stink outa the plant, in addition to this water even an irreligious person could walk on, so they did a consent. The plant upgraded its waste treatment, and did a sound-baffle wall all around, and planted trees so people wouldn't have to look at the wall, and now those trees are all big, you'd think it's a forest there, except the two drives in, with the gates, one for the workers and one for deliveries, and they're both around on the stream side, no houses across the way."

Dortmunder said, "We'd have to go up there, ahead of time, take a look at this place."

"Definitely," Kelp said.

"That's a good idea," Querk said, "you can help me refine the details. I could drive you up there tomorrow, I've got my cousin's van, I've been sleeping in it down in Greenwich Village."

"Nice neighborhood," May commented.

"Yeah, it is."

Dortmunder said, "We oughta have our own wheels, we'll drive up, meet you there."

Grinning, Querk said, "Another doctor gonna be on his feet?"

"Possibly," Kelp said. "You say this place is a hundred miles upstate? About two hours?"

"Yeah, no more. You go up the Taconic."

Dortmunder said, "If this is a plant, with workers, there's probably a place to eat around it."

"Yeah, just up from the bridge, you know, where the dam is, there's a place called Sycamore House. It's mostly a bar, but you can get lunch."

Dortmunder nodded. "You got a problem, up there, being seen with us?"

"No, it's not *that* small a town. You're just people I happen to know, passing through."

"So before you leave here," Dortmunder said, "do a little map, how we find this town, we'll get some lunch there, come out at one o'clock, there you are."

"Fine," Querk said.

Kelp said, "What if there's an emergency around there, the night we go, and we've got the generator truck?"

"For three hours in the middle of night in August?" Querk shrugged. "There isn't gonna be a blizzard. The three vehicles in the garage are in separate bays, so even if they come for the fire engine or the ambulance, which would almost never happen, middle of the summer, they still won't see the generator truck's gone."

"But what if," Kelp said.

"Then we're screwed," Querk said. "Me more than you guys, because there won't be any question who put the generator truck in the printery, and there goes my quiet life not being on the run."

Kelp said, "So you'll take the chance."

"The odds are so extreme," Querk said. "I mean, unless one of you guys is a Jonah, I don't see I've got anything to worry about. I'll risk it."

Nobody said anything.

7

First Querk split, and then Kelp, and then Dortmunder filled May in on the rest of the setup; Rodrigo, and the half of a half of a half, and the barely mentioned female travel agent.

"Well, she's the one behind it all," May said.

"Yeah, I got that part," Dortmunder said. "So what was your reading on the guy?"

"Rabbity."

"Yeah."

"Something's bothering you," May said.

Dortmunder shook his head. "I don't even know what it is. The thing is, this job *seems* to be doing everything you shouldn't do, and yet somehow it doesn't. You should never rip off the place where you work or you used to work, because you're who they look at, but that's what Querk's doing, but this time it's supposed to be okay, because, like Querk says, nobody's supposed to know any rip-off happened. If they know there's a hundred billion siapas gone missing, then the job's no good."

"I can't imagine money like that," May said. "But how do you get *your* money, that's the question. The dollars."

"We gotta work on that," Dortmunder said. "So far, Querk hasn't made any suggestions. And the other thing, I keep thinking about what Harry Matlock said, how he knew Querk was all right, not a star, when he was just a sideman in somebody else's scheme, but he couldn't say how Querk would be when the scheme was his own. And this is a weird scheme."

"In parts," May agreed.

"In all the parts. You got a factory closed because they open the dam to help out the fish downstream, you like that part?"

"Well, if that's what they do," May said.

"I guess." Dortmunder frowned, massively. "It's the country, see, I don't know what makes sense in the country. So that's what's got me geechy. Querk talks about how he isn't comfortable in the city any more, but you know, I *never* been comfortable in the country. Why can't they print these siapas in the city? In Brooklyn somewhere."

"Well," May said, "there isn't any fish downstream in the city."

"Oh, yes, there is," Dortmunder said. "I just hope I'm not one of them."

8

As Querk walked toward Cousin Claude's van, he thought what a pity it was he couldn't phone now, give this progress report. But it was after five, so Seven Leagues was closed, and he couldn't call her at home, even if she'd got home so soon. Well, he'd see her in the morning, when he drove up to Sycamore, so he'd tell her then.

And what he'd tell her was that it was all coming together. Yes, it was. The two guys he'd wound up with were sharp enough to do the job without lousing anything up, but not so sharp as to be trouble later. He had a good feeling about them.

Walking along, he kept his hands in his pockets, even though it was a very hot August afternoon, because otherwise they'd shake like buckskin fringe at the ends of his arms. Well, when this was over, when at last they'd be safe—and rich—he wouldn't tremble at *all*. Hold a glass of wine, not a single wave in it.

Traveling from Dortmunder's place on East 19th Street to where he'd parked the van in the West Village seemed to just naturally lead Querk along West 14th Street, the closest thing Manhattan has to a casbah. Open-fronted stores with huge signs, selling stuff you never knew you wanted, but cheap. Gnomish customers draped with gnomish children and lugging shopping bags half their size roamed the broad littered sidewalk and oozed in and out of the storefronts, adding more and more *things* to their bags.

What got to Querk in this spectacle, though, was the guard on duty in front of every one of those stores. Not in a uniform or anything, usually in just jeans and a T-shirt, bulky stern-looking guys positioned halfway between the storefront and curb, some of them sitting on top of a low ladder, some of them just standing there in the middle of the sidewalk, but all of them doing nothing but glaring into their store. Usually, they had their arms folded, to emphasize their muscles, and a beetle-browed angry look on their faces to emphasize their willingness to dismember shoplifters.

Walking this gauntlet, Querk was sorry his hands were in his pockets, because those guys could see that as a provocation, particularly in this August heat, but he figured, if they saw him trembling all over instead that would not be an improvement in his image.

Finally, he got off 14th Street and plodded on down to 12th, which was much more comforting to walk along, being mostly old nineteenth-century townhouses well-maintained, intermixed with more recent bigger apartment buildings that weren't as offensive as they might be. The pedestrians here were less frightening, too, being mostly people either from the townhouses or who had things to do with the New School for Social Research, and therefore less likely to be homicidal maniacs than the people on 14th Street or up in Midtown.

When Greenwich Village becomes the West Village, the numbered grid of streets common to Manhattan acts all at once as though it's been smoking dope, at the very least. Names start mingling with the numbers—Jane, Perry, Horatio, who *are* these people?—and the numbers themselves turn a little weird. You don't, for instance, expect West 4th Street to *cross* West 10th Street, but it does . . . on its way to cross West 11th Street.

Cousin Claude's van was parked a little beyond that example of street-design as funhouse mirror, on something called Greenwich Street, lined with low dark apartment buildings and low dark warehouses, some of those being converted into low dark apartment buildings. The van was still there—it always surprised him, in New York City, when something was still there after he'd left it—and Querk unlocked his way in.

This was a dirty white Ford Econoline van that Claude used mostly for fishing trips or other excursions, so behind the bucket front seats he had installed a bunk bed and a small metal cabinet with drawers that was bolted to the side wall. Querk could plug his electric razor into the cigarette lighter, and could wash and brush teeth and do other things in restaurant bathrooms.

It was too early for dinner now, not yet six, so he settled himself behind the wheel, looked at the books and magazines lying on the passenger seat, and tried to decide what he wanted to read next. But then, all at once, he thought: Why wait? I'm done here. I don't have to wait here all night and drive up there in the morning. It's still daylight, I'm home before eight o'clock.

Home.

Janet.

Key in ignition. Seatbelt on. Querk drove north to West 11th Street, seeming none the worse for wear after its encounter with West 4th Street, turned left, turned right on the West Side Highway, and joined rush hour north. Didn't even mind that it was rush hour; just to be going home.

After a while he passed the big Fairway billboard on top of the Fairway supermarket. Those two guys sure know the city, don't they?

Well, Querk knew Sycamore.

9

In the end, Kelp decided to leave the medical profession alone this morning and rent a car for the trip upstate, which would mean fewer nervous looks in the rearview mirror for a hundred miles up and a hundred miles back. Less eyestrain, even though this decision meant he would have to go promote a credit card, which in turn meant a visit to Arnie Albright, a fence, which was the least of the things wrong with him.

Kelp truly didn't want to have to visit with Arnie Albright, but when he dropped by at John's apartment at eight-thirty in the morning, just in time to wish May bon voyage on her journey to Safeway, to suggest that *John* might be the one to go promote the credit card, John turned mulish. "I've done my time with Arnie Albright," he said. "Step right up to the plate."

Kelp sighed. He knew, when John turned mulish, there was no arguing with him. Still, "You could wait out front," he suggested.

"He could look out the window and see me."

"His apartment's at the back."

"He could *sense* me. You gonna use O'Malley's?"

"Sure," Kelp said. O'Malley's was a single-location car rental agency that operated out of a parking garage way down on the Bowery near the Manhattan Bridge. Most of the clientele were Asians, so O'Malley mostly had compact cars, but more important, O'Malley did *not* have a world-wide interconnected web of computers that could pick up every little nitpick in a customer's credit card and driver's license, so whenever Kelp decided to go elsewhere than doctors for his wheels it was O'Malley got the business.

"I'll meet you at O'Malley's," John demanded, "at nine-thirty."

So that was that. Kelp walked a bit and took a subway a bit and walked a bit and pretty soon there he was on 89th Street between Broadway and West End Avenue, entering the tiny vestibule of Arnie's building. He pushed the button next to *Albright*, waited a pretty long time, and suddenly the intercom snarled, "Who the hell is that?"

"Well, Andy Kelp," Kelp said, wishing it weren't so.

"What the hell do *you* want?"

He wants me to tell him *here*? Leaning confidentially closer to the intercom—he'd been leaning fastidiously away from it before this— Kelp said, "Well, I wanna come upstairs and tell you *there*, Arnie."

Rather than argue any more, Arnie made the awful squawk happen that let Kelp push the door open and go inside to a narrow hall that smelled of cooking from some ethnicity that made you look around for shrunken heads. Seeing none, Kelp went up the long flight of stairs to where the unlovely Arnie stood at his open door, glaring out. A grizzled gnarly guy with a tree-root nose, he had chosen to welcome summer in a pair of stained British Army shorts, very wide, a much-too-big bilious green polo shirt, and black sandals that permitted views of toes like rotting tree stumps; not a wise decision.

"It's buy or sell," this gargoyle snarled as Kelp neared the top of the stairs, "buy or sell, that's the only reason anybody comes to see Arnie Albright. It's not my lovable *personality* is gonna bring anybody here."

"Well, people know you're busy," Kelp said, and went past Arnie into the apartment.

"Busy?" Arnie snarled, and slammed the door. "Do I look *busy*? I look like somebody where the undertaker said, 'Don't do the open coffin, it would be a mistake,' and the family went ahead anyway, and now they're sorry. That's what *I* look like."

"Not that bad, Arnie," Kelp assured him, looking around at the apartment as a relief from looking at Arnie, who, in truth, would look much better with the lid down.

The apartment was strange in its own way. Small underfurnished rooms with big dirty viewless windows, it was decorated mostly with samples from Arnie's calendar collection, Januarys down the ages, girls with their skirts blowing, Boy Scouts saluting, antique cars, your ever-popular kittens in baskets with balls of wool. Among the Januarys starting on every possible day of the week, there were what Arnie called his "incompletes," calendars hailing June or September.

Following Kelp into the living room, Arnie snarled, "I see John Dortmunder isn't with you. Even *he* can't stand to be around me any more. Wha'd you do, toss a coin, the loser comes to see Arnie?"

"He wouldn't toss," Kelp said. "Arnie, the last time I saw you, you were taking some medicine to make you pleasant."

"Yeah, I was still obnoxious, but I wasn't angry about it any more."

"You're not taking it?"

"You noticed," Arnie said. "No, it made me give money away."
Kelp said, "What?"

"I couldn't believe it myself, I thought I had holes in my pockets, the super was coming in to lift cash—not that he could *find* the upstairs in this place, the useless putz—but it turned out, my new pleasant personality, learning to live with my inner scumbag, every time I'd smile at somebody, like out in the street, and they'd smile back, I'd give them money."

"That's terrible," Kelp said.

"You know it is," Arnie said. "I'd rather be frowning and obnoxious and *have* money than smiling and obnoxious and throwing it away. I suppose you're sorry you didn't get some of it."

"That's okay, Arnie," Kelp said, "I already got a way to make a living. Which by the way—"

"Get it over with, I know," Arnie said. "You want outa here, and so do I. You think I *enjoy* being in here with me? Okay, I know, tell me, we'll get it over with, I won't say a word."

"I need a credit card," Kelp said.

Arnie nodded. As an aid to thought, he sucked at his teeth. Kelp looked at Januarys.

Arnie said, "How long must this card live?"

"Two days."

"That's easy," Arnie said. "That won't even cost you much. Lemme try to match you with a signature. Siddown."

Kelp sat at a table with incompletes shellacked on the top—aircraft carrier with airplanes flying, two bears and a honeypot—while Arnie went away to rummage and shuffle in some other room, soon returning with three credit cards, a ballpoint pen, and an empty tissue box.

"Hold on," he said, and ripped the tissue box open so Kelp could write on its inside. "I'll incinerate it later."

Kelp looked at his choice of cards. "Howard Joostine looks pretty good."

"Give it a whack."

Kelp wrote *Howard Joostine* four times on the tissue box, then compared them with the one on the credit card. "Good enough for O'Malley," he said.

10

Dortmunder's only objection to the car was the legroom, but that was objection enough. "This is a *sub*-compact," he complained.

"Well, no," Kelp told him. "With the sub-compact, you gotta straddle the engine block."

They were not the only people fleeing the city northbound on this bright hot morning in August, but it is true that most of the other people around them, even the Asians, were in cars with more legroom. (O'Malley's bent toward Oriental customers was because his operation was on the fringe of Chinatown. However, he was also on the fringe of Little Italy, but did he offer bulletproof limos? No.)

In almost every state in the Union, the state capital is not in the largest city, and the reason for that is, the states were all founded by farmers, not businessmen or academics, and farmers don't trust cities. In Maryland, for instance, the city is Baltimore and the capital is Annapolis. In California, the city is Los Angeles and the capital is Sacramento. And in New York, the capital is Albany, a hundred fifty miles up the Hudson.

When the twentieth century introduced the automobile, and then the paved road, and then the highway, the first highway in every state was built for the state legislators; it connected the capital with the largest city, and let the rest of the state go fend for itself. In New York State, that road is called the Taconic Parkway, and it's *still* underutilized, nearly a century later. That's planning.

But it also made for a pleasant drive. Let others swelter in bumper-to-bumper traffic on purpose-built roads, the Taconic was a joy, almost as empty as a road in a car commercial. The farther north of the city you drove, the fewer cars you drove among (and no trucks!), while the more beautiful became the mountain scenery through which this empty road swooped and soared. It was almost enough to make you believe there was an upside to the internal combustion engine.

After a while, the congeniality of the road and the landscape soothed Dortmunder's put-upon feelings about legroom. He figured out a way to disport his legs that did not lead immediately to cramps, his upper body settled comfortably into the curve of the seat, and he spent his time, more fruitfully than fretting about legroom, thinking about what could go wrong.

An emergency in town while they were in possession of the generator truck, that could go wrong. The woman travel agent who was running Querk, and whose bona fides and motives were unknown, she could go wrong. (Harry Matlock's instincts had been right, when he'd said he could recommend Querk as a follower but not as a leader. He was still a follower. The question was, who vouched for the leader?)

Other things that could go wrong. Rodrigo, for one. No, Rodrigo for four or five. Described as mostly a hustler down on his home turf, he could run foul of the law himself at just the wrong moment, and have neither the cash nor the leisure to take delivery on the print job. Or, as unknown as the travel agent, he could be planning a double-cross from the get-go. Or, he could be reasonably trustworthy himself, but unaware of untrustworthy friends waiting just out of sight. Or, he could get one of those South American illnesses that people get when they leave the five boroughs, and die.

All in all, it was a pleasant drive.

Querk's instructions had said to exit the Taconic at Darby Corners and turn east and then north, following the signs past Darbyville, where Querk lived temporarily with his cousin, and on to Sycamore, where the Sycamore Creek Printery stood in woodland disguise beside Sycamore Creek.

They approached Sycamore from the south, while the creek approached the town from the north, so for the last few miles they were aware of the stream in the woods and fields off to their right, spritzing in the sun as it rushed and tumbled the other way.

There were farmhouses all along the route here, some of them still connected to farms, and there were fields of ripe corn and orchards of almost-ripe apples. The collapse of the local dairy farming industry due to the tender loving care of the state politicians meant several of the farms they passed were growing things that would have left the original settlers scratching their heads: llamas, goats, anemones, ostriches, Christmas trees, Icelandic horses, long-horn cattle.

The town was commercial right from the city line: lumberyard on the left, tractor dealership on the right. Far ahead was the only traffic light. As they drove toward it, private housing was mixed with shops on the left, but after the tractor man it was all forested on the right almost all the way to the intersection, where an Italian restaurant on that side signaled the return of civilization.

"That'll be it in there," Kelp said, taking a hand off the steering wheel to point at the dubious woodland.

"Right."

"And all evergreens, so people don't have to look at it in winter, either."

"Very tasteful," Dortmunder agreed.

It wasn't quite eleven-thirty. The traffic light was with them, so Kelp drove through the intersection, and just a little farther, on the right, they passed Sycamore House, where they would eat lunch. It was a very old building, two stories high, the upper story extending out over and sagging down toward an open front porch. The windows were decorated with neon beer logos.

A little beyond Sycamore House a storefront window proclaimed SEVEN LEAGUES TRAVEL. This time, Kelp only pointed his nose: "And there *she* is."

"Got it."

Kelp drove to the northern end of town—cemetery on left, church on right, "Go and Sin no More" the suggestion on the announcement board out front—where he made a U-turn through the church's empty parking lot and headed south again. "We'll see what we see from the bridge," he said.

Here came the traffic light, this time red. Moderate traffic poked along, locals and summer folk. Kelp turned left when he could, and now the pocket forest was on their right, and the creek up ahead. Just before the creek, where the bosk ended, a two-lane road ran off to the right, between the evergreens and creek, marked at the entrance by a large black-on-white sign:

PRIVATE
SYCAMORE CREEK PRINTERY
NO TRESPASSING

Right after that, there was what seemed to be a lake on their left, and a steep drop to a stream on their right, so the road must be the dam. Dortmunder craned around, banging his legs into car parts, trying to see something other than pine trees along the streamside back there, and just caught a glimpse of something or other where the private road turned in. "Pretty hid," he said.

There were no intersections on the far side of the creek, and in fact no more town over here. All the development was behind them, along the west side of the creek. On this side the land climbed steeply through a more diversified woods, the road twisting back and forth, and when they finally did come to a turnoff, seven miles later, it was beyond the crest, and the turnoff was to a parking area where you could enjoy the view of the Berkshire Mountains in Massachusetts, farther east.

They didn't spend a lot of time contemplating the Berkshires, but drove back to Sycamore, ignoring the traffic that piled up behind them because they insisted on going so slowly down the twisty road, trying to see signs of the printing plant inside the wall of trees. Here and there a hint, nothing more.

"So if he's careful," Kelp said, "with the light and the noise, it should be okay."

"I'd like to get in there," Dortmunder said, "just give it the double-o."

"We'll discuss it with him," Kelp said.

11

It was still too early for lunch. Kelp parked the little car in the parking lot next to Sycamore House, in among several cars owned by people who didn't know it was too early for lunch, and they got out to stretch, Dortmunder doing overly elaborate knee-bends and massaging of his thighs that Kelp chose not to notice, saying, "I think I'll take a look at the League."

"I'll walk around a little," Dortmunder said, sounding pained. "Work the kinks out."

They separated, and Kelp walked up the block to Seven Leagues Travel, the middle shop in a brief row of storefronts, a white clapboard one-story building, with an entrance and a plate glass display window for each of the three shops. The one on the right was video rental and the one on the left was a frame shop.

Kelp pushed open the door for Seven Leagues, and a bell sounded. He entered and shut the door, and it sounded again, and a female voice called, "Just a minute! I got a bite!"

A bite? Kelp looked around an empty room, not much deeper than it was wide. Filing cabinets were along the left wall and two desks, one behind the other, faced forward on the right. Every otherwise empty vertical space was covered with travel posters, including the side of the nearest filing cabinet and the front of both desks. The forward desk was as messy as a Texas trailer camp after a tornado, but the desk behind it was so neat and empty as to be obviously unused. At the rear, a door with a travel poster on it was partly open, showing just a bit of the lake formed by the dam and the steep wooded slope beyond.

Kelp, wondering if assistance was needed here—if a person was being bitten, that was possible—walked down the length of the room past the desks, pulled the rear door open the rest of the way, and leaned out to see a narrow roofless porch and a woman on it fighting with a fishing pole. She was middle-aged, which meant impossible to tell exactly, and not too overweight, dressed in full tan slacks, a blue man's dress shirt open at the collar and with the sleeves cut off above the elbow, huge dark sunglasses, and a narrow-brimmed cloth cap with a lot of fishing lures and things stuck in it.

"Oh!" he said. "A *bite*!"

"Don't break my concentration!"

So he stood there and watched. A person, man or woman, fighting a fish can look a little odd, if the light is just so and the fishing line can't be seen. There she was with the bent rod, and nothing else visible, so that she looked as though she were doing one of those really esoteric Oriental exercise routines, bobbing and weaving, hunching her shoulders, kicking left and right, spinning the reel first one way, then the other, and muttering and grumbling and swearing beneath her breath the entire time, until all at once a *fish* jumped out of the water and flew over the white wood porch railing to start its own energetic exercise program on the porch floor. The fish was about a foot long, and was a number of colors Kelp didn't know the names of.

She was gasping, the woman (so was the fish), but she was grinning as well (the fish wasn't). "Isn't he a beauty?" she demanded, as she leaned the pole against the rear wall.

"Sure," Kelp said. "What is it? I mean, I know it's a fish, but what's his name?"

"Trout," she said. "I can tell already, I give you one more word, it's gonna get too technical."

"Trout is good enough," he agreed. "They're good to eat, aren't they?"

"They're wonderful to eat," she said. "But not this one." Going to one knee beside the flopping fish, she said, "We do catch and release around here."

Kelp watched her stick a finger into the fish's mouth to start working the hook out of its lower lip. He imagined a hook in his own lower lip, then was sorry he'd imagined it, and said, "Catch and *release*? You let it go again?"

"Sure," she said. Standing, she scooped the fish up with both hands and, before it could shimmy away from her, tossed it well out into the lake. "See you again, fella!" she called, then said to Kelp, "Just let me wash my hands, I'll be right with you."

They both went back into the office and she headed for the bathroom, a separate wedge in the rear corner of the room. Opening its door, she looked back at him and waved her free hand toward her desk. "Take a seat, I'll be right with you."

He nodded, and she went inside, shutting the door. He walked over to the diorama of tornado damage and noticed, half-hidden under a cataract of various forms and brochures, one of those three-sided brass plaques with a name on it, this one JANET TWILLEY.

He wandered around the room, looking at the various travel posters, noting there was none to tout Guerrera, and that in fact the only South American poster showed some amazing naked bodies in Rio, and then the toilet flushed and a minute later Janet Twilley came out, shut the bathroom door, frowned at Kelp, and said, "I told you, take a seat."

"I was admiring the posters."

"Okay." Coming briskly forward, she gestured at the chair beside the front desk. "So *now* you can take a seat."

Bossy woman. They both sat, and she said, "So where did you want to go?"

"That's why I was looking at the posters," he said. He noticed she kept her sunglasses on. Then he noticed a little discoloration visible around her left eye.

She peered at him through the dark glasses. "You don't know where you want to *go*?"

"Well, not exactly," he said.

She disapproved. "That's not the usual way," she said.

"See," he told her, "I have this problem with time zones."

"Problem?"

"I change time zones, it throws me off," he explained, "louses up my sleep, I don't enjoy the trip."

"Jet lag," she said.

"Oh, good, you know about that."

"Everybody knows about jet lag," she said.

"They do? Well, then, you know what I mean. Me and the wife, we'd like to go somewhere that we don't change a lot of time zones."

"Canada," she said.

"We been to Canada. Very nice. We were thinking of somewhere else, some other direction."

She shook her head. "You mean Florida?"

"No, a different country, you know, different language, different people, different cuisine."

"There's Rio," she said, nodding at the poster he'd been admiring.

"But that's so far away," he said. "I mean, really far away. Maybe somewhere not quite that far."

"Mexico has many—"

"Oh, Mexico," he said. "Isn't that full of Americans? We'd like maybe somewhere a little off the beaten path."

Over the next ten minutes, she suggested Argentina, Belize, Peru, Ecuador, all of the Caribbean, even Colombia, but not once did she mention the name Guerrera. Finally, he said, "Well, I better discuss this with the missus. Thank you for the suggestions."

"It would be better," she told him, a little severely, "if you made your mind up *before* you saw a travel agent."

"Yeah, but I'm closing with it now," he assured her. "You got a card?"

"Certainly," she said, and dumped half the crap from her desk onto the floor before she found it.

12

The less said about lunch, the better. After it, Dortmunder and Kelp came out to find Querk perched on the porch rail out front. Dortmunder burped and said, "Well, look who's here."

"Fancy meeting you two," Querk said.

Kelp said, "We should all shake hands now, surprised to see each other."

So they did a round of handshakes, and then Dortmunder said, "I feel like I gotta see the plant."

"I could show you a little," Querk said. "Not inside the buildings, though, around the machines, the management gets all geechy about insurance."

"Just for the idea," Dortmunder said.

So they walked to the corner, crossed with the light, and turned left, first past the Italian restaurant (not open for lunch, unfortunately), and then the abrupt stand of pines. Looking into those dense branches, Dortmunder could occasionally make out a blank grayness back in there that would be the sound-baffle wall.

At the no-trespassing sign, they turned right and trespassed, walking down the two-lane blacktop entrance drive with the creek down to their left, natural woods on the hillside across the way, and the "forest" on their right.

A big truck came slowly toward them from the plant entrance, wheezing and moving as though it had rheumatism. The black guy driving—moustache, cigar stub, dark blue Yankees cap—waved at Querk, who waved back, then said, "He delivers paper. That's what I'll be doing this afternoon, move that stuff around." With a look at his watch, he said, "I should of started three minutes ago."

"Stay late," Dortmunder suggested.

At the entrance, the shallowness of the tree-screen became apparent. The trees were barely more than two deep, in complicated diagonal patterns, not quite random, and behind them loomed the neutral gray wall, probably ten feet high.

Passing through the entrance, Dortmunder saw tall gray metal gates opened to both sides, and said, "They close those when the plant is shut?"

"And lock them," Querk said. "Which is my specialty, remember. I could deal with them before we get the truck, leave them shut but unlocked."

And the closed gates, Dortmunder realized, would also help keep light in here from being seen anywhere outside.

They walked through the entrance, and inside was a series of low cream-colored corrugated metal buildings, or maybe all one building, in sections that stretched to left and right and were surrounded by blacktop right up to the sound-baffle wall, which on the inside looked mostly like an infinitude of egg cartons. The only tall item was a gray metal water tower in the middle of the complex, built on a roof. The roofs were low A shapes, so snow wouldn't pile too thick in the winter.

Directly in front of them was a wide loading bay, the overhead doors all open showing a deep, dark, high-ceilinged interior. One truck, smaller than the paper deliverer, was backed up to the loading bay and cartons were being unloaded by three workmen while the driver leaned against his truck and watched. Beyond, huge rolls of paper, like paper towels in Brobdingnag, were strewn around the concrete floor.

"My work for this afternoon," Querk said, nodding at the paper rolls.

"That driver's doing okay," Dortmunder said.

Querk grinned. "What did Jesus Christ say to the Teamsters? 'Do nothing till I get back.'"

Dortmunder said, "Where's the presses?"

"All over," Querk said, gesturing generally at the complex of buildings. "The one we'll use is down to the right. We'll be able to park down there, snake the wires in through the window."

Kelp said, "Alarm systems?"

"I've got keys to everything," Querk said. "I studied this place, I could parade elephants through here, nobody the wiser." Here on his own turf he seemed more sure of himself, less, as May had said, rabbity.

Kelp said, "Well, to me it looks doable."

Querk raised an eyebrow at Dortmunder. "And to you?"

"Could be," Dortmunder said.

"I like your enthusiasm," Querk said. "Shall we figure to do it one night next week?"

"I got a question," Dortmunder said, "about payout."

Querk looked alert, ready to help. "Yeah?"

"When do we get it?"

"I don't follow," Querk said.

Dortmunder pointed at the building in front of them. "When we leave there," he said, "what we got is siapas. *Money* we get from Rodrigo."

"Sure," Querk said.

"How? When?"

"Well, first the siapas gotta go to Guerrera," Querk said, "and then Rodrigo has stuff he's gonna do, and then the dollars come up here."

"What if they don't?" Dortmunder said.

"Listen," Querk said, "I trust Rodrigo, he'll come through."

"I dunno about this," Dortmunder said.

Querk looked at his watch again. He was antsy to get to work. "Lemme get a message to him," he said, "work out a guarantee. What if I come back to the city this Saturday? We'll meet. Maybe your place again?"

"Three in the afternoon," Dortmunder said, because he didn't want to have to give everybody lunch.

"We'll work it out then," Querk said. "Listen, I better get on my forklift, I wouldn't want to get fired before vacation time."

He nodded a farewell and walked toward the loading bay, while Dortmunder and Kelp turned around and headed out. As they walked toward the public street, Kelp said, "Maybe the dollars should come up *before* the siapas go down."

"I was thinking that," Dortmunder said. "Or maybe one of us rides shotgun."

"You mean, *go* to this place?" Kelp was astonished. "Would you wanna do that?"

"No," Dortmunder said. "I said, 'one of us.'"

"We'll see how it plays," Kelp said. They turned toward the intersection, and he said, "I talked to Seven Leagues."

"Yeah?"

"Her name is Janet Twilley. She's bossy, and she's got a black eye."

"Oh, yeah?" Dortmunder was surprised. "Querk doesn't seem the type."

"No, he doesn't. I think we oughta see is there a Mr. Twilley."

13

Roger Twilley's shift as a repairman for Darby Telephone & Electronics (slogan: "The 5th Largest Phone Co. in New York State!") ended every day at four, an hour before Janet would close her travel agency, which was good. It gave him an hour by himself to listen to the day's tapes.

Twilley, a leathery, bony, loose-jointed fellow who wore his hair too long because he didn't like barbers, was known to his co-workers as an okay guy who didn't have much to say for himself. If he ever *were* to put his thoughts into words (which he wouldn't), their opinion would change, because in fact Twilley despised and mistrusted them all. He despised and mistrusted everybody he knew, and believed he would despise and mistrust everybody else in the world if he got to know them. Thus the tapes.

Being a phone company repairman, often alone on the job with his own cherry picker, and having a knack with phone gadgets he'd developed over the years on the job, Twilley had found it easy to bug the phones of everybody he knew that he cared the slightest bit about eavesdropping on. His mother, certainly, and Janet, naturally, and half a dozen other relatives and friends scattered around the general Sycamore area. The bugs were voice-activated, and the tapes were in his "den" in the basement, a room Janet knew damn well to keep out of, or she knew what she'd get.

Every afternoon, once he'd shucked out of his dark blue Darby Telephone jumpsuit and opened himself a can of beer, Twilley would go down to the den to listen to what these people had to say for themselves. He knew at least a few of them were scheming against him—mom, for instance, and Janet—but he hadn't caught any of them yet. It was, he knew, only a matter of time. Sooner or later, they'd condemn themselves out of their own mouths.

There are a lot of factors that might help explain how Twilley had turned out this way. There was his father's abrupt abandonment of the family when Twilley was six, for instance, a betrayal he'd never gotten over. There was his mother's catting around for a good ten years or more after that first trauma, well into Twilley's sexually agonized teens. There was the so-called girlfriend, Renee, who had publicly humiliated him in seventh grade. But the fact is, what it came down to, Twilley was a jerk.

The jerk now sat for thirty-five minutes at the table in his den, earphones on as he listened to the day the town had lived through, starting with Janet. Her phone calls today were all strictly business, talking to airlines, hotels, clients. There was nothing like the other day's "wrong number," somebody supposedly asking for somebody named Frank, that Twilley had immediately leaped on as code. A signal, some kind of signal. He'd played that fragment of tape over and over— "Is Frank there?" "Is Frank there?" "Is Frank there?"— and he would recognize that voice if it ever called again, no matter what it had to say.

On to the rest of the tapes. His mother and her friend Helen yakked the whole goddam day away, as usual—they told each other recipes, bird sightings, funny newspaper items, plots of television shows—and as usual Twilley fast-forwarded through it all, just dropping in for spot checks here and there— ". . . and she said Emmaline looked pregnant to *her* . . ."—or he'd be down here in the den half the night, listening to two women who had raised boringness to a kind of holy art form. Stained glass for the ear.

The rest of the tapes contained nothing useful. Twilley reset them for tomorrow and went upstairs. He sat on the sofa in the living room, opened the drawer in the end table beside him, and his tarot deck had been moved. He frowned at it. He always kept it lined up in a neat row between the coasters and the notepad, and now all three were out of alignment, the tarot deck most noticeably.

He looked around the room. *Janet* wouldn't move it. She wouldn't open this drawer. Had somebody been in the house?

He walked through the place, a small two-bedroom Cape Cod, and saw nothing else disturbed. Nothing was missing. He must have jostled the table one time, walking by.

He did a run of the cards on the living room coffee table, a little more hastily than usual, to be done before Janet got home. He wasn't embarrassed by the cards and his daily consultation of them, he could certainly do anything he damn well pleased in his own home, but it just felt a little awkward somehow to shuffle the deck and deal out the cards if he knew Janet could see him.

Nothing much in the cards today. A few strangers hovered here and there, but they always did. Life, according to the tarot deck, was normal.

He put the deck away, neatly aligned in the drawer, and when Janet came home a quarter hour later he was sprawled on the sofa, watching the early news. She took the sunglasses off right away, as soon as she walked in the door, to spite him. He squinted at her, and that shouldn't look that bruised, not four, five days later. She must be poking her thumb in her eye to make it look worse, so he'd feel bad.

You want somebody to poke a thumb in your eye, is that it? Is that what you want? "How was your day?" he said.

"I caught a fish." She'd been speaking to him in a monotone for so long he thought it was normal. "I'll see about dinner," she said, and went on through toward the kitchen.

Watching antacid commercials on television, Twilley told himself he *knew* she was up to something, and the reason he knew, she didn't fight back any more. She didn't get mad at him any more, and she almost never tried to boss him around any more.

Back at the beginning of the marriage, years ago, she had been an improver and he had been her most important project. Not her only project, she bossed everybody around, but the most important one. She'd married him, and they both knew it, because she'd believed he needed improving, and further believed he'd be somebody she'd be happy to live with once the improvement was complete.

No. Nobody pushes Roger Twilley. Roger Twilley pushes back.

But she wasn't pushing any more, hardly at all, only in an automatic unguarded way every once in a while. Like a few days ago. So that's how he knew she was up to something. Up to something.

"Is Frank there?"

14

Since he didn't plan to stay overnight in the city this time, Querk didn't borrow Claude's van but drove his own old clunker of a Honda with the resale value of a brick. But it would take him to New York and back, and last as long as he'd need it, which wouldn't be very long at all.

Three o'clock. He walked from his parked heap to the entrance to Dortmunder's building and would have rung the bell but Kelp was just ahead of him, standing in front of the door as he pulled his wallet out. "Whadaya say, Kirby?" he said, and withdrew a credit card from the wallet.

A credit card? To enter an apartment building? Querk said, "What are you doing?" but then he saw what he was doing, as Kelp slid the credit card down the gap between door and frame, like slicing off a wedge of soft cheese, and the door sagged open with a little forlorn *creak*.

"Come on in," Kelp said, and led the way.

Following, Querk said, "Why don't you ring the doorbell?"

"Why disturb them? This is just as easy. And practice."

Querk was not pleased, but not surprised either, when Kelp treated the apartment door upstairs the same way, going through it like a movie ghost, then pausing to call down the hallway, "Hello! Anybody there?" He turned his head to explain over his shoulder, "May doesn't like me to just barge in."

"No," agreed Querk, while down the hall Dortmunder appeared from the living room, racing form in one hand, red pencil in the other and scowl on face.

"God damn it, Andy," he said. "The building spent a lot of money on those doorbells."

"People spend money on anything," Kelp said, as he and Querk entered the apartment, Querk closing the door, yet wondering why he bothered.

Dortmunder shook his head, giving up the fight, and led the way into the living room as Kelp said, "May here?"

"She's doing a matinee." Dortmunder explained to Querk, "She likes movies, so if I got something to do she goes to them."

"You don't? Like movies?"

Dortmunder shrugged. "They're okay. Siddown."

Querk took the sofa, Dortmunder and Kelp the chairs. Kelp said, "So here we all are, Kirby, and now you're going to ease our minds."

"Well, I'll try." This was going to be tricky now, as Querk well knew. He said, "Maybe I should first tell you about the other person in this."

"Rodrigo, you mean," Kelp said.

"No, the travel agent."

"*That's* right," Kelp said, "you said there was a travel agent, he's the one gonna ship the siapas south."

"She," Querk corrected him. "Janet Twilley, her name is. She's got a travel agency, up there in Sycamore."

"Oh, ho," said Kelp. He looked roguish. "A little something happening there, Kirby?"

"No no," Querk said, because he certainly didn't want them to think *that*. "It's strictly business. She and I are gonna split our share, the same as you two."

"Half of a half," Kelp said.

"Right."

Dortmunder said, "You trust this person."

"Oh, absolutely," Querk said.

Dortmunder said, "Without anything special between you, just a business thing, you trust her."

Treading with extreme caution, Querk said, "To tell you the truth, I think she's got an unhappy marriage. I think she wants money so she can get away from there."

"But not with you," Kelp said.

"No, not with an ex-con." Querk figured if he put himself down it would sound more believable. "She just wants to use me," he explained, "to make it so she can get out of that marriage."

Dortmunder shrugged. "Okay. So she's the one takes the siapas to Rodrigo. *You* trust her to come back with the dollars. But we still got the same question, why do *we* trust her?"

"We talked about that," Querk said, "Janet and me, and the only thing we could come up with is, one of you has to travel with her."

Kelp nodded at Dortmunder. "Told you so."

"See," Querk said, hurrying through the story now that they'd reached it, "she's putting together this travel package, I dunno, fifteen or twenty people on this South American bus tour. Plane down, then bus. And she'll have the boxes in with the whole container load of everybody's luggage. So what she can do, she can slip in one more person, and she'll get the ticket for free, but you'll have to tell me which one so she'll know what name to put on the ticket."

Dortmunder and Kelp looked at each other. Kelp sighed. "I knew this was gonna happen," he said.

Querk said, "It won't be bad. A few days' vacation, and you come back."

Kelp said, "Can she promote two tickets?"

"You mean, both of you go down?"

"No," Kelp said. "I mean my lady friend. I could see myself doing this, I mean it would be easier, if she could come along."

"Sure," Querk said, because why not, and also because this was turning out to be easier than he'd feared. "Just give me her name. Write it down on something."

Dortmunder, rising, said, "I got a pad in the kitchen. Anybody want a beer?"

Everybody wanted a beer. Dortmunder went away, and Kelp said to Querk, "Her name is Anne Marie Carpinaw. Your friend— Janet?—they'll like each other."

"I'm sure they will," Querk said. Then, because he was nervous, he repeated himself, saying, "It won't be bad. A few days' vacation, that's all. You'll have a good time."

"Sure," Kelp said.

Dortmunder came back with a notepad and three unopened beer cans. "Here, everybody can open their own," he said.

Kelp took the pad and wrote his lady friend's name on it, while the other two opened their beer cans, Dortmunder slopping beer onto his pants leg. "Damn!"

"Here it is," Kelp said, and handed the slip of paper to Querk.

"Thanks." Querk pocketed the paper and lifted his beer. "What was that toast of yours? To crime."

Kelp offered the world's blandest smile. "To crime, with good friends," he said.

"Hear, hear," Dortmunder and Querk said.

15

Wednesday. The last thing Janet did before shutting Seven Leagues for the day was cut the two tickets, in the names of Anne Marie Carpinaw and Andrew Octavian Kelp, JFK to San Cristobal, Guerrera, change in Miami, intermediate stop in Tegucigalpa, Honduras, departure 10 P.M. tomorrow night, arrival 6:47 A.M., first leg Delta, second leg the charter carrier InterAir. She tucked these two tickets into her shoulder bag, put on her sunglasses, locked up the shop, took a last long look at it through the front plate glass window, and drove home to the rat.

At almost the exact same instant Janet was opening the door of her hated home, Kelp was opening the driver's door of another O'Malley special (small but spunky) rented with another short-life-expectancy credit card. Dortmunder tossed his bag in the back and slid in beside Kelp.

Kirby Querk, being on vacation along with the entire workforce of Sycamore Creek Printery, spent the afternoon fishing with a couple of friends from the plant, well downstream from town. (It was while fishing this part of this stream, almost a year ago, that he'd first met Janet, beautiful in her fishing hat and waders.) The unusually high water made for a rather interesting day, with a few spills, nothing serious. The influx of water from the opened dam starting last Saturday had roiled the streambed for a while, making turbid water in which the fishing would have been bad to useless, but by Wednesday Sycamore Creek was its normal sparkling self and Querk spent a happy day playing catch and release with the fish. There were times he almost forgot his nervousness about tonight.

Roger Twilley watched television news every chance he got, a sneer on his face. He despised and mistrusted them all, and watched mainly so he could catch the lies. A lot of the lies got past him, he knew that, but some of them he caught, the blatant obvious untruths the powers that be tell to keep the shmos in line. Well, Roger Twilley was no shmo; he was on to them, there in their 6:30 network news.

Meanwhile Janet, allegedly in the kitchen working on dinner, was actually in the bedroom, packing a small bag. Toiletries, cosmetics, a week's worth of clothing. She left much more than she took, but still the bag was crammed full when she was finished, and surprisingly heavy. She lugged it from the bedroom through the kitchen, out the back door, and around to the side of the house where a band of blacktop had been added, for her to keep her car. (*His* car got the attached garage, of course, which was all right in the summer, less so in the winter.) She heaved the bag into the trunk, which already contained her fishing gear, and went back into the house to actually make dinner, asking herself yet again, as she did every evening at this time, why she didn't just go ahead and poison the rat. But she answered the question, too, as she always did, with the knowledge that she'd simply never get away with it. A battered wife and a poisoned husband; even a Darby County cop could draw that connector.

Using the same credit card that had promoted the rental car, outside which now Dortmunder was stretching and groaning and wailing, "Why me?" Kelp took two adjoining rooms in the Taconic Lakes Motel, just about twenty miles north of Sycamore. It was not quite 7:30; even leaving the city in the middle of rush hour, they'd made good time.

Querk ate a bland dinner (meat loaf, mashed potatoes, green beans, water) with Cousin Claude and Eugenia and the two kids, then went into "his" room and packed his own bag. His years of being in and out of various jails had left him a man of very few possessions, all of which either fit into the bag or he wouldn't mind leaving behind. He put the bag on the floor next to the bed, on the side away from the door, and went out to watch television with the family.

Dortmunder and Kelp, after resting a little while in the motel, drove down to Sycamore and had dinner in the Italian restaurant by the traffic light there, the printery's forest crowding in on it from two sides. Dinner wasn't bad, and the same credit card still had some life in it. After dinner, they strolled around town a while, seeing how absolutely dense and black that forest was. There was some traffic, not much, and by evening the other joint in town, Sycamore House, where they'd had that lunch they were trying to forget, turned out to be where the rowdies hung out, the kind of place where the usual greeting is, "Wanna fight?" Their bark was presumably worse than their bite, though, because there was absolutely no police presence in town, neither around Sycamore House nor anywhere else, nor did it appear to be needed. Maybe on weekends.

When Janet washed her hair, which she usually did about three evenings a week, she was in the bathroom absolutely *forever*. This was a one-bathroom house, so Roger complained bitterly about the time she hogged in the bathroom, forcing him to go outside to piss on the lawn, but secretly this was the time he would take to search her possessions. Sooner or later, she would slip, leave something incriminating where he could find it.

And tonight, by God, was it! His hand shook, holding the airline tickets, and something gnawed at his heart, as though in reality he'd never wanted to find the proof of her perfidy after all, which was of course nonsense. Because here it was. *She* was Anne Marie Carpinaw, of course, a stupid alias to try to hide behind. But who was Andrew Octavian Kelp?

Cousin Claude and his family were early to bed, early to rise, and usually so was Querk; jail does not encourage the habit of rising late. This evening, as usual, the entire household was tucked in and dark before eleven o'clock, but this evening Querk couldn't sleep, not even if he wanted to, which he didn't. He lay in the dark in "his" room, the packed bag a dark bulk on the floor beside the bed, and he gazed at the ceiling, thinking about the plan he and Janet had worked out, seeing how good it was, how really good. They'd gone over it together he didn't know how many times, looking for flaws, finding some, correcting them. By now, the plan was honed as smooth as a river rock.

Janet almost always went to bed before Roger, and by the time he got there she would be asleep or at least pretending. Tonight, without a word, she went off to the bedroom and their separate beds just as he started watching the eleven o'clock news. He listened, and when he heard the bedroom door close he quietly got up, went to the kitchen, then through the connecting door to the garage. There was an automatic electric garage door opener, but it was very loud, and it caused a bright light to switch on for three minutes, so tonight Roger opened his car door to cause the interior light to go on, and by that light he found the red-and-white cord he could pull to separate the door from the opener, designed for emergencies like the power being off. Then he lifted the door by hand, leaned into the car to put it in neutral, and pushed it backward out of the garage. There was a slight downhill slope from garage to street, so the car did get away from him just a little bit, but there was no traffic on this residential side street this late at night, so he just followed it, and it stopped of its own accord when the rear wheels reached the street. He turned the wheel through the open window, and wrestled the car backward in a long arc until it was parked on the opposite side of the street one door down. A dark street, trees in leaf, a car like any other. Janet would have no reason to notice it. He went back to the house, into the garage, and pulled the door down. He could reattach the cord in the morning.

11:45 said Querk's bedside clock, red numbers glowing in the dark. He got up, dressed quickly and silently, picked up his bag, and tiptoed from the house. Tonight, he had parked the Honda down the block a ways. He walked to it, put the bag on the passenger seat, and drove away from there.

In their separate beds in the dark room, Janet and Roger were each convinced the other was asleep. Both were fully clothed except for their shoes under the light summer covers, and both worked very hard to breathe like a sleeping person. They had each other fooled completely.

Every time Janet, lying on her left side, cautiously opened her right eye to see the table between the beds, plus the dark mound of Roger over there, the illuminated alarm clock on the table failed to say midnight. She had no fear of accidentally falling asleep, not tonight of all nights, but why did time have to *creep* so? But then at last she opened that eye one more time and now the clock read *11:58*, and darn it, that was good enough. Being very careful, making absolutely no noise—well, a faint rustle or two—she rolled over and rose from the bed. She stooped to pick up her shoes, then carried them tiptoe from the room.

The instant he heard Janet move, Roger tensed like a bowstring. He forced himself to keep his eyes shut, believing eyes reflect whatever light might be around and she might see them and know he was awake. It wasn't until the rustle of her movements receded toward the bedroom door that he dared to look. Yes, there she goes, through the doorway, open now because it was only shut if she was in bed while he was watching television.

Janet turned left, toward the kitchen, to go out the back door and around to the car. It was too bad she'd have to start its engine so close to the house, but the bedroom was way on the other side, with the bulk of the house and the garage in between, so it should be all right. In any case, she was going.

The instant Janet disappeared from the doorway, Roger was up, stepping into his loafers, streaking silently through the house to the front door, out, and running full tilt across the street to crouch down on the far side of his car. Hunkered down there, he heard her car motor start, saw the headlights switch on, and then saw the car come out and swing away toward town, which is what he'd been hoping. It meant his car was faced the right way. He let her travel a block, then jumped into the car, started it, didn't turn the lights on, and drove off in pursuit.

12:20 by the dashboard clock, and Querk parked in the lot next to Sycamore House. There was no all-night street parking permitted in Central Sycamore, but there were always a few cars left at Sycamore House, by people whose friends had decided maybe they shouldn't drive home after all, so the Honda wouldn't attract attention. He got out and walked down the absolutely deserted silent street to the traffic light doggedly giving its signals to nothing, then crossed and walked to the entrance to Sycamore Creek and on in.

There was no problem unlocking the main gate, nor temporarily locking it again behind him. He crossed to the building, unlocked the one loading bay door with a faulty alarm he happened to know about, and made his way through the silent, dark, stuffy plant to the managers' offices, where it was a simple matter to disarm the alarm systems, running now on the backup batteries. Then he retraced his steps, out to the street.

Janet had expected to be the only person driving around this area this late at night, but partway to town another car's headlights appeared in her rearview mirror. Another night owl, she thought, and hoped he wasn't a drunken speed demon who would try to pass her. These roads were narrow and twisty. But, no; thankfully, he kept well back. She drove on into town, turned into the Sycamore House parking lot, recognized the Honda right away, and parked next to it.

Roger had kept well back, sorry he had to use his headlights at all but not wanting to run into a deer out here, the deer population having exploded in this part of the world once all of the predator animals had been removed, unless you count hunters, and don't. He followed the car ahead all the way into town, and when he saw the brake lights go on he thought at first she was braking for the traffic light up ahead, but then she suddenly made the left turn into the Sycamore House parking lot. Damn! He hadn't expected that. Should he go past? Should he stop? If he tried to park along here, you just knew some damn cop would pop out of nowhere to give him both a hard time and a ticket, while Janet got away to who knows where. Guerrera, that's where. San Cristobal, Guerrera.

He drove on by, peering in at the Sycamore House parking lot, but she'd switched her lights off and there was nothing to see. He got to the corner, and the light was against him, so he stopped, while no traffic went by in all directions. Diagonally across the street was Luigi's, the Italian restaurant, and at the far end of it, he knew, was a small parking lot, hemmed in by the fake forest. He could leave the car there and hoof it back to Sycamore House, just as soon as this damn light changed. When would it—? Ah! At last.

He drove across the empty intersection, turned left at the small and empty parking lot, and stopped, car's nose against pine branches. He switched off lights and engine, so now it was only by the vague streetlight glow well behind him that he saw, in his rearview mirror, the apparition rise from the floor behind the front seat, *exactly* like all those horror stories! He stared, convulsed with terror, and the apparition showed him a wide horrible smile, a big horrible pistol and a pair of shiny horrible handcuffs. "Didn't that tarot deck," it asked him, "tell you not to go out tonight?"

16

When Querk walked back into the Sycamore House parking lot, Janet's Chrysler Cirrus was parked next to his little Honda; a bigger, more comfortable car, though not very new. She must have seen him in the rearview mirror because she popped out of her car, the brief illumination of the interior light showing the hugeness of her smile but still the dark around her left eye. Then the door closed, the light went out, and she was in his arms.

They embraced a long time, he feeling her body tremble with the release of weeks of tension. Months. But now it was over. He was off parole, a free man. She was out of that house, a free woman. Start here.

At last he released her and whispered, "Everything's going fine. Three, four hours, it'll be all over."

"I know you'll do it," she whispered, then shook a finger at him. "Don't let them get any ideas."

"I won't."

He took his bag from the Honda and put it in the Chrysler, then kissed her one last time, got into the Honda, and drove out to the street. He turned left, ignored the red light, drove through the intersection, and stopped next to the Hess station across the street from Luigi's. Promptly, Dortmunder stepped out of the dimness inside the phone booth there, crossed the sidewalk, and slid in next to him.

Querk looked around. "Where's Kelp?"

"A couple things came up," Dortmunder told him, "nothing to do with us. He'll take care of them, then catch up with us later."

Querk didn't like this, didn't like the idea that one of his partners was going to be out of sight while the job was going down. "We're gonna need Kelp in the plant there," he said.

"He'll be there," Dortmunder promised. "He'll be right there when we get back with the truck."

There was nothing Querk could do about this development short of to call the whole thing off, which he didn't want to do, so he nodded reluctantly and said, "I hope nothing's gonna get screwed up."

"How could it? Come on, let's go."

The Combined Darby County Fire Department and Rescue Squad existed in an extremely fireproof brick building in the middle of nowhere. Seven local volunteer fire departments and two local volunteer ambulance services, each with its own firehouse or garage, had been combined into this organization, made necessary by the worsening shortage of volunteers, and political infighting had made it impossible to use any of the existing facilities. A local nob had donated land here in the middle of the responsibility area, and the building was erected, empty and alone unless a fund-raiser dinner were being held or the volunteers' beepers sounded off.

Querk parked the Honda behind the building, out of sight, and used a copy of Cousin Claude's key to unlock the right garage door. He lifted it, stepped inside, and drove out the truck, which was red like a fire engine, with high metal sides full of cubicles containing emergency equipment, a metal roof, but open at the back to show the big generator bolted to the truck body in there.

Querk waited while Dortmunder lowered the garage door and climbed up onto the seat next to him. "Pretty good machine," he said.

"It does the job," Querk said.

It was with relief that Querk saw Kelp actually standing there next to the NO TRESPASSING sign. Kelp waved, and Dortmunder waved back, while Querk drove down to the closed entrance gates. "They're unlocked," he assured Dortmunder, who climbed out to open the gates, then close them again after the truck and Kelp had both entered.

Driving slowly alongside the building toward the window he wanted, Querk saw in all his rearview mirrors, illuminated by a smallish moon, Dortmunder and Kelp walking along in his wake, talking together. Kelp must be telling Dortmunder what he'd done about whatever problem he'd gone off to fix.

Querk wondered; should he ask Kelp what the problem was? No, he shouldn't. Dortmunder had said it was nothing to do with tonight's job, so that meant it was none of his business. The fact that Kelp was here was all that mattered. A tight-lipped man knows when other people expect him to be tight-lipped.

17

Dortmunder was bored. There was nothing to do about it but admit it; he was bored.

Usually, in a heist, what you do is, you case the joint, then you plan and plan, and then there's a certain amount of tension when you break into whatever the place is, and then you *grab* what you came for and you get *out* of there.

Not this time. This time, the doors are open, the alarms are off, and nobody's around. So you just waltz in. But then you don't *grab* anything, and you certainly don't get *out* of there.

What you do instead, you shlep heavy cable off a wheel out of the generator truck, shove it through a window Querk has opened, and then shlep it across a concrete floor in the dark, around and sometimes into a lot of huge machines that are not the machine Querk wants, until at last you can hook the cables to both a machine and a control panel. This control panel also controls some lights, so finally you can see what you're doing.

Meanwhile, Querk has been collecting his supplies. He needs three different inks, and two big rolls of special paper, that he brings over with his forklift. He needs one particular size of paper cutter, a wickedly sharp big rectangle criss-crossed with extremely dangerous lines of metal, that has to be slid into an opening in the side of the machine without sacrificing any fingers to it, and which will, at the appropriate moments, descend inside the machine to slice sheets of paper into many individual siapas.

The boxes for the siapas already exist, but laid out flat, and have to be inserted into a wide slot in the back of the machine. The nasty wire bands to close the boxes—hard, springy, with extremely sharp edges—have to be inserted onto rolls and fed into the machine like feeding movie film into a projector. Having three guys for this part is a help, because it would take one guy working alone a whole lot longer just to set things up, even if he could wrestle the big paper roll into position by himself, which he probably couldn't.

But after everything was in position, then you *really* needed three guys. It was a three-guy machine. Guy number one (Querk) was at the control panel, keeping an eye on the gauges that told him how the ink flow was coming along, how the paper feed was doing, how the boxes were filling up. Guy number two (Kelp) was physically all around the machine, which was a little delicate and touchy, following Querk's orders on how to adjust the various feeds and watch the paper, which would have liked to jam up if anybody looked away for a minute.

And guy number three, Dortmunder, was the utility man. It was his job to replenish the ink supply when needed, which was rarely. It was also his job to wrestle the full boxes off the end of the chute at the back of the machine, but since in three hours there were only going to be five boxes, that didn't take up a lot of his time. It was also his job occasionally to go out to see how the generator truck was coming along, which was fine. In addition, it was his job to keep checking on the laid-out boxes inside the machine with the money stacking up on them, and the alignment of the big paper-cutter, to make sure nothing was getting off kilter and to warn Querk to shut down temporarily if something did, which only happened twice. And generally it was his job to stand chicky; but if anybody were to come into the plant that they wouldn't like to come in, it would already be too late to do anything about it.

So here he was, the gofer in a slow-motion heist, and he was bored. It was like having an actual job.

They'd started at ten after one, and it was just a few ticks after four when the last of the paper rolled into the machine and Querk started shutting its parts down, one section at a time until the fifth and final box came gliding out of the chute and Dortmunder wrestled it over onto the concrete floor with the others. Five boxes, very heavy, each containing a thousand bills compressed into the space, a thousand twenty million siapa notes per box, for a value of a hundred thousand dollars per box. In Guerrera.

Dortmunder stepped back from the final box. "Done," he said. "At last."

"Not exactly done," Querk said. "Remember, this run never happened. We gotta clean up everything in here, put it all back the way it was."

Yes; exactly like having a job.

18

Querk's nervousness, once they'd driven the generator truck actually onto the plant property, had turned into a kind of paralysis, a

cauterizing in which he couldn't feel his feelings. He was just doing it, everything he'd been going over and over in his mind all this
time, acting out the fantasy, reassuring Janet and himself that
everything would work out just fine, playing it out in his head again
and again so that, when the time came to finally *do* it, actually in
the real world do it, it was as though he'd already done it and this
was just remembering.

And the job went, if anything, even better than the fantasy,
smooth and quick and easy. Not a single problem with the two guys
he'd found to help, and that had always been one of the scarier parts
of the whole thing. He couldn't do it alone, but he couldn't use locals, none of these birds around here had the faintest idea how to
keep their mouths shut. Amateurs. He had to use pros, but he didn't
know anybody any more.

Nevertheless, if he was going to do it, he would have to reach out,
find *somebody* with the right résumé that he could talk into the job, and
boy, did he come up lucky. Dortmunder and Kelp were definitely pros,
but at the same time they were surprisingly gullible. He could count
on them to do the job and to keep their mouths shut, and he could also
count on them to never even notice what he was really up to.

The cleaning up after the print job took another half hour. The
next to the last thing they did, before switching off the lights, was
forklift the five boxes of siapas out to the generator truck, where they
fit nicely at the back. Then it was disconnect the cables, reel them
back into the truck, and drive out of there, pausing to lock the big
gates on the way by.

Still dark on the streets of Sycamore. Still no vehicles for the du-
tiful traffic light to oversee. Dortmunder and Kelp rode on the wide
bench seat of the truck beside Querk, who drove down the street to
stop in front of Seven Leagues. "I'll just unlock the door," he said, as
he climbed down to the street.

The story he'd told them was that the travel group going down
there to Guerrera contained a bunch of evangelicals, looking for con-
verts, so Janet would ship the boxes out of the United States as
missals and hymnals. Tonight, they'd leave the boxes at Seven
Leagues, and in the morning she'd cover them with all the necessary
tags and stickers, and the van carrying all the tour group's luggage
would come by to pick them up and take them down to JFK.

Once the boxes had been lugged into Seven Leagues and the door relocked, Querk said, "You fellas need a lift to your car?"

"No, that's okay," Kelp said, pointing vaguely north, out of town. "We're parked just up there."

Dortmunder said, "You want to get the truck back."

"I sure do."

Should he shake hands with them? He felt he should; it would be the more comradely thing to do. Sticking his hand out in Kelp's direction, he said, "It's been good working with you."

Kelp had a sunny smile, even in the middle of the night. Pumping Querk's hand, he said, "I wouldn't miss it for the world."

Shaking Dortmunder's hand, bonier than Kelp's but less powerful, Querk said, "We'll be in touch."

"You know it," Dortmunder said.

"You know where to find me."

"Sure do," Dortmunder said.

Well. That was comradely enough. "I better get this truck back before sunup," he said.

"Sure," they said, and waved at him, and he got into the truck.

He had to make a K turn to go back the other way, cumbersome with this big vehicle. He headed toward the traffic light as Dortmunder and Kelp walked off northward, disappearing almost immediately into the darkness, there being streetlights only here in the center of town.

As he drove toward the traffic light, he passed Sycamore House on his left, and resisted the impulse to tap the horn. But Janet would see him, and a horn sounding here in the middle of the night might attract attention. Attention from Dortmunder and Kelp, in any case.

So he drove on, the traffic light graciously turning green as he reached the intersection. Behind him, Janet in the Cirrus would now have seen the truck go by twice, and would know the job had gone well. He could hardly wait to get back to her.

Querk grinned all the way to the garage, where he put the truck away, backing it in the way it had been before. Then he got into the Honda for the last time in his life and drove it back to Sycamore, not only grinning now but also humming a little and at times even whistling between his teeth. To his right, the sky was just beginning to pale; dawn was on the way.

Sycamore. Once again the traffic light gave him a green. He drove through the intersection, turned into the Sycamore House parking lot, and put the Honda next to the Cirrus. He switched off the lights and the engine and stepped out to the blacktop, leaving the keys in the car. Turning to the Cirrus, he expected Janet to either start the engine or step out to speak to him. When she did neither, he bent to look into the car, and it was empty.

What? Why? They'd agreed to meet here when the job was done, so what happened? Where was she?

Maybe she'd needed to go to the bathroom. Or maybe she started to get uncomfortable in the car, after almost four hours, and decided to go wait in the office instead. The whole purpose of her being here the whole time was so he'd have his own backup means of escape in case anything were to go wrong with the job. Once she'd seen the truck, she had to know the job had gone well.

So she must be up at Seven Leagues. Querk left the parking lot and walked up the street, taking the Seven Leagues key out of his pocket. When he reached the place, there were no lights on inside. That was strange.

He unlocked the door, entered, closed the door, felt around on the wall for the light switch, found it, and stared, unbelieving.

"Surprise," Dortmunder said.

19

Between dinner and the job, in fact, Dortmunder and Kelp had found a number of things to keep them interested, if not completely surprised. Primarily, they'd wanted to know what part Janet Twilley planned to take in tonight's exercises, if any, and so had driven out to the Twilley house a little before eleven, seeing lights still on in there. They'd visited that house last week, learning more about Roger Twilley than anybody else on Earth, and had found none of it pleasant. If Janet Twilley wanted to begin life anew with Kirby Querk, they couldn't argue the case, not with what they knew of Roger, just so she didn't plan to do it with their siapas.

They were parked down the block from the Twilley residence, discussing how to play this—should Kelp drive Dortmunder back to town, to keep an eye on the plant, while Kelp kept the car and maintained an observation post chez Twilley—when Roger decided their moves for them. The first thing they saw was the garage door open over there.

"The light didn't come on," Dortmunder said.

"I knew there was something," Kelp said.

Next, a car backed out of the garage, also with no lights on, and moving very slowly. Not only that, Roger himself came trotting out of the garage right after the car, so who was driving?

Turned out, nobody. Fascinated, they watched Roger push his car around in a great loop to park it on their side of the street, about two houses away.

"He, too, knows something's up," Kelp said.

Dortmunder said, "But he doesn't know what."

"He's gonna follow her."

"So we," Dortmunder said, "follow him."

"I got a better idea," Kelp said. "Have we got that bag in the back?"

"In the trunk? Yeah."

On an outing like this, they always traveled with that bag. Small, it was packed with extra materials that, who knew, might come in handy. Tools of various kinds, ID of various kinds, weapons of various kinds, and handcuffs of just one kind.

"What do you need from it?" Dortmunder asked.

"The cuffs. I'll ride in the back of the peeping tom's car, take him out if there's a problem, borrow it myself if she doesn't come out to be followed. You stash this car in town, tell Kirby I'll meet up with you guys at the plant."

So that's what they did, Dortmunder learning some more along the way, beginning with the fact that the driver's seat had even less legroom than the passenger seat. He stashed the compact in the Sycamore House parking lot, but stayed with it, and was there when Querk arrived, parked his Honda, and went off to set things up over at the printery.

A little later, he was also about to leave when Janet Twilley drove in, shut down, but didn't get out of her car. That was interesting. Not wanting to call attention to himself, he removed the bulb from the compact's interior light so that everything remained dark when he eased out of the car and out of the parking lot to go over to the Hess station and wait for Querk.

One thing about the phone booth outside the Hess station; it had legroom. Dortmunder leaned his back against the phone, folded his arms, and watched the traffic light change. After a while he saw Querk cross the street and walk north, and then here he came in the Honda south.

After the job at the plant and the departure of Querk to return the generator truck, there'd been nothing left to do but gather up Janet Twilley, still at her post in her Chrysler Cirrus, and use her keys to gain entrance to Seven Leagues. As for her husband, he could stay where he was, trussed up on the floor of his own car down by Luigi's. Good place for him.

And now it was simply a matter of waiting for Querk. And here he is.

20

Querk stared, pole-axed with shock. Janet was gagged and tied to her office chair, wide-eyed and trembling. Even her bruise was pale. Kelp, still with that sunny smile, sat near her in the client's chair. And Dortmunder stood near Querk; not too near, but close enough so that, if Querk decided to spin around and pull the door open and run, it wouldn't happen.

Stammering, the tremble in his hands back and worse than ever, Querk said, "What? What happened?"

"We came to settle up," Dortmunder said, while Kelp got to his feet, walked back to the unused desk, took the client's chair from it, and brought it back to stand facing himself and Janet. "Take a load off," he offered.

Dortmunder said, "Andy, turn the desk light on, will you? It's too bright in here."

Kelp did, and Dortmunder switched off the overheads that Querk had switched on. It became much dimmer in the long room, the light softer, though not what Querk thought of as cozy. Watching all this, he tried desperately to think, without much success. What was going on? What were they going to do? He said, "What's wrong? Fellas? I thought everything was okay."

"Not exactly okay," Dortmunder said, as he perched on the corner of Janet's desk.

Kelp said, "Come on, Kirby, take a chair. We'll tell you all about it."

So Querk sat in the chair Kelp had brought for him, and folded his shaking hands in his lap. He could feel Janet's eyes on him, but he couldn't bring himself to look directly at her. He was supposed to make things *better* for her. Tied up in a chair by two heisters from New York wasn't *better*.

Kelp said, "You know, Kirby, the thing was, at first we believed there really was a Rodrigo." He still seemed cheerful, not angry or upset, but Querk didn't believe any of it.

"You got us there, for a while," Dortmunder agreed. He sounded sullen, and that Querk could believe.

"What we figured," Kelp said, "why would you go through this whole scheme unless you had a payout coming? So that's why we believed in Rodrigo. Until, of course, we heard about Janet. Just as a by the by."

"Just dropped in the conversation," Dortmunder said.

"And Harry Matlock said you were a better follower than a leader," Kelp said, "so we began to wonder, who exactly were you following? So when we came up here last week, I stopped in to see Janet."

What? Querk now did stare directly at Janet, and she was frantically nodding, eyebrows raised almost to her hairline. "She—" Querk had to clear his throat. "She didn't tell me."

"She didn't know," Kelp said. "See, I was a customer, I was interested in going somewhere in South America, I wasn't sure where, and we talked about, oh . . ." He looked at Janet, amiable, inquiring. "About fifteen minutes, right?" Looking at Querk again, he said, "And the funny thing, never once did she mention that tour going to Guerrera. In fact, she never even mentioned Guerrera, the whole country."

"Probably," Querk said, even though he knew it was hopeless, "the tour was full by then."

"Which gets to how easy the extra two tickets were," Kelp said. "First she can wangle one ticket, but then two tickets is easy, no sweat, you don't even have to check back with her. But I'm getting ahead of my story."

"I thought you were buying it," Querk said.

Kelp's grin got even wider. "Yeah, I know. Anyway, when I was here that time, I noticed the shiner on Janet, and you didn't seem the type—"

"We both thought that," Dortmunder said.

"Thank you," Querk said.

"So we checked out her house," Kelp said, "and that's some winner she decided to marry."

"I guess he didn't seem that bad at first," Querk said.

"Maybe," Kelp said. "Anyway, here's this bossy woman—"

Janet gave him a glare, which Kelp ignored.

"—with a shiner and a bad husband. And here's you, likes to be bossed around. So we decided, what it was, you didn't have any Rodrigo, because how is this Janet here in upstate New York gonna make that kinda connection. Also, this is not a really successful travel agency here, which you can see by the fact that the other desk isn't used, so if she ever had an assistant or a partner the business couldn't support that person. So *maybe*, just maybe, the idea is, you'll run these half million dollars' worth of siapas, and you and Janet will *drive* to Guerrera, down through Mexico and all that, maxing out your credit cards along the way. And when you get there, you find a nice place to stay, you start living on the siapas. You put 'em in a few banks down there, you can even come back up to the States sometimes and spend them like money. Of course, there wouldn't be any for *us*."

"I'm sorry," Querk said.

Dortmunder nodded. "You certainly are."

"You needed two guys," Kelp said. "You couldn't go with local amateurs, so you had to reach out for pros, and what you got was us."

"I underestimated you," Querk said.

"Don't feel bad," Kelp advised him. "That's what *we* specialize in. So here you are, you've kissed us off, and Anne Marie and me are gonna feel really stupid tomorrow night at JFK with those imitation tickets—"

"I'm sorry," Querk said again.

"We know," Dortmunder said. He didn't sound sympathetic.

"But, you know," Kelp said, "this is better for you, because *Roger* knew something was up. You know, the paranoid is sometimes right, and Roger was right. So he was following Janet tonight, and if it hadn't been for us, Roger would be making a whole lot of trouble for you people right now."

Querk was rather afraid of Roger Twilley. "Roger?" he said. "Where is he?"

"Tied up in his car, down at Luigi's."

Dortmunder said, "You owe us for that one."

"Well," Kelp said, "he owes us for the whole score."

"That's true," Dortmunder said.

Rising, Kelp said, "I'll go get our wheels, you explain it."

Kelp was the pleasant one. Why couldn't Dortmunder go get their car? But, no; Kelp nodded at Querk and left the shop, and it was Dortmunder who said, "This is what we're gonna do. We're gonna leave you one box of the siapas, that's a hundred grand you can take down to Guerrera, get you started. In six months, you come up to New York, you buy at least one more box from us, half price. Fifty grand for a hundred grand of siapas. You can buy them all then, or you can buy a box every six months."

Querk said, "Where am I gonna get that money?"

"You're gonna steal it," Dortmunder told him. "That's what you do, remember? You gave up on reform."

Querk hung his head. The thought of a Guerreran jail moved irresistably through his mind.

Meanwhile, Dortmunder said, "If you *don't* show up in six months, the four boxes go to the cops with an anonymous letter with your names and a description of the scheme and where you're hiding out, and the probable numbers on your siapas. And then you've got nothing."

"Jeez," Querk said.

"Look at it this way," Dortmunder suggested. "You lied to us, you abused our trust, but we aren't getting even, we aren't hurting you. Because all we want is what's ours. So, one way or another, you keep your side of the bargain, and we keep ours." Looking past Querk at the window, he said, "Here's the goddam compact. I hope we can fit these boxes in there. Come on, Querk, help me carry the loot."

"All right." Rising, Querk said, "What do we do about Roger?"

"Nothing," Dortmunder said. "Luigi's cook'll find him in the morning, let *him* decide what to do. Come on, grab a box."

So Querk did, the two of them shlepping the boxes one at a time, Kelp busily moving crap around inside the car. They managed to cram three of the boxes into the trunk and one on its side on the alleged back seat, with their luggage on top.

At the end, feeling humble, Querk said to them both, on the sidewalk, "I wanna thank you guys. You could of made things a lot tougher for me."

"Well," Dortmunder said, "I wouldn't say you were getting off scot free." He nodded at Seven Leagues. "Sooner or later, you're gonna have to take off that gag."

ANNE PERRY

Anne Perry is the bestselling author of two Victorian detective series that are practically mandatory reading for any aficionado of the historical mystery. Her Thomas Pitt series and the William and Hester Monk series, although both set in the same nineteenth-century London, take very different looks at English society. She is also writing another acclaimed historical series set during the French Revolution, and consisting of the books *A Dish Taken Cold* and *The One Thing More*. She has also started another series set during World War I, which launched with the acclaimed novel *No Graves As Yet*. Besides this, she has also written a fantasy duology, *Tathea* and *Come Armageddon*. But no matter what genre she writes in, her deft, detailed research, multifaceted characters, and twisting plots have garnered her fans around the world. In her spare time she lectures on writing in such places as the cruise ship the *Queen Elizabeth II*. Recent books include *A Christmas Journey*, featuring a secondary character from the Thomas Pitt novels taking center stage, and the second volume in her World War I series, *Shoulder the Sky*. She makes her home in the highlands of Scotland.

HOSTAGES

Anne Perry

Bridget folded the last pair of trousers and put them into the case. She was looking forward to the holiday so much there was a little flutter of excitement in her stomach. It would not be the west coast she loved with its clean wind off the Atlantic and the great waves pounding in, because that would mean crossing the border into Eire, and they could not do that. But the north coast held its own beauty, and it would be away from Belfast, from Connor's responsibilities to the church, and most of all to the political party. There was always something he had to do, a quarrel to arbitrate, someone's bereavement to ease, a weakness to strengthen, a decision to make, and then argue and persuade.

It had been like that as long as she had known him, as it had been for his father. But then the Irish Troubles were over three hundred years old, in one form or another. The courage with which you fought for your beliefs defined who you were.

There was room for more in the suitcase. She looked around to see what else to put in just as Liam came to the door. He was sixteen, tall and lean like Connor, not yet filled out with muscle, and very conscious of it.

"Are you packed yet?" she asked.

"You don't need that much, Mum," he said dismissively. "We're only going for a week, and you can wash things, you know! Why are we going anyway? There's nothing to do!"

"That's exactly what I want to go for," she answered with a smile. "Your father needs to do nothing."

"He'll hate it!" Liam responded. "He'll be fretting all the time in case he's missing something, and when he comes home he'll only have to work twice as hard to put right whatever they've fouled up."

"Has it ever occurred to you," she said patiently, "that nothing will go wrong, and we'll have a good time? Don't you think perhaps it would be nice to be together, with no one else to think about, no one demanding anything, just for a few days?"

Liam rolled his eyes. "No," he said candidly. "It'll bore me out of my mind, and Dad too. He'll end up half the time on the phone anyway."

"There's no phone there," she told him. "It's a beach house."

"The mobile!" he said impatiently, his voice touched with contempt. "I'm going to see Michael."

"We're leaving in a couple of hours!" she called after him as he disappeared, and she heard his footsteps light and rapid along the passage, and then the back door slammed.

Connor came into the room. "What are you taking?" he asked, looking at the case. "What have you got all those trousers for? Haven't you packed any skirts? You can't wear those all the time."

She could, and she intended to. No one would see them. For once appearance would not matter. There would be no one there to criticize or consider it was not the right example for the wife of a minister and leader of the Protestant cause. Anyway, what she wore had nothing to do with the freedom of faith he had fought for since he was Liam's age, costing him the lightheartedness and the all too brief irresponsibility of his youth.

But was it worth arguing now, on the brink of this rare time together? It would sour it from the outset, make him feel thwarted, as if she were deliberately challenging him. It always did. And she wanted this week for them to have time away from anxiety and the constant pressure and threat that he faced every day at home, or in London.

Wordlessly she took the trousers out, all but one pair, and replaced them with skirts.

He did not say anything, but she saw the satisfaction in his face. He looked tired. There was a denser network of fine lines around his eyes and he was greyer at the temples than she had realized. A tiny muscle ticked intermittently in his jaw. Although he had complained about it, denied it, he needed this holiday even more than she did. He needed days without duty, without decisions, nights of sleep without interruption from the telephone, a chance to talk without weighing every word in case it were misjudged, or misquoted. She felt the little flutter of pleasure again, and smiled at him.

He did not notice. He left, closing the door behind him.

She was crushed, even as she knew it was stupid. He had far too much else on his mind to bother with emotional trivialities. He had every right to expect that she should take such things for granted. In the twenty-four years of their marriage he had never let her down. He never let anyone down! No matter what it cost, he always kept his word. The whole of Northern Ireland knew that, Catholic and Protestant. The promise of Connor O'Malley could be trusted, it was rock solid, as immutable as the promise of God—and as hard.

She heard the words in her mind with horror. How could she even think such a thing, let alone allow it to come into her head. He was engaged in a war of the spirit, there was no room for half measures, for yielding to the seduction of compromise. And he used the right words, she could feel her own temptation to water down the chastenings, in order to achieve a little peace, to yield on truth just for respite from the constant battle. She was heart and soul weary of it. She hungered for laughter, friendship, the ordinary things of daily life, without the pressure of outward righteousness and inner anger all the time.

And he would see that as weakness, even betrayal. Right cannot ever compromise with wrong. It is the price of leadership that there can be no self-indulgence. How often had he said that, and lived up to it?

She looked at the trousers she had taken out of the case. They were comfortable, and she could wear flat, easy shoes with them. This was supposed to be a holiday. She put two pairs of them back in again, at the bottom. She would do the unpacking anyway, and he would never know.

It was not difficult to pack for him: pyjamas, underwear, socks, plenty of shirts so he would always have a clean one, sweaters, lighter coloured casual trousers, toiletries. He would bring his own books and papers; that was an area she was not expected to touch.

Three middle-sized cases and Connor's briefcase would fit into the trunk of the car easily. The bodyguards, Billy and Ian, would come separately, following in another car, and they were not her responsibility. In fact she would try to imagine they were not there. They were necessary, of course, as they always were. Connor was a target for the I.R.A., although as far as she knew they had never physically attacked him. It would be a politically stupid thing to do; it would be the one thing that would unite all the disparate Protestant factions in one solid outrage.

And for the verbal attacks, he gave as good as he received, or better. He had the gift of words, the knowledge, and above all the passion so that his sermons, and his political speeches, almost interchangeable, erupted like lava to scorch those who were against his vision of Protestant survival and freedom. Sometimes it was directed just as fiercely at those on his own side who wavered, or in his view committed the greatest sin of all, betrayal. He despised a coward even more than he hated an open enemy.

The doorbell rang, and then, before anyone had had time to answer it, she heard the door open, and then Roisin's voice call out. "Hello, Mum! Where are you?"

"Bedroom!" Bridget answered. "Just finishing the packing. Like a cup of tea?"

"I'll make it," Roisin answered, arriving in the doorway. She was twenty-three, slim, with soft, brown hair like Bridget's, only darker, no honey fair streaks. She had been married just over a year and still had that glow of surprise and happiness about her. "You all ready?" she asked.

Bridget heard a slight edge to her voice, a tension she was trying to conceal. Please heaven it was not a difference with Eamonn. They were sufficiently in love it would all iron out, but Bridget did not want to go away for a week leaving Roisin emotionally raw. She was too vulnerable, and Eamonn was like Connor, passionate about his beliefs, committed to them, and expecting the same kind of commitment from those he loved, unaware of how little of himself he gave to his family, forgetting to put into word or touch what he expected them to know. "What is it?" she said aloud.

"I've got to speak to Dad," Roisin answered. "That's what I came for, really."

Bridget opened her eyes wide.

Roisin took a quick breath. "Sorry, Mum," she apologized. "I came to wish you a good holiday too. Heaven knows, you need it. But I could have done that over the phone."

Bridget looked at her more closely. She was a little flushed and her hands were stiff at her sides. "Are you alright?" she said with a pinch of anxiety. She almost asked her if she were pregnant, there was something about her which suggested it, but it would be intrusive. If it were so, Roisin would tell her when she was ready.

"Yes, of course I am!" Roisin said quickly. "Where's Dad?"

"Is it political?" It was a conclusion more than a question. She saw the shadow deepen in Roisin's eyes, and her right hand clench. "Couldn't it wait until we get back? Please!"

Roisin's face was indefinably tighter, more closed. "Eamonn asked me to come over," she answered. "Some things don't wait, Mum. I'll put the kettle on. He's not out, is he?"

"No . . ." Before she could add anything else, Roisin twisted around and was gone. Bridget looked around, checking the room for the last time. She always forgot something, but it was usually a trivial thing she could do without. And it was not as if they were going abroad. The house on the shore was lonely, that was its greatest charm, but the nearest village was a couple of miles away, and they would have the car. Even though they took bread and potatoes and a few tins, they would still need to go for food every so often.

She went through to the kitchen and found Roisin making the tea, and Connor standing staring out of the window into the back garden. Bridget would like to have escaped the conflict, but she knew there was no point. She would hear what had been said sooner or later. If they agreed it would be a cause for celebration, and she would join in. If they didn't, it would be between them like a coldness in the house, a block of ice sitting in the kitchen to be walked around.

Roisin turned with the teapot in her hand. "Dad?"

He remained where he was, his back to the room.

She poured three cups. "Dad, Eamonn's been talking with some of the moderates about a new initiative in education . . ." She stopped as she saw his shoulders stiffen. "At least listen to them!" Her voice was tight and urgent, a kind of desperation lifting it a pitch higher. "Don't refuse without hearing what it is!"

He swung around at last. His face was bleak, almost grey in the hard light. He sounded weary and bitter. "I've heard all I need to about Catholic schools and their methods, Rosie. Wasn't it the Jesuits who said 'Give me a child until he's seven, and I'll give you the man'? It's Popish superstition founded on fear. You'll never get rid of it out of the mind. It's a poison for life."

She swallowed. "They think the same about us!" she argued. "They aren't going to give in on teaching their children as they want, they can't afford to, or they won't carry their own people!"

"Neither am I," he replied, nothing in his face yielding, his jaw set, his blue eyes cold.

Bridget ached to interrupt, but she knew better. He found her ideas woolly and unrealistic, a recipe for evasion, and inch by inch surrender without the open honesty of battle. He had said so often enough. She had never stood her ground, never found the words or the courage to argue back. Somebody had to compromise or there would never be peace. She was tired of the cost of anger, not only the destruction of lives, the injury and the bereavement, but the loss of daily sanity, laughter and the chance to build with the hope of something lasting, the freedom from having to judge and condemn.

Roisin was still trying. "But Dad, if we gave a little on the things that don't matter, then we could stick on the things that do, and at least we would have started! We would look reasonable, maybe win over some of the middle parties."

"To what?" he asked.

"To join us, of course!" She spoke as if the answer were obvious.

"For how long?" There was challenge in his voice, and something close to anger.

She looked puzzled.

"Rosie, we're different parties because we have different principles," he said wearily. "The door has always been open for them to join us, if they will. I am not adulterating my beliefs to please the crowd or to win favours of anyone. I won't do it because it's wrong, but it's also foolish. As soon as they've got one concession, they'll want another, and another, until there's nothing left of what we've fought for, and died for all these years. Each time we give in, it'll be harder to stand the next time, until we've lost all credibility, and our own can't trust us any more. You're one or another. There's no half way. If Eamonn doesn't know that now, he'll learn it bitterly."

She would not retreat. She was beaten on logic, but not on will. "But Dad, if no one ever moves on anything, we'll go on fighting each other for ever. My children will live and die for exactly the same things your parents did, and we're doing now! We've got to live together some day. Why not now?"

Connor's face softened. He had more patience with her than he did with Bridget. He picked up his cup in both hands, as if he were cold and warming himself on it. "Rosie, I can't afford to," he said quietly. "I've made promises I have to keep. If I don't, I have no right to ask for their trust. It's my job to bind them together, give them courage and hope, but I can only lead where they are willing to follow. Too far in front, and I'll lose them. Then I'll have accomplished nothing. They'll feel betrayed and choose a new leader, more extreme, and less likely to yield to anything than I am."

"But Dad, we've got to yield over something!" she persisted, her voice strained, her body awkward as she leaned across the table. "If you can't in education, then what about industry, or taxes, or censorship? There's got to be somewhere we can meet, or everything's just pointless, and we're all playing a charade that's going to go on and on forever, all our lives! All of us caught in a madman's parade, as if we hadn't the brains or the guts to see it and get out. It isn't even honest! We pretend we want peace, but we don't! We just want our own way!"

Bridget heard the hysteria in her voice, and at that moment she was sure Roisin was pregnant. She had a desperation to protect the future that was primal, higher and deeper than reason. Perhaps it was the one real hope? She stepped forward, intervening in her own instinct to shield.

"They're just people with a different faith and political aim," she said to Connor. "There must be a point where we can meet. They've moderated a lot in the last twenty years. They don't insist on Papal censorship of books any more . . ."

Connor looked at her in amazement, his eyebrows rising sharply. "Oh! And you call that moderation, do you? We should be grateful to be allowed to choose for ourselves what we can read, which works of philosophy and literature we can buy and which we can't, instead of being dictated to by the Pope of Rome?"

"Oh, come on, Dad!" Roisin waved her hand sharply. "It's not like it used to be . . ."

"We are not living under Roman Catholic laws, Roisin, not on marriage and divorce, not on birth control or abortion, not on what we can and cannot think!" His voice was grating hard, and he too leaned forward as if some physical force impelled him. "We are part of the United Kingdom of Great Britain and Northern Ireland, and that is the guarantee of our freedom to have laws that are the will of the people, not of the Roman Catholic Church. And I will die before I will give away one single right to that." His fist was clenched on the table top. "I don't move from here!"

Roisin looked pale and tired, her eyes stunned with defeat. When she spoke it was quietly. "Dad, not everyone in the party is behind you, you know. There are many who want at least to listen to the other side and make a show of being reasonable, even if at the end we don't change anything that matters." She half reached towards him, hesitated, then her hand fell away. "It's dangerous to appear as if we won't move at all." She was not looking at him, as if she dared not, in case she did not complete what she felt compelled to say. "People get impatient. We're tired of killing and dying, of seeing it going on and on without getting any better. If we're ever to heal it, we've got to begin somewhere."

There was sadness in Connor's face, Bridget could see it and pity wrenched inside her, because she knew what he was going to say. Maybe once there had been a choice, but it had gone long ago.

"We don't begin by surrendering our sovereignty, Roisin," he said. "I've tried all my life to deal with them. If we give an inch they'll take the next, and the next, until we have nothing left. They don't want accommodation, they want victory." He let his breath out in a sigh. "Sometimes I'm not even sure they want peace. Who do they hate, if not us? And who can they blame every time something goes wrong? No." He shook his head. "This is where we stand. Don't try to push me again, and tell Eamonn to do his own errands, not send you." He reached across as if to touch her hair, but she backed away, and Bridget saw the tears in her eyes.

"I'm frightened for you," Roisin said softly.

He straightened up, away from her. Her movement had hurt, and that surprised him.

"If you stand for your beliefs, there'll always be people who fight you," he answered, his lips tight, his eyes bitter. "Some of them violently."

Bridget knew he was thinking of the bombing nearly ten years ago in which his mentor had lost both his legs, and his four grandchildren with him had been killed. Something in Connor had changed then, the pain of it had withered compassion in him.

"Would you rather I were a coward?" he demanded, looking at Roisin. "There are different kinds of deaths," he went on. "I'll face mine forwards, trusting in God that He will protect me as long as I am in His service." Emotion twisted his face, startlingly naked for an instant. "Do you admire a man who bends with the wind because it might cost him to stand straight, Rosie? Is that what I've taught you?"

She shook her head, the tears spilling over. She leaned forward very quickly and brushed his cheek with her lips, but was gone past him before he could reach out his arm to hold her, and respond. She looked at Bridget for an instant, trying to smile. Her voice trembled too much to say more than a word of good-bye, and she hurried out. They heard her feet down the hall, and the front door slammed.

"It's Eamonn," Connor said grimly, avoiding meeting her eyes.

"I know," she agreed. She wanted to excuse Roisin and make him understand the fear she felt, the fierce driving need to protect the child Bridget was more than ever sure she was carrying. And she wanted to ease the hurt in Connor because he was being questioned and doubted by the daughter he loved, even if she had no idea how much, and he did not know how to tell her, or why she needed to know.

"He wants to impress her," she tried to explain. "You're the leader of Protestantism in Ireland, and he's in love with your daughter. He needs her to see him as another strong man, like you, a leader not a follower. He admires you intensely, but he can't afford to stand in your shadow—not with her."

Connor blinked and rubbed his hand wearily across his face, but at last he looked at her, surprise and a fleeting gratitude in his eyes.

Bridget smiled. "It's happened as long as young men have courted great men's daughters, and I expect it always will. It's hard to fall in love with a man who's in your own father's mould, just younger and weaker. He has to succeed for himself. Can't you see that?" She had felt that about Connor twenty-five years ago. She had seen the strength inside him, the fire to succeed. His unbreakable will had been the most exciting thing she could imagine. She had dreamed of working beside him, of sharing defeat and victory, proud just to be part of what he did. She could understand Roisin so well it was as if it were herself all over again.

Bridget had been lovely then, as Roisin was now. She had had the passion and the grace, and perhaps a little more laughter? But the cause had grown grimmer and more violent since then, and hope a little greyer. Or perhaps she had only seen more of the price of it, been to more funerals, and sat silently with more widows.

Connor stiffened. The moment was past. He looked at his watch. "It's nearly time we were going. Be ready in twenty minutes. Where's Liam?" He expected her to know, even though she had been here in the kitchen with him. The requirement for an answer was in his voice.

"He's gone to see Michael. He knows when to be back," she answered. She did not want an argument just as they were leaving, and they would have to sit together in the car all the way to the coast, verbally tiptoeing around each other. Liam would side with his father, hungry for his approval whatever the cost. She had seen his unconscious imitating of Connor, then catching himself, and deliberately doing differently, not even realizing it when he began to copy again. He was always watching, weighing, caught between admiration and judgment. He wanted to be unique and independent, and he needed to be accepted.

Connor walked past her to the door. "He'd better be here in ten minutes," he warned.

The journey to the coast was better than she had feared. The bodyguards followed behind so discreetly that most of the time she was not even aware of them. Usually she did not even know their names, only if she looked at them carefully did she notice the tension, the careful eyes, and perhaps the slight bulge of a weapon beneath their clothes if they turned a particular way, or the wind whipped a jacket hard against the outline of a body. She wondered sometimes what kind of men they were, idealists or mercenaries? Did they have wives at home, and children, mortgages, a dog? Or was this who they were all the time? They drove in the car behind, a faintly comforting presence in the rearview mirror.

She still wished they were all going west to the wildness of the Atlantic coast with its dark hills, heather-purpled in places, bog-deep, wind-scoured. It was a vast, clean land, always man's master, never his servant. But even this gentler coast would be good. They would have time together to be at ease, to talk of things that mattered only to them, and rediscover the small sanities of ordinary life.

Perhaps they would even recapture some of the laughter and the tenderness they had had before. Surely neither of them had changed too much for that?

She spoke little, content to listen to Liam and Connor talk about football, what they thought would happen in the new season, or the possibilities of getting any really good fishing in the week, where the best streams were, the best walks, the views that were worth the climb, and the secret places only the skilled and familiar could find.

She smiled at the thought of the two of them together doing things at which they were equally skilled, no leader, no follower. She was prepared to stand back and let that happen, without thinking of herself, or allowing herself to miss Connor because he gave his time, and his pleasure in it, to someone else. She was glad he had the chance to let go of the responsibility, not have to speak to anyone from the Party, and above all not to have to listen to their bickering and anger. She would be happy to walk alone along the beach and listen to the sound of the water, and let its timelessness wrap itself around her and heal the little scratches of misunderstanding that bled and ached at home.

They reached the village a little after five. The sun was still above the hills and only beginning to soften the air with gold. They stopped to buy fresh milk, eggs, an apple pie and a barbecued chicken to add to what they had brought, then drove on around the curve of the bay to the farther headland. Even Connor seemed to be excited when they pulled up at the cottage standing alone in a sheltered curve, almost on the edge of the sand. He looked around at the hills where they could climb, then across at the windows of the village where the first lights were beginning to flicker on, the dark line of the jetty cutting the golden water and the tender arch of the fading sky above. He said nothing, but Bridget saw his body relax and some of the tension iron out of his face, and she found herself smiling.

They unpacked the car, the guards, Billy and Ian, helping, Billy slender and energetic, his dark hair growing in a cowslick over his forehead, Ian fair-haired with freckles and strong, clever hands. It was he who got the gas boiler going, and unjammed the second bedroom window.

When everything was put away they excused themselves. "We'll go up the rise a little," Billy said, gesturing roughly behind him. "Set up our tent. It's camouflaged pretty well, and in the heather up there it'll be all but invisible."

"But don't worry, sir," Ian added. "One of us will be awake and with our eyes on you all the time." He gave a slight laugh. "Not that I don't feel a fraud, taking money to sit here in the sun for a week. Have a nice holiday, Mr. O'Malley. If ever a man deserved it, you do." He glanced at Bridget, smiling a little shyly. "And you, ma'am."

She thanked them and watched the two of them get back into their car and drive away up the hill until they disappeared into what seemed to be a hollow where the track ended, and she turned back and went inside. The air was growing cool and she realized how happy she was.

They ate cold chicken and salad, and apple pie. Liam went to his room with a book.

Bridget looked across at Connor. It was twilight now and the lamp on the table cast his face into shadows, emphasising the hollows under his cheeks and the lines around his mouth.

"Would you like to go for a walk along the beach?" she invited.

He looked up as if the question had intruded on his thoughts.

"Please?" she added.

"I'm tired, Bridget," he said, his voice flat. "I don't feel like talking, especially if you're going to try explaining Roisin to me. You don't need to. I understand perfectly well that she's young, thinking of having children, and she wants peace. Just leave it alone."

"I wasn't going to talk!" she said angrily. "About Roisin, or anything else. I just wanted to be outside." She added in her own mind that there used to be a time when they could have talked about anything, just for the pleasure of sharing ideas, feelings, or being together, but it sounded sentimental, and it exposed her hurt too clearly. And companionship was of no value once you had had to ask for it.

She went out of the door onto the hard earth, and then a dozen yards across it, past the washing line and through the sea grass to where the sand was softer, cool and slithering away under her feet. The evening was calm, the wave edge barely turning over, pale under the starlight. She walked without thinking, and trying to do it without even dreaming. By the time she came back her face and hands were cold, but there was a warmth inside her.

In the morning Connor seemed to be more relaxed. He was even enthusiastic about going fishing with Liam, and hummed to himself as he sorted out and chose his tackle, instructing Liam what he should take. Liam looked over his shoulder at Bridget and raised his eyebrows, but he accepted the advice goodnaturedly, secretly pleased. They took sandwiches, cold pie and bottles of water, and she watched them climb up the slope side by side, talking companionably, until they disappeared over the crest.

It was a long day without them, but she was happy knowing how much it would please Liam. Connor had sacrificed much for the cause, and perhaps one of the most costly was time with his son. He had never spoken of it, but she had seen the regret in his face, the tightening of his muscles when he had to explain why he could not be at a school prize-giving, or a football match, or why he could not simply talk, instead of working. At times it had seemed that everyone else mattered more to him than his own family, even though she knew it was not true.

At midday Ian came down to make sure everything was still working in the house, and she did not need anything. Billy had followed Connor and Liam, at a discreet distance, of course.

"It's fine, thank you," she told Ian.

He leaned against the door in the sun, and she realized with surprise that he was probably no more than thirty-two or three.

"Would you like lunch?" she offered impulsively. "There's still some apple pie—enough for one, and I don't want it."

He smiled. "I'd love it, Mrs. O'Malley, but I can't come inside for more than a moment or two. Can't see the road."

"Then I'll put the pie on a plate, and you take it," she said, going inside to fetch it before he could refuse.

He accepted it with evident pleasure, thanking her and striding away up the hill again, waving for a moment before he disappeared.

Connor and Liam came back, faces flushed, delighted with their success. For the first time in months Bridget heard him laugh.

"We've caught more than enough for us," he said triumphantly. "Do you want to go and ask Ian and Billy if they'd like a couple?" He turned to Bridget. "You'll cook them, won't you?"

"Of course," she agreed, liking the thought, and beginning immediately as Liam went out of the back door. She had them ready for the pan when he came back again, walking straight past her to the sitting room. "Dad, I can't find them!"

"Go back and look properly!" Connor said with impatience. "And hurry up! Ours'll be ready to eat in a few minutes."

"I have looked," Liam insisted. "And I called out."

"Then look again," Connor ordered. "They can't be far. At least one of them is on duty. The other one could have taken the car for something. Maybe gone to the pub to fetch a crate of Guinness."

"The car's there," Liam told him.

Connor put his newspaper down. Bridget heard the rustle of it. "Do I have to go and look myself?" he demanded.

"I'll go!" Liam was defensive, the friendship and the equality of the afternoon were gone. He marched past Bridget without looking at her, angry that she should have seen it shatter, and went outside into the darkness.

She took the frying pan off the heat.

It was another ten minutes before Liam came back alone. "They're not there," he said again, this time his voice was sharp, edged with fear.

Connor slammed the newspaper down and came out of the sitting room, his face tight and hard, the muscle jumping in his jaw. He walked past both of them and went outside. They heard him shouting, the wind carrying his voice, fading as he went up the hill.

Liam said nothing. He stood awkwardly in the kitchen, looking suddenly vulnerable, and acutely aware of it. He was waiting for Connor to return, successful where he had failed. He dreaded looking stupid in his father's eyes, far more than anything Bridget might think of him.

But when Connor came in quarter on an hour later his face was white and his body rigid, shoulders stiff. "They're not there," he said angrily. "Damn it, they must have walked over to the pub in the village." His mouth closed in a thin line and there was an icy rage in his eyes.

For the first time Bridget was touched with real fear, not of his temper but of something new, and far uglier. "They won't be far," she said aloud, and the moment the words were out of her mouth she realized how pointless they were.

He spun round on her. "They're out of earshot!" he said between his teeth. "If you screamed now, who'd hear you? For God's sake, Bridget, use your brains! They're supposed to be bodyguards! We may not be in Belfast, but we're still in Ireland! I'll have them dismissed for this."

Bridget felt the heat burn up her face, for Ian and Billy who had taken trouble to help, and even more for herself. She knew her words had been foolish, but he had had no need to belittle her in front of Liam. His lack of regard for her hurt more than she wanted to face. It was probably part of growing up, separating the man from the boy. But she was losing him, and each new widening of the gap twisted inside her.

"Don't worry, Dad," Liam said awkwardly. "No one else knows we're here. We'll be okay. We can always fry them up tomorrow."

Connor hesitated, his anger easing out of him. "Of course we will," he agreed. "It's a matter of discipline, and loyalty." He turned to Bridget, no warmth in his eyes. "You'd better put the extra fish in the fridge, and do ours. It's late."

She did as she was told, and they ate in silence. It was a long evening. Connor and Liam talked a little, but not to her. She did not intrude, she knew she would gain nothing by it, and only invite them to make her exclusion more obvious. She saw Liam glance at her once or twice, anxious and a little embarrassed, but he did not know what to say.

She went to bed early. She was still awake an hour later, and heard Connor come in, but she made no movement, and he did not attempt to waken her, as if it had not even occurred to him.

She woke to hear a steady banging, and it was several minutes before she understood what it was. There was someone at the door. It must be Billy and Ian back, probably full of remorse. They were wrong to have gone, but she wanted to protect them from Connor's anger. In theory it could have cost him his life, but actually no harm had come of it. They wouldn't have been gone no more than that brief half hour of suppertime. And no one had ever attempted to harm him physically. It was all just threat.

She swung her feet out of bed, slipped her coat over her night-gown, and went to answer before Connor heard them. She closed the bedroom door softly and tiptoed across the hall to the front door. She opened it.

It was not Billy and Ian there, but three men she had never seen before. The first was tall and lean with fair brown hair and a slightly crooked face that looked as if he laughed easily. The one to the left of him was darker, his features more regular, but there was a seriousness in him that was heavy, almost brooding. The third man was thin with bright blue eyes and hair with a strong tinge of auburn in it.

"Good morning, Mrs. O'Malley," the first one said with a smile. "It's a beautiful day, is it not?" But he did not look at the sweep of the bay, glittering in the sun, or the dark headland behind them.

It was a moment before the chill struck her that he knew her name. Then it came with a cold, tight knot.

He must have seen it in her eyes, but his expression altered only fractionally. "My name's Paddy." He gestured to the dark man. "This is Dermot." He motioned the other way. "And this is Sean. We've brought some fresh eggs with us from the farm over the way, and perhaps you'd be good enough to cook them for us, and we'll all have breakfast together—you and Mr. O'Malley, and us—and the boy, of course." He was polite, still smiling, but there was no question in his voice, no room for refusal.

She backed away from him. It occurred to her for an instant to close the door on him, but she knew he could force his way in if he wanted. "Come back in half an hour, when we're up," she said quite sure even as she spoke that he would refuse.

"We'll wait in the sitting room." He took a step towards her, holding out the open box of eggs, smooth and brown, faintly speckled. There were at least a dozen of them. "We'll have them fried, if that's alright with you? Sean here has a fresh loaf of bread, and a pound of butter as well. Here, Sean, give it to Mrs. O'Malley."

Sean held them out and Bridget took them from him. She needed time to think. She was angry at the intrusion, but she dared not show it. As she led the way to the sitting room and watched them go in easily, as if they had a right to be there, she thought how often she was angry, and suppressed it because she was afraid of making it worse, and losing what she already had. She had done it for so long it was habit.

Connor was sitting up when she returned to the bedroom.

"Where have you been?" he said irritably. "Did you go out to warn Billy and Ian? I know you!" He swung his feet out of bed and stood up. "You've no idea of the gravity of it. I don't tell you of the threats I get, there's no need for you to know, but going off as they've done is a betrayal of me—and the cause."

"No, I didn't!" she said curtly. She was frightened and angry, and the accusation was true in spirit. She would have, had they been there. "There are three men in the sitting room to speak to you . . ."

For an instant he was motionless, frozen in time and place. Then slowly he turned to stare at her. "What men?" His mouth was so dry his voice was husky. "What men, Bridget?"

She swallowed. "I don't know. But they won't go until you speak to them. They're waiting in the sitting room. They told me to get them breakfast."

He was incredulous. "They what?"

"I don't mind!" she protested, wanting to stop him from quarrelling with them needlessly. She was used to men with that hard, underlying anger in them, and the threat of violence close under the surface. Religious politics always seemed to be like that. She wanted it over as soon as possible. Let the wind and the sea wash them clean from the taste of it. She started to dress.

"Where the hell are Billy and Ian?" She heard the first cutting edge of fear in his voice, higher and sharper than the anger. It startled her. She swung around to look at him, but it was gone from his face, only fury remaining.

"Don't you dare make their breakfast!" he ordered. "Tell them to come back when I'm shaved and dressed . . . and I've eaten."

"I already did, and they won't do it," she replied, fastening her skirt. "Connor . . ." she gulped. She felt separate from him and she needed intensely to have the safety, the courage of being together. "Connor . . . they aren't going to go until they want to. Just listen to them . . . please?"

"What are they going to say? Who are they?" He demanded it as if he believed she already knew.

It was ridiculous, but her throat tightened as if she was going to cry. "I don't know." This time she went out, leaving him alone to shave and dress. In the kitchen she started making breakfast for five. Liam was still asleep, and perhaps he would stay that way until after the men had gone.

By the time Connor appeared she had laid the table and made tea and toast and was ready to serve the eggs and bacon.

"Very civil of you, Mrs. O'Malley," Paddy said appreciatively, taking the seat at the head of the table. The other two sat at the sides, leaving spaces for Connor and Bridget between them.

A flicker of annoyance crossed Connor's face, but he accepted and sat also, and started to eat. It was a race against time until either Billy or Ian should appear, or better still, both of them. They were armed and would get rid of Paddy and his friends in moments. Then Connor would crucify them for not having prevented it in the first place. She dreaded that. They were lax, but years of physical safety had left them unprepared for the reality of such intrusion. They would be horribly ashamed, and she would have given them a second chance.

"Now, Mr. O'Malley," Paddy said, putting his knife and fork together on his empty plate. "To business."

"I have no business with you," Connor replied, his eyes level, his voice flat.

"Well that's a shame now." Paddy did not lose his slight smile. "But I'm not easy put off. You see, I'm after peace, not all of a hurry, because it's not a simple thing, but just a beginning."

"So am I," Connor answered. "But only on my terms, and I doubt they're yours, but put them, if you want."

"I doubt that we can agree, Mr. O'Malley. I know right enough what your terms are. It's not as if you were backward about it, or had ever shifted your ground."

"Then where have you shifted?" Connor asked. "And who do you represent, anyway?"

Paddy leaned back in his chair, but the other two remained exactly as they were, vigilant. "Well I haven't shifted a great deal either," Paddy said. "And that's the trouble. We need to have a change, don't you think?" He did not stop long enough for Connor to answer. "This is getting nowhere, and sure enough, I don't see how it can. I'm a moderate man, Mr. O'Malley, reasonable, open to argument. And you're not."

A shred of a smile touched Connor's lips, but Bridget could see half under the table where his fists were clenched and his feet were flat on the floor to balance if he moved suddenly.

"That's the change I propose," Paddy went on.

"You've already said that you know I won't change," Connor pointed out, a very slight sneer on his face.

"Perhaps I haven't made myself plain." Paddy said it as a very slight apology. "I'm suggesting that you step down as leader, and allow a more amenable man into your place." He stopped as Connor stiffened. "Someone who's not tied by past promises," Paddy went on again. "A fresh start."

"You mean I should abandon my people?" Connor's eyebrows rose. "Walk away from them and leave the leadership open to someone of your choosing, that you can manipulate! You're a fool, Paddy—whoever you are, and you're wasting my time, and yours. You've had your breakfast, now take your friends and get out. Leave my family alone. You're . . ." He stopped.

Bridget was certain that he had been going to say that they were lucky the bodyguards had not come in and thrown them out, then he had realized that they had been here half an hour already, in fact thirty-five minutes by the kitchen clock, and neither Billy nor Ian had come. Why not? Where were they? The flicker of fear was stronger inside her and more like a bird's wing than a moth's. Was that why he had stopped, because he had felt that as well?

Paddy made no move at all, he did not even straighten in his chair. "Give it a bit of thought now, Mr. O'Malley," he persisted. "I'm sure you don't want all this trouble to go on. If there's ever going to be peace, there's got to be compromise. Just a little here and there."

"Get out," Connor repeated.

There was a slight movement in the hall doorway and as one man they all looked at Liam, in his pyjama trousers, blinking at them, his face half asleep, confused.

"And you'll be Liam," Paddy remarked. "Wanting your breakfast, no doubt. Come on in, then. Your mother'll lay a place for you. There's plenty of food left—eggs and bacon, fresh from the farm, they are."

Liam blushed. "Who are you? Where are Billy and Ian?"

"My name's Paddy, and these are my friends, Dermot and Sean. We just dropped by to have a word with your father. Have a cup of tea." He gestured to Sean. "Get up now, and let the boy have your place."

Wordlessly Sean obeyed, taking his used dishes to the sink.

Bridget stood up. "Sit," she told Liam. "I'll fry you some eggs."

Connor's face was white. "You'll do no such thing!" he said furiously. "Liam, go and get dressed! You don't come to the table like that, and you know it."

Liam turned to go.

Sean moved to the door to block his way.

Liam stopped.

Connor swivelled around in his chair.

"Come back to the table, Liam," Paddy said levelly. "It's a fine morning. You'll not be cold. Get him his breakfast, Mrs. O'Malley. Feed the boy."

Connor drew in his breath sharply, his face now twisted with anger. Bridget dreaded what punishment Ian and Billy would get when they finally showed up. It would finish their careers, perhaps even finish them ever getting work in Belfast. Connor would never forgive them for allowing him to be humiliated like this in his own house.

Then like having swallowed ice water she realized that Billy and Ian were prisoners somewhere else, just as they were here. They had not come because they could not. She turned to face Paddy and he looked across at her. She tried to mask the knowledge in her eyes, but it was too late. He had already seen it. He said nothing, but the understanding was like a rod of iron between them.

Liam sat down, looking at his father, then away again, embarrassed.

Bridget relit the gas and moved the frying pan over onto the heat.

"Are you sure you won't think again, Mr. O'Malley?" Paddy asked gently. "There are men just a little more to the centre than you are, who could afford to yield a point or two, and still hold to the rest. You've had your day at the top. It's not as if you'd not made it . . ."

"You arrogant fool!" Connor exploded. "Do you think that's what it's about—being leader?" His voice burned with contempt. He half rose in his seat, leaning across the table towards Paddy who still lounged in his chair. "It's about principle, it's about fighting for the freedom to make our own laws according to the will of the people, not the Church of Rome! I don't care that much," he snapped his fingers, "who's leader, as long as they do it with honour and the courage to yield nothing of our rights, whoever threatens them or promises money or power in exchange for the surrender of our birthright."

Liam straightened up in his chair, squaring his bare shoulders.

Bridget put bacon into the frying pan, and two eggs. She had known that was what Connor would say, and there was a kind of pride in her for his courage, but larger than that, overtaking it, was pity and anger, and sick fear.

"That's right, Mr. O'Malley," Paddy said calmly. "You're hostage to all the fine speeches you've made one time or another. I understand that you can't go back on them. You've left yourself no room. That's why I'm thinking it'd be a fine idea for you to step down now, and allow someone new to take over—someone who has a little space to move."

"Never!" Connor forced the word between his teeth. "I've never yielded to threats in my life, and I'm not beginning now. Get out of my house." He straightened up, standing tall, almost to attention. "Now!"

Paddy smiled very slightly. "Don't be hasty, Mr. O'Malley. Give it some thought before you answer."

Bridget had the frying pan in her hand, full of hot fat, the eggs and bacon sizzling.

"I wouldn't do that, Mrs. O'Malley," Paddy said warningly.

Connor swivelled around, his jaw slack for an instant, then he realized what Paddy meant. He leaned across the table and picked up the teapot and flung it not at Paddy, but at Sean standing in the doorway. It hit him in the chest, knocking him off balance and he staggered backwards.

Suddenly Dermot was on his feet, a gun in his hand. He pointed it at Liam.

"Sit down, Mr. O'Malley," Paddy said quietly, but there was no gentleness in his voice any more. "I'm sorry you won't be reasonable about this. It puts us all in an unpleasant situation. Perhaps you should consider it a little longer, don't you think? When you've finished the boy's breakfast, how about another cup of tea, Mrs. O'Malley." It was an order.

Connor sank to his chair. It seemed he had only just grasped the reality that they were prisoners. He was shaking with anger, his hands trembled and the muscle in his jaw flicked furiously.

Bridget picked up the spatula and served the eggs and bacon, using two hands because she was shaking as well, and she thought of the mess she would make on the floor if she dropped the plate.

Liam seemed about to refuse it, then met Paddy's eyes, and changed his mind.

Bridget returned the teapot to the stove, and cleaned up the spilled leaves and water on the floor. She boiled the kettle again and made more. Paddy thanked her. The minutes ticked by. No one spoke.

Liam finished his meal. "Can I go and get dressed?" he asked Paddy.

Connor's temper flared, but he did not speak.

"Sure you can," Paddy answered. "Sean'll go with you, just to make sure you don't forget to come back."

When they were gone he turned to Connor. "We've got all week, Mr. O'Malley, but it'll be nicer for everyone if you make the right decision sooner rather than later. Then you can have a nice holiday here with your family, and enjoy it just as you intended to."

"I'll see you in hell first," Connor replied.

"Now that's a shame," Paddy answered. "Hell's surely a terrible place, so I hear the preachers say. But then you're a preacher aren't you, so you'll know that already."

"You'll know it yourself, soon enough!" Connor returned.

Dermot rose to his feet. "That's your last answer, is it?"

"It is."

He shrugged. "Sean!" he called out.

Sean reappeared, Liam behind him, fully dressed now.

"Mr. O'Malley's not for changing his mind," Dermot said. "Leave the boy here. You and I have a job to do."

Sean pushed Liam, nudging him forward into the kitchen.

"What?" Connor demanded.

"You're staying here," Dermot told him. He signalled to Sean and the two of them went outside. Paddy stood up, revealing the gun in his hand also. He lounged against the door post, but it would have taken less than a second for him to straighten up and raise the barrel if one of them threatened him.

There were several moments' silence, then a shout from outside. Paddy looked up sharply, but it was Connor's name that was called. He lowered the gun and Connor walked to the outside door and opened it.

Bridget followed a step behind him.

On the tussock grass just beyond the gate Ian and Billy stood facing Dermot; their hands were tied behind their backs. Dermot jerked the gun up, gesturing with his other arm.

Billy knelt down.

Dermot put the gun to Billy's head and a shot rang out, sharp and thin in the morning air, sounding surprisingly far away. Billy fell forward. Ian swayed.

Dermot pointed again. Ian knelt. A second shot cracked. Ian fell forward.

Connor gave a strangled cry in his throat and staggered over to the sink as if he could be sick. He dry-retched and gulped air.

Bridget felt the room reel around her, her legs turn to jelly. She clasped onto the door jamb until the nausea passed, then turned to look at Liam, ashen-faced by the table, and Paddy by the stove, the gun still in his hand.

A terrible sadness overwhelmed her. It was a moment that divided forever the past from the present. Billy and Ian were dead. They had helped her, casually, smiling, not knowing what was ahead of them. They had never deserted their posts, and they were lying out there with bullets through their heads, butchered almost without thought.

Liam was ashen. Connor looked as if he might be sick.

Bridget ached to be able to help someone, help herself, undo the moment and see Billy and Ian alive again. And it was all impossible, and far too late.

She made a move towards Liam, and he jerked away from her, too hurt to be touched, blaming her in some way, as if she could have prevented it. School friends had been caught in bomb blasts. He had seen plenty of injury and bereavement, but this was the first murder he had seen. Connor went to him, holding out his hand, wordlessly. Liam took it.

Time stretched on. Bridget washed the dishes and put them away. Sean and Dermot returned. She noticed that their boots had earth on them, and there were marks of sweat on their shirts, as if they had been involved in some heavy physical exertion.

Connor stood up.

"Sit down," Dermot said pleasantly, but he stood still, waiting to be obeyed.

"I'm going to the bathroom!" Connor snapped.

"Not yet," Dermot answered. "My hands are dirty. Sean's too. We'll go and wash, then you can. And don't lock yourself in. We'll only have to break the door down, then Mrs. O'Malley'll have no privacy, and you don't want that, do you?"

"For God's sake, you can't . . ." Connor began, then he knew that they could—they would.

The morning passed slowly, all of them in the kitchen except when someone needed to use the bathroom. Bridget made them tea, and then started to peel potatoes for lunch.

"We haven't enough food for five," she pointed out. "Not beyond this evening, anyway."

"They'll be gone before then!" Connor snapped at her.

"If you've made the right decision," Paddy agreed. He turned to Bridget. "Don't worry, we've got plenty, and it's no trouble to get more. Just make what you've got, Mrs. O'Malley."

"You don't tell her what to do!" Connor turned on him.

Dermot smiled. "Sure he does, Mr. O'Malley. She knows that, don't you, Bridget?"

Connor was helpless, it was naked in his face, as if something were stripped from him.

Bridget longed to protect him, but he had made it impossible. Everything that came to her mind to say would only have made it worse, shown up the fact that she was used to being ordered around, and he was not. She realized it with a shock. Usually it was Connor, for different reasons, and now it was two strangers, but the feeling of being unable to retaliate was just the same.

"We've got to eat," she said reasonably. "I'd rather cook it myself than have one of them do it, even if I had the choice."

Connor said nothing.

Liam groaned and turned away, then slowly looked up at his father, anxiety in his face, and fear, not for himself.

Bridget dug her nails into the palms of her hands. Was Liam more afraid that Connor would be hurt, or that he would make a fool of himself, fail at what he needed to do, to be?

"You'll pay for this," Connor said at last. "No matter what you do to me, or my family, you won't change the core of the people. Is this your best argument—the gun? To hold women and children hostage?" His voice descended into sarcasm, and he did not notice Liam's sudden flush of anger and shame. "Very poor persuasion! That's really the high moral ground!"

Dermot took a step toward him, his hand clenched.

"Not yet!" Paddy said warningly. "Let him be."

Dermot glared at him, but he dropped his hand.

Bridget found herself shaking so badly she was afraid to pick up anything in case it slipped through her fingers. "I'm going to the bathroom," she said abruptly, and pushed past Sean and out of the door. No one followed her.

She closed the bathroom door and locked it, then stood by the basin, her stomach churning, nausea coming over her in waves. They were prisoners. Billy and Ian were dead. Connor was frightened and angry, but he was not going to yield, he couldn't. He had spent all his life preaching the cause, absolutism, loyalty to principles whatever the cost. Too many other men had died, and women and children, he had left himself no room to give anything away now. He might have, even yesterday, when it was only Roisin who asked him, but today it would be seen as yielding to force, and he could never do that.

They were prisoners until someone rescued them, or Dermot and Sean killed them all. Would Connor let that happen? If he gave in to save them, he would hate them for it. She knew without hesitation that he would resent them for ever for being the cause of his weakness, the abandoning of his honour, even his betrayal of all his life stood for.

How blindingly, ineffably stupid! For a sickening moment rage overtook her for the whole idiotic religious divide, which was outwardly in the name of Christianity!

But of course it wasn't. It was human arrogance, misunderstanding, rivalry, one wrong building on another, and the inability to forgive the terrible, aching losses on both sides. Religion was the excuse they clothed it in, to justify it. They created God in their own image: vengeful, partisan, too small of mind to love everyone, incapable of accepting differences. You might fear a god like that, you could not love him.

She dashed cold water over her face and dried it on the rough towel. She hung it up and saw that they were going to run out of toilet paper with six of them in the house. And laundry powder. She would have to tell Paddy that, as well as getting food.

"I'll remember," he said with a smile when she told him early in the afternoon. The others were still in the sitting room and she was in the kitchen going through the store cupboard to see what there was.

"And washing-up liquid," she added.

"Of course. Anything else?"

She straightened up and looked at him. He was still smiling, his slightly lopsided face softened by humour.

"How long are you going to stay here?" she asked.

There was a shadow around his eyes. It was the first uncertainty she had seen in him. She did not find it comforting. Suddenly she was aware, with a sharp pain of fear, how volatile the situation was. He did not know the answer. Perhaps he really had expected Connor to step down, and now that he knew he would not, he did not know how to proceed. She felt cold inside.

"That's all," she said without waiting for him to answer. "Except some bread, I suppose. And tea, if you want it." She moved past him, brushing his arm as she went back to the sitting room.

Connor was standing looking out of the window, his shoulders stiff. She could imagine the expression on his face by seeing his back. Liam was huddled in the armchair, watching his father. His unhappiness was written in every line of his body. Sean was lounging against the door. Dermot was nowhere to be seen.

The afternoon wore on in miserable silence, sporadic anger, and then silence again. Dermot returned at last. He looked at his watch. "Half past five," he observed. "I think we'll eat at seven, Mrs. O'Malley." His eyes flickered to Connor and saw the dull flash of anger in his face. A tiny smile touched his mouth. "And you can go to bed at nine, after you've done the dishes."

The muscle in Connor's jaw twitched. He was breathing slowly, trying to control himself. Liam stared at him, fear and embarrassment struggling in his eyes. He was mortified to see his father humiliated, and yet he was also deeply afraid that if he showed any courage at all he would be hurt, and then humiliated even more. Bridget found his confusion painful to watch, but she had no idea how to help. Exactly the same fear twisted inside her stomach, making her swallow to keep from being sick.

"How about a cup of tea?" Dermot went on.

She moved to obey, and saw his satisfaction.

"Get your own tea!" Connor said curtly. "Bridget! Don't wait on them!"

"I don't mind," she told him. "I've nothing else to do."

"Then do nothing!" He swung around to face her. "I told you not to wait on them. For God's sake, they're not so stupid they can't boil water!"

She saw Paddy's expression, and realized with surprise that Connor had spoken to her in exactly the same tone of voice that

Dermot had used. Was that deliberate—Dermot mimicking Connor? And she was so accustomed to obeying that she was going to do it automatically.

Now she was totally undecided. If she obeyed Dermot she would further reduce Connor, and if she did not she might provoke the violence she feared, or at best make him exert his control in some other way.

They were all watching her, waiting, particularly Liam.

"Actually I'm going to do the laundry," she said. "Just because we're prisoners here doesn't mean we shouldn't have clean underwear. If any of you can be bothered to follow me you can, but it's pretty stupid. You know I'm not going to leave. You've got my family here." And without looking at Paddy or Dermot, she walked out and went to the bedrooms to collect whatever she could find to wash. No one came after her.

The evening passed slowly, with tension in the air so brittle every time anyone moved suddenly, or made a sound with knife on china, or Liam dropped his fork, they all stiffened, and Sean in the doorway lifted the barrel of his gun.

Bridget washed the dishes and Liam dried them. They went to bed at nine o'clock, as ordered.

As soon as the bedroom door was closed Connor turned on Bridget.

"Why are you obeying them?" he said furiously, his face mottled dark with rage. "How can I make a stand against them if you defy me all the time?"

"You can't make a stand against them," she replied wearily. "They've got guns." She started to undress, hanging her skirt and blouse up in the wardrobe.

"Don't turn your back on me when I'm talking to you!" His voice shook.

She turned around. It was only one full day, not even a night, and already he was losing his mastery of himself, because nothing was in his control. She looked at him steadily, unblinking.

"We have no choice, Connor. I'm not defying you, I'm just not making them angry when there's no point. Besides, I'm used to doing what someone else tells me to."

"What do you mean by that?"

She turned back to the wardrobe. "Go to bed."

"You don't care, do you!" he accused. "You think I should give in to them, let them have whatever they want, buy our freedom now by surrendering everything we've fought for all our lives!"

"I know you can't do that." She went on undressing, looking out a clean nightgown because she had washed the other one, for something to do. "You haven't left yourself room. I don't suppose they have either. That's the trouble with all of us, we're hostage to the past we've created. Go to bed. Staying up all night isn't going to help."

"You're a coward, Bridget. I didn't think I'd ever be ashamed of my own wife."

"I don't suppose you thought about it at all," she replied. "Not really, not about me, I mean." She walked past him, putting the nightgown on and climbed into her side of the bed.

He was silent for several minutes. She heard him taking off his clothes, hanging them up as well, then she felt the bed move a little as he got in.

"I'll excuse that, because you're afraid," he said at last.

She did not answer. She was not helping him, and she felt guilty, but it was his intransigence that had made dealing with him impossible. It was a matter of principle, and she knew he could not help it, not now, anyway. He had ordered her around for years, just the way Dermot was ordering him. And it was her fault too, for obeying. She had wanted peace, wanted him happy, not always for his sake but for hers, because he was kinder then, closer to the man she wanted him to be, the man who made her laugh sometimes, who enjoyed the small things, as well as the great, and who loved her. She should have been honest years ago.

Now she could not even protect Liam from the disillusion that was already beginning to frighten him more deeply than the threat of violence from Dermot or Sean. There was nothing she could do. She slid down a little further, and pretended to be asleep.

The next day was worse. Tempers were tighter, edges more raw. There was nothing to do, and they were all cramped inside the cottage. Sean, Paddy, and Dermot took turns watching and sleeping. They had nailed the windows closed, so the air was stuffy, and there was no escape except through one of the two doors.

"What the hell are they waiting for?" Connor demanded when he and Bridget were alone in the bedroom, Sean just beyond the door.

"I don't know," she replied. "I don't know what can happen. You aren't going to change, and neither are they." What was really in her mind was Billy and Ian murdered in front of them and buried somewhere up the hillside, only she did not want to acknowledge it in words. Then she would have to face the consequences of what it meant, and the possibilities it closed off.

"Then what are they waiting for?" he repeated. "Have they asked somebody for money? Or are they going to keep me here until someone else has taken power?"

She had not thought of that. It was a relief, because it made sense. "Yes," she said aloud. "That could be it." Then doubt came to her again. She had become aware that Dermot was waiting, just small signs, a turning when there was a sound, a half listening attitude, a certain tension in him that was not in Paddy. Sean she saw far less of—in fact she had not watched him at all.

"You sound pleased," Connor said.

She looked at him. His face was deeply lined, his eyes pink-rimmed as if he had not slept at all. The muscle in his jaw jumped erratically. "I'm not pleased," she said gently. "I'm just glad you thought of something that makes sense. It's easier to deal with."

"Deal with?"

"Live with," she corrected. "I'm going back out, before they come for us." She left him alone because she did not know what more to say.

It was the third day when she was standing in the back garden, picking a handful of mint for the potatoes, and staring across the stretch of tussock grass towards the sea, when she was aware of someone behind her.

"I'm coming," she said a little tartly. Dermot was irritating her. She had watched him deliberately baiting Connor, ordering him in small, unnecessary things. She swung around, to find Paddy a yard away.

"No hurry," he answered, looking beyond her to the water, barely restless in the slight wind, the waves no more than rustling as they turned over on the sand.

She followed his glance. It had beauty, but she ached for the wilder Atlantic shore with its vast width, the skies that stretched for ever, the wind so hard and clean it blew mares tails of spume off the incoming rollers so that when they crashed on the sand the streamers of foam trailed behind them.

"I miss the west," she said impulsively.

"And of course you can't go there any more." His voice was quiet, almost gentle. "It's a high price we pay, isn't it?"

She drew in her breath to challenge him for including himself, then she realized that perhaps he too was bound by choices he had made long ago, things other people expected of him, as Connor had always expected of her.

"Yes," she agreed. "Penny by penny, over the years."

He said nothing for a little while, just watching the water, as she did.

"Do you come from the west?" she asked.

"Yes." There was regret in his voice.

She wanted to ask him how he had come to be here, holding Connor at gunpoint, what had happened in his life to change a crusade for his beliefs into this kind of violence, but she did not want to anger him with what was undoubtedly intrusive. Perhaps like her, he had started by wanting to please someone he loved, to live up to their ideas of courage and loyalty, and ended clinging onto the shreds of love, because that was all there was left, hoping for something that honesty would have told him did not exist. She had not wanted to face that. It invalidated too much she had paid for with years of trying, swinging from hope to defeat, and then creating hope again.

He started to speak, and stopped.

"What were you going to say?" she asked.

"I was going to ask you something it's none of my business to know," he replied. "And maybe I'd rather not, anyway. I know what you'd say, because you'd be loyal, and perhaps I'd believe you, perhaps not. So maybe it's better we just stand and look at the water. The tides will come and go, the seabirds will call exactly the same, whatever we do."

"He won't change," she said.

"I know. He's a hard man. His time is past, Bridget. We've got to have change. Everyone's got to yield something."

"I know. But we can't take the hard liners with us. They'll call him a traitor, and he couldn't bear that."

"Captain going down with the ship?" He had a slight, wry humour in his voice, but a knowledge of tragedy as well.

"I suppose so," she agreed.

A gull wheeled above them, and soared up in the wind. They both watched it.

She thought of asking him what they were waiting for, but she was not certain that Paddy was waiting, not as Dermot was. Should she warn him, say that Dermot was different, darker? Perhaps he already knew, and it would be disloyal to Connor if she were to say anything to Paddy that could be of help to him. Perhaps she shouldn't be speaking to him at all, more than was necessary.

"I must go in," she said aloud, turning towards the kitchen door.

He smiled at her, not moving from her path, so she passed almost close enough to brush him. She smelled a faint odour of aftershave, clean cotton from the shirt she had laundered. She forced the thoughts out of her mind and went inside.

The evening was tedious and miserable. Connor paced back and forth until Dermot lost his temper and told him to stop. Connor glared at him, and kept pacing. Dermot walked over to Liam and lifted the gun, held by the barrel.

"You don't need to do that!" Paddy said angrily. "Mr. O'Malley's going to do as he's told. He doesn't have the control of his nerves that Bridget has. He doesn't take easily to not being master of his fate."

The dull red colour rose up Connor's face, but he did not take his eyes off Dermot, the gun still within striking distance of Liam's head.

Liam sat motionless, white with misery, not fear for himself, but embarrassment for his father, and helpless anger that Bridget had been singled out for strange and double-edged praise. His loyalties were torn apart. The world which had been difficult enough had become impossible.

"I'm going to bed!" Connor said in a voice so hard it rasped on the ear.

"Good," Paddy agreed.

Dermot relaxed.

Liam stumbled to his feet. "So am I! Dad! Wait for me!"

Bridget was left alone with Paddy and Dermot. She did not want to stay, but she knew better than to follow Connor yet. He needed time on his own, to compose himself, and to pretend to be asleep

when she came. There was nothing she could say to comfort him. He
did not want her understanding, he would only take it for pity. He
wanted respect, not companionship, honour, loyalty and obedience,
not the vulnerability of love.

She would stay here for at least another hour, saying nothing,
making tea for them if they wanted it, fetching and carrying, doing as
she was told.

The morning began the same, but at quarter to ten suddenly Dermot stiffened, and the moment after, Bridget also heard the whine of
an engine. Then it cut out. Sean went to the door. Everyone else
waited.

The silence was so heavy the wind in the eaves was audible, and
the far cry of seabirds. Then the footsteps came, light and quick on
the path. The door opened and Roisin came in. She looked at Bridget, at her father, then at Paddy.

Paddy beckoned her to follow him, and they went into Liam's
bedroom.

Dermot started to fidget, playing with the gun in his hand, his
eyes moving from Connor to the door, and back again.

Connor stared at Bridget.

"I don't know," she whispered. "Some kind of a message?"

"Maybe it's money . . ." he mouthed the words.

"Where would she get money?"

"The party," Liam was close beside them. "They'd pay for you,
Dad. Everybody'd give."

Bridget looked at him, he was thin, very young. In the sunlight
from the window she could see the down on his cheek. He shaved,
but he didn't really need to. He was desperate to believe that his father was loved, that the party respected him and valued him enough
to find whatever money was demanded. She was afraid they would
be politically astute enough to see the value of a martyr—three
martyrs—four if Roisin were included. Please God she wasn't! Why
had Eamonn sent her, instead of coming himself?

The door opened and Roisin came out, Paddy on her heels.

Dermot stared at him, the question in his eyes.

Connor was so stiff he seemed in danger of losing his balance.

Paddy faced him. "There's been a slight change, Mr. O'Malley," he said softly, his voice a trifle husky. "One of your lieutenants, Michael Adair, has gone over to the moderate camp."

"Liar," Connor said immediately. "Adair would never desert. I know him."

Bridget felt her stomach clench inside her. Connor spoke as if to change one's mind were a personal affront to him. She had felt Adair's doubt for several months, but Connor never listened to him, he always assumed he knew what he was going to say, and behaved as if he had said it. Almost as he did with her!

"It's not desertion, Dad," Roisin said awkwardly. "It's what he believes."

Connor's eyebrows rose. "Are you saying it's true? He's betrayed us?" His contempt was like a live thing in the air.

"He has either to betray you or himself," Roisin told him.

"Rubbish! You don't know what you're talking about, Rosie. I've known Adair for twenty years. He believes as I do. If he's turned his coat it's for money, or power, or because he's afraid."

Roisin seemed about to say something, then she turned away.

"Traitor!" Liam said, his pent-up fury breaking out at last. "You're best without him, Dad. Someone like that's worth nothing to them, or to us."

Connor touched his hand to Liam's shoulder in the briefest gesture, then he turned to Paddy. "It makes no difference. If you thought it would, then you're a fool!"

"Adair carries weight," Paddy answered. "He represents many. He could still carry most of your party, if you gave him your backing."

"My backing?" Connor was incredulous. "A traitor to the cause? A man who would use my imprisonment by you to seize the leadership? He's a greedy, disloyal coward, and you'd deal with him? You're an idiot! Give him a chance and he'll turn on you too."

"He's doing what he believes," Roisin repeated, but without looking at her father.

"Of course he is!" Connor spat. "He believes in opportunism, power at any price, even betrayal. That's so plain only a fool couldn't see it."

Paddy glanced at Bridget, but she knew the denial was in his eyes, and she looked away. Roisin was right. Connor had expected, bullied, ignored argument and difference, until Adair had been silenced. Now in Connor's absence, and perhaps hearing that he was hostage, he had found the courage to follow his own convictions. But she did not want Paddy even to guess that she knew that. It seemed like one more betrayal.

Paddy smiled, a funny, lopsided gesture with self-mocking in it as well as humour, and a touch of defiance. "Well, Mr. O'Malley, aren't there enough fools? But for the sake of argument, what if you were to give Adair your support, written in your own hand, for Roisin here to take back, would that not be the best choice open to you now? All things considered, as it were?"

"Ally myself with traitors?" Connor said witheringly. "Endorse what has happened, as if I'd lost my own morality? Never."

"Then maybe you could just retire, on grounds of health?" Paddy suggested. He was leaning against the kitchen bench, his long legs crossed at the ankle, the light from the window shining on his hair. The lines on his face marked his tiredness. He had seemed younger at the beginning, now it was clear he was over forty. "Give it some thought."

"There's nothing wrong with my health!" Connor said between his teeth.

Dermot twisted his gun around. "We could always do something about that," he said with a curl to the corners of his mouth that lacked even the suggestion of humour.

"And explain it as what?" Paddy rounded on him. "A hunting accident? Don't be stupid." He turned back to Connor before he saw the moment of bleak, unadulterated hatred pass over Dermot's face, making it dead, like a mask. Then he controlled it again, and was merely flat, watchful. It touched Bridget with a quite different, new fear, not just for herself but for Paddy.

"You're wasting your time," Connor answered, exactly as Bridget had known he would. He was not even considering it, not acknowledging change, he never had. Now he did not even know how to. He had made his own prison long before Paddy and his men came here with guns.

"Are you sure about that?" Paddy said softly.

"Of course he is!" Dermot cut across him. "He was never going to agree to anything. I could have told you that the day you set out." He jerked his head towards Sean, standing at the far door and the way out to the beach. Sean straightened up, holding his gun steady in front of him.

Paddy was still staring at Connor, as if he believed that he might yet change his mind. He did not see Dermot move behind him, raise his arm and bring it across sharply on the side of his jaw. Paddy crumpled to his knees, and then forward onto the floor.

"Don't!" Sean warned as Connor gasped, and Roisin made a sharp move towards Paddy. "He'll be alright."

Dermot was taking the gun out of Paddy's waistband. He stood up again, watching Bridget rather than Connor or Liam. "Just don't do anything heroic, and you'll be alright."

"Alright?" Connor was stupefied. "What the hell's the matter with you? He's your own man!"

Roisin ignored him and bent to Paddy who was already stirring. She held out her arms and helped him to climb up, slowly, his head obviously paining him. He looked confused and dizzy. He was gentle with Roisin, but did not speak to her. Awkwardly he turned to Dermot, who was careful to keep far enough away from him he was beyond Paddy's arm's length. He held the gun high and steady.

Sean was watching the rest of them. "The first one to move gets shot," he said in a high-pitched voice, rasping with tension. "None of you'd want that, now would you?"

"Dermot?" Paddy said icily.

"Don't be losing your temper, now," Dermot answered. "We did it your way, and it didn't work. Not that I thought it would, mind. O'Malley wasn't even going to change. He can't. Hasn't left himself room. But you wouldn't be told that, you and your kind. Now we'll do it our way, and you'll take the orders."

"You fool!" Paddy's voice was bitter and dangerous. "You'll make a hero out of him! Twice as many will follow him now!"

"Not the way we'll do it," Dermot answered him. "And stop giving me orders, Paddy. You're the one that'll do as you're told now."

"I'm not with you. This is the wrong way. We already decided . . ."

"You did! Now I'm in charge . . ."

"Not of me. I told you, I'm not with you," Paddy repeated.

Dermot's smile was thin as arctic sunshine. "Yes, you are, Paddy, my boy. You can't leave us. For that matter, you never could—at least not since we shot those two lads up the hill, and buried them. Markers are left, just so we could direct anyone to find them, if it were ever in our interest." He raised his black eyebrows in question.

The blood drained out of Paddy's skin, leaving him oddly grey.

He was not old, yet Bridget, looking at him, could see the image of when he would be.

"That's why you killed them . . ." he said with understanding at last.

"We killed them, Paddy," Dermot corrected. "You were part of it, just like us. Law makes no difference who pulls the trigger. Isn't that right, Mr. O'Malley?" He glanced at Connor, who was still standing motionless. Then the ease in Dermot's face vanished and his voice was savage. "Yes of course that's why we did it! You're one of us, whether you like it or not. No way out, boy, none at all. Now are you going to take your gun and behave properly? Help us to keep all these people good and obedient, until we decide exactly what's to be done with them. Now we've got the pretty Roisin as well, perhaps Mr. O'Malley will be a bit more amenable, not to mention her husband. Though to tell the truth, maybe we'd be better not to mention him for yet a while, don't you think?"

Paddy hesitated. Again there was silence in the kitchen, except for the wind and the sound of the gulls along the shore.

Liam stared at his father, waiting.

At last Paddy held out his hand.

"For the gun?" Dermot enquired. "In a little while, when I'm satisfied you've really grasped your situation. Now, Mrs. O'Malley." He turned to Bridget. "We've one extra to feed. You'd best take a good look at your rations, because there'll be no more for a while. I'm not entirely for trusting Paddy here, you see. Not enough to send him off into the village, that is. So be sparing, eh? No seconds for anyone, in fact you'd best be cutting down a bit on firsts as well. D'you understand me?"

"Of course I understand you," she replied. "We've got a whole sack of potatoes. We'll live on those if we have to. We haven't much to season them with, but I suppose that doesn't matter a lot. Connor, you'd better move in with Liam, and Roisin can come in with me. I'll wash the sheets. It's a good day for drying."

"That's a good girl, now," Dermot approved. "Always do what you're told, don't you! I'd like a woman like you for myself, one day. Or maybe with a bit more fire. You can't be much fun. But then I don't suppose Mr. O'Malley is much of a man for fun, is he? Got a face like he bit on a lemon, that one. What do you see in him, eh?"

She stopped at the doorway into the hall and looked directly at him. "Courage to fight for what he believes, without violence," she answered. "Honour to keep his word, whatever it cost him. He never betrayed anyone in his life." And without waiting to see his reaction, or Connor's, she went out across the hall and into first Liam's bedroom, taking the sheets off the bed, then her own. They could watch her launder them if they wanted to. She wouldn't have gone anywhere before, but with Roisin here as well, she was even more of a prisoner.

There was a separate laundry room with a big tub, a washboard, plenty of soap, a mangle to squeeze out the surplus water, and a laundry basket to carry them out to the line where the sea wind would blow them dry long before tonight.

She began to work, because it was so much easier than simply standing or sitting, as Connor and Liam were obliged to do.

She had filled the tub with water and was scrubbing the sheets rhythmically against the board, feeling the ridges through the cotton, when she heard the footsteps behind her. She knew it was Roisin.

"Can I help, Mum?" she asked.

"It doesn't take two of us," Bridget replied. "But stay if you want to."

"I can put them through the mangle," Roisin offered.

They worked without speaking for several minutes. Bridget didn't want to think about why Roisin was here, who had sent her with the message, but the thoughts crowded into her mind like a bad dream returning, even when her eyes were open. She was the only one they had told where they were going, not even Adair knew. Roisin had tried so hard to persuade Connor to moderate his position on education before they left. Bridget had never seen her argue with such emotion before. When he had refused, she had looked defeated, not just on a point of principle, but as if it hurt her profoundly, emotionally. The loss was somehow permanent.

"You're pregnant, aren't you?" she said aloud.

Roisin stopped, her hands holding the rinsed sheets above the mangle. The silence was heavy in the room. "Yes," she said at last. "I was going to tell you, but it's only a few weeks. It's too soon."

"No, it isn't," Bridget said quietly. "You know, that's all that matters." She wanted to be happy for her, congratulate her on the joy to come, but the words stuck in her throat. It was why Roisin had betrayed her father to the moderates, and for Eamonn. She not only wanted peace, she needed it, for her child. Everything in her now was bent on protecting it. It was part of her, tiny and vulnerable, needing her strength, her passion to feed it, keep it warm, safe, loved, defended from the violence of men who cared for ideas, not people. Perhaps Bridget would have done the same. She remembered Roisin when she was newborn. Yes, she would have done whatever was necessary to protect her, or Liam, or any child.

Roisin started the mangle again, keeping her face turned away; she did not yet realize that Bridget knew. She would have done it for Eamonn as well. He was another idealist, like Connor. Roisin was vulnerable herself. It was her first child. She might be ill with it. She would certainly be heavy, awkward, needing his love and his protection, his emotional support. She might even be afraid. Childbirth was lonely and painful, full of doubts that the baby would be well, that she would be able to look after it properly, do all the things she should to see nothing went wrong, that the tiny, demanding, infinitely precious life was cherished. She would be desperately tired at times. She would need Eamonn. Perhaps she had no choice either.

"Your father doesn't know," she said aloud.

Roisin pulled the wrung sheet out from between the rollers and put it into the basket, ready for the line. "I'll tell him in a couple of months."

"Not about the child." Bridget passed her the next sheet. "He doesn't know that you told the I.R.A., or whoever Paddy is, where we are."

Roisin froze, hands in the air. There was no sound but the dripping water.

"I know why you did it," Bridget went on. "I might have done the same, to protect you, before you were born. But don't expect him to understand. I don't think he will. Or Liam."

Roisin's face pinched, looking bruised as if some deep internal injury were finally showing. Roisin realized she had always expected her father to reject her, but she had not thought about Liam before. It was a new pain, and the reality of it might be far worse than the idea, even now.

"I thought when he realized how many of us want peace, he might change, even a little," she said. "Someone has to! We can't go on like this, year after year, hating and mourning, then starting all over again. I won't!" She bit her lips. "I want something better."

"We all do," Bridget said quietly. "The difference is in how much we are prepared to pay for it."

Roisin turned away, blinking, and bent her attention to the sheets.

When they were finished Bridget took them out and hung them on the line, propping up the middle of it with the long pole, notched at the end to hold the rope taut so the sheets did not touch the ground.

How could she protect Connor from the disillusion he would feel when he knew that it was Roisin who had betrayed him? All the reasoning in the world would not make any difference to the pain. Even if his mind understood, his emotions would not. First Adair, now his own daughter.

And what would Liam make of it? He was confused, all his previous certainties were slipping away. His father, whom he had believed to be so strong he wavered in nothing, was losing control of his temper, being ordered around by men he despised, and he did nothing about it. Now his sister was the cause of it all, and for an emotion and a loyalty he could only guess at.

She yanked up the heavy pole, awkward, tipping in her hands from the weight of the wet sheets with the wind behind them. Suddenly it eased and she lurched forward, straight into Paddy.

"Sorry," he apologized, propping the pole up for her.

"Thank you," she said abruptly, realizing he had done it to help. The wind filled the sheets, bellying them high and wide, temporarily shielding them from view of the house.

"Your husband'll work it out that it was her," he said quietly. "You can't stop it."

"I know." She was not sure if she resented his understanding, or in an obscure way it was a comfort not to face it alone. No, that was absurd. Of course she was alone. Paddy was the enemy. Except that he too had been betrayed by someone he had trusted, and it had been very neatly done, using his own plan against him, enmeshing him in a double murder so he had no retreat. He must feel like a complete fool.

"It doesn't seem as if either of us can stop much, does it?" she said drily.

He looked at her with a black laughter in his eyes, self-mocking.

He was trying to hide the hurt, and she knew in that instant that it was deep, and there were probably years of long and tangled debt behind it, and perhaps love of one sort or another. She was not sure if she wanted to know the story or not. She might understand it more than she could afford to.

She glanced at him again. He was staring out towards the horizon, his eyes narrowed against the light off the water, even though the sun was behind them.

"It didn't go where you expected, did it?" she said aloud.

"No," he admitted. "I never thought Connor would yield easily, but I thought he would, when he realized Adair had crossed over. I misjudged him. I guess the ransom for freeing him from old promises was too high. Too high for him, I mean."

"I know what you mean," she answered. "I'm not sure he knows how to escape now. He's more hostage to the past than he is to you. You're just more physically apparent, that's all. It's . . ." She thought how she was going to phrase what she wanted to say. She was thinking aloud, but if she spoke to anyone at all, it would be to Paddy.

"It's a matter of admitting it," he said for her, watching to see if she understood. "We've invested so much of ourselves, our reason for living, whatever it is that makes us think we matter, into a set of ideals. It takes a hell of a lot of courage to say that we didn't get it right—even in the silence of the small hours, staring up at the bedroom ceiling, let alone to all the angry men who've invested the same, and can't face it either. Some of us will die of pride, I think. If you don't believe in yourself, what have you got left?"

"Not much," she replied. "At least—not here. Ireland doesn't forgive—not politically. We're too good at remembering all the wrong things. We don't learn to forget and start again."

He smiled, turning to look at the water again. "Could we, do you think, then? There'd be a lot of things I'd do differently and dear God, but wouldn't I!" He swivelled suddenly to stare very directly at her. "What would you do differently, Bridget?"

She felt the colour rise up her face. His eyes were too frank, far too gentle, intruding into her thoughts, the hopes and sorrows she needed to keep locked inside herself. And yet she allowed him to go on looking at her, the wind streaming past them, the sun bright, the gulls wheeling and crying above.

"You won't tell me, will you?" he said at last, his voice urgent.

She lowered her gaze. "No, of course I won't. None of it matters anyway, because we can't."

"But I would like to have known," he said, as she started to walk back in again, forgetting the laundry basket half hidden by the blowing sheets.

She did not answer. He did know. He had seen it in her face.

Inside the house the tension was almost unbearable. Everyone was in the kitchen, so Dermot and Sean could watch them. Liam was sitting at the table swinging his legs and alternately kicking and missing the opposite chair. Dermot was glaring at him, obviously irritated. Now and then Liam looked up at him, sullen and miserable, almost daring to defy him, then backing off again.

Sean was standing in his usual place against the door frame to the hall and the bedrooms and bathroom. Connor stood by the sink and the window to the side, and the long view of the path winding up over the hill, where he and Liam had gone fishing on the first day.

Roisin was looking through the store cupboards putting things in and out, as if it made any difference.

"Stop doing that," Connor told her. "Your mother knows what we've got. We'll have to live on potatoes, until Dermot here gets tired of them."

Roisin kept her back to him, and replaced the tins and packets, such as they were, exactly where she had found them. She was stiff, her fingers fumbling. Twice she lost her grip on a tin and knocked one over. Bridget realized she was waiting for Connor to piece the facts together and realize it was she who had betrayed them.

It was still early, but she wanted to break the prickling, near silence, the tiny, meaningless remarks.

"I'll make lunch," she said to no one in particular.

"Too soon," Dermot told her. "It's only half past eleven. Wait an hour."

"I'll make a fish pie," she answered. "It takes a while. And I could bake something at the same time. There's flour."

"Don't bake for them!" Connor ordered.

"Good idea," Dermot responded instantly. "You do that, Mrs. O'Malley. Bake us something. Can you do a cake?"

"Don't be ridiculous!" Connor moved forward as if he would

stop her physically. "For God's sake, Bridget! Adair's betrayed us, told these terrorists where we are, so he can take my place and sell out the party! We're prisoners until God knows when, and you're going to bake a cake! Haven't you the faintest understanding of what's happening?"

She walked past him to the cupboard and bent down in front of it. She was aware of Paddy by the back door, and knew he was watching her. She needed to defend herself.

"Not eating isn't going to help," she replied. "And you may be perfectly happy to have potatoes for every meal, but I'd rather have something else as well. A cake is one of the few things we have the ingredients for. I'd rather bake than just stand here."

"You're playing into their hands! Don't you give a damn that Adair betrayed us? Billy and Ian are lying dead up there. Doesn't that mean something to you? You knew them for months! Ian helped you mend the gas. He stood in this kitchen only a couple of days ago." His voice was shaking. "How can you bake a cake, when this man tells you to?" He jerked his arm towards Dermot. "Are you so afraid you'll do anything at all?"

She stood up slowly and turned around to face him. "No, Connor, I'm not. I'm baking a cake because I want to. I haven't forgotten what happened to Billy and Ian, but nothing's going to change that now. Maybe we could have when we had the chance, but now it's too late. And fighting over what we eat isn't brave, it's just stupid. Please move away from the bench, so I can use it."

Connor remained where he was.

Liam was watching them, his eyes wide, the muscles in his face drawn tight with fear.

"Please, Dad?" Roisin said urgently.

He raised his head and looked at her.

Bridget watched them. It was as if time stood still. She could hear the ticking of the clock on the wall as the second hand jumped. She knew what was going to happen before it did, in the endless moment from one word to the next.

"You want me to do what he says?" Connor asked. "Why is that, Rosie? I told Adair we were going away for a week. I didn't tell him where to. Who did?"

Whether she could have lied or not, Bridget did not know, but

Roisin must have felt her face give her away. The tide of colour must have burned.

"Eamonn!" Connor said bitterly. "You told him, and he told Adair!"

"No," Roisin looked straight back at him. "Adair never knew. He still doesn't, so far as I know. I told Paddy, because you won't listen and you won't change. I'm going to have a child, and I'm tired of endless fighting and killing from one generation to the next, with no hope of ever being different. I want peace for my children to grow up in. I don't want them afraid all the time, as I am, and everyone I know. No sooner do we build something than it's broken again. Everybody I know has lost someone, either dead, or maimed. Everybody's got to move. If you won't, then we need somebody else to lead us who will!"

"You did?" He said the words as if he could hardly believe them. He swayed a little, and gripped hard on the edge of the bench, his knuckles white. "You betrayed me, the cause? My own daughter? You got Billy and Ian murdered, and the rest of us, your mother and your brother held here at gunpoint—because you're going to have a baby? Great heaven, girl, do you think you're the only woman in Ireland to have a child?"

Bridget stepped forward. "Leave her alone, Connor. She did what she thought was right. She thought you'd change. She was wrong. But I think I'd have done the same thing in her place. We protect our children. We always have."

He stared at her. "You sound as if you agree with her?" It was an accusation.

Bridget heard Paddy move a little to her left, towards Connor, but closer to her also. She was afraid he was going to say something to protect her, then she realized how stupid that was, but the feeling was still there. She rushed into speech to prevent it. "I understand. It's not the same thing. Please, Connor, this isn't the time for us to quarrel, and not here."

His face twisted in scorn. "You mean in front of this lot?" he jabbed his elbow to indicate Dermot and Sean. "Do you think I give a damn what they think about me, or anything else?"

"Perhaps you don't," she replied. "Have you considered that I might? Or Roisin, or Liam?"

"Liam's with me," he stared at her icily. "As far as Roisin is concerned, she is no longer part of my family. She is Eamonn's wife, not my daughter. That's what she has chosen." He moved fractionally so he turned his shoulder away from Roisin, as if physically cutting her out of his sight, and his knowledge.

Bridget saw her face pale, and the tears fill her eyes, but she did not defend herself. Bridget understood why Connor had said it, she could feel his hurt as if it were a tangible thing in the room, but she still was angry with him for his reaction. He should have been larger, braver of heart than to cut Roisin off. She was not betraying for money or power, but because she believed differently, even though she had deceived him.

"What she did was wrong, at least the way she did it," she said aloud. "But you contributed to that also."

"I what?" he shouted.

"You contributed to that also! You don't listen. You never really listen to anybody else, unless they agree with you." She stopped abruptly as she saw Connor's face.

Behind her Dermot was applauding. She turned and saw his smile, a wide, curling leer. His hands were held up, clapping where the others could see them.

"It's a crusade of hate, with you, isn't it!" she said to him with disgust. "It's nothing to do with religion, or freedom, or any of the other things you talk about with such affected passion. It's about power and hate. The only way you can make anybody notice you is with a gun in your hand." Her contempt was so fierce, carrying her shame for Connor, her pain for all of them, that her voice was laden with it.

Dermot swung his arm back to strike her, and Paddy lunged forward and took the blow on his forearm, sending him off balance a little, landing against the table.

Dermot swivelled to face him, his lips drawn back in a snarl. Then suddenly he stopped, and a hard, artificial smile replaced his anger. "Oh, very good!" he said sarcastically. "But I'm not that stupid, Paddy. A grandstand rescue isn't going to make any difference now. You're with us, like it or not. Remember Billy and whatever his name is, up on the hillside? You put them there just as much as we did, so you can forget trying to win Mrs. O'Malley over. She can't help you, and she won't."

"She's right," Paddy said bitterly. "You only know how to destroy."

"I know how to clear the ground, before I build," Dermot said between his teeth. "More than you do, Paddy. You're soft. You haven't the guts to go through with it, or the judgement to know who's strong and who's weak."

"Or who's honest and who isn't," Paddy added, but he did not move.

By the far door Sean relaxed a little. "I'm going to cook," Bridget said abruptly. "If you want to eat, you'll let me get on with it. If you don't, there's not much but raw potatoes. Take your choice." And without waiting for permission she went to the sink, filled the bowl with water, and took a dozen large potatoes out of the sack and began to scrub them.

Silence descended again until every movement she made sounded like a deliberate noise. The wind was rising. She heard Connor say he was going to the bathroom. There was a brief altercation with Dermot, and then he went.

She looked at Liam, still sitting at the kitchen table, and saw the misery in him. He glared back at her, as if she were the enemy. He was furious with her because she was not defending Connor. She had seen his defeat, and Liam could not forgive her for that. It confirmed it in his own mind, and made his confusion deeper. He so desperately wanted certainty, a cause to believe in and someone to admire, and in the space of a few days it had all been torn away and the flaws exposed, the fear and the weaknesses, the self-absorption.

She turned back at the potatoes. They were half done. She had to persuade Connor and Paddy both to run, in opposite directions. Paddy must know Dermot wasn't going to let them live? Was that regret deep enough in him for him to risk his life? Or would he sacrifice them all for his own chance?

And what about Connor? Would he risk himself, to save his family? Or did he really believe it was his duty to live, that only he was fit to lead the cause? She remembered him in her mind's eye as he had been when they first met, his face smooth and eager, his eyes full of dreams. There had been something beautiful in him then.

She was nearly finished with the potatoes. How long had she got left before Dermot made his decision? Once he moved it would be too late. Little time, very little. She must think of a way to persuade each person to do what she needed them to. With Paddy and Connor it would have to be without their knowing.

She cut the potatoes into manageable pieces, awkward with the one blunt slice they had left her, and put them into the largest saucepan, then covered them with cold water. They were going to be very bland. There was a little bacon left, and some eggs, but she did not want to use them now. It would betray the fact that she knew that there was no tomorrow. She must behave as if she believed rescue, or at least release, was only a matter of time. There was no ideological difference between Connor and Eamonn, or Adair, only the means to attain the goal of Protestant safety. Just as there was none between Dermot and Paddy, only the means to unite Ireland under Catholic rule. No one expected anyone to cross the gulf between them. Their quarrels with each other were nothing compared with the enmity that stretched down the generations dividing Catholic from Protestant, Southern Ireland from the North. Paddy might not be on Dermot's side, but he would never be against him. There was all the difference in the world between those two things. She must not trust him.

But she did not have to tell the truth—to anyone!

She looked at the potatoes. They needed salt, and flavour. An idea began in her mind. It was small, not very good, but there was not time to spend waiting for something better. Dermot was nervous, shifting uneasily already. How much longer would it be before he decided to act? He could shoot them, her whole family, everyone she loved most in the world. Paddy would be upset, for a while, caught in an act of barbarity he had not intended, but violence was part of Irish life. Almost every week someone was killed. It would not make any difference to him, in the long run.

"Liam!" she said suddenly. "I want to move something in my room. Will you come and help me please?"

Sean looked up suspiciously.

"In my bedroom I'd rather have my son, thank you," she said sharply. "Liam!"

He stood up slowly, unwilling. He looked for a moment at his father, and received no response. He followed Bridget along the short corridor to the bedroom.

"What is it?" he said as soon as they were inside.

"Close the door," she told him

He frowned.

"Be quick!"

"What is it?" He looked puzzled now, and a little alarmed, but he obeyed.

"Listen to me, Liam." She swallowed down the tension inside her, and deliberately banged the chair on the floor as if moving it. There was no time to think of the risk she was taking, or whether this might be the most costly mistake in her life. "Dermot can't afford to let us go. He killed Billy and Ian, and there isn't going to be any resolution to this. He'll realize it soon, and then he'll kill us."

His eyes were dark, wide with horror at what she had said, and the leap to denial.

"It's true," she said with as much firmness as she could put into her trembling voice. "One of us has to escape and get to the village."

"But, Mum . . ." he began.

"It has to be you," she cut across him. "There's no time to argue. Roisin can't do it, your father won't. I can't outrun them, but you might. I'm going to try and make Dermot think both Paddy and your father are escaping, in opposite directions, which should occupy Sean as well. When you see the chance, run for it. Don't go straight to the village, it's what they would expect. Go round the shore, and bring help back, as soon as you can. Do you understand?"

He stood silently, absorbing what she had said.

"Do you understand?" she repeated, her ears straining to catch the sound of Sean or Dermot in the passage outside. "There's no time to think of anything better."

"Are you sure?" he asked, his voice was tight, high pitched with fear.

"Yes. He can't let us go. Your father will hunt him down for ever. You know that!"

"Yes. Okay. When?"

"In a few minutes." She gulped. "If I can make Paddy and your father go in opposite directions—or I can make Dermot and Sean think they have."

"Does Dad know?"

"No. If I tell anyone else it'll raise their suspicions. Now go back and behave just the same. Go on."

He hesitated only a second, started to say something, then swallowed it back and went out. She followed a moment later.

In the kitchen everything was exactly as they had left it, Sean standing by the door, Dermot by the window behind the table,

Roisin at the stove and Connor sitting on the hard-backed chair near-est to the back door. Bridget went back to the sink and ran the tap until it was hot, replaced the water over the potatoes, put in salt, and set them on the stove.

She must do it now, before thinking about it sapped away her courage. She had nothing to lose. She must keep that in mind all the time. If Dermot realized, and acted before she did, they would all be dead.

She started to speak, but her mouth was too dry. She licked her lips and started again. "This is going to be very bland. I need some-thing with a bit of flavour to add to it." She turned to Connor. "There are some wild onions growing up the hillside, about a hun-dred yards or so. Can you go and dig them up?"

He looked surprised.

"Please?" She must not make it too urgent, or Dermot would suspect. Surely worrying about food would sound so normal, so sure of tomorrow and the next day?

"Send Liam," Connor replied, without moving from his seat.

Dermot straightened up. "You're neither of you going! Do you think I'm stupid? A hundred yards up the hill, and I'd never see you again. How do I know there even are onions up there?"

Liam raised his head. "There are," he replied, without looking at Bridget.

"Then Paddy can get them," Dermot said. He looked at Paddy. "Do you know an onion when you see it?"

"Probably not," Paddy said with a half smile. "But I can smell one, or taste it." He turned to Bridget. "Do you want them dug up, or pulled, or what?"

"Dig up two or three," she told him. "There's a small garden fork just outside the back door. Thank you." She could not meet his eyes for more than a moment, but by then he was gone anyway, closing the door after him.

Now she had to get Connor to go in the other direction, or at the worst to make Dermot think he had. She glanced at Dermot. The slight sneer was still on his face. Could she trick him into doing what she wanted? Had she understood him?

She turned back to Connor. "Will you help me get the sheets in, please? It's a lot easier to fold them with two. Roisin, watch the potatoes."

"Liam can do it," Connor replied, remaining where he was.

Bridget let her annoyance show in her face. "Why can't you do something for once?" she answered back.

Liam's head turned from Bridget to Connor and back again. He was very pale.

"Liam, do as you're told," Connor said abruptly. "Help your mother with the laundry."

Uncertainly Liam started to climb to his feet.

"Sit down!" Dermot snapped. "O'Malley, she's right. You go and do something for a change. Help her fold the sheets! Move!"

Sean was smiling, leaning against the door to the passage, his gun also raised.

Slowly Connor rose to his feet, his face red, his lips in a tight, thin line. He opened the back door and Bridget followed him out. He walked ahead, without looking at her, and went straight to the line.

She hesitated. Now that the moment had come she found it desperately hard to do, almost too hard.

"Don't," she said as he unpegged the first end.

"What the hell's the matter now?" he snapped.

She moved closer to him, making him back behind the billowing sheet and he grabbed at it with his left hand.

"Connor, they won't let us go," she said levelly. "Dermot can't. And as soon as he realizes you aren't going to give in, which will be any moment, he'll shoot us. He has no choice. He'll go back over the border into Southern Ireland, and at least he'll have a head start before anybody even knows what's happened to us."

"They'll hunt him down like a rat," Connor said contemptuously.

"How? Who'll be alive to say it was him?"

The full horror of it dawned on him. She saw it in the void of his eyes.

There was a shout from the house. She could not tell from where, because the sheets were in the way, but it was Sean's voice. There was no time to hesitate.

"We've got to go! Now, while there's time," she urged. Was Sean coming after them already? What about Paddy up the hill? If he'd kept on looking for the onions, which didn't exist, he should be over the slight rise and out of sight. Why wasn't one of them looking for him? Surely after their betrayal of him they couldn't trust him, could they? Not enough to let him out of their sight, this side of the border?

Then she heard Sean's voice again, calling Paddy's name, sharp and angry.

"Is this what you intend to do?" Connor demanded. "Turn and run, and leave Liam and Rosie to take Dermot's rage when he finds we've escaped? And you were the one who said you understood Rosie putting her baby before the cause, sacrificing her morality to save her child! You disgust me, Bridget. I thought I knew you, and you were better than that. You've betrayed not only me, but everything you said you believed in, everything you are."

"Don't stand there preaching!" She heard her voice rising out of control. "Run! While there's time! For the cause, if not for yourself!"

There was a shout of rage from up the hill, and then another. They both turned towards the sound, but they could see nothing. Then there was a scream, a shot, and then silence again.

The back door slammed open and for an instant she saw Dermot's head and shoulders outlined against the house, his arm raised.

"Run!" she yelled at Connor. Then in case Dermot had not heard her, she did it again.

This time Connor obeyed. At least they were drawing one of them away from the house, and there had been no shots inside. She caught up and grasped his hand, leaping over the sea grass and running down onto the beach, towards the low rise of the sandhills twenty yards away, where at least there was a little shelter.

They were racing over the beach near the tide line where it was hard and firm when the shot rang out. Connor stumbled and pitched forward, his hand going to the scarlet stain spreading across his chest and shoulder. He rolled over and over, carried by the impetus of his speed, then lay still.

Bridget stopped abruptly, and turned back. Dermot was standing on the soft sand just in front of the sea grass, the gun still held out stiffly in front of him. He could pull the trigger again any moment, all he had to do was tighten his grip.

She waited. Oddly, she did not feel a terrible loss. As long as Liam had got away, something was saved. Perhaps Rosie had even gone with him, at least far enough to be out of sight of the house. If they were alive, that was enough. This was a clean way to go, here on the wind-scoured sand, one shot, and then oblivion. It was a bad time, but a good place to die.

Dermot lowered the gun, not right down, he still held it in his hand. He started walking towards her, slowly, evenly.

She did not know if Connor was dead or not. A chest wound might be fatal, but it looked to be closer to the shoulder. Just in case he was still alive, she moved away from him, and began to walk up towards Dermot. If he came down for her, he might shoot Connor again, to make sure. She increased her speed. Strange how she could walk so easily even where the wet sand changed to dry, slithering under her feet. She stopped a couple of yards from Dermot. He was smiling. "You don't care that I shot him, do you!" he said, his eyes wide, his face pale, with two spots of colour high on his cheeks.

"You have no idea what I care about," she answered coldly.

"You'd rather have Paddy, wouldn't you!" he said, his lip curling in disgust. "He'd use you, and throw you away."

"It really doesn't matter what you think," she said wearily, surprised that now it was almost over, that was the exact truth. All she needed was time for Liam to get away, and Rosie if possible.

He jerked the gun towards the house. "Well, let's see, shall we? Is the Reverend O'Malley's wife as cold as she looks? Or his daughter, the pretty turncoat, Roisin?"

If she refused to move, she had no doubt he'd shoot her where she stood. Walking would gain a little more time, only minutes, but minutes might count. She obeyed slowly, passing him and walking ahead. She stepped carefully through the clumps of sea grass and onto the level stretch at the beginning of the lawn, or what passed for it. The sheets were still billowing. She had no idea where Paddy or Sean were. There was no sign of life from the house, and no sound.

She reached the sheets blowing towards her. The plastic laundry basket was just in front of her, empty. Why should she go into the house with him without a fight? It was ridiculous. Rosie might be in there. Even if she wasn't, why should Bridget herself let it be easy?

She picked up the laundry basket and threw it at his feet just as he emerged between the sheets.

He had not had time to see it and dodge. It caught him below the knee, hard enough to cost him his balance. He stumbled forward, still clutching the gun. He was on his hands and knees, his face twisted with rage, already beginning to scramble up again.

She reached for the clothes prop, grasping it with both hands, yanking it out from the line and swinging it wide in a half circle, low and with all her weight behind it. The end of it caught him on the side of the head with a crack she felt all the way through her own body. He fell over sideways and lay motionless, the gun on the ground six inches away from his limp hand.

She scrambled over to him, her body shaking. She picked up the gun, then looked at him. The upper side of his head was bleeding, but not heavily. She knew from the angle of it that he had to be dead. His neck was broken.

She felt sick. But she still needed to face Sean and Paddy.

She walked shakily over to the back door and opened it. The kitchen was empty. "Roisin!" she called.

"Mum!"

The bedroom door crashed wide and Roisin came out, her eyes hollow with fear.

There was no time for hugging, for any kind of emotion. "Where's Liam?" Bridget asked. "And Sean?"

"Liam's gone, as you told him," Roisin answered. "Sean went up the hill after Paddy. I heard him shout. I don't think he came back. Where's Dad?" The look in her face betrayed that she knew.

"On the beach," Bridget replied. "Dermot's dead. I don't know how your father is, I hadn't time to look. Take the tea towels and see what you can do."

"What about you?"

"I've got the gun. I have to find Paddy and Sean."

"But . . ."

"I'll shoot them if I have to." She meant it. She could, to save herself and Roisin. "Go."

Roisin obeyed, and Bridget set off carefully up the slope, watching all the time, keeping both hands on the gun, ready to use it the moment she saw any kind of movement in the tussock and heather.

She had followed the track all the way to the ridge and beyond when she saw Paddy's body lying in a clear patch of grass, his shirt a pale blur against the green, except for the wide, bright red stain of blood across his chest, right in the middle.

Where was Sean? There was no time to allow herself grief now, or any understanding of the waste. She had heard only one shot.

Sean was alive somewhere, maybe waiting, watching her right now. Then why had he not shot her too?

She turned around slowly, searching for him, expecting the noise and the shattering weight of the bullet any moment. But all she could hear was the distant sound of the waves, and bees in the heather. She could see where it had been broken, trampled down around Paddy as if there had been a fight there. Stems were snapped off, the damp earth gouged. The trail led to the edge of a little gully.

Very carefully she walked over towards it, holding the gun in front of her, ready to squeeze the trigger. She looked from right to left, and back again. If Sean was still here, why did he do nothing?

She came to the edge and looked over. She saw him immediately, lying on his back, his body twisted, hips and legs crooked, right thigh bent half under him. His eyes were still open and the gun in his hand.

He shot at her, but it went wide. The angle was wrong, and he could not move to correct it.

She thought of shooting him, but it was cold-blooded, unnecessary. She also thought of saying something, but that was unnecessary too. His pelvis was broken, and at least one leg. He was not going to get out of the gully until someone came and carried him.

She turned away and walked back down the path to the house, and into the kitchen. It was empty. The pan of potatoes, half cooked, stood in the sink. Roisin had thought to take them off before she went into the bedroom.

She should go down to the sand and see if Connor was alive, and if she could do anything for him. At least she could help Roisin. She picked up a couple of bath towels and went out of the back door and past Dermot's body, over the edge of the sea grass and down the sand. Roisin was walking towards her, Connor lay beyond, where he had fallen, but she could not see clearly enough to know whether he was in exactly the same position or not.

Roisin stopped as Bridget reached her. Her face was wet with tears.

"He won't let me do anything," her voice choked. "He won't even listen to me."

So he was alive! And conscious. For an instant Bridget did not even know if she was glad or not. It was as if walls had closed around her again.

"Mum?"

Yes, of course she must be pleased. He didn't deserve to die. And she didn't have to stay inside the walls. It was her choice. If she paid her ransom she could escape. She must never forget that again.

"He may change his mind," she said gently, looking at Roisin. "But if he doesn't, you'll have to accept that. You made your choice, it's your husband and your child. It doesn't matter what I think, it's what you think. But if you care, I believe it's the right choice. And whether I like what you do or not, I shall always love you . . . as you will love your child." She touched Roisin for a moment, just the tips of her fingers to her cheek, then she walked on down the sand to Connor.

He looked at her as she knelt beside him. He was very white and there was a lot of blood on his shirt, but he seemed quite conscious. The tea towels were on the sand. She picked them up, rolled them into pads, and placed them firmly on the wound.

He winced and cried out.

"You should have let Rosie do it," she told him. "It would have cost you less blood."

"Never!" he said between clenched teeth, gasping as the pain washed through him in waves. "I don't have a daughter."

"That's your choice, Connor." She took one of the long towels to put it round him as well as she could to keep the pads in place. "I expect she'll forgive you for your part in this. Whether you forgive her or not is up to you, but I can tell you now, if you don't, you'll lose more than she will. By the way, you might like to know that Sean killed Paddy, but his own pelvis is broken, and he's lying up the hill in a gully. He'll be there until someone carries him out."

He stared at her as if he had never seen her before.

"And I killed Dermot." She could hardly believe her own words, though they were terribly, irrevocably true.

He blinked.

"Liam's gone for the police," she added. "I expect they'll be here soon. And a doctor."

"I can't feel my left arm," he said.

She rolled up the other towel and eased it under his head. "I'll go up to the house and get a blanket. You should be kept warm."

"No!" He breathed in and out slowly. "Stay with me!"

"Oh, I probably will," she replied. "But on my terms, Connor, not on yours. And I'm going to get the blanket. Shock can kill, if you get cold." She rose to her feet, smiling very slightly to herself, and walked back up the sand.

SHARYN MCCRUMB

Sharyn McCrumb holds degrees from the University of North Carolina and Virginia Tech. She lives in Virginia's Blue Ridge Mountains but travels the United States and the world lecturing on her work, most recently leading a writer's workshop in Paris in summer 2001. Her Ballad series, beginning with *If Ever I Return, Pretty Peggy-O* (1990), has won her numerous honors, including the Appalachian Writers Association's Award for Outstanding Contribution to Appalachian Literature and several listings as *New York Times* and *Los Angeles Times* notable books. In the introduction to her short-story collection *Foggy Mountain Breakdown and Other Stories*, she details the family history in North Carolina and Tennessee that contributed to her Appalachian fiction. One of the continuing characters, Sheriff Spencer Arrowood, takes his surname from ancestors on her father's side, while Frankie Silver ("the first woman hanged for murder in the state of North Carolina"), whose story McCrumb would incorporate in *The Ballad of Frankie Silver*, was a distant cousin. "My books are like Appalachian quilts," she writes. "I take brightly colored scraps of legends, ballads, fragments of rural life, and local tragedy, and I place them together into a complex whole that tells not only a story, but also a deeper truth about the nature of the mountain south." The seventh and most recent title in the Ballad series, *Ghost Riders*, appeared in 2003. Her most recent novel is *St. Dale*.

THE RESURRECTION MAN

Sharyn McCrumb

Haloed in lamplight the young man stands swaying on the threshold for an instant, perhaps three heartbeats, before the scalpel falls from his fingers, and he pitches forward into the dark hallway, stumbling toward the balcony railing where the stairwell curves around the rotunda. From where he stands outside the second floor classroom, it is thirty feet or more to the marble floor below.

The old man in the hall is not surprised. He has seen too many pale young men make just such a dash from that room, from its stench of sweet decay, hardly leavened by the tobacco spit that coats the wooden floor. They chew to mask the odor—this boy is new, and does not yet know that trick. The tobacco will make him as sick as the other at first. It is all one.

He makes no move to take hold of the sufferer. They are alone in the building, but even so, these days such a thing would not be proper. The young man might take offense, and there is his own white linen suit to be thought of. He is not working tonight. He only came to see why there was a light in the upstairs window. More to the point, he has long ago lost the desire to touch human flesh. He stays in the shadows and watches the young man lunge for cold air in the cavernous space beneath the dome.

But the smell of the dissecting room is not escaped so easily, and the old man knows what will happen if the student does not get fresh air soon. Somebody will have to clean up the hall floor. It won't be the old man. He is too grand for that, but it will be one of the other employees, some acquaintance of his, and it is easy enough to spare a cleaner more work and the young man more embarrassment. Easy enough to offer the fire bucket as an alternative.

A gallon bucket of sand has been set outside the dissection room in case a careless student overturns an oil lamp, and in one fluid motion he hoists it, setting it in front of the iron railing, directly in the path of the young man, who has only to bend over and exhale to make use of it, which he does, for a long time. He coughs and retches until he can manage only gasps and dry heaves. By the time he is finished he is on his knees, hunched over the bucket, clutching it with both hands. The retching turns to sobbing and then to soft cursing.

A few feet away the old man waits, courteously and without much interest in the purging process. If the student should feel too ill to return to his work, he will call someone to tend to him. He will not offer his shoulder unless the tottering young man insists. He does not care to touch people: The living are not his concern. Most of the students know him, and would shrink from him, but this one is new. He may not know whom he has encountered in the dark hallway. For all the boy's momentary terror and revulsion, he will be all right. He will return to his task, if not tonight then tomorrow. It is the night before his first dissection class, after all, and many a queasy novice has conquered his nerves and gone on to make a fine doctor.

The young man wipes his face with a linen handkerchief, still gulping air as if the motion *in* will prevent the motion *out*. "I'm all right," he says, aware of the silent presence a few feet away.

"Shouldn't come alone," the old man says. "They make you work together for a reason. 'Cause you joke. You prop up one another's nerve. Distractions beguile the mind, makes it easier, if you don't think too much."

The young man looks up then, recognizing the florid speech and the lilt of a Gullah accent beneath the surface. Pressing the handkerchief to his mouth, he takes an involuntary step backward. He does know who this is. He had been expecting to see a sweeper, perhaps, or one of the professors working here after hours, but this apparition, suddenly recognized, legendary and ancient even in his father's student days, fills him with more terror than the shrouded forms in the room he has just quit.

He is standing in the hall, beside a bucket filled with his own vomit, and his only companion is this ancient black man, still straight and strong-looking in a white linen suit, his grizzled hair shines about his head in the lamplight like a halo, and the student knows that he looks a fool in front of this old man who has touched more dead people than live ones. He peers at the wrinkled face to see if there is some trace of scorn in the impassive countenance.

"I was here because I was afraid," he says, glancing back at the lamp-lit room of shrouded tables. He does not owe this man an explanation, and if asked, he might have replied with a curt dismissal, but there is only silence, and he needs to feel life in the dark hall. "I thought I might make a fool of myself in class tomorrow—" He glances toward the bucket, and the old man nods. "—And so I came along tonight to try to prepare myself. To see my—well, to see it. Get it over with. Put a cloth over its eyes." He dabbed at his mouth with the soiled handkerchief. "You understand that feeling, I guess."

"I can't remember," said the old man. He has always worked alone. He pulls a bottle out of the pocket of his black coat, pulls out the cork, and passes it to the young man. It is half full of grain alcohol, clear as water.

The young man takes a long pull on the bottle and wipes his mouth with the back of his hand. The two of them look at each other and smile. Not all of the students would drink from the same bottle as a black man. Not in this new century. Maybe once, but not now. The prim New Englanders would not, for his race is alien to them, and while they preach equality, they shrink from proximity. The crackers would not, because they must always be careful to enforce their precarious rank on the social ladder, even more so since Reconstruction. But this boy is planter class, and he has no need for such gestures. He has traded sweat and spit with Negroes since infancy, and he has no self-consciousness, no need for social barriers. It is the way of his world. They understand each other.

"You don't remember?" The young man smiles in disbelief as he hands back the bottle. "But how could you not recall the first time you touched the dead?"

Because it has been nigh on sixty years, the old man thinks. He points to the bucket. "Do you remember the first time you ever did that?"

His life is divided into *before the train* and *after the train*. Not after the war. Things for him did not so much change after the war as this new century's white folks might suppose. The landmark of his life was that train ride down from Charleston. He remembers some of his earliest life, or perhaps he has imagined parts of it for so long that they have taken on a reality in his mind. He remembers a rag quilt that used to lay atop his corn shuck mattress. It had been pieced together from scraps of cloth—some of the pieces were red and shiny, probably scavenged from silk dresses worn by the ladies up at the house. His memories are a patchwork as well: a glimpse of dark eyes mirroring firelight; the hollowed shell of a box turtle . . . someone, an old man, is making music with it, and people are dancing . . . he is very young, sitting on a dirt floor, watching legs and calico skirts flash past him, brushing him sometimes, as the dancers stamped and spun, the music growing louder and faster . . .

There was a creek, too . . . He is older by then . . . Squatting on a wet rock a little way out into the water, waiting for the frog . . . waiting . . . So still that the white birds come down into the field for the seeds as if he were not there . . . Then crashing through the cattails comes Dog, reeking of creek water and cow dung, licking his face, thrashing the water with his muddy tail . . . frogs scared into kingdom come. What was that dog's name? It is just sounds now, that name, and he isn't sure he remembers them right, but once they meant something inside his head, those sounds . . . He has never heard them since.

Older still . . . Now he has seen the fields for what they are: not a place to play. Sun up to sun down . . . Water in a bucket, dispensed from a gourd hollowed out to make a dipper . . . the drinking gourd. He sits in the circle of folks in the dark field, where a young man with angry eyes is pointing up at the sky. The *drinking gourd* is a pattern of stars. They are important. They lead you somewhere, as the Wise Men followed stars . . . But he never set off to follow those stars, and he does not know what became of the angry young man who did. It is long ago, and he resolved to have nothing to do with drinking gourds—neither stars nor rice fields.

He listened to the old people's stories, of how the trickster rabbit smiled and smiled his way out of danger, and how the fox never saw the trap for the smile, and he reckoned he could do that. He could smile like honey on a johnny cake. Serenity was his shield. You never looked sullen, or angry, or afraid. Sometimes bad things happened to you anyway, but at least, if they did, you did not give your tormentor the gift of your pain as well. So he smiled in the South Carolina sunshine and waited for a door to open somewhere in the world, and presently it did.

The sprawling white house sat on a cobblestone street near the harbor in Charleston. It had a shady porch that ran the length of the house, and a green front door with a polished brass door knocker in the shape of a lion's head, but that door did not open to the likes of him. He used the back door, the one that led to the kitchen part of the house.

The old woman there was kind. To hear anyone say otherwise would have astonished her. She kept slaves as another woman might have kept cats—with indulgent interest in their habits, and great patience with their shortcomings. Their lives were her theatre. She was a spinster woman, living alone in the family house, and she made little enough work for the cook, the maid, and the yard man, but she must have them, for the standards of Charleston's quality folk must be maintained.

The old woman had a cook called Rachel. A young girl with skin the color of honey, and still so young that the corn pone and gravy had not yet thickened her body. She was not as pretty as some, but he could tell by her clothes and the way she carried herself that she was a cherished personage in some fine house. He had met her at church, where he always took care to be the cleanest man there with the shiniest shoes. If his clothes were shabby, they were as clean and presentable as he could make them, and he was handsome, which went a long ways toward making up for any deficiency in station. By then he was a young man, grown tall, with a bronze cast to his skin, not as dark as most, and that was as good as a smile, he reckoned, for he did not look so alien to the white faces who did the picking and choosing. He was a townsman, put to work on the docks for one of the ship's chandlers at the harbor. He liked being close to the sea, and his labors had made him strong and lean, but the work was hard, and it led nowhere. The house folk in the fine homes fared the best. You could tell them just by looking, with their cast-off finery and their noses in the air, knowing their station—higher than most folks.

The fetching little cook noticed him—he took care that this should be so, but he was patient in his courting of her, for he had more on his mind than a tumble on a corn shuck mattress. For many weeks he was as gentlemanly as a prince in a fairy story, taking no more liberties than pressing her hand in farewell as they left the church service. Finally when the look in her eyes told him that she thought he'd hung the moon, he talked marriage. He could not live without her, he said. He wanted no more of freedom than the right to grow old at her side.

Presently the determined Rachel ushered him into the presence of her mistress, the old woman who kept her servants as pets, and he set out to charm her with all the assurance of golden youth, condescending to old age. The gambit would not work forever, but this time it did, and he received the mistress's blessing to wed the pretty young cook. The mistress would buy him, she said, and he could join the household, as butler and coachman—or whatever could be done by an assiduous young man with strength and wit.

The joining took place in a proper white frame church, presided over by a stately clergyman as dignified and elegant as any white minister in Charleston. No broom jumping for the likes of them. And the mistress herself even came to the wedding, sat there in the pew with two of her lady friends and wept happy tears into a lace handkerchief.

Then the newlyweds went back to their room behind the kitchen that would be their home for the next dozen years. Being a town servant was easy, not like dock work. The spinster lady didn't really need a coachman and butler, not more than a few hours a week, so she let him hire out to the inn to work as a porter there, and she even let him keep half of what he earned there. He could have saved up the coins, should have perhaps. One of the cooks there at the inn had been salting away his pay to purchase his freedom, but he didn't see much point in that. As it was, he and Rachel lived in a fine house, ate the same good food as the old lady, and never had to worry about food or clothes or medicine. The free folks might give themselves airs, but they lived in shacks and worked harder than anybody, and he couldn't see the sense of that. Maybe someday they'd think about a change, but no use to deprive himself of fine clothes and a drink or two against that day, for after all, the old missus might free them in her will, and then all those years of scrimping would have been for naught.

All this was *before the train ride . . .*

Dr. George Newton—1852

Just as Lewis Ford and I were setting out from the college on Telfair Street, one of the local students, young Mr. Thomas, happened along in his buggy and insisted upon driving us over the river to the depot at Hamburg so that we could catch the train to Charleston. When Thomas heard our destination, he began to wax poetic about the beauties of that elegant city, but I cut short his rhapsody. "We are only going on business, Dr. Ford and I," I told him. "We shall acquire a servant for the college and come straight back tomorrow."

The young man left us off the depot, wishing us godspeed, but I could see by his expression that he was puzzled, and that only his good manners prevented his questioning us further. *Going to Charleston for a slave?* he was thinking. *Whatever for? Why not just walk down to sale at the Lower Market on Broad Street here in Augusta?*

Well, we could hardly do that, but I was not at liberty to explain the nature of our journey to a disinterested party. We told people that we had gone to secure a porter to perform custodial services for the medical college, and so we were, but we wanted no one with any ties to the local community. Charleston was just about far enough away, we decided.

For all that the railroad has been here twenty years, Lewis claims he will never become accustomed to jolting along at more than thirty miles per hour, but he allows that it does make light of a journey that would have taken more than a day by carriage. I brought a book along, though Lewis professes astonishment that I am able to read at such a speed. He contented himself with watching the pine trees give way to cow pastures and cotton fields and back again.

After an hour he spoke up. "I suppose this expense is necessary, Newton."

130 SHARYN McCRUMB

"Yes, I think so," I said, still gazing out the window. "We have all discussed it, and agreed that it must be done."

"Yes, I suppose it must. Clegg charges too much for his services, and he really is a most unsatisfactory person. He has taken to drink, you know."

"Can you wonder at it?"

"No. I only hope he manages to chase away the horrors with it. Still, we cannot do business with him any longer, and we have to teach the fellows somehow."

"Exactly. We have no choice."

He cleared his throat. "Charleston. I quite understand the need for acquiring a man with no ties to Augusta, but Charleston is a singular place. They have had their troubles there, you know."

I nodded. Thirty years ago the French Caribbean slave Denmark Vesey led an uprising in Charleston, for which they hanged him. All had been quiet there since, but Dr. Ford is one of nature's worriers. "You may interview the men before the auction if it will ease your mind. You will be one-seventh owner," I reminded him. We had all agreed on that point: All faculty members to own a share in the servant, to be bought out should said faculty member leave the employ of the college.

He nodded. "I shall leave the choosing to you, though, Newton, since you are the dean."

"Very well," I said. Dr. Ford had been my predecessor—the first dean of the medical college—but after all it was he who had engaged the services of the unsatisfactory Clegg, so I thought it best to rely upon my judgment this time.

"Seven hundred dollars, then," said Ford. "One hundred from each man. That sum should be sufficient, don't you think?"

"For a porter, certainly," I said. "But since this fellow will also be replacing Clegg, thus saving us the money we were paying out to him, the price will be a bargain."

"It will be if the new man has diligence and ingenuity. And if he can master the task, of which we are by no means certain," said Ford.

"He will have to. Only a slave can perform the task with impunity."

We said little else for the duration of the journey, but I was hoping for a good dinner in Charleston. After my undergraduate days at the University of Pennsylvania, I went abroad to study medicine in Paris.

There I acquired a taste for the fine food and wines that Charleston offers in abundance. It is the French influence—all those refugees from the French Caribbean improved the cuisine immeasurably.

When we had disembarked and made our way to the inn to wash off the dust of the journey, there were yet a few hours of daylight before dinner, and after I noted down the costs of our train fares and lodging for the college expense record, I decided that it would be prudent to visit the market in preparation for the next day's sale. Slaves who are to be auctioned are housed overnight in quarters near the market, and one may go and view them, so as to be better prepared to bid when the time came.

It was a warm afternoon, and I was mindful of the mix of city smells and sea air as I made my way toward the old market. I presented myself at the building quartering those who were to be sold the next day, and a scowling young man ushered me inside. No doubt the keeping of this establishment made for unpleasant work, for some of its inhabitants were loudly lamenting their fate, while others called out for water or a clean slop bucket, and above it all were the wails of various infants and snatches of song from those who had ceased to struggle against their lot.

It was a human zoo with but one species exhibited, but there was variation enough among them, save for their present unhappiness. I wanted to tell them that this was the worst of it—at least I hoped it was.

I made my way into the dimly lit barracks, determined to do my duty despite the discomfort I felt. *Slave* . . . We never use that word. *My servant*, we say, or *my cook*, or *the folks down on my farm . . . my people . . . Why, he's part of the family*, we say . . . We call the elderly family retainers by the courtesy title of Uncle or Aunt . . . Later, when we have come to know and trust them and to presume that they are happy in our care, it is all too easy to forget by what means they are obtained. From such a place as this.

In truth, though, it hardly matters that I am venturing into slave quarters, for I am not much at ease anywhere in the company of my fellow creatures. Even at the orphan asylum supported by my uncle, my palms sweat and I shrink into my clothes whenever I must visit there, feeling the children's eyes upon me with every step I take. I find myself supposing that every whisper is a mockery of me, and that all eyes upon me are judging me and finding me wanting. It is a childish fear, I suppose, and I would view it as such in anyone other than myself, but logic will not lay the specter of ridicule that dogs my steps, and so I tread carefully, hearing sniggers and seeing scorn whether there be any or not.

Perhaps that is why I never married, and why, after obtaining my medical degree, I chose the role of college administrator to that of practicing physician—I hope to slip through life unnoticed. But I hope I do my duty, despite my personal predilections, and that evening my duty was to enter this fetid human stable and to find a suitable man for the college. I steeled myself to the sullen stares of the captives and to the cries of their frightened children. The foul smell did not oppress me, for the laboratories of the college are much the same, and the odor permeates the halls and even my very office. No, it was the eyes I minded. The cold gaze of those who fear had turned to rage. I forced myself to walk slowly, and to look into the face of each one, nodding coolly, so that they would not know how I shrank from them.

"Good evening, sir." The voice was deep and calm, as if its owner were an acquaintance, encountering me upon some boulevard and offering a greeting in passing.

I turned, expecting to see a watchman, but instead I met with a coffee-colored face, gently smiling: an aquiline nose, pointed beard, and sharp brown eyes that took in everything and gave out nothing. The man looked only a few years younger than myself—perhaps thirty-five—and he wore the elegant clothes of a dandy, so that he stood out from the rest like a peacock among crows.

The smile was so guileless and open that I abandoned my resolve of solemnity and smiled back. "How do you do?" I said. "Dreadful place, this. Are you here upon the same errand as I?" Charleston has a goodly number of half castes, a tropical mixture of Martinique slaves and their French masters. They even have schools here to educate them, which I think a good thing, although it is illegal to do so in Georgia. There are a good many freedmen in every city who have prospered and have taken it in turn to own slaves themselves, and I supposed that this light-colored gentleman must be such a free man in need of a workman.

There was a moment's hesitation and then the smile shone forth again. "Almost the same," he said. "Are you here in search of a servant? I am in need of a new situation."

In momentary confusion I stared at his polished shoes, and the white shirt that shone in the dimness. "Are you—"

He nodded, and spoke more softly as he explained his position. For most of his adult life he had been the principal manservant of a spinster lady in Charleston, and he had also been permitted in his free time to hire out to a hotel in the city, hence his mannered speech and the clothes of a dandy.

"But—you are to be sold?"

He nodded. "The mistress is ailing, don't you know. Doesn't need as much help as before, and needs cash money more. The bank was after her. So I had to go. Made me no never mind. I'll fetch a lot. I just hope for a good place, that's all. I'm no field hand."

I nodded, noting how carefully he pronounced his words, and how severely clean and well-groomed his person. Here was a man whose life's course would be decided in seconds tomorrow, and he had done all he could to see that it went well.

"And the mistress, you know, she cried and carried on to see me go. And she swore that she would never part with my wife."

I nodded. It is regrettable that such things happen. Money is the tyrant that rules us all. I said, "I am the dean of a medical college in Augusta. In Georgia. Do you know where that is?"

"A good ways off, sir."

"Half a day's journey south by train. Over the Savannah River and into the state of Georgia."

"A college. That sounds like a fine situation indeed, sir. What kind of place is it?"

"We teach young men to be doctors and surgeons."

"No, sir," He smiled again. "The *place*. The position you've come here wanting to fill."

"Oh, that." I hesitated. "Well—Porter, I suppose you'd say. General factotum about the college. And *something else*, for which, if the man were able to do it, we should *pay*." I did not elaborate, but I thought he could read expressions much better than I, for he looked thoughtful for a few moments, and then he nodded.

"You'd pay . . . Enough for train fare?"

"If the work is satisfactory. Perhaps enough, if carefully saved, to make a larger purchase than that. But the extra duty . . . it is not pleasant work."

He smiled. "If it was pleasant, you wouldn't pay."

And so it was done. It was not the sordid business of buying a life, I told myself, but more of a bargain struck between two men of the world. True, he would have to leave his wife behind in Charleston, but at least we were saving him from worse possible fates. From cane fields farther south, or from someone who might mistreat him. He could do worse, I told myself. And at least I saved him from one ordeal—that of standing upon the block not knowing what would become of him. I thought the man bright enough and sufficiently ambitious for the requirements of our institution. It may seem odd that I consulted him beforehand as if he had a choice in his fate, but for our purposes we needed a willing worker, not a captive. We needed someone dependable, and I felt that if this man believed it worth his while to join us, we would be able to trust him.

They must have thought him wonderfully brave the next day. On the block, before upturned white faces like frog spawn, peering up at him, he stood there smiling like a missionary with four aces. It was over in the space of a minute, only a stepping stone from one life to the next, crossed in the blink of an eye.

Seven hundred dollars bid and accepted in the span of ten heart-beats, and then the auctioneer moved on to the next lot, and we went out. As we counted out the gold pieces for the cashier, and signed the account book, Lewis Ford was looking a little askance at the whole procedure.

"So you're certain of this fellow, Newton?"

"Well, as much as one can be, I suppose," I said. "I talked at length with him last evening. Of course I did not explain the partic-ulars of the work to him. That would have been most imprudent."

Lewis Ford grunted. "Well, he has the back for it, I grant you that. And, as you say, perhaps the temperament as well. But has he the stomach for it? After our experience with Clegg, that's what I wonder."

"Well, *I* would, Dr. Ford. If my choice in life was the work we have in store for this fellow or a short, hard life in the cane fields fur-ther south, by God, I would have the stomach for it."

"Indeed. Well, I defer to your judgment. I don't suppose what we're asking of him is much worse than what we do for a living, af-ter all."

"We'll be serving the same master, anyhow," I said. "The col-lege, you know, and the greater good of medicine."

"What is the fellow's name, do you know?"

I nodded. "He told me. It is Grandison. Grandison Harris."

"Odd name. I mean they *have* odd names, of course. Xerxes and Thessalonians, and all that sort of thing. People will give slaves and horses the most absurd appellations, but I wouldn't have taken Grandison for a slave name, would you?"

I shrugged. "Called after the family name of his original owner, I should think. And judging by the lightness of his skin, there's some might say he's entitled to it."

Grandison Harris had never been on a train before, and his interest in this new experience seemed to diminish what regrets he might have about leaving his home in Charleston. When the train pulled out of the depot, he leaned out the window of the car and half stood until he could see between the houses and over the people all the way to the bay—a stand of water as big as all creation, it looked from here. Water that flowed into the sky itself where the other shore ought to be. The glare of the afternoon sun on the water was fierce, but he kept on twisting his head and looking at the diminishing city and the expanse of blue.

"You'll hurt your eyes staring out at the sun like that," I said.

He half turned and smiled. "Well, sir, Doctor," he said, "I mean to set this place in my memory like dye in new-wove cloth. My eyes may water a little, but I reckon that's all right, for dyes are sot in salt. Tears will fix the memories to my mind to where they'll never come out."

After that we were each left alone with our thoughts for many miles, to watch the unfamiliar landscapes slide past the railway carriage, or to doze in relief that, although the future might be terrible, at least this day was over.

Instead of the sea, the town of Augusta had the big Savannah River running along beside it, garlanded in willows, dividing South Carolina from the state of Georgia. From the depot in Hamburg they took a carriage over the river into town, but it was dark by then, and he couldn't see much of the new place except for the twinkling lights in the buildings. Wasn't as big as Charleston, though. They boarded him for the night with a freed woman who took in lodgers, saying that they would come to fetch him in the morning for work.

For a moment in the lamplight of the parlor, he had taken her for a white woman, this haughty lady with hair the brown of new leather and green eyes that met everybody's gaze without a speck of deference. Dr. Newton took off his hat to her when they went in, and he shook her hand and made a little bow when he took his leave.

When he was alone with this strange landlady, he stared at her in the lamplight and said, "Madame, you are a red bone, not?"

She shrugged. "I am a free person of color. Mostly white, but not all. They've told you my name is Alethea Taylor. I'll thank you to call me Miz Taylor."

"You sure look white," he said. *Act it, too*, he thought.

She nodded. "My mama was half-caste and my daddy was white. So was my husband, whose name I ought to have. But it was Butts, so maybe I don't mind so much."

She smiled at that and he smiled back.

"We married up in Carolina where I was born. It's legal up there. I was given schooling as well. So don't think this house is any low class place, because it isn't. We have standards."

The new lodger looked around at the tidy little parlor with its worn but elegant mahogany settee and a faded turkey carpet. A book shelf stood beside the fireplace, with a big leather Bible on top in pride of place. "Your white husband lives here, too?" he asked.

"Of course not." Her face told him that the question was foolish. "He was rich enough to buy up this whole town, Mr. Butts was. But he's dead now. Set me and our children free, though, when he passed. Seven young'uns we had. So now I do fine sewing for the town ladies, and my boys work to keep us fed. Taking in a lodger helps us along, too. Though I'm particular about who I'll accept. Took you as a favor to Dr. George Newton. Would you tell me your name again?"

"Grandison Harris," he said. "I guess the doctors told you: I'm the porter at the college."

She gave him a scornful look. "'Course you are. Dr. Newton's uncle Tuttle is my guardian, so I know all about the college."

"Guardian?"

"Here in Georgia, freed folk have to have white guardians."

"What for?"

She shrugged. "To protect us from other white men, I suppose. But Mr. Isaac Tuttle is a good man. I can trust him."

He watched her face for some sign that this Tuttle was more to her than a disinterested legal guardian, but she seemed to mean no more than what she said. It made no difference to him, though. Who she shared her bed with was none of his business, and never would be. She had made her opinion of him plain. He was a slave, and she was a free woman, his landlady, and a friend of his owners. You couldn't cross that gulf on a steamboat.

"It's late," she said, "But I expect you are hungry as well as tired. I can get you a plate of beans if you'd care to eat."

"No, ma'am, I'm good 'til morning. Long day."

She nodded, and her expression softened. "Well, it's over now. You've landed on your feet."

"The college—It's a good place, then?" he asked.

"Hard work," she said. She paused as if she wanted to say more, but then she shook her head. "Better than the big farms, anyhow. Dr. George is a good man. Lives more in his books than in the world, but he means well. Those doctors are all right. They treat sick black folks, same as white. You will be all right with them if you do your job. They won't beat you to show they're better than you." She smiled. "Doctors think they are better than most everybody else, anyhow, so they don't feel the need to go proving it with a bull whip."

"That's good to hear."

"Well, just you mind how *you* treat *them*," she said. "You look like you wouldn't be above a little sharp practice, and those doctors can be downright simple. Oh, they know a lot about doctoring and a lot about books, but they're not very smart about people. They don't expect to be lied to. So you take care to be straight with them so that you can keep this good place."

He followed her meekly to a clean but spartan room. A red rag quilt covered the bed, and a chipped white pitcher and basin stood on a small pine table next to a cane-seat chair. Compared to the faded splendor of Miz Taylor's parlor, the room was almost a prison cell, but he was glad enough to have it. Better here with a family than in some makeshift room at the medical college. He wasn't sure whether the doctors kept sick people around the place, but he didn't like the thought of sleeping there all the same. In a place of death. The best thing about this small bare room was what it did *not* contain: no shackles, no lock on the door or barred window. He was a boarder in a freedman's house.

He turned to the woman, who stood on the threshold holding the lamp.

"Aren't they afraid I'll run off?" he asked.

She sighed. "I told you. They don't have good sense about people. I reckon they figure you'd be worse off running than staying here. You know what happens to runaways."

He nodded. He had seen things in Charleston, heard stories about brandings and toes lopped off. And of course the story of Denmark Vesey, whose rebellion had consisted mostly of talk, was never far from the surface of any talk about running or disobedience.

She set the lamp beside the basin. "I'll tell you what's the truth, Mr. Harris. If you give satisfaction at the college—do your work and don't steal, or leastways don't get caught at it—those doctors won't care about what you do the rest of the time. They won't remember to. They don't want to have to take care of a servant as if he were a pet dog. All they want is a job done with as few ructions as possible, and the less trouble you give them, the happier they'll be. You do your job well, you'll become invisible. Come and go as you please. You'll be a freedman in all but name. That's what I think. And I know the doctors, you see?"

"I won't give them no trouble," he said.

"See you don't. Can you read, Mr. Harris?"

He shook his head. There had been no call for it, and the old miss in Charleston wasn't averse to her folks getting book learning, but she had needed him to work.

"Well," she said, "I school my young'uns every evening. If you would like to join us, one of my girls can start by teaching you your letters."

"I thank you."

She nodded and turned to leave. "Reading is a good skill," she said as she closed the door. "You can write out your own passes."

He had seen fine buildings in Charleston, but even so, the Medical College on Telfair Street was a sight to behold. A white temple, it was, with four stone columns holding up the portico and a round dome atop the roof, grand as a cathedral, it was. You stepped inside to an open space that stretched all the way up to the dome, with staircases curving up the sides that led to the upper floor rooms. The wonder of it wore off before long, but it was grand while it lasted. Soon enough the architectural splendor failed to register, and all he saw were floors that needed mopping and refuse bins that stank.

For the first couple of days he chopped firewood, and fetched pails of water when they needed them.

"Just until you are settled in," Dr. Newton had said. "Then we will have a talk about why you are here."

He didn't see much of the doctors during the couple of days they gave him to get acquainted with his new surroundings. Perhaps they were busy with more pressing matters, and, remembering Alethea Taylor's advice about giving no trouble, he got on with his work and bothered no one. At last, though, clad in one of the doctors' clean cast-off suits, he was summoned into the presence, a little shy before the all-powerful strangers, but not much afraid, for they had paid too much good money for him to waste it by harming him.

For a night or two he had woken up in the dark, having dreamed that the doctors were going to cut him open alive, but this notion was so patently foolish that he did not even mention it to his landlady, whose scorn would have been withering.

George Newton was sitting behind his big desk, tapping his fingers together, looking as if his collar were too tight. "Now Grandison," he began, "you have settled in well? Good. You seem to be a good worker, which is gratifying. So now I think we can discuss that other task that your duties entail."

He paused, perhaps to wait for a question, but he saw only respectful interest in the man's face. "Well, then . . . This is a place where men are taught to be doctors. And also to be surgeons. A grim task, that: the cutting open of living beings. Regrettably necessary. A generation ago there was an English surgeon who would vomit before every operation he performed. Do you know why?"

The listener shook his head.

"Because the patient is awake for the operation, and because the pain is so terrible that many die of it. We lose half the people on whom we operate, even if we do everything right. They die of shock, of heart failure, perhaps, from the pain. But despite these losses, we are learning. We *must* learn. We must help more people, and lessen the torture of doing so. This brings me to your function here at the college." He paused and tapped his pen, waiting in case the new servant ventured a question, but the silence stretched on. At last he said, "It was another English surgeon who said, *we must mutilate the dead in order not to mutilate the living.*" Another pause. "What he meant was that we physicians must learn our way around the human body, and we must practice our surgical skills. It is better to practice those skills upon a dead body rather than a living one. Do you see the sense of that?"

He swallowed hard, but finally managed to nod. "Yes, sir."

George Newton smiled. "Well, if you *do* understand that, Grandison, then I wish you were the governor of Georgia, because *he* doesn't. The practice is against the law in this state—indeed, in all states—to use cadavers for medical study. People don't want us defiling the dead, they say—so, instead, out of ignorance, we defile the living. And that cannot be permitted. We must make use of the dead to help the living."

"Yes, sir," he said. The doctor still seemed lost in thought, so he added encouragingly, "It's all right with me, sir."

Again the smile. "Well, thank you, Grandison. I'm glad to have your permission, anyhow. But I'm afraid we will need more than that. Tell me, do you believe that the spirits of the dead linger in the graveyard? Object to being disturbed? That they'd try to harm anyone working on their remains?"

He tried to picture dead people loitering around the halls of the college, waiting for their bodies to be returned. This was a place of death. He didn't know whether to smile or weep. Best not to think of it at all, he decided. "They are gone, ain't they?" he said at last. "Dead. Gone to glory. They're not sitting around waiting for Judgment Day in the grave, are they?"

Another doctor sighed. "Well, Grandison, to tell you the truth, I don't know where the souls of the dead are. That is something we don't teach in medical college. However, I don't believe they're sitting out there in the graveyard, tied to their decaying remains. I think we can be sure of that."

"And you need the dead folks to learn doctoring on?"

Dr. Ford nodded. "Each medical student should have a cadaver to work on, so that he can learn his trade without killing anyone in the learning process. That seems a sufficiently noble reason to rob graves, doesn't it?"

He considered it, more to forestall the rest of the conversation than anything else. "You could ask folks before they dies," he said. "Tell them how it is, and get them to sign a paper for the judge."

"But since the use of cadavers is against the law, no judge would honor such a paper, even if people could be persuaded to sign it, which most would not. I wish there were easy answers, but there aren't. You know what we must ask of you."

"You want me to bring you dead folks? Out the graveyard?"

"Yes. There is a cemetery on Watkins Street, not half a mile from here, so the journey would not be long. You must go at night, of course."

He stood quite still for some time before he spoke. It was always best to let white folks think you took everything calmly and agreed with them on every particular. To object that such a deed would frighten or disgust him would make no difference. The doctor would dismiss his qualms as fear or superstition. The doctors had explained the matter to him, when they could have simply given him an order. That was something, anyhow. At last he nodded. The matter was settled, and the only considerations now were practical ones. "If I get caught, what then?"

"I don't suppose you will *get caught*, as you put it, if you are the least bit clever about it, but even if you should, remember that slaves are not prosecuted for any crime. They are considered property and therefore not subject to prosecution. The authorities simply hand them back over to their masters." Newton smiled. "And you don't suppose that *we* would punish you for it, do you?"

The others nodded in agreement, and the matter was settled.

He was given a lantern and a shovel, and a horse-drawn cart. Dr. Newton had written out a pass, saying that the bearer, Grandison Harris, servant of the medical college, was allowed to be abroad that night to pick up supplies for the doctors. "I doubt very much that the city's watchmen can read," Newton had told him. "Just keep this pass until it wears out, and then one of us will write you a new one."

He kept the pass in his jacket pocket, ready to produce if anyone challenged him, but he had met no one on his journey from Telfair Street to the burying ground. It was well after midnight, and the sliver of moon had been swallowed by clouds, so he made his way in darkness. Augusta was a smaller place than Charleston. He had walked around its few streets until he knew it by day and by night, and he had been especially careful of the route to Cedar Grove, where the town buried its slaves and freedmen. Now he could navigate the streets without the help of the lantern. Only the horse's footfalls broke the silence. Nearer to the town center, perhaps, people might still be out drinking and wagering at cards, but no sounds of merriment reached him here on the outskirts of town. He would have been glad of the sound of laughter and music, but the silence blanketed everything, and he did not dare to whistle to take his mind off his errand.

Do you want me to dig up just any old grave? he had asked the doctor.

No. There were rules. A body rots quick. Well, he knew that. Look at a dead cat in the road, rippling with maggots. After two, three days, you'd hardly know what it was. *Three days buried and no more*, the doctor told him. *After that, there's no point in bringing the corpse back up; it's too far gone to teach us anything. Look for a newly-dug grave*, Newton told him. Flowers still fresh on a mound of newly-spaded earth. *Soon*, he said, *you will get to know people about the town, and you will hear about deaths as they happen. Then you can be ready. This time, though, just do the best you can.*

He knew where he was going. He had walked in the graveyard that afternoon, and found just such a burial plot a few paces west of the gate: a mound of brown dirt, encircled by clam shells, and strewn across it a scattering of black-eyed susans and magnolia flowers, wilting in the Georgia sun, but newly placed there.

He wondered whose grave it was. No mourners were there when he found it. Had there been, he would have hesitated to inquire, for fear of being remembered if the theft were ever discovered. There was no marker to tell him, either, even if he had been able to read. The final resting place of a slave—no carved stone. Here and there, crude wooden crosses tilted in the grass, but they told him nothing.

He reached the cemetery gate. Before he began to retrace his steps to the new grave, he lit the lantern. No one would venture near a burying ground so late at night, he thought, and although he had paced off the steps to the grave, he would need the light for the task ahead.

Thirty paces with his back to the gates, then ten paces right. He saw the white shape of shells outlining the mound of earth, and smelled the musk of decaying magnolia. He stood there a long time staring down at the flower-strewn grave, a colorless shape in the dimness. All through the long afternoon he had thought it out, while he mopped the classroom floors and emptied the waste bins, and waited for nightfall. His safety lay in concealment: No one must suspect that a grave had been disturbed. No one would look for a grave robber if they found no trace of the theft. The doctor had told him over and over that slaves were not jailed for committing a crime, but he did not trust laws. Public outrage over this act might send him to the end of a rope before anyone from the college could intervene. Best not to get caught.

He would memorize the look of the burial plot: the position of the shells encircling the mound, and how the flowers were placed, so that when he had finished his work he could replace it all exactly as it had been before.

Only when he was sure that he remembered the pattern of the grave did he thrust his shovel into the soft earth. He flinched when he heard the rasp of metal against soil, and felt the blade connect with the freshly-spaded dirt. The silence came flowing back. What had he expected? A scream of outrage from beneath the mound? When he had first contemplated the task before him, he had thought he could endure it by thinking only of the physical nature of the work: It is like digging a trench, he would tell himself. Like spading a garden. It is just another senseless task thought up by the white people to keep you occupied. But here in the faint lantern light of a burying ground, he saw that such pretenses would not work. The removing of dirt from a newly-filled hole was the least of it. He must violate consecrated ground, touch a corpse, and carry it away in darkness to be mutilated. He could not pretend otherwise.

All right, then. If the spirits of the dead hovered outside the lantern light, watching him work, so be it. Let them see. Let them hear his side of it, and judge him by that.

"Don't you be looking all squinty-eyed at me," he said to the darkness as he worked. "Wasn't my doing. You all know the white folks sent me out here. Say they need to study some more on your innards."

The shovel swished in the soft earth, and for a moment a curve of moon shimmered from behind a cloud, and then it was gone. He was glad of that. He fancied that he could make out human shapes in the shadows beneath the trees. Darkness was better. "You all long dead ones don't have no quarrel with me," he said, more loudly now. "Doctors don't want you if you gone ripe. You all like fish—after three days, you ain't good for nothing except fertilizer."

He worked on in the stillness, making a rhythm of entrenchment. The silence seemed to take a step back, giving him breathing room as he worked. Perhaps two hours now before cock crow.

He struck wood sooner than he had expected to. Six feet under, people always said. But it wasn't. Three feet, more like. Just enough to cover the box and then some for top soil. Deep enough, he supposed, since the pine boards would rot and the worms would take care of the rest.

He didn't need to bring up the coffin itself. That would disturb too much earth, and the doctors had no use for the coffin, anyhow. Dr. Newton told him that. It might be stealing to take a coffin, he had said. Wooden boxes have a monetary value. Dead bodies, none.

He stepped into the hole, and pushed the dirt away from the top of the box. The smell of wet soil made him dizzy, and he willed himself not to feel for worms in the clods of earth. He did not know whose grave this was. They had not told him, or perhaps they didn't know.

"You didn't want to be down there anyhow," he said to the box. "Salted away in the wet ground. You didn't want to end up shut away in the dark. I came to bring you back. If the angels have got you first, then you won't care, and if they didn't, then at least you won't be alone in the dark any more."

He took the point of the shovel and stove in the box lid, pulling back when he heard the wood splinter, so that he would not smash what lay beneath it. On the ground beside the grave, he had placed a white sack, big enough to carry away the contents of the box. He pulled it down into the hole, and cleared away splinters of wood from the broken box, revealing a face, inches from his own.

Its eyes were closed. Perhaps—this first time—if they had been open and staring up at him, he would have dropped the shovel and run from the graveyard. Let them sell him south rather than to return to such terrors. But the eyes were shut. And the face in repose was an old woman, scrawny and grizzled, lying with her hands crossed over her breast, and an expression of weary resignation toward whatever came next.

He pulled the body out through the hole in the coffin lid, trying to touch the shroud rather than the flesh of the dead woman. She was heavier than he had expected from the look of her frail body, and the dead weight proved awkward to move, but his nerves made him hurry, and to finish the thing without stopping for breath: only get her into the sack and be done with it.

He wondered if the spirit of the old woman knew what was happening to her remains, and if she cared. He was careful not to look too long at the shadows and pools of darkness around trees and gravestones, for fear that they would coalesce into human shapes with burning eyes.

"Bet you ain't even surprised," he said to the shrouded form, as he drew the string tight across the mouth of the sack. "Bet you didn't believe in that business about eternal rest, no more'n the pigs would. Gonna get the last drop of use out you, same as pigs. But never mind. At least it ain't alone in the dark."

She lay there silent in the white sack while he spent precious long minutes refilling the hole, smoothing the mound, and placing the shells and flowers back exactly as he had found them.

He never found out who the old woman was, never asked. He had trundled the body back to the porter's entrance of the medical college, and steeped her in the alcohol they'd given him the money to buy as a preservative. Presently, when the body was cured and the class was ready, the old woman was carried upstairs to perform her last act of servitude. He never saw her again—at least not to recognize. He supposed that he had seen remnants of her, discarded in bits and pieces as the cutting and the probing progressed. That which remained, he put in jars of whiskey for further study or scattered in the cellar of the building, dusting it over with quicklime to contain the smell. What came out of the classes was scarcely recognizable as human, and he never tried to work out whose remains he was disposing of in a resting place less consecrated than the place from which he had taken them.

"Well, I suppose the first one is always the worst," said Dr. Newton the next day when he had reported his success in securing a body for the anatomy class. He had nodded in agreement, and pocketed the coins that the doctor gave him, mustering up a feeble smile in response to the pat on the back and the hearty congratulations on a job well done.

The doctor had been wrong, though. The first one was not the worst. There were terrors in the unfamiliar graveyard, that was true, and the strange feel of dead flesh in his hands had sent him reeling into the bushes to be sick, so that even he had believed that the first time was as bad as it could get, but later he came to realize that there were other horrors to take the place of the first ones. That first body was just a lump of flesh, nothing to him but an unpleasant chore to be got over with as quick as he could. And he would have liked for them all to be that way, but he had a quota to fill, and to do that he had to mingle with the folks in Augusta, so that he could hear talk about who was ailing and who wasn't likely to get well.

He joined the Springfield Baptist Church, went to services, learned folks' names, and passed the time of day with them if he happened to be out and about. Augusta wasn't such a big town that a few months wouldn't make you acquainted with almost the whole of it. He told people that he was the porter up to the medical college, which was true enough as far as it went, and no one seemed to think anything more about him. Field hands would have been surprised by how much freedom you could have if you were a town servant in a good place. There were dances and picnics, camp meetings and weddings. He began to enjoy this new society so much that he nearly forgot that they would see him as the fox in the henhouse if they had known why he was set among them.

Fanny, Miz Taylor's eldest girl, made sport of him because of his interest in the community. "I declare, Mister Harris," she would say, laughing, "You are worse than two old ladies for wanting to know all the goings-on, aren't you?"

"I take an interest," he said.

She shook her head. "Who's sick? Who's in the family way? Who's about to pass?—Gossip! I'd rather talk about books!" Miss Fanny, with her peach-gold cheeks and clusters of chestnut curls, was a pretty twelve-year-old. She and her young sister Nannie were soon to be sent back to South Carolina for schooling, so she had no time for the troubles of the old folks in dull old Augusta.

When she thought he was out of earshot, Fanny's mother reproved her for her teasing. "Mary Frances," she said. "You should not poke fun at our lodger for taking an interest in the doings of the town. Do you not think he might be lonely, with no family here, and his wife back in Charleston? It is our Christian duty to be kind to him."

"Oh, *duty*, mama!"

"And, Fanny, remember that a lady is always kind."

But he had not minded Miss Fanny's teasing. To be thought a nosey "old lady" was better than to be suspected of what he really was. But in the few months before she left for school, Miss Fanny had made an effort to treat him with courtesy. She was well on her way to being a lady, with her mother's beauty and her father's white skin. He wondered what would become of her.

He was in the graveyard again, this time in the cold drizzle of a February night. He barely needed a lantern anymore to find his way to a grave, so accustomed had he become to the terrain of that hallowed field. And this time he would try to proceed without the light, not from fear of discovery but because he would rather not see the face of the corpse. Cheney Youngblood, a soft-spoken young woman whose sweet serenity made her beautiful, had gone to death with quiet resignation on Saturday night. It had been her first child, and when the birthing went wrong, the midwife took to drink and wouldn't do more than cry and say it weren't her fault. At last Miz Taylor was sent for, and she had dispatched young Jimmie to fetch Dr. Newton. He had come readily enough, but by then the girl had been so weak that nothing could have saved her. "I'd have to cut her open, Alethea," Dr. Newton had said. "And she'd never live through that, and I think the baby is dead already. Why give her more pain when there's nothing to be gained from it?"

At dawn the next morning he had just been going out the door to light the fires at the college when Alethea Taylor came home, red-eyed and disheveled from her long night's vigil. "It's over," she told him, and went inside without another word.

The funeral had been held the next afternoon. Cheney Youngblood in her best dress had been laid to rest in a plain pine box, her baby still unborn. He had stood there before the flower-strewn grave with the rest of the mourners, and he'd joined in the singing and in the prayers for her salvation. And when the minister said, *Rest in peace*, he had said "Amen" with the rest of them. But he knew better.

Three-quarters of an hour in silence, while the spadefuls of earth fell rhythmically beside the path. He would not sing. He could not pray. And he tried not to look at the shadows that seemed to grow from the branches of the nearby azaleas. At last he felt the unyielding wood against his spade, and with hardly a pause for thought, he smashed the lid, and knelt to remove the contents of the box. There had been no shroud for Cheney Youngblood, but the night was too dark for him to see her upturned face, and he was glad.

"Now, Cheney, I'm sorry about this," he whispered, as he readied the sack. "You must be in everlasting sorry now that you ever let a man touch you, and here I am seeing that you will get more of the same. I just hope you can teach these fool doctors something about babies, Cheney. So's maybe if they see what went wrong, they can help the next one down the road."

He stood at the head of the coffin, gripping her by the shoulders, and pulled until the flaccid body emerged from the box. Fix his grip beneath her dangling arms, and it would be the act of a moment to hoist the body onto the earth beside the grave, and then into the sack. He did so, and she was free of the coffin, but not free.

Attached by a cord.

He stood there unmoving in the stillness, listening. Nothing.

He lit the lamp, and held it up so that he could see inside the box.

The child lay there, its eyes closed, fists curled, still attached to its mother's body by the cord.

His hand was shaking as he set down the lantern on the edge of the grave, and reached down for the child. After so much death, could he possibly restore to life . . . He took out his knife, but when he lifted the cord, it was withered and cold—like a pumpkin vine in winter.

Dr. Newton sat before the fire in his study, clad in a dressing gown and slippers. First light was a good hour away, but he had made no complaint about being awakened by the trembling man who had pounded on his door in the dead of night, and, when the doctor answered, had held out a sad little bundle.

He was sitting now in a chair near the fire, still shaking, still silent.

Dr. Newton sighed, poured out another glass of whiskey, and

held it out to his visitor. "You could not have saved it, Grandison," he said again. "It did not live."

The resurrection man shook his head. "I went to the burying, Doctor. I was there. I saw. Cheney died trying to birth that baby, but she never did. She was big with child when they put her in the ground."

"And you think the baby birthed itself there in the coffin and died in the night?"

He took a gulp of whiskey, and shuddered. "Yes."

"No." Newton was silent for a moment, choosing his words carefully. "I saw a man hanged once. I was in medical school in those days, and we were given the body for study. When we undressed the poor fellow in the dissecting room, we found that he had soiled himself in his death agonies. The professor explained to us that when the body dies, all its muscles relax. The bowels are voided . . . And, I think, the muscles that govern the birth process must also relax, and the gases build up as the body decays, so that an infant in the birth canal is released in death."

"And it died."

"No. It never lived. It never drew breath. It died when its mother did, not later in the coffin when it was expelled. But it does you credit that you tried to save it."

"I thought the baby had got buried alive." The doctor shook his head, and Grandison said, "But people do get buried alive sometimes, don't they?"

Newton hesitated, choosing his words carefully. "It has happened," he said at last. "I have never seen it, mind you. But one of my medical professors in Paris told the tale of a learned man in medieval times who was being considered for sainthood. When the church fathers dug him up, to see if his body was in that uncorrupted state that denotes sanctity, they found the poor soul lying in the coffin on his back, splinters under his fingernails and a grimace of agony frozen on his withered features." He sighed. "To add insult to injury, they denied the fellow sainthood on the grounds that he seemed to be in no hurry to meet his Maker."

They looked at each other and smiled. It was a grim story, but not so terrible as the sight of a dead child wrapped in its mother's winding sheet. Besides, first light had just begun to gray the trees and the lawn outside. That night was over.

Cheney Youngblood had been early on, though. And he was sorry for her, because she was young and kindly, and he had thought her child had lived, however briefly. A year or so after that—it was hard to remember after so long a time, with no records kept—a steaming summer brought yellow fever into Augusta, and many died, burning in their delirium and crying for water. Day after day wagons stacked with coffins trundled down Telfair Street, bound for the two cemeteries, black and white. The old people and the babies died first, and here and there someone already sick or weakened by other ailments succumbed as well. New graves sprouted like skunk cabbage across the green expanse of the burying field.

Now he could dig and hoist with barely a thought to spare for the humans remains that passed through his hands. By now there had been too many dark nights, and too many still forms to move him to fear or pity. His shovel bit into the earth, and his shoulders heaved as he tossed aside the covering soil, but his mind these days ranged elsewhere.

"I want to go home," he told George Newton one night, after he had asked for the supplies he needed.

The doctor looked up, surprised and then thoughtful. "Home, Grandison?"

His answer was roundabout. "I do good work, do I not, doctor? Bring you good subjects for the classes, without causing you any trouble. Don't get drunk. Don't get caught."

"Yes. I grant you all that, but where is home, Grandison?"

"I have a wife back in Charleston."

Dr. Newton considered it. "You are lonely? I know that sometimes when people are separated by circumstance, they find other mates. I wonder if you have given any thought to that—or perhaps she—"

"We were married legal," he said. "I do good work here. Y'all trust me."

"Yes. Yes, we do. And you want to go back to Charleston to see your wife?"

He nodded. No use in arguing about it until the doctor thought it out.

At last Newton said, "Well, I suppose it might be managed. We could buy you a train ticket. Twelve dollars is not such a great sum, divided by the seven of us who are faculty members." He tapped his fingers together as he worked it out. "Yes, considered that way, the cost seems little enough, to ensure the diligence of a skilled and steady worker. I think I can get the other doctors to go along. You would have to carry a pass, stating that you have permission to make the journey alone, but that is easily managed."

"Yes. I'd like to go soon, please." He was good at his job for just this reason, so that it would be easier to keep him happy than to replace him.

Not everyone could do his job. The free man who was his predecessor had subsided into a rum-soaked heap; even now he could be seen shambling along Bay Street, trying to beg or gamble up enough money to drown the nightmares.

Grandison Harris had no dreams.

"Excuse me, Dr. Newton, but it's time for my train trip again, and Dr. Eve said it was your turn to pay."

"Hmm . . . what? Already?"

"Been four weeks." He paused for a moment, taking in the rumpled figure elbow-deep in papers at his desk. "I know you've had other things on your mind, sir. I'm sorry to hear about your uncle's passing."

"Oh, yes, thank you, Grandison." George Newton ran a hand through his hair, and sighed. "Well, it wasn't a shock, you know. He was a dear old fellow, but getting up in years, you know. No, it isn't so much that. It's the chaos he's left me."

"Chaos?"

"The mess. In his will my uncle left instructions that his house be converted to use as an orphanage, which is very commendable, I'm sure, but he had a houseful of family retainers, you know. And with the dismantling of his household on Walker Street, they have all moved in with me on Greene Street. I can't walk for people. Eleven of them! Women. Children. Noise. Someone tugging at my sleeve every time I turn around. And the Tuttle family heirlooms, besides. It's bedlam. And Henry, my valet, is at his wit's end. He's getting on in years, you know, and accustomed to having only me to look after. I would not dream of turning them out, of course, but . . ."

Grandison nodded. Poor white folks often thought that servants solved all the problems rich people could ever have, but he could see how they could be problems as well. They had to be fed, clothed, looked after when they got sick. It would be one thing if Dr. George had a wife and a busy household already going—then maybe a few extra folks wouldn't make much difference, but for a bachelor of forty-five used to nobody's company but his own, this sudden crowd of dependents might prove a maddening distraction. It would never occur to George Newton to sell his uncle's slaves, either. That was to his credit. Grandison thought that things ought to be made easier for them so he wouldn't be tempted to sell those folks to get some peace. He considered the situation, trying to think of a way to lighten the load. He said, "Have you thought about asking Miz Alethea if she can help you sort it out, Doctor?"

"Alethea Taylor? Well, I am her guardian now, I know." Newton smiled. "Is she also to be mine?"

"You know she does have seven young'uns. She's used to a house full. Maybe she could set things in order for you."

George Newton turned the idea over in his mind. Women were better at managing a household and seeing to people's needs. He had more pressing matters to contend with here at the medical school. He reached into his pocket and pulled out a roll of greenbacks. "Well, we must get you to Charleston," he said. "Twelve dollars for train fare, isn't it? And, thanks. I believe I will take your advice and ask Alethea to help me."

George Newton's problems went out of his head as soon as the door shut behind him. He went off to the depot to wait for the train, and he wanted no thought of Augusta to dampen his visit to Rachel.

Three days later he walked into Alethea Taylor's parlor near suppertime, and found that one of the family was missing. "Where's Miss Mary Frances?" he asked as they settled around the big table.

Young Joseph waved a drumstick and said, "Oh, Mama sent her over to Dr. George's house. You know how he's been since Mr. Tuttle passed. People just running all over him, asking for things right and left. And Mr. George he can't say no to anybody, and he has about as much common sense as a day-old chick. He asked Mama to come help him, but she's too busy with her sewing work. So we sent Fanny instead."

Jane, who was ten, said, "Mama figured Fanny would put a stop to that nonsense. She'll sort them all out, that's certain. Ever since she got back from that school in South Carolina she's been bossing all of us something fierce, so I'm glad she's gone over there. It'll give us a rest."

"But she's what—seventeen?"

Joseph laughed. "Sixteen going-on-thirty," he said. "Those folks at Newton's will think a hurricane hit 'em. Fanny's got enough sand to take on the lot of them, and what's more she won't need a pass to go there, either."

Harris nodded. No, she wouldn't need a pass. Fanny Taylor was a gray-eyed beauty, whiter than some of the French Creole belles he'd seen in Charleston. With her light skin, her education and her poise, she could go anywhere unchallenged, and she had the same fire and steel as Miss Alethea, so he didn't think she'd be getting any back talk from the Newton household.

"She's living over there now?"

Jim laughed. "No-oo, sir! Mama wouldn't sit still for that." He glanced at his mother to see if it was safe to say more, but her expression was not encouraging.

"She'll be home directly," said Anna. "She goes first thing in the morning and she comes home after dinner time."

Miss Alethea spoke up then. "Children, where are your manners? Pass Mr. Harris those fresh biscuits and some gravy, and let him talk for once. Hand round the chicken, Jim. Mr. Harris, how was your journey?"

"The day was fine for a train ride," he said, careful to swallow the last bit of chicken before he spoke. The Taylors were sticklers for table manners. "Though we did have to stop once for some cows had got out and would not leave the track."

Miss Alethea was not interested in cows. "And your wife, Mr. Harris? I hope you found her well?"

"She's well enough." He hesitated. "She is with child."

Miss Alethea glanced at her own brood, and managed to smile. "Why, don't say that news with such a heavy heart, Mr. Harris. This will be your first born, won't it! You should be joyful!"

He knew it was his child. The old miss would never permit any goings-on in her house. Not that he thought Rachel would have countenanced it anyhow. But a child was one more millstone of Charleston to burden him. He couldn't be with his child, couldn't protect it. And the old missus professed to be delighted at this new addition to the household, but he was afraid that a baby on the premises would be more annoying to her than she anticipated. He thought of Dr. George's fractious household. Might the old missus part with Rachel and the infant to restore her house to its former peacefulness? Was it any wonder that he was worried?

Miss Alethea gave her children a look, and one by one they left the table, as if a command had been spoken aloud. When the two of them were alone, she said, "It's not right to separate a husband from his wife. I don't know what Dr. George was thinking when he brought you here to begin with."

"No, I asked him to. It seemed for the best. And my Rachel wasn't to be sold, so there wasn't any question of bringing her, too."

"Be that as it may, you have been here now, what? Three years? It is high time that Medical College did something about your situation. And a baby on the way as well. Yes, they must see about that."

"I suppose the doctors thought—"

"I know what they thought. They thought what all you men think—that you'd replace your wife and be glad of the chance. Folks said that about Mr. Butts, too, but they were wrong. Seven children we had, and he stayed with me until the day he died. Those doctors must see by now that you have not deserted your wife. You going so faithful on the train to see her every chance you get. Well, it's early days still. The baby not born yet, and many a slip, as they say. Let us wait and see if all goes well, and if it does, one day we will speak to Dr. George about it."

The anatomy classes did not often want babies. He was glad of that. He thought he might take to drink as old Clegg had done if he'd had to lift shrouded infants out of the ground during the months that he waited for his own child to be born in Charleston.

Women died in childbirth. No one knew better than he. The men he pulled from their shrouds in Cedar Grove were either old husks of humanity, worn out by work and weariness at a great age, or else young fools who lost a fight, or died of carelessness, their own or someone else's. But the women . . . It was indeed the curse of Eve. Sometimes the women died old, too, of course. Miss Alethea herself had borne seven babies, and would live to make old bones. She came of sturdy stock. But he saw many a young woman put into the clay before her time, with her killer wrapped in swaddling cloths and placed in her arms.

And the doctors did want those young mothers. Their musculature was better for study than the stringy sinews of old folks, Dr. Newton had told him. "A pregnant woman will make a good subject," he said, examining the body Grandison had brought in just before dawn. "Midwives see to all the normal births, of course, but when something goes wrong, they'll call in a doctor. When we attend a birth, it's always a bad sign. We need to know all we can."

"But why does birthing kill them?" Grandison had asked. It was when he'd first learned about Rachel, and he wondered if the doctors here had some new sliver of knowledge that might save her, if it came to that. Surely this long procession of corpses had amounted to something.

George Newton thought the matter over carefully while he examined the swollen form of the young woman on the table before them. In the emptiness of death she looked too young to have borne a child. Well, she did not bear it. It remained inside her, a last secret to take away with her. Grandison stared at her, trying to remember her as a living being. He must have seen her among the crowds at the city market, perhaps, or laughing among the women on the lawn outside the church. But he could not place her. Whoever she had been was gone, and he was glad that he could summon no memory to call her back. It was easier to think of the bodies as so much cordwood to be gathered for the medical school. Had it not been for her swollen belly, he would not have given her a thought.

At last Dr. Newton said, "Why do they die? Now that's a question for the good Reverend Wilson over at the Presbyterian church across the street. He would tell you that their dying was the will of God, and the fulfillment of the curse on Eve for eating the apple, or some such nonsense as that. But I think . . ." He paused for a moment, staring at the flame of his match as if he'd forgotten the question.

"Yes, doctor? Why do you think they die?"

"Well, Grandison, I spent my boyhood watching the barn cats give birth and the hounds drop litters of ten at a time, and the hogs farrow a slew of piglets. And you know, those mothers never seemed to feel any pain in those birthings. But women are different. It kills some and half kills the rest. And I asked myself why, same as you have, and I wondered if we could find something other than God to blame for it."

"Did you? Find something to blame besides God?"

Dr. Newton smiled. "Ourselves, I guess. The problem in child-birth is the baby's head. The rest of that little body slides through pretty well, but it's the head that gets caught and causes the problems. I suppose we need those big heads because our brains are bigger than a dog's or a pig's, but perhaps over the eons our heads have outgrown our bodies."

He thought it over. "But there's nothing I can do about that," he said, "I can't help Rachel."

The doctor nodded. "I know," he said. "Perhaps in this case Reverend Wilson would be more help to you than we doctors are. He would prescribe prayer, and I have nothing better to offer."

Newton turned to go, but another thought occurred to him. "Grandison, why don't you come in to class today?" He nodded toward the girl's swollen body. "She will be our subject today. Perhaps you'll feel better if you understood the process."

Grandison almost smiled. It would never occur to the studious bachelor that a man with a pregnant wife might be appalled by such a sight. Dr. George considered learning a cure in itself. Grandison did not think that was the case, but since learning was often useful for its own sake, he would not refuse the offer. And he would take care not to show disgust or fear, because that might prevent other offers to learn from coming his way. Doctoring would be a good skill to know. He had seen enough of death to want to fight back.

He had watched while the doctors cut open the blank-faced woman, and now he knew that the womb looked like a jellyfish from the Charleston docks, and that the birth canal made him think of a snake swallowing a baby rabbit, but the knowledge did nothing to allay his fears about Rachel's confinement. It was all right, though, in the end. Whether the prayers accomplished their object or whether his wife's sturdy body and rude good health had been her salvation, the child was safely delivered, and mother and baby thrived. He called that first son "George," in honor of Dr. Newton, hoping the gesture would make the old bachelor feel benevolent toward Rachel and the boy.

After that he got into the habit of sitting in on the medical classes when he could spare the time from his other duties. Apart from the big words the doctors used, the learning didn't seem too difficult. Once you learned what the organs looked like and how to find them in the body, the rest followed logically. They were surprised to learn that he could read—his lessons with the Taylor children had served him well. After a while, no one took any notice of him at all in the anatomy classes, and presently the doctors grew accustomed to calling on him to assist them in the demonstrations. He was quiet and competent, and they noticed his helpfulness, rather than the fact that he, too, was learning medicine.

He had been in Augusta four years. By now he was as accustomed to the rhythm of the academic year as he had once been attuned to the seasonal cadence of the farm. He had taken Alethea Taylor's advice and made himself quietly indispensable, so that at work the doctors scarcely had to give him a thought, except to hand over money for whatever supplies he needed for the task at hand or for his personal use. No one ever questioned his demands for money these days. They simply handed over whatever he asked for, and went back to what they had been doing before he had interrupted.

Sixteen bodies per term for the anatomy class. He could read well now, thanks to the Taylor daughters, although they would be shocked if they knew that he found this skill most useful in reading the death notices in the *Chronicle*. When there were not enough bodies available in the county to meet this need, Grandison was authorized to purchase what he needed. A ten-dollar gold piece for each subject. Two hundred gallons of whiskey purchases each year for the preservation of whole corpses or of whatever organs of interest the doctors wished to keep for further study, and if he bought a bit more spirits than that amount, no one seemed to notice. It never went to waste.

He tapped on the door of George Newton's office. "Morning, Dr. George. It's train time again."

The doctor looked up as if he had forgotten where he was. "Train time?—Oh, yes, of course. Your family. Sit down, Grandison. Perhaps we should talk."

He forced himself to keep smiling, because it didn't do any good to argue with a man who could break your life in two. He wasn't often asked to sit down when he talked to the doctors, and he made no move toward the chair. He assumed an expression of anxious concern. "Is there anything I can help you with, Dr. George?" he said.

The doctor tapped his pen against the ledger. "It's just that I've been thinking, you know. Twelve dollars a month for train fare, for you to go and see your wife."

"And child," said Grandison, keeping his voice steady.

"Yes, of course. Well, I was thinking about it, and I'll have to talk it over with the rest of the faculty—"

I could take a second job, he was thinking. *Maybe earn the money for train fare myself . . .*

But Dr. George said, "I shall persuade them to purchase your family."

It took him a moment to sort out the words, so contrary were they to the ones he had anticipated. He had to bite back the protests that had risen in his throat. "Buy Rachel and George?"

The doctor smiled. "Oh, yes. I shall explain that we could save enough money in train fare to justify the purchase price within a few years. It does make fiscal sense. Besides, I have lately come to realize how much you must miss them."

Grandison turned these words over in his mind. If one of the cadavers had got up from the dissecting table and walked away, he could not have been more surprised. He never mentioned his wife and son except to respond with a vague pleasantry on the rare occasion that someone asked after them. Why had the doctor suddenly taken this charitable notion? Why not when the baby was first born? Dr. George was a kind man, in an absent-minded sort of way, but he hardly noticed his own feelings, let alone anybody else's. Grandison stood with his back to the door, the smile still frozen to his lips, wondering what had come over the man.

George Newton rubbed his forehead and sighed. He started to speak, and then shook his head. He began again, "It may be a few months before we can find the money, mind you. It should take about thirteen hundred dollars to buy both your wife and son. That should do it, surely. I'll write to your wife's mistress in Charleston to negotiate the purchase."

Grandison nodded. "Thank you," he whispered. The joy would come later, when the news had sunk in. Just now he was still wondering what had come over Dr. George.

"I'm going to be moving out one of these days," he told Alethea Taylor that night after supper.

She sat in her straight-backed chair closest to the lamp, embroidering a baby dress. "You'll be needing to find a place for your family to live," she said, still intent upon her work.

He laughed. "The world can't keep nothing from you, Miz Taylor. Dr. George told you?"

"Fanny told me." She set the baby dress down on the lamp table, and wiped her eyes. "She's been after George to bring them here, and he promised he would see to it."

"I wondered what put it into his head. Saying he was going to buy them, right out of the blue, without me saying a word about it. I can't make out what's come over him."

She made no reply, but her frown deepened as she went on with her sewing.

"I don't suppose you know what this is all about?"

She wiped her eyes on the hem of the cloth. "Yes. I know. I may as well tell you. Dr. George and Fanny are—well, man and wife, I would say, though the state of Georgia won't countenance it. Fanny has a baby coming soon."

He was silent for a bit, thinking out what to say. Dr. George was in his forties, and looked every minute of it. Fanny was a slender and beautiful sixteen. He knew how it would sound to a stranger, but he had known Dr. George five years now, and for all the physician's wealth and prominence, he couldn't help seeing him as a gray-haired mole, peering out at the world from his book-lined burrow, while the graceful Fanny seemed equal to anything. He knew—he *knew*—of light-skinned women forced to become their owners' mistresses, but Fanny was free, and besides he couldn't see her mother allowing such a thing to happen. Miss Alethea did not have all the rights of a white woman, though you'd take her for one to look at her, but still, there were some laws to protect free people of color. Through her dress-making business, Miss Alethea had enough friends among her lady clientele that if she'd asked, some lady's lawyer husband would have intervened. The white ladies hated the idea of their menfolk taking colored mistresses, and they'd jump at the chance to put a stop to it. Someone would have been outraged by such a tale, and they would have been eager to save Miss Alethea's young daughter from a wicked seducer. But . . . *Dr. George?* He couldn't see it. Why, for all his coolness in cutting up the dead, when it came to dealing with live folks, Dr. George wouldn't say boo to a goose.

"He didn't . . . force her?" he asked, looking away as he said it. But when he looked back and saw Miss Alethea's expression, his lips twitched, and then they both began to laugh in spite of it all.

Miss Alethea shook her head. "*Force? Dr. George?* Oh, my. I can't even think it was his idea, Mr. Harris. You know how he is."

"Well, is Miss Fanny happy?" he said at last.

"Humph. Sixteen years old and a rich white doctor thinks she hung the moon. What do you think?" She sighed. "When a man falls in love for the first time when he's past forty, it hits him hard. Seems like he's taken leave of his senses."

"Oh. Well," he cast about for some word of comfort, and settled on, "I won't tell anybody."

She stabbed her needle at the cloth. "Shout it from the rooftops if you feel like it, Mr. Harris. It's not as if *they're* keeping it a secret. He wants to marry her."

He smiled. "Anybody would, Miss Alethea. Mary Frances is a beautiful girl."

"You misunderstand, Mr. Harris. I'm saying that he *means* to marry her."

"And stay here? And let folks know about it?"

She nodded. "I'm saying. Live as man and wife, right there on Greene Street."

Now he realized why George Newton had suddenly understood the pain of his separation from Rachel, but he felt that the doctor's newfound wisdom had come at the price of folly. St. Paul's seeing the light on the road to Damascus might have been a blessed miracle, but Dr. George's light was more likely to be a thunderbolt. "He can't do that," he said. "Set her up as his wife."

"Not without losing his position he can't." The needle stabbed again. "Don't you think I've told them that?"

"And what did he say?"

"He's going to resign from the medical school, that's what. Says he has money enough. Going to continue his work in a laboratory at home. Huh!" She shook her head at the folly of it.

He thought about it. Perhaps in Charleston such a thing might work. Down in the islands, certainly. Martinique. Everybody knew that the French . . . But *here*?

"I even asked him, Mr. Harris, I said straight out, *Do you remember Richard Mentor Johnson?*" His expression told her that he did not remember, either. But she did. "Richard Mentor Johnson of Kentucky. He was the vice president of the United States, back when I was a girl. Under President Van Buren. Folks said that he had killed the Indian chief Tecumseh, which they thought made him a hero. But then he had also married a woman of color, and when word of that got out, they tried to run him out of office on account of it. When his first term was over, he gave up and went home to Kentucky. And, do you know, Mr. Johnson's wife wasn't even alive by that time. She had died before he ever went to Washington to be vice president. Just the memory of her was enough to ruin him. Now, how well does Dr. George think he will fare in Georgia with a *live* colored wife in his house?"

"But Miss Fanny—to look at her—"

"I know. She's whiter to look at than some of the doctors' wives, but that makes no difference. This is a small town, Mr. Harris. Everybody knows everybody. Fanny can't pass in Augusta, and they both say they've no mind to go elsewhere."

He thought he had made all the proper expressions of sympathy and commiseration, but he was thinking just as much about the effect that Dr. George's folly would have on him. Would this change of heart mean no more robbing Cedar Grove? Or in his madness would the doctor insist on obtaining an equal number of bodies from the white burying ground? Equality was a fine thing, but not if it got him hanged by a white lynch mob.

He swept the upstairs hall four times that morning, waiting for Dr. George to be alone in his office. Finally the last visitor left, and he tapped on the door quickly before anyone else could turn up. "Excuse me, Dr. George. We're getting low on supplies for the anatomy classes," he said.

He always said "supplies" instead of "bodies" even when they were alone, just in case anyone happened to overhear.

Dr. George gave him a puzzled frown. "Supplies? Oh—oh, I see. Not filled our quota yet? Well, are there any fresh ones to be had?"

"A burying today," he said. "Little boy fell off a barn roof. I just wondered if you wanted me to take him."

"Yes, I suppose so. He's needed. Though we could use a yellow fever victim if you hear of one. Must teach the Southern diseases, you know. Medical schools up north don't know a thing about them." Dr. George looked up. "Why did you ask about this boy in particular? Do you know him?"

That didn't matter. He had known them all for years now. Some he minded about more than others, but all of them had long ceased to be merely lumps of clay in his hands. "It's all right," he said. "I don't mind bringing him in. I just wondered what you wanted me to do, and if there's to be a new dean—"

The doctor leaned back in his chair and sighed. "Yes, I see, Grandison. You have heard."

"Yes."

"It's true that I am resigning the post of dean. I felt that it was better for the college if I did so." He picked up a sheaf of papers from his desk and held it out with a bemused smile. "But it seems that I shall be staying on as Emeritus Professor of Anatomy, after all. This is a petition, signed by all of the students and faculty, asking that I stay. And the Board of Trustees has acceded to their request."

"Do they know?"

"About Fanny? They do. They profess not to care. I suppose when one is a doctor, one sees how little difference there really is between the races. Just a thin layer of skin, that's all, and then it's all the same underneath. Whatever the reason, they insist that I stay on in some capacity, and I shall."

"So nothing will change? For me, I mean?"

George Newton shook his head. "We still must have bodies, and the only safe place to obtain them is from Cedar Grove. That has not changed. And I fancy that I shall still have enough influence to bring your family to Augusta. I do not intend to shirk my duty, so you may go and see to yours."

———

Madison Newton was born on the last day of February, red-faced, fair-haired, and hazel-eyed, looking like a squashed cabbage leaf, but a white one, after all.

"It's a fine baby," he had said to Fanny, when she brought the baby to her mother's house on a mild day in March.

Fanny switched the blanket back into place, so that only the infant's nose peeped out. "People only want to look at him to see what color he is," she said. "What do they expect? He had sixteen great-great grandparents, same as everybody, and only one of them was colored. All the rest of him from then on down is white. Of course, that doesn't change what he is to most folks' way of thinking."

He had kept smiling and said the plain truth: that the infant was a fortunate child, but he had been angry, and his annoyance had not left him. That night in Cedar Grove in a fine mist of rain, he dug as if he could inflict an injury upon the earth itself. "I reckon Miss Fanny is whiter in her head than she is on her face," he said to the darkness, thrusting the shovel deep into the ground. "Feeling sorry for a light-eyed baby born free, his daddy a rich white doctor. I guess pretty Miss Fanny wants the moon, even when it's raining."

He spared hardly a thought for the man in the box below. Some drunken laborer from the docks, hit too hard over the head in a brawl. He had even forgotten the name. An easy task tonight. No shells or flowers decorated this grave site. The dead man had been shunted into the ground without grief or ceremony. Just as well take him to the doctors, where he could do some good for once. His thoughts returned to his grievance. Spoiled Miss Fanny had never given a thought to his baby when she was complaining about her own son's lot in life. How would she have liked to be Rachel— separated from her husband, and left to raise a child without him, knowing that at any time old missus might take a notion to sell that child, and nothing could be done to stop it.

He brushed the dirt from the pine box, and stove in the lid with his shovel point. Miss Fanny Taylor didn't know what trouble was, complaining about—

A sound.

Something like a moan, coming from inside the smashed coffin. He forgot about Fanny and her baby, as he knelt in the loose dirt of the open grave, pressing his ear close to the lid of the box. He held his breath, straining to hear a repetition of the sound. In the stillness, with all his thoughts focused on the dark opening before him, he realized that something else was wrong with the grave site. The smell was wrong. The sickly sweet smell of newly decaying flesh should have been coming from the box, but it wasn't. Neither was the stench of voided bowels, the last letting-go of the dead. All he smelled was rotgut whiskey.

He gripped the corpse under the armpits and pulled it out of the grave, but instead of sacking it up, he laid the body out on the damp grass. It groaned.

He had heard such sounds from a corpse before. The first time it happened, he had been unloading a sack from the wagon into the store room at the medical college. He had dropped the sack and gone running to Dr. George, shouting that the deader from the burying ground had come back to life.

George Newton had smiled for an instant, but without a word of argument, he'd followed the porter back to the store room and examined the sacked-up body. He had felt the wrist and neck for a pulse, and even leaned into the dead face to check for breath, but Grandison could tell from his calm and deliberate movements that he knew what he would find. "The subject is dead," he said, standing up, and brushing traces of dirt from his trousers.

"It just died then. I heard it moan."

Dr. George smiled gently. "Yes, I believe you did, Grandison, but it was dead all the same."

"A ghost then?"

"No. Merely a natural process. When the body dies, there is still air trapped within the lungs. Sometimes when that air leaves the lungs it makes a moaning sound. Terrifying, I know. I heard it once myself in my student days, but it is only a remnant of life, not life itself. This poor soul has been dead at least a day."

He never forgot that sound, though in all the bodies that had passed through his hands on the way to the dissecting table, he had never heard it since.

The sound coming now from the man stretched out on the grass was different. And it changed—low and rumbling at first, and then louder. He knelt beside the groaning man and shook his shoulder.

"Hey!" he said. "Hey, now—" His voice was hoarse and unnaturally loud in the still darkness of Cedar Grove. *What can you say to a dead man?*

The groan changed to a cough, and then the man rolled over and vomited into the mound of spaded earth.

He sighed, and edged away a few feet. He had seen worse. Smelled worse. But finding a live body in the graveyard complicated matters. He sat quietly, turning the possibilities over in his mind, until the retching turned to sobbing.

"You're all right," he said, without turning around.

"This is the graveyard. Badger Benson done killed me?"

"I guess he tried. But you woke up. Who are you, anyhow?"

"I was fixing to ask you that. How did you come to find me down in the ground? You don't look like no angel."

He smiled. "Might be yours, though. You slave or free, boy?"

"Belong to Mr. Johnson. Work on his boat."

"Thought so. Well, you want to go back to Mr. Johnson, do you?"

The man stretched and kicked his legs, stiff from his interment. "I dunno," he said. "Why you ask me that?"

" 'Cause you were dead, boy, as far as anybody knows. They buried you this morning. Now if you was to go back to your master, there'd be people asking me questions about how I come to find you, and they'd take you back to Johnson's, and you'd still be a slave, and like as not I'd be in trouble for digging you up. But if you just lit out of here and never came back, why nobody would ever even know you were gone and that this grave was empty. You're dead. You don't let 'em find out any different, and they'll never even know to hunt for you."

The man rubbed the bruise on the back of his head. "Now how did you come to find me?"

Grandison stood up and retrieved the shovel. "This is where the medical school gets the bodies to cut up for the surgery classes. The doctors at the college were fixing to rip you open. And they still can, I reckon, unless you light out of here. Now, you tell me, boy, do you want to be dead again?"

The young man raised a hand as if to ward off a blow. "No. No!— I understand you right enough. I got to get gone."

"And you don't go back for nothing. You don't tell nobody good-bye. You are dead, and you leave it at that."

The young man stood up and took a few tentative steps on still unsteady legs. "Where do I go then?"

Grandison shrugged. "If it was me, I would go west. Over the mountains into Indian country. You go far enough, there's places that don't hold with slavery. I'd go there."

The man turned to look at him. "Well, why don't you then?" he said. "Why don't *you* go?"

"Don't worry about me. I'm not the one who's dead. Now are you leaving or not?"

"Yeah. Leaving."

"You've got three hours before sunup." He handed the shovel to the resurrected man. "Help me fill in your grave, then."

DR. GEORGE NEWTON—DECEMBER 1859

It is just as well that I stepped down as dean of the medical college. I haven't much time to wind up my affairs, and the fact that Ignatius Garvin is ably discharging my former duties leaves me with one less thing to worry about. If I can leave my dear Fanny and the babies safely provided for, I may leave this world without much regret. I wish I could have seen my boy grow up . . . wish I could have grown old with my dearest wife . . . . And I wish that God had seen fit to send me an easier death.

No one knows yet that I am dying, and it may yet be weeks before the disease carries me off, but I do not relish the thought of the time before me, for I know enough of this illness to tremble at the thought of what will come. I must not do away with myself, though. I must be brave, so as not to cause Fanny any more pain than she will feel at losing me so soon.

So many papers to sift through. Investments, deeds, instructions for the trustees—my life never felt so complicated. Soon the pain will begin, and it may render me incapable of making wise decisions to safeguard my little family. At least I have safeguarded the family of our faithful college servant, Grandison Harris. Thank God I was able to do that in time, for I had long promised him that I would bring his Rachel and her boy to Augusta, so I did a few months back. I am not yet fifty, sound in body and mind, and newly married. I thought I had many years to do good works and to continue my medical research. I suppose that even a physician must think that he will

never face death. Perhaps we would go mad if we tried to live thinking otherwise.

I wonder how it happened. People will say it was the buggy accident just before Christmas, and perhaps it was. That gelding is a nervous horse, not at all to be depended upon in busy streets of barking
dogs and milling crowds. I must remember to tell Henry to sell the
animal, for I would not like to think of Fanny coming to harm if
the beast became spooked again. I was shaken and bruised when he
dumped me out of the carriage and into the mud, but did I sustain
any cuts during the fall? I do not remember any blood.

Dr. Eve came to look me over, and he pronounced me fit
enough, with no bones broken, and no internal injuries. He was right
as far as it went. My fellow physicians all stopped by to wish us good
cheer at Christmas, and to pay their respects to their injured friend.
They did not bring their wives, of course. No respectable white
woman accepts the hospitality of this house, for it is supposed that
Fanny's presence taints the household. We are not, after all, legally
married in the eyes of the law here. Fanny professes not to care. *Dull
old biddies*, anyhow, she declares. But she has certainly charmed the
gentlemen, who consider me a lucky man. And so I was, until this
tragedy struck—though none of those learned doctors suspected it.

I wish that I had not. I wish that I could go innocently into the
throes of this final illness, as would a child who had stepped on a
rusty nail, not knowing what horrors lay before me. But I am a
trained physician. I do know. And the very word clutches at my
throat with cold fingers.

Tetanus.

Oh, I know too much, indeed. Too much—and not enough. I
have seen people die of this. The muscles stretch and spasm, in the
control of the ailment rather than the patient, an agonizing disten-
sion such as prisoners must have felt upon the rack in olden days.
The body is tortured by pain beyond imagining, but beyond these
physical torments, the patient's mind remains clear and unaffected. I
doubt that the clarity is a blessing. Delirium or madness might prove
a release from the agony, yet even that is denied to the sufferer. And
there is no cure. Nothing can stop the progression of this disease,
and nothing can reverse its effects. I have, perhaps, a week before
the end, and I am sure that by then I will not dread death, but rather
welcome it as a blessed deliverance.

Best not to dwell on it. It will engulf me soon enough. I must send for James Hope. I can trust him. As the owner of the cotton mill, he will be an eminently respectable guardian for my wife's business interests, and since James is a Scotsman by birth, and not bound by the old Southern traditions of race and caste, he will see Fanny as the gentlewoman that she is. He treats her with all the courtly gentility he would show to a duchess, and that endears him to both of us. Yes, I must tell James what has happened, and how soon he must pick up where I am forced to leave off.

My poor Fanny! To be left a widow with two babies, and she is not yet twenty. I worry more over her fate than I do my own. At least mine will be quick, but Fanny has another forty years to suffer if the world is unkind to her. I wish that the magnitude of my suffering could be charged against any sorrow God had intended for her. I must speak to James Hope. How aptly named he is! I must entrust my little family to him.

It was nearly Christmas, and Rachel had made a pound cake for the Newtons. He was to take it around to Greene Street that afternoon, when he could manage to get away from his duties. Grandison looked at the cake, and thought that Dr. George might prefer a specimen from the medical school supply for his home laboratory, but he supposed that such a gesture would not be proper for the season. Rachel would know best what people expected on social occasions. She talked to people, and visited with her new friends at church, while he hung back, dreading the prospect of talking to people that he might be seeing again some day.

He took the cake to the Newton house, and tapped on the back door, half expecting it to open before his hand touched the wood. He waited a minute, and then another, but no one came. He knocked again, harder this time, wondering at the delay. As many servants as the Newtons had, that door ought to open as soon as his foot hit the porch. What was keeping them so busy?

Finally, after the third and loudest spate of knocking, Fanny herself opened the door. He smiled and held out his paper-wrapped Christmas offering, but the sight of her made him take a step backward. His words of greeting stuck in his throat. She was big-bellied with child again, he knew that. She looked as if it could come at any moment, but what shocked him was how ill she looked, as if she had not eaten or slept for a week. She stared out at him, hollow-eyed and trembling, her face blank with weariness. For a moment he wondered if she recognized him.

"My Rachel made y'all a pound cake. For Christmas," he said.

She nodded, and stepped back from the door to admit him to the kitchen. "Put it on the table," she said.

He set down the cake. The house was unnaturally quiet. He listened for sounds of baby Madison playing, or the bustle of the servants, who should have been making the house ready for the holiday, but all was still. He looked back at Fanny, who was staring down at the parcel as if she had never seen one before, as if she had forgotten how it got there, perhaps.

"Are you all right?" he asked. "Shall I fetch Miss Alethea for you?"

Fanny shook her head. "She's been already. She took Madison so that I can stay with George," she whispered. "And I've sent most of the others around there, too. Henry stayed here, of course. He won't leave George."

Something was the matter with Dr. George, then. It must be bad. Fanny looked half dead herself. "Shall I go for Dr. Eve?" he asked.

"He was here this morning. So was Dr. Garvin. Wasn't a bit of use. George told me that from the beginning, but I wouldn't have it. I thought with all those highfalutin doctors somebody would be able to help him, but they can't. They can't."

"Is he took bad?"

"He's dying. It's the lockjaw. You know what that is?"

He nodded. Tetanus. Oh, yes. They had covered it in one of the medical classes, but not to consider a course of treatment. Only to review the terrible symptoms and to hope they never saw them. He shivered. "Are they sure?"

"George is sure. Diagnosed himself. And the others concur. I was the only one who wouldn't believe it. I do now, though. I sit with him as long as I can. Hour after hour. Watch him fighting the pain. Fighting the urge to scream. And then I go and throw up, and I sit with him some more."

"I could spell you a while."

"*No!*" She said it so harshly that he took a step back in surprise. She took a deep breath, and seemed to swallow her anger. "No, thank you very kindly, Mr. Harris, but I will not let you see him."

"But if Dr. George is dying—"

"That's exactly why. Don't you think I know what you do over there at the medical college? Porter, they call you. *Porter.* I know what your real duties are, Mr. Harris. Known for a long time. And that's fine. I know doctors have to learn somehow, and that nothing about doctoring is pretty or easy. But you are not going to practice your trade in this house. You are not going to take my husband's body, do you hear?"

He said softly, "I only wanted to help you out, and maybe to tell him good-bye."

"So you say. But he is weak now. Half out of his mind with the pain, and he'd promise anything. He might even suggest it himself, out of some crazy sense of duty to the medical college, but I won't have it. My husband is going to have a proper burial, Mr. Harris. He has suffered enough!"

It doesn't hurt, he wanted to tell her. *You don't feel it if you're dead.* He did not bother to speak the words. He knew whose pain Fanny was thinking of, and that whatever Dr. George's wishes might be, it was the living who mattered, not the dead. Best to soothe her quickly and with as little argument as possible. He did not think that the other doctors would accept George Newton's body anyhow. That would be bringing death too close into the fold, and he was glad that he would not be required to carry out that task. Let the doctor lie in consecrated ground: There were bodies enough to be had in Augusta.

"I'll go now, Miss Fanny," he said, putting on his best white folks manners, if it would give her any comfort. "But I think one of the doctors should come back and take a look at you." He nodded toward her distended belly. "And we will pray for the both of you, my Rachel and I. Pray that he gets through this." It was a lie. He never prayed, but if he did, it would be for Dr. George's death to come swiftly—the only kindness that could be hoped for in a case of tetanus.

Dr. George died after the new year in 1860. The illness had lasted only two weeks, but the progress of the disease was so terrible that it had begun to seem like months to those who could do nothing but wait for his release from the pain. Grandison joined the crowd at the doctor's funeral, though he took care to keep clear of Fanny, for fear of upsetting her again. In her grief she might shout out things that should not be said aloud in Augusta's polite society. The doctors knew his business, of course, but not the rest of the town. He reckoned that most of Augusta would have been at the funeral if it weren't for the fact of the doctor's awkward marriage arrangements. As it was, though, his fellow physicians, the students, and most of the town's businessmen came to pay their respects, while their wives and daughters stayed home, professing themselves too delicate to endure the sight of the doctor's redbone widow. Not that you could see an inch of her skin, whatever its color, for she was swathed from head to foot in black widow's weeds and veils, leaning on the arm of Mr. James Hope, as if he were the spar of her sinking ship.

"Left a widow at eighteen," said Miss Alethea, regal in her black dress, her eyes red from tears of her own. "I had hoped for better for my girl."

He nodded. "She will be all right," he said. "Dr. George would have seen to that."

Miss Alethea gave him the look usually reserved for one of her children talking foolishness. "She's back home again, you know. Dr. George was too clouded at the last to do justice to a will, and Mr. James Hope had to sell the house on Greene Street. He vows to see her settled in a new place, though, over on Ellis, just a block from Broad Street. Having it built. There's all Dr. George's people to be thought of, you know, and the Tuttle folks, as well. Fanny has to have a house of her own, but I'm glad to have her by me for now, for the new baby is due any day—if it lives through her grief. We must pray for her, Mr. Harris."

Grandison looked past her at the tall, fair-haired Scotsman, who was still hovering protectively beside the pregnant young widow, and wondered if the prayer had already been answered.

The cellar was paved with bones now. Each term when the anatomy class had finished with its solemn duties of dissection, the residue was brought to him to be disposed of. He could hardly rebury the remains in any public place or discard them where they might be recognized for what they were. The only alternative was to layer them in quicklime in the basement on Telfair Street. How many hundred had it been now? He had lost count. Mercifully the faces and the memories of the subjects' resurrection were fading with the familiarity of the task, but sometimes he wondered if the basement resounded with cries he could not hear, and if that was why the building's cat refused to set foot down there. The quicklime finished taking away the flesh and masked the smell, but he wondered what part of the owners remained, and if that *great getting up in the morning* that the preacher spoke of was really going to come to pass on Judgment Day. And who would have to answer for the monstrous confusion and scramble of bones that must follow? Himself? Dr. George? The students who carved up the cadavers? Sometimes as he scattered the quicklime over a new batch of discarded bones, he mused on Dr. George peering over the wrought iron fence of white folks' heaven at an angry crowd of colored angels shaking their fists at him.

"Better the dead than the living, though," he would tell himself.

Sometimes on an afternoon walk to Cedar Grove, he would go across to the white burying ground to pay his respects to Dr. George, lying there undisturbed in his grave, and sometimes he would pass the time of day with the grassy mound, as if the doctor could still hear him. "Miss Mary Frances finally birthed that baby," he said one winter day, picking the brown stems of dead flowers off the grave. "Had a little girl the other day. Named her Georgia Frances, but everybody calls her Cissie, and I think that's the name that's going to stick. She's a likely little thing, pale as a Georgia peach. And Mr. James Hope is building her that house on Ellis like he promised, and she's talking about having her sister Nannie and young Jimmie move in along with her. I thought maybe Mr. James Hope would be moving in, too, the way he dotes on her, but he's talking about selling the factory here and going back to New York where his family is, so I don't think you need to linger on here if you are, sir. I think everything is going to be all right."

Dr. George hadn't been gone hardly more than two years when the war came, and that changed everything. Didn't look like it would at first, though. For the rest of the country, the war began in April in Charleston, when Fort Sumpter fell, but Georgia had seceded in

January, leaving Augusta worried about the arsenal on the hill, occupied by federal troops. Governor Joe Brown himself came to town to demand the surrender of the arsenal, and the town was treated to a fine show of military parades in the drizzling rain. Governor Brown himself stood on the porch of the Planters Hotel to watch the festivities, but Captain Elzey, who was in command of the eighty-two men at the arsenal, declined to surrender it. He changed his mind a day or so later when eight hundred soldiers and two brigadier generals turned up in the rain to show the arsenal they meant business. Then Captain Elzey sent for the governor to talk things over, and by noon the arsenal and its contents had been handed over to the sovereign State of Georgia, without a shot fired. That, and a lot of worrying, was pretty much all that happened to Augusta for the duration of the war.

When the shooting actually started in Charleston, he was glad that Rachel and the boy were safe in Augusta, instead of being caught in the middle of a war, though personally he would have liked to see the battle for the novelty of it. Everybody said the war was only going to last a few weeks, and he hated to have missed getting a glimpse of it.

Folks were optimistic, but they were making preparations anyhow. Two weeks after Fort Sumpter, Augusta organized a local company of home guards, the Silver Grays, composed mostly of men too old to fight in the regular army. Mr. James Hope came back from New York City to stand with the Confederacy and got himself chosen second member of the company, after Rev. Joseph Wilson, who was the first. Rev. Wilson's boy Tommy and little Madison Newton were the same age, and they sometimes played together on the lawn of the Presbyterian church, across the road from the college. Sometimes the two of them would come over and pepper him with questions about bodies and sick folks, and he often thought that you'd have to know which boy was which to tell which one wasn't the white child. Fanny kept young Madison as clean and well-dressed as any quality child in Augusta.

The months went by, and the war showed no signs of letting up. One by one the medical students drifted away to enlist in regiments back home.

"I don't suppose you'll have to worry about procuring any more cadavers for classes, Grandison," Dr. Garvin told him.

"No, sir," he said. "I've heard a lot of the students are fixing to quit and join up."

Dr. Garvin scowled. "I expect they will, but even if the school stays open, this war will produce enough cadavers to supply a thousand medical schools before it's over."

There wasn't any fighting in Augusta, but they saw their share of casualties anyhow. A year into the war, the wounded began arriving by train from distant battlefields, and the medical school suspended operation in favor of setting up hospitals to treat the wounded. The City Hotel and the Academy of Richmond County were turned into hospitals in '62 to accommodate the tide of injured soldiers flowing into the city from far off places with unfamiliar names, like Manassas and Shiloh. Many of the faculty members had gone off to serve in the war as well. Dr. Campbell was in Virginia with the Georgia Hospital Association, seeing to the state's wounded up there; Dr. Miller and Dr. Ford were serving with the Confederate forces at different places up in Virginia, and Dr. Jones was somewhere on the Georgia coast contributing his medical skills to the war effort.

Grandison worked in one of the hospitals, assisting the doctors at first, but as the number of casualties strained their ability to treat them, he took on more and more duties to fill the gap.

"I don't see why you are working so hard to patch those Rebels up," one of the porters said to him one day, when he went looking for a roll of clean bandages. "The Federals say they are going to end slavery, and here you are helping the enemy."

He shrugged. "I don't see any Federals in Augusta, do you? I don't see any army coming here to hand me my freedom. So meanwhile I do what I'm supposed to do, and we'll see what transpires when the war is over." Besides, he thought, it was one thing to wish the Confederacy to perdition, and quite another to ignore the suffering of a single boy soldier who couldn't even grow a proper beard yet.

Sometimes he wondered what had happened to the man he "resurrected" who wasn't dead—whether the fellow had made it to some free state beyond the mountains, and whether that had made any difference.

He didn't know if freedom was coming, or what it would feel like, but for the here and now there was enough work for ten of him.

So he stitched, and bandaged, and dressed wounds. *I've handled dead people*, he told himself. *This isn't any worse than that*.

But of course it was.

The boy was a South Carolina soldier, eighteen or so, with copper-colored hair and a sunny nature that not even a gaping leg wound could dampen. The pet of the ward, he was, and he seemed to be healing up nicely what with all the rest and the mothering from Augusta's lady hospital visitors. The nurses were already talking about the preparations to send him home.

Grandison was walking down the hall that morning, when one of the other patients came hobbling out into the hall and clutched at his coat sleeve. "You got to come now!" the man said. "Little Will just started bleeding a gusher."

He hurried into the ward past the crippled soldier and pushed his way through the patients clustered around the young man's cot. A blood-soaked sheet was pulled back revealing a skinny white leg with a spike of bone protruding through the skin. Jets of dark blood erupted from the bone splinter's puncture. Without a word Grandison sat down beside the boy and closed his fingers over the ruptured skin.

"I just tried to walk to the piss pot," the boy said. He sounded close to passing out. "I got so tired of having to be helped all the time. I felt fine. I just wanted to walk as far as the wall."

He nodded. The mending thigh bone had snapped under the boy's weight, severing a leg artery as the splintered bone slid out of place. The men crowded around the bed murmured among themselves, but no one spoke to the boy.

"Shall I fetch the surgeon?" one of the patients asked Grandison.

He shook his head. "Surgeon's amputating this morning. Wouldn't do no good to call him anyhow."

The boy looked up at him. "Can you stop it, sir?"

He looked away, knowing that the *sir* was for his medical skills and not for himself, but touched by it all the same. The red-haired boy had a good heart. He was a great favorite with his older and sadder comrades.

"Get a needle?" somebody said. "Sew it back in?"

He kept his fingers clamped tight over the wound, but he couldn't stay there forever. He wanted to say: *Y'all ever see a calf killed? Butcher takes a sharp knife and slits that cord in his throat, and he bleeds out in—what? A minute? Two?* It was the same here. The severed artery was not in the neck, no, but the outcome would be the same—and it was just as inevitable.

"But I feel all right," said the boy. "No pain."

He ignored the crowd around the bed and looked straight into the brown eyes of the red-haired boy. "Your artery's cut in two," he said. "Can't nothing remedy that."

"Can you stop the bleeding?"

He nodded toward his fingers pressed against the pale white skin. The warmth of the flesh made him want to pull away. He took a deep breath. "I have stopped it," he said, nodding toward his hand stanching the wound. "But all the time you've got is until I let go."

The boy stared at him for a moment while the words sunk in. Then he nodded. "I see," he said. "Can you hold on a couple minutes? Let me say a prayer."

Somebody said, "I got paper here, Will. You ought to tell your folks good-bye. I'll write it down."

The boy looked the question at Grandison, who glanced down at his hand. "Go ahead," he said. "I can hold it."

In a faltering voice the boy spoke the words of farewell to his parents. He sounded calm, but puzzled, as if it were happening to someone else. That was just as well. Fear wouldn't change anything, and it was contagious. They didn't need a panic in the ward. The room was silent as the boy's voice rose and fell. Grandison turned away from the tear-stained faces to stare at a fly speck on the wall, wishing that he could be elsewhere while this lull before dying dragged on. These last minutes of life should not be witnessed by strangers.

The letter ended, and a few minutes after that the prayers, ending with a whispered amen as the last words of the Lord's Prayer trailed off into sobs.

He looked at the boy's sallow face, and saw in it a serenity shared by no one else in the room. "All right?" he said.

The boy nodded, and Grandison took his hand away.

A minute later the boy was dead. Around the bedstead the soldiers wept, and Grandison covered the still form with the sheet and went back to his duties. He had intended to go to the death room later to talk to the boy, to tell him that death was a release from worse horrors and to wish him peace, but there were so many wounded, and so much to be done that he never went.

The war came to Augusta on stretchers and in the form of food shortages and lack of mercantile goods—but never on horseback with flags flying and the sound of bugles. Augusta thought it would, of course. When Sherman marched to the sea by way of Savannah, troops crowded into the city to defend it, and the city fathers piled up bales of cotton, ready to torch them and the rest of the town with it to keep the powder works and the arsenal out of Union hands, but Sherman ignored them and pushed on north into South Carolina.

Three months later the war ended, and federal troops did come to occupy the city.

"I am a throne, Grandison!" Tommy Wilson announced one May morning. "And Madison here, he's only a dominion."

"That's fine," he said without a glance at the two boys. He was cleaning out the little work room at the college on Telfair Street. It had been his headquarters and his storage room for thirteen years now, but the war was over and he was free. It was time to be his own master now somewhere else. He thought he might cross the river to Hamburg. Folks said that the Yankees over there were putting freedmen into jobs to replace the white men. He would have to see.

Tommy Wilson's words suddenly took shape in his mind. "A throne?" he said. "I thought a throne was a king's chair."

"Well, a throne can be that," said Tommy, with the air of one who is determined to be scrupulously fair. "But it's also a rank of angels. We're playing angels, me and Madison. We're going to go out and convert the heathens."

"Well, that's a fine thing, boys. You go and—*what* heathens?"

"The soldiers," said Madison.

Tommy nodded. "They misbehave something awful, you know. They drink and fight and take the Lord's name in vain."

"And by God we're gonna fix 'em," said Madison.

"Does your father know where you are?"

Tommy nodded. "He said I could play outside."

Madison Newton shrugged. "Mr. Hope don't care where I go.

He's living up at my house now, but he's not my daddy. He says he's gonna take Momma and their new babies up north with him, but me and Cissie can't go."

Grandison nodded. Fanny Newton was now called Fanny Hope, and she had two more babies with magnolia skin and light eyes. He wondered what would become of Dr. George's two children.

"Don't you go bothering the soldiers now," he told the boys. "They might shoot the both of you."

Tommy Wilson grinned happily. "Then we shall be angels for real."

"Do we call you *judge* now, Mr. Harris?" Either the war or the worry of family had turned Miss Alethea into an old woman. Her hair was nearly white now, and she peered up at him now through the thick lenses of rimless spectacles.

He had taken his family to live across the river in South Carolina, but he still came back to Augusta on the occasional errand. That morning he had met Miss Alethea as she hobbled along Broad Street, shopping basket on her arm, bound for the market. He smiled and gave her a courtly bow. "Why, you may call me judge if it pleases you, ma'am," he said. "But I don't expect I'll be seeing you in court, Miss Alethea. I'll be happy to carry your shopping basket in exchange for news of your fine family. How have you been?"

"Oh, tolerable," she said with a sigh. "My eyes aren't what they used to be—fine sewing in a bad light, you know. The boys are doing all right these days, grown and gone you know. But I do have young Madison and Cissie staying with me now. Mr. James Hope has taken their mother off to New York with him. Their little girls, too. You know they named the youngest after me? Little Alethea." She sighed. "I do miss them. But tell me about you, Mr. Harris. A judge now, under the new Reconstruction government! What's that like?"

He shrugged. "I don't do big law. Just little matters. Fighting drunks. Disturbing the peace. Stealing trifling things—chickens, not horses." They both smiled. "But when I come into the court, they all have to stand up and show me respect. I do like that. I expect Fanny—er, Mrs. Hope—knows what I mean, being up there in New York and all."

The old woman sighed. "She hates it up there—would you credit it? Poor James Hope is beside himself with worry. Thought he was handing her heaven on a plate, I reckon. Come north where there's been no slaves for fifty years, and maybe where nobody knows that Fanny is a woman of color anyhow. Be really free." She shook her head. "Don't you suppose he expected her to thank God for her deliverance and never want to come back."

"I did suppose it," he said.

"So did the Hopes. But she's homesick and will not be swayed. Why, what do you suppose Mr. James Hope did? He took Fanny to meet with Frederick Douglass. The great man himself! As if Mr. Douglass didn't have better things to do than to try to talk sense into a little Georgia girl. He did his best, though, to convince her to stay. She'll have none of it."

"Do you hear from her, Miz Alethea?"

She nodded. "Regular as clockwork. In every letter she sounds heartbroken. She misses me and her brothers and sisters. Misses Madison and Cissie something fierce. She says she hates northern food. Hates the cold weather and that ugly city full of more poor folks and wickedness than there is in all of Georgia. Fanny has her heart set on coming home."

"But if she stays up there, she could live white, and her children could be white folks."

Alethea Taylor stared. "Why would she want to do that, Mr. Harris?"

She already knew the answer to that, of course, but stating the truth out loud would only incur her wrath, so he held his peace, and wished them all well.

A year later, James and Fanny Hope did return to take up residence in Augusta, and perhaps it was best that they had, for Miz Alethea died before another year was out. At least she got to be reunited with her family again, and he was glad of that.

He did not go to the burying. They laid her to rest in Cedar Grove, and he forced himself to go for the sake of their long acquaintance. At least she would rest in peace. He alone was sure of that.

He wished that she had lived to see her new grandson, who was born exactly a year after his parents returned from the North. The Hopes named the boy John, and he was as blond and blue-eyed as any little Scotsman.

Privately Grandison had thought Fanny had been crazy to come back south when she could have passed in New York and dissolved her children's heritage in the tide of immigrants. But before the end of the decade, he knew he had come round to her way of thinking, for he quit his post of judge in South Carolina, and went back over the river to work at the medical school. Perhaps there were people talking behind his back then, calling him a graven fool, as he had once thought Fanny Hope, but now he had learned the hard way. For all the promises of the Reconstruction men, he got no respect as a judge. The job was a sham whose purpose was not to honor him or his people, but to shame the defeated Rebels. He grew tired of being stared at by strangers whose hatred burned through their feigned respect, and as the days went by, he found himself remembering the medical school with fondness.

He had been good at his job, and the doctors had respected his skills. Sometimes he even thought they forgot about his color. Dr. George had said something once about the difference being a thin layer of skin, and then underneath it was all the same. Many of the faculty had left during the war, but one by one they were coming back now to take up their old jobs at the medical college, and he knew that he was wishing he could join them as well.

He was wearing his white linen suit, a string tie, and his good black shoes. He stood in front of the desk of Dr. Louis Dugas, hat in hand, waiting for an answer.

Dugas, a sleek; clean-shaven man who looked every inch a French aristocrat, had taken over as dean of the college during the war years. In his youth he had studied in Paris, as Dr. George had, and it was Dugas who had traveled to Europe to purchase books for Augusta's medical library. It was said that he had dined with Lafayette himself. Now he looked puzzled. Fixing his glittering black eyes on Harris's face in a long-nosed stare, he said, "Just let me see if I understand you, my good man. You wish to leave a judiciary position across the river and come back here to work as a porter."

Grandison inclined his head. "I do, sir."

"Well, I don't wish to disparage the virtues of manual labor, as I am sure that the occupation of porter is an honorable and certainly a necessary one, but could you just tell me why it is that you wish to abandon your exalted legal position for such a job?"

He had been ready for this logical question, and he knew better than to tell the whole truth. The law had taught him that, at least. Best not to speak of the growing anger of defeated white men suddenly demoted to second-class citizens by contemptuous strangers. He'd heard tales of a secret society that was planning to fight back at the conquerors and whoever was allied with them. But as much as the rage of the locals made him uneasy, the patronizing scorn of his federal overseers kindled his own anger. They treated him like a simpleton, and he came to realize that he was merely a pawn in a game between the white men, valued by neither side. It would be one thing to have received a university education and then to have won the job because one was qualified to do it. Surely they could have found such a qualified man of color in the North, and if not, why not? But to be handed the job only as a calculated insult to others—that made a mockery of his intelligence and skills. At least the doctors had respected him for his work and valued what he did. Fifteen years he'd spent with them.

Best not to speak of personal advantage—of the times in the past when he had prevailed upon one or another of the doctors to treat some ailing neighbor or an injured child who might otherwise have died. The community needed a conduit to the people in power—he could do more good there than sentencing his folks to chain gangs across the river.

Best not to say that he had come to understand the practice of medicine and that, even as he approached his fiftieth year, he wanted to know more.

At last he said simply, "I reckon I miss y'all, Dr. Dugas."

Louis Dugas gave him a cold smile that said that he himself would never put sentiment before other considerations, but loyalty to oneself is a hard fault to criticize in a supplicant. "Even with the procuring of the bodies for the dissection table? You are willing to perform that task again as before?"

We must mutilate the dead so that we do not mutilate the living. He must believe that above all.

He nodded. "Yes, sir."

"Very well then. Of course we must pay you now. The rate is eight dollars per month, I believe. Give your notice to the South Carolina court and you may resume your post here."

And it was done. What he had entered into by compulsion as a

slave so many years before, he now came to of his own volition as a
free man. He would return to the cart and the lantern and the shovel
and begin again.

Well, all that was a long time ago. It is a new century now, and much
has changed, not all of it for the better.

He steps out into the night air. The queasy medical student has
tottered away to his rooms, and now the building can be locked again
for the night. He still has his key, and he will do it himself, although
his son George is the official porter now at the medical college—not
as good as he himself once was, but what of that? Wasn't the faculty
now packed with pale shadows—the nephews and grandsons of the
original doctors? A new century, not a patch on the old one for all its
motorcars and newfangled gadgets.

He will walk home down Ellis Street, past the house where
James and Fanny Hope had raised their brood of youngsters. One of
the Hope daughters lived there now, but that was a rarity these days.
There was a colored quarter in Augusta now, not like the old days
when people lived all mixed together and had thought nothing
about it.

James and Fanny Hope had enjoyed eight years in that house on
Ellis Street, before a stroke carried him off in 1876. They had let his
white kinfolk take him back to New York for burying. Better to have
him far away, Fanny Hope had said, than separated from us by a
cemetery wall here in Augusta.

Fanny raised her brood of eight alone, and they did her credit.
She had lived three years into the twentieth century, long enough to
see her offspring graduate from colleges and go on to fine careers.
Little blue-eyed John Hope was the best of them, folks said. He had
attended Brown University up north, and now he was president of a
college in Atlanta. So was little Tommy Wilson, the white preacher's
son, who now went by his middle name of Woodrow, and was a
"throne" at Princeton College up north. You never could tell about a
child, how it would turn out.

Though he never told anyone, Grandison had hoped that Dr.
George's son Madison might be the outstanding one of Fanny's children, but he had been content to work at low wage jobs in Augusta

and to care for his aging mother. He and Dr. George had that in common—neither of the sons had surpassed them.

Funny to think that he had outlived the beautiful Fanny Hope. In his mind she is still a poised and gentle young girl, and sometimes he regrets that he did not go to her burying in Cedar Grove. The dead rested in peace there now, for the state had legalized the procuring of cadavers by the medical schools some twenty years back, but around that time, rumors had surfaced in the community about grave robbing. Where had the doctors got the bodies all those years for their dissecting classes? Cedar Grove, of course. There was talk of a riot. Augusta had an undertaker now for people of color. The elegant Mr. Dent, with his fancy black oak hearse with the glass panels, and the plumed horses to draw it along in style. Had John or Julia Dent started those rumors to persuade people to be embalmed so the doctors wouldn't get you? There had been sharp looks and angry mutterings at the time, for everyone knew who had been porter at the medical college for all these years, but he was an old man by then, a wiry pillar of dignity in his white suit, and so they let him alone, but he did not go to buryings any more.

The night air is cool, and he takes a deep breath, savoring the smell of flowers borne on the wind. He hears no voices in the wind, and dreams no dreams of dead folks reproaching him for what he has done. In a little while, a few months or years at most, for he is nearly ninety, he too will be laid to rest in Cedar Grove among the empty grave sites, secret monuments to his work. He is done with this world, with its new machines and the new gulf between the races. Sometimes he wonders if there are two heavens, so that Fanny Hope will be forever separated from her husbands by some celestial fence, but he rather hopes that there is no hereafter at all. It would be simpler so. And in all his dissecting he has never found a soul.

He smiles on the dark street, remembering a young minister who had once tried to persuade him to attend a funeral. "Come now, Mr. Harris," the earnest preacher had said. "There is nothing to fear in a cemetery. Surely those bodies are simply the discarded husks of our departed spirits. Surely the dead are no longer there."

BIBLIOGRAPHY

Allen, Lane. "Grandison Harris, Sr.: Slave, Resurrectionist and Judge." Athens, GA: *Bulletin of the Georgia Academy of Science*, 34:192–199.

Ball, James M. *The Body Snatchers*. New York: Dorset Press, 1989.

Blakely, Robert L., and Judith M. Harrington. *Bones in the Basement: Post Mortem Racism in Nineteenth Century Medical Training*. Washington, DC: Smithsonian Institution, 1997.

Burr, Virginia Ingraham, ed. *The Secret Eye: The Journal of Ella Gertrude Clanton Thomas, 1848–1889*. Chapel Hill, NC: UNC Press, 1990.

Cashin, Edward J. *Old Springfield: Race and Religion in Augusta, Georgia*. Augusta, GA: The Springfield Village Park Assoc. 1995.

Corley, Florence Fleming. *Confederate City: Augusta, Georgia 1860–1865*. Columbia, SC: The USC Press; Rpt. Spartanburg, SC: The Reprint Company, 1995.

Davis, Robert S. *Georgia Black Book: Morbid Macabre and Disgusting Records of Genealogical Value*. Greenville, SC: Southern Historical Press, 1982.

Fido, Martin. *Body Snatchers: A History of the Resurrectionists*. London: Weidenfeld & Nicolson, 1988.

Fisher, John Michael. Fisher & Watkins Funeral Home, Danville, VA. Personal Interview, March 2003.

Kirby, Bill. *The Place We Call Home: A Collection of Articles About Local History from the Augusta Chronicle*. Augusta, GA: *The Augusta Chronicle*, 1995.

Lee, Joseph M. III. *Images of America: Augusta and Summerville*. Charleston, SC: Arcadia Publishing, 2000.

Spalding, Phinizy. *The History of the Medical College of Georgia*. Athens, GA: The University of Georgia Press, 1997.

Torrence, Ridgely. *The Story of John Hope*. New York: Macmillan, 1948.

United States Census Records: Richmond County, GA: 1850; 1860; 1870; 1880; 1990.

JOHN FARRIS

John Farris began writing fiction in high school. At 22, while he was studying at the University of Missouri, his first major novel, *Harrison High*, was published; it became a bestseller. He has worked in many genres—suspense, horror, mystery—while transcending each through the power of his writing. The *New York Times* noted his talent for "masterfully devious plotting" while reviewing *The Captors*. *All Heads Turn When the Hunt Goes By* was cited in an essay published in *Horror: 100 Best Books*, which concluded, "The field's most powerful individual voice ... when John Farris is on high-burn, no one can match the skill with which he puts words together." In the 1990s he turned exclusively to thrillers, publishing *Dragonfly, Soon She Will Be Gone, Solar Eclipse,* and *Sacrifice,* of which Richard Matheson wrote, "John Farris has once again elevated the terror genre into the realm of literature." Commenting on *Dragonfly*, Ed Gorman said, "*Dragonfly* has style, heart, cunning, terror, irony, suspense, and genuine surprise—and an absolutely fearless look into the souls of people very much like you and me." And *Publishers Weekly* concluded, "(he writes with) a keen knowledge of human nature and a wicked sense of humor." John Farris received the 2001 Lifetime Achievement Award from the Horror Writers Association. His latest novel is *Phantom Nights*.

THE RANSOME WOMEN

John Farris

ONE

Echo Halloran first became aware of the Woman in Black during a
visit to the Highbridge Museum of Art in Cambridge, Massachusetts. Echo and her boss were dealing that day with the chief curator
of the Highbridge, a man named Charles Carwood. The Highbridge
was in the process of deacquisitioning, as they say in the trade, a
number of paintings, mostly by twentieth-century artists whose
stock had remained stable in the fickle art world. The Highbridge
was in difficulty with the IRS and Carwood was looking for around
thirty million for a group of Representationalists.

Echo's boss was Stefan Konine, director of Gilbard's, the New
York auction house. Stefan was a big man, florid as a poached salmon,
who lied about his age and played the hayburners for recreation. He
wore J. Dege & Sons suits with the aplomb of royalty. He wasn't
much interested in Representationalists and preferred to let Echo,
who had done her thesis at NYU on the Boquillas School, carry the
ball while the paintings were reverently brought, one by one, to their
attention in the seventh floor conference room. The weather outside
was blue and clear. Through a nice spread of windows the view to
the south included the Charles River.

Echo had worked for Konine for a little over a year. They had established an almost familial rapport. Echo kept busy with her laptop on questions of provenance while Stefan sipped Chablis and regarded each painting with the same dyspeptic expression, as if he were trying to digest a bowling ball he'd had for lunch. His mind was mostly on the Trifecta he had working at Belmont, but he was alert to the nuances of each glance Echo sent his way. They were a team. They knew each other's signals.

Carwood said, "And we have this exquisite David Herrera from the Oppenheim estate, probably the outstanding piece of David's Big Bend Cycle."

Echo smiled as two museum assistants wheeled in the oversize canvas. She was drinking 7-Up, not Chablis.

The painting was in the style of Georgia O'Keeffe during her Santa Fe incarnation. Echo looked down at her laptop screen, hit a few keys, looked up again. It was a long stare, as if she were trying to see all the way to the Big Bend country of Texas. After a couple of minutes Stefan raised a spikey eyebrow. Carwood fidgeted on his settee. His eyes were on Echo. He had done some staring himself, from the moment Echo was introduced to him.

There are beauties who stop traffic and there are beauties who grow obsessively in the hearts of the susceptible; Echo Halloran was one of those. She had a full mane of wraparound dark hair. Her eyes were large and round and dark as polished buckeyes, deeply flecked with gold. Spright as a genie, endowed with a wealth of breeding and self-esteem, she viewed the world with an intensity of favor that piqued the wonder of strangers.

When she cleared her throat Carwood started nervously. Stefan looked lazily at his protégée, with the beginning of a wise smile. He sensed an intrigue.

Carwood said, "Perhaps you'd care to have a closer look, Miss Halloran? The light from the windows—"

"The light is fine." Echo settled back in her seat. She closed her eyes and touched the center of her forehead with two fingers. "I've seen enough. I'm very sorry, Mr. Carwood. But that canvas isn't David Herrera's work."

"Oh, my *dear*," Carwood said, drawing a pained breath as if he were trying to decide whether a tantrum or a seizure was called for, "you must be extremely careful about making potentially actionable judgments—"

"I am," Echo said, and opened her eyes wide, "always careful. It's a fake. And not the first fake Herrera I've seen. Give me a couple of hours and I'll tell you which of his students painted it, and when."

Carwood attempted to appeal to Stefan, who held up a cautionary finger.

"But that will cost you a thousand dollars for Miss Halloran's time and expertise. A thousand dollars an hour. I would advise you to pay it. She's very good. As for the lot you've shown us today—" Stefan got to his feet with a nod of good cheer. "Thank you for considering Gilbard's. I'm afraid our schedule is unusually crowded for the fall season. Why don't you try Sotheby's?"

For a man of his bulk, Stefan did a good job of imitating a capering circus bear in the elevator going down to the lobby of the Highbridge.

"Now, Stefan," Echo said serenely.

"But I *loved* seeing dear old Carwood go into the crapper."

"I didn't realize he was another of your old enemies."

"Enemy? I don't hold Charles in such high regard. He's simply a pompous ass. If he were mugged for his wits, he would only impoverish the thief. So tell me, who perpetrated the fraud?"

"Not sure. Either Fimmel or Arzate. Anyway, you can't get a fake Herrera past me."

"I'm sure it helps to have a photographic memory."

Echo grinned.

"Perhaps you should be doing my job."

"Now, Stefan." Echo reached out to press the second-floor button.

"Some day you *will* have my job. But you'll have to pry it from my cold, dead fingers."

Echo grinned again. The elevator stopped on two.

"What are you doing? Aren't we leaving?"

"In a little while." Echo stepped off the elevator and beckoned to Stefan. "This way."

"What? Where are you dragging me to? I'm desperate to have a smoke and find out how My Little Margie placed in the fourth."

Echo looked at her new watch, a twenty-second birthday present from her fiancé that she knew had cost far more than either of them should have been spending on presents.

"There's time. I want to see the Ransome they've borrowed for their show of twentieth-century portraitists."

"Oh, dear God!" But he got off the elevator with Echo. "I detest Ransome! Such transparent theatrics. I've seen better art on a sailor's ass."

"Really, Stefan?"

"Although not all that recently, I'm sorry to say."

The gallery in which the exhibition was being mounted was temporarily closed to the public, but they wore badges allowing them access to any part of the Highbridge. Echo ignored frowns from a couple of dithering functionaries and went straight to the portrait by Ransome that was already in place and lighted.

The subject was a seated nude, blond, Godiva hair. Ransome's style was impressionistic, his canvas flooded with light. The young woman was casually posed, like a Degas girl taking a backstage break, her face partly averted. Stefan had his usual attitude of near-suicidal disdain. But he found it hard to look away. Great artists were hypnotists with a brush.

"I suppose we must give him credit for his excellent eye for beauty."

"It's marvelous," Echo said softly.

"As Delacroix said, 'One never paints violently enough.' We must also give Ransome credit for doing violence to his canvases. And I must have an Armagnac, if the bar downstairs is open. Echo?"

"I'm coming," she said, hands folded like an acolyte's in front of her as she gazed up at the painting with a faintly worshipful smile.

Stefan shrugged when she failed to budge. "I don't wish to impose on your infatuation. Suppose you join me in the limo in twenty minutes?"

"Sure," Echo murmured.

Absorbed in her study of John Leland Ransome's technique, Echo didn't immediately pay attention to that little barb at the back of her neck that told her she was being closely observed by someone.

When she turned she saw a woman standing twenty feet away ignoring the Ransome on the wall, staring instead at Echo.

The woman was dressed all in black, which seemed to Echo both obsessive and oppressive in high summer. But it was elegant, tasteful couture. She wasn't wearing jewelry. She was, perhaps, excessively made up, but striking nonetheless. Mature, but Echo couldn't guess her age. Her features were immobile, masklike. The directness of her gaze, a burning in her eyes, gave Echo a couple of bad moments. She knew a pickup line was coming. She'd averaged three of these encounters a week since puberty.

But the stare went on, and the woman said nothing. It had the effect of getting Echo's Irish up.

"Excuse me," Echo said. "Have we met?" Her expression read, *Whatever you're thinking, forget it, Queenie.*

Not so much as a startled blink. After a few more seconds the woman looked rather deliberately from Echo to the Ransome painting on the wall. She studied that for a short time, then turned and walked away as if Echo no longer existed, heels clicking on the gallery floor.

Echo's shoulders twitched in a spidery spasm. She glanced at a portly museum guard who also was eyeing the woman in black.

"Who is *that*?"

The guard shrugged. "Beats me. She's been around since noon. I think she's from the gallery in New York." He looked up at the Ransome portrait. "His gallery. You know how fussy these painters get about their placement in shows."

"Uh-huh. Doesn't she talk?"

"Not to me," the guard said.

The limousine Stefan had hired for the day was parked in a taxi zone outside the Highbridge. Stefan was leaning on the limo getting track updates on his BlackBerry. There was a *Racing Form* lying on the trunk.

He put away his BlackBerry with a surly expression when Echo approached. My Little Margie must have finished out of the money.

"So the spell is finally broken. I suppose we could have arranged for a cot to be moved in for the night."

"Thanks for being so patient with me, Stefan."

They lingered on the sidewalk, enjoying balmy weather. New York had been a stewpot when they'd left that morning.

"It's all hype, you know," Stefan said, looking up at the gold and glass façade of the Cesar Pelli–designed building. "The Ransomes of the art world excel at manipulation. The scarcity of his work only makes it more desirable to the *Vulturati*."

"No, I think it's the quality that's rare, Stefan. Courbet, Bonnard, he shares their sense of . . . call it a divine melancholy."

"'Divine melancholy.' Nicely put. I must remember to filch that one for my *Art News* column. Where are we having dinner tonight? You *did* remember to make reservations? Echo?"

Echo was looking past him at the Woman in Black, who had walked out of the museum and was headed for a taxi.

Stefan turned. "Who, or what, is that?"

"I don't know. I saw her in the gallery. Caught her staring at me." Uncanny, Echo thought, how much she resembled the black queen on Echo's chessboard at home.

"Apparently, from her lack of interest now, you rebuffed her."

Echo shook her head. "No. Actually she never said a word. Dinner? Stefan, I'm sorry. You're set at Legal's with the Bronwyns for eight-thirty. But I have to get back to New York. I thought I told you. Engagement party tonight. Peter's sister."

"Which sister? There seems to be a multitude."

"Siobhan. The last one to go."

"Not that huge, clumsy girl with the awful bangs?"

"Hush. She's really very sweet."

"Now that Peter has earned his gold shield, am I correct to assume the next engagement party will be yours?"

"Yes. As soon as we all recover from this one."

Stefan looked deeply aggrieved. "Echo, have you any idea what child-bearing will do to your lovely complexion?"

Echo looked at her watch and smiled apologetically.

"I can just make the four o'clock Acela."

"Well, then. Get in."

Echo was preoccupied with answering e-mail during their short trip up Memorial Drive and across the river to Boston's North Station.

She didn't notice that the taxi the Woman in Black had claimed was behind them all the way.

> Hi Mom
> Busy day. I had to hustle but I made the four o'clock
> train. I'll probably go straight to Queens from the
> station so won't be home until after midnight.
> Scored points with the boss today; tell you all about
> it at breakfast. Called Uncle Rory at the Home, but
> the Sister on his floor told me he probably wouldn't
> know who I was . . .

The Acela was rolling quietly through a tunnel on its way out of the city. In her coach seat Echo, riding backwards, looked up from the laptop she'd spent too much time with today. Her vision was blurry, the back of her neck was stiff and she had a headache. She looked at her reflection in the window, which disappeared as the train emerged into bright sunlight. She winced and closed her laptop after sending the message to her mother, rummaged in her soft-leather shoulder bag for Advil and swallowed three with sips of designer water. Then she closed her eyes and rubbed her temples.

When she looked up again she saw the Woman in Black, looking solemnly at her before she opened the vestibule door and disappeared in the direction of the club car.

The look didn't mean anything. The fact that they were on the same train didn't mean anything either. Even so for a good part of the trip to New York, while Echo tried to nap, she couldn't get the woman out of her mind.

Two

After getting eight stitches to close the cut near his left eye at the hospital in Flatbush, Peter O'Neill's partner Ray Scalla drove him to the 7-5 station house, where Pete retrieved his car and continued home to Bayside, Queens. By then he'd put in a twelve-hour day, but he had a couple of line-of-duty off days coming.

The engagement party for his sister Siobhan was roaring along by the time he got to the three-story brick-and-shingle house on

Compton Place, and he had to hunt for a parking space a block and a half away. Walked back to the house swapping smack with neighborhood kids on their bikes and skateboards. The left eye felt swollen. He needed an ice bag, but a cold beer would be the first order of business. Make it two beers.

The O'Neill house was lit up to the roof line. Floodlights illuminated half a dozen guys playing a scuffling game of basketball in the driveway. Peter was related one way or another to all of them, and to everyone on the teeming porch.

His brother Tommy, a freshman at Hofstra on a football scholarship, fished in a tub of cracked ice and pitched Pete a twelve-ounce Rolling Rock as he walked up to the stoop. Kids with Gameboys cluttered the steps. His sister Kathleen, just turned thirty, was barefoot on the front lawn, gently rocking to sleep an infant on her shoulder. She gave Pete a kiss and frowned at the patched eye.

"So when's number four due?"

"You mean number five," Kathleen said. "October ninth, Petey."

"Guess I got behind on the count when I was workin' undercover." Pete popped the tab top on the icy Rock and drank half of it while he watched some of the half-court action on the driveway. He laughed. "Hey, Kath. Tell your old man to give up pasta or give up hoops."

Brother Tommy came down to the walk and put an arm around him. He was a linebacker, three inches taller than the five-eleven Peter but no wider in the shoulders. Big shoulders were a family hallmark, unfortunately for the women.

One of the basketball players got stuffed driving for a layup, and they both laughed.

"Hey, Vito!" Pete called. "Come on hard or keep it in your pants!" He finished off the beer and crushed the can. "Echo make it back from Boston?" he asked Tommy.

"She's inside. Nice shiner."

Pete said ruefully, "My collar give it to me."

"Too bad they don't hand out Purple Hearts downtown."

"Yeah, but they'll throw you a swell funeral," Pete said, forgetting momentarily what a remark like that meant to the women in a family of cops. Kathleen set him straight with a stinging slap to the back of his head. Then she crossed herself.

"God and Blessed Mother! Don't you ever say that again, Petey!"

Like the rest of the house, the kitchen was full of people helping themselves to beer and food. Peter gave his mom a kiss and looked at Echo, who was taking a pan of hors d'oeuvres out of the oven with insulated mittens. She was moist from the heat at her temples and under her eyes. She gave Pete, or the butterfly patches above his eye, a look and sat him down on a stool near the door to the back porch for a closer appraisal. Pete's middle sister Jessie handed him a bulging hero.

"Little bitty girl," Pete said. "One of those wiry types, you know? She was on crank and I don't know what else."

"Just missed your eye," Echo said, tight-lipped.

"Live and learn." Peter bit into his sandwich.

"You get a tetanus booster?"

"Sure. How was your day?"

"I did great," Echo said, still finding small ways to fuss over him: brushing his hair back from his forehead with the heel of one hand, dabbing at a drip of sauce on his chin with a napkin. "I deserve a raise."

"About time. How's your mom?"

"Didn't have a real good day, Julia said. Want another beer?"

"Makes you think I had one already?"

"Ha-ha," Echo said; she went out to the porch to fish the beer from the depths of the cooler. Peter's sister Siobhan, the bride-to-be, followed her unsteadily inside, back on her heels from an imaginary gale in her face. Her eyes not tracking well. She embraced Peter with a goofy smile.

"I'm so happy!"

"We're happy for you, Siobhan." At thirty-five she was the oldest of the seven O'Neill children, and the least well favored. Putting it mildly.

Her fiancé appeared in the doorway behind Siobhan. He was a head shorter, gap-toothed, had a bad haircut. A software salesman. Doing very well. He drove a Cadillac, had put a down payment on a condo in Vally Stream and was planning an expensive honeymoon cruise. The diamond on Siobhan's finger was a big one.

Peter saluted the fiancé with his can of beer. Siobhan straightened unsteadily and embraced Echo too, belching loudly.

"Oops. Get any on ya?"

"No, sweetie," Echo said, and passed her on to the fiancé, who chuckled and guided her through the kitchen to a bathroom. Peter shook his head.

"What they say about opposites."

"Yeah."

"Siobhan has a lot to learn. She still thinks 'fellatio' is an Italian opera."

"You mean it's not?" Echo said, wide-eyed. Then she patted his cheek. "Lay off. I love Siobhan. I love all your family."

Peter put the arm on his fourteen-year-old brother Casey as he came inside from the porch, and crushed him affectionately.

"Even the retards?"

"Get outta here," Casey said, fighting him off.

"Casey's no retard, he's a lover," Echo said. "Gimme kiss, Case."

"No way!" But Echo had him grinning.

"Don't waste those on that little fart," Pete said.

Casey looked him over. "Man, you're gonna have a shiner."

"I know." Pete looked casually at Echo and put his sandwich down. "It's a sweatbox in here. Why don't we go upstairs a little while?"

Casey smiled wisely at them. "Uh-uh. Aunt Pegeen put the twins to sleep on your bed." He waited for the look of frustration in Peter's eyes before he said, "But I could let you use my room if you guys want to make out. Twenty bucks for an hour sound okay?"

"Sounds like you think I'm a hooker," Echo said to Casey. Staring him down. Casey's shoulders dropped; he looked away uneasily.

"I didn't mean—"

"Now you got a good reason not to skip confession again this week," Peter said. Glancing at Echo, and noticing how tired she looked, having lost her grip on her upbeat mood.

Driving Echo back to the city, Pete said, "I just keep goin' round and round with the numbers, like a dog chasin' its tail. You know?"

"Same here."

"Jesus, I'm twenty-six, ought to have my own place already instead of living home."

"*Our* own place. Trying to save anything these days. The taxes.

Both of us still paying off college loans. Forty thousand each. My mom sick. Your mom was sick—"

"We both got good jobs. The money'll come together. But we'll need another year."

Peter exited from the Queensboro Bridge and took First uptown. They were nearing 78th when Echo said, "A year. How bad can that be?" Her tone of voice said, *miserable.*

They waited on the light at 78th, looking at each other as if they were about to be cast into separate dungeons.

"Gotta tell you, Echo. I'm just goin' nuts. You know."

"I know."

"It hasn't been easy for you either. Couple close calls, huh?" He smiled ruefully.

She crossed her arms as if he'd issued a warning. "Yeah."

"You know what I'm sayin'. We are gonna be married. No doubt about that. Is there?"

"No."

"So—how big a deal is it, really? An act of contrition—"

"Pete, I'm not happy being probably the only twenty-two-year-old virgin on the face of the earth. But confession's not the same as getting a ticket fixed. You know how I was brought up. It's *God's law.* That has to mean something, or none of it does."

The light changed. Peter drove two blocks and parked by a fire hydrant a few doors down from Echo's brownstone.

"Both your parents were of the cloth," he said. "They renounced their vows and they made you. Made you for me. I can't believe God thought that was a sin."

Blue and unhappy, Echo sank lower in her seat, arms still crossed, over her breasts and her crucifix.

"I love you so much. And I swear to Him, I'll always take care of you."

After a long silence Echo said, "I know. What do you want me to do, Pete?"

"Has to be your call."

She sighed. "No motels. I feel cheap that way, I can't help myself. Just know it wouldn't work."

"There's this buddy of mine at the squad, he was in my year at the Academy, Frank Ringer. Like maybe you met him at the K of C picnic in July?"

"Oh. Yeah. Got a twitch in one eye? Really ripped, though."

"Right. Frank Ringer. Well, his uncle's got a place out on the Island. Way out, past Riverhead on Peconic Bay I think."

"Uh-huh."

"Frank's uncle travels a lot. Frank says he could make arrangements for us to go out there, maybe this weekend—"

"So you and Frank been having these discussions about our sex life?"

"Nothing like that. I just mentioned we'd both like to get off somewhere for some R and R, that's all."

"Uh-huh."

"So in exchange for the favor I'd cover Frank's security job for him sometime. Echo?"

"Guess I'd better be getting on up, see how mom is. Might be a long night; you know, I read to her when she can't—"

"So what do I tell Frank?"

Echo hesitated after she opened the door.

"This weekend sounds okay," she said. "Does his uncle have a boat?"

Three A.M. and John Leland Ransome, the painter, was up and prowling barefoot around his apartment at the Pierre Hotel on Fifth Avenue. The doors to his terrace were open; the sounds of the city's streets had dwindled to the occasional swish of cabs or a bus seven stories below. There was lightning in the west, a plume of yellow-tinged dark clouds over New Jersey or the Hudson. Some rain moving into Manhattan, stirring the air ahead of it. A light wind that felt good on his face.

Ransome had a woman on his mind. Not unusual; his life and career were dedicated to capturing the essence of a very few uniquely stunning creatures. But this was someone he'd never seen or heard of until approximately eight o'clock of the night before. And the few photos he'd seen, taken with a phonecam, hadn't revealed nearly enough of Echo Halloran to register her so strongly on his imagination.

Anyway, it was too soon, he told himself. Better just to forget this one, the potential he'd glimpsed. His new show, the first in four years, was being mounted at his gallery. Five paintings only, his usual output after as much as eighteen painful months of work. He wouldn't be ready to pick up a brush for at least that length of time. If ever again.

And half the world's population was women. More or less. A small but dependable percentage of them physically ravishing.

But this one was a painter herself, which intrigued him more than the one good shot of her he'd seen, taken on the train, Echo sitting back in her seat with her eyes closed, unaware that she was being photographed.

Ransome wondered if she had promise as a painter. But he could easily find out.

He lingered on the terrace until the first big drops of rain fell. He went inside, closing the doors, walked down a marble hall to the room in which Taja, wearing black silk lounging pajamas, was watching *Singin' in the Rain* on DVD. Another insomniac. She saw his reflection on the plasma screen and looked around. There was a hint of a contrite wince in her smile.

"I'll want more photos," he said. "Complete background check, of course. And order a car for tomorrow. I'd like to observe her myself."

Taja nodded, drew on a cigarette and returned her attention to the movie. Donald O'Connor falling over a sofa. She didn't smile. Taja never smiled at anything.

THREE

It rained all day Thursday; by six-thirty the clouds over Manhattan were parting for last glimpses of washed-out blue; canyon walls of geometric glass gave back the brassy sunset. Echo was able to walk the four blocks from her Life Studies class to the 14th Street IRT station without an umbrella. She was carrying her portfolio in addition to a shoulder tote and computer, having gone directly from her office at Gilbard's to class.

The uptown express platform was jammed, the atmosphere underground thick and fetid. Obviously there hadn't been a train for a while. There were unintelligible explanations or announcements on the P.A. Someone played a violin with heroic zeal. Echo edged her way up the platform to find breathing room where the first car would stop when the train got there.

Half a dozen Hispanic boys were scuffling, cutting up; a couple of the older ones gave her the eye. One of them, whom she took in at a glance, looked like trouble. Tats and piercings. Full of himself.

A child of the urban jungle, Echo was skilled at minding her own business, building walls around herself when she was forced to linger in potentially bad company.

She pinned her bulky portfolio between her knees while she retrieved a half-full bottle of water from her tote. She was jostled from behind by a fat woman laden with shopping bags and almost lost her balance. The zipper on her portfolio had been broken for a while. A few drawings spilled out. Echo grimaced, nodded at the woman's brusque apology and tried to gather up her life studies before someone else stepped on them.

One of the younger Hispanic kids, wearing a do-rag and a Knicks jersey, came over to give her a hand. He picked up a charcoal sketch half-soaked in a puddle of water. Echo's problem had attracted the attention of all the boys.

The one she'd had misgivings about snatched the drawing from the hand of the Knicks fan and looked it over. A male nude. He showed it around, grinning. Then backed off when Echo held out a hand, silently asking for the return of her drawing. She heard the uptown express coming.

The boy looked at her. He wore his Cholo shirt unbuttoned to his navel.

"Who's this guy? Your boyfriend?"

"Give me a break, will you? I've had a long day, I'm tired, and I don't want to miss my train."

The boy pointed to the drawing and said, "Man, I seen a bigger tool on a gerbil."

They all laughed as they gathered around, reinforcing him.

"No," Echo said. "*My* boyfriend is on the cops, and I can arrange for you to meet him."

That provoked whistles, snorts, and jeers. Echo looked around at the slowing express train, and back at the boy who was hanging onto her drawing. Pretending to be an art critic.

"Hey, you're good, you know that?"

"Yes, I know."

"You want to do me, I can *arrange* the time." He grinned around at his buddies, one of whom said, "*Draw* you."

"Yeah, man. That's what I said." He feigned confusion. "That ain't what I said?" He looked at Echo and shrugged magnanimously. "So first you draw me, then you can *do* me."

Echo said, "Listen, you fucking little idiot, I want my drawing *now*, or you'll be in shit up to your bull ring."

The express screeched to a stop behind her. A local was also approaching on the inside track. The boy made a show of being astonished by her threat. As if he were trembling in fright, his hands jerked and the drawing tore nearly in half.

"Oh, sorry, man. Now I guess you need to get yourself another naked guy." He finished ripping her drawing.

Echo, losing it, dropped her computer case and hooked a left at his jaw. She was quick on her feet; it just missed. The *cholo* danced away with the halves of the drawing in each hand, and bumped into a woman walking the yellow platform line of the local track as if she were a ballet dancer. The headlight of the train behind her winked on the slim blade of a knife in her right hand.

With her left hand she took hold of the boy by his bunchy testicles and lifted him up on his toes until they were at eye level.

The Woman in Black stared at him, and the point of the knife was between two of his exposed ribs. Echo's throat dried up. She had no doubt the woman would cut him if he didn't behave. The boy's mouth was open, but he could have screamed without being heard as the train thundered in a couple of feet away from them.

The woman cast a long look at Echo, then nodded curtly toward the express.

The kid in the Knicks jersey picked up Echo's computer and shoved it at her as if he suspected that she too might have a blade. The doors of the local opened and there was a surge of humanity across the platform to the parked express. Echo let herself be carried along with it, looking back once as she boarded. Another glimpse of the Woman in Black, still holding the *cholo* helpless, getting a few looks but no interference. Echo's pulses throbbed. The woman was like a walking superstition, with a temperament as dark and lurking as paranoia.

Who was she? And why, Echo wondered as the doors closed, does she keep showing up in *my* life?

She rode standing up to 86th in the jam of commuters, her face expressionless, presenting a calm front but inside just a blur, like a traumatized bird trying to escape through a sealed window.

Echo didn't say anything to Peter about the Woman in Black until Friday evening, when they were slogging along in oppressive traffic on the 495 eastbound, on their way to Mattituck and the cozy weekend they'd planned at the summer house of Frank Ringer's uncle.

"No idea who she is?" Peter said. "You're sure you don't know her from somewhere?"

"Listen, she's the kind, see her once, you never forget her. I'm talking spooky."

"She pulled a knife in the subway? Switchblade?"

"Maybe. I don't know much about knives. It was the look in her eyes, man. That *cholo* must've went in his pants." Echo smiled slightly, then her expression turned glum. "So, the first couple times, okay. Coincidence. A third time in the same week, uh-uh, I don't buy it. She must've been following me around." Echo shrugged again, and her shoulders stayed tight. "I didn't sleep so good last night, Pete."

"You ever see her again, make it your business to call me right away."

"I wonder if maybe I should—"

"*No*. Stay away from her. Don't try to talk to her."

"You're thinking she could be some sort of psycho?"

"That's New York. Ten people go by in the street, one or two out of the ten, something's gonna be seriously wrong with them mentally."

"Great. Now I'm scared."

Peter put an arm around her.

"You just let me handle this. Whatever it is."

"Engine's overheating." Echo observed.

"Yeah. Fucking traffic. Weekend, it'll be like this until ten o'clock. Might as well get off, get something to eat."

The cottage that had been lent to them for the weekend wasn't impressive in the headlights of Peter's car; it looked as if Frank Ringer's uncle had built it on weekends using materials taken from various construction or demolition sites. Mismatched windows, missing clapboards, a stone chimney on one side that obviously was out of plumb; the place had all the eye appeal of a bad scab.

"Probably charming inside," Echo said, determined to be upbeat about a slow start to their intimate weekend.

Inside the small rooms smelled of mildew from a leaky roof. There were curbsides in Manhattan that were better furnished on trash pickup days.

"Guess it's kind of like men only out here," Pete said, not concealing his disbelief. "I'll open a couple of windows."

"Do you think we could clean it up some?" Echo said.

Peter took another look around.

"More like burn it down and start over."

"It's such a beautiful little cove."

There was so much dismay in her face it started him laughing. He put an arm around her, guided her outside, and locked the door behind them.

"Live and learn," he said.

"Your house or mine?" Echo said.

"Bayside's closest."

The O'Neill house in Bayside didn't work out, either; overrun with relatives. At a few minutes past ten Echo unlocked the door of the Yorktown apartment where she lived with her mother and Aunt Julia, from her late father's side of the family. She looked at Peter, sighed, kissed him.

Rosemay and Julia were playing Scrabble at the dining room table when Echo walked in with Peter. She had left her weekend luggage in the hall by her bedroom door.

"This is a grand surprise," Rosemay said. "Echo, I thought you were stayin' over in Queens."

Echo cleared her throat and shrugged, letting Peter handle this one.

Peter said, "My uncle Dennis, from Philly? Blew into town with his six kids. Our house looks like a day camp. They been redoin' the walls with grape jelly." He bent over Rosemay, putting his arms around her. "How're you, Rosemay?"

Rosemay was wearing lounging pajamas and a green eyeshade.

There were three support pillows in the chair she occupied, and one under her slippered feet.

"A little fatigued, I must say."

Julia was a roly-poly woman who wore thick eyeglasses. "Spent most of the day writing," she said of Rosemay. "Talk to your ma about eating, Echo."

"Eat, mom. You promised."

"I had my soft-boiled egg with some tea. It was, oh, about five o'clock, wasn't it, Julia?"

"Soft-boiled eggs. Wants nought but her bit of egg."

"They go down easy," Rosemay said, massaging her throat. Words didn't come easily, at least at this hour of the night. But for Rosemay sleep was elusive as well.

"All that cholesterol," Peter chided.

Rosemay smiled. "Nothing to worry about. I already have one fatal disease."

"None of that," Peter said sternly.

"Go on, Petey. You say what is. At least my mind will be the last of me to go. Pull up some chairs, we'll all play."

The doorbell rang. Echo went to answer it.

Peter was arranging chairs around the table when he heard Echo unlock the door, then cry out.

"Peter!"

"Who is it, Echo?" Rosemay called, as Peter backtracked through the front room to the foyer. The door to the hall stood half open. Echo had backed away from the door and from the Woman in Black who was standing outside.

Peter took Echo by an elbow and flattened her against the wall behind the door, saying to the Woman in Black, "Excuse me, can I talk to you? I'm the police."

The Woman in Black looked at him for a couple of seconds, then reached into her purse as Peter filled the doorspace.

"Don't do that!"

The woman shook her head. She pulled something from her purse but Peter had a grip on her gloved wrist before her hand fully cleared. She raised her eyes to him but didn't resist. There was a white business card between her thumb and forefinger.

Still holding onto her wrist, Peter took the card from her with his left hand. Glanced at it. He felt Echo at his back, looking at the woman over his shoulder. The woman looked at Echo, looked back at Peter.

"What's going on?" Echo said, as Rosemay called again.

Peter let go of the Woman in Black, turned and handed Echo the card.

"Echo! Peter!"

"Everything's fine, mom," Echo said, studying the writing on the card in the dim foyer light.

Peter said to the Woman in Black, "Sorry I got a little rough. I heard about that knife you carry, is all."

This time it was Echo who moved Peter aside, opening the door wider.

"Peter, she can't—"

"Talk. I know." He didn't take his eyes off the woman in black. "You've got another card, tells me who you are?"

She nodded, glanced at her purse. Peter said, "Yeah, okay." This time the woman produced her calling card, which Echo took from her.

"Your name's Taja? Am I saying that right?"

The woman nodded formally.

"Taja what?"

She shrugged slightly, impatiently; as if it didn't matter.

"So I guess you know who *I* am. What did you want to see me about? Would you like to come in?"

"Echo—" Peter objected.

But the woman shook her head and indicated her purse again. She made an open-palm gesture, hand extended to Echo, slow enough so Peter wouldn't interpret it as hostile.

"You have something for me?" Echo said, baffled.

Another nod from Taja. She looked appraisingly at Peter, then returned to her purse and withdrew a cream-colored envelope the size of a wedding announcement.

Peter said, "Echo tells me you've been following her places. What's that about?"

Taja looked at the envelope in her hand as if it would answer all of their questions. Peter continued to size the woman up. She used cosmetics in almost theatrical quantities; that overload plus Botox, maybe, was enough to obscure any hint of age. She wore a flat-crowned hat and a long skirt with large fabric-covered buttons down one side. A scarlet puff of neckerchief was Taja's only concession to color. That, and the rose flush of her cheeks. Her eyes were almond-shaped, creaturely bold, intelligent. One thing about her, she didn't blink very often, which enhanced a certain robotic effect.

Echo took the envelope. Her name, handwritten, was on it. She smiled uncertainly at Taja, who simply looked away—something dismissive in her lack of expression, Peter thought.

"Just a minute. I'd like to ask you—"

The Woman in Black paused on her way to the stairs.

Echo said, "Pete? It's okay. Taja?"

Taja turned.

"I wanted to say—thank you. You know, for the subway, the other day?"

Taja, after a few moments, did something surprisingly out of character, considering her previous demeanor, the rigid formality. She responded to Echo with an emphatic thumbs-up before soundlessly disappearing down the stairs. Peter had the impression she'd enjoyed intimidating the *cholo* kid. Might have enjoyed herself even more if she'd used the knife on him.

Echo had a hand on his arm, sensing his desire to follow the Woman in Black.

"Let's see what this is," she said, of the envelope in her other hand.

"She looks Latin to me, what d'you think?" Peter said to Echo as they returned to the front room. Rosemay and Julia began talking at the same time, wanting to know who was at the door. "Messenger," Peter said to them, and looked out the windows facing the street.

Echo, preoccupied, said, "You're the detective." She looked for a letter opener on Rosemay's writing table.

"Jesus above," Julia said. "Sounded like a ruckus. I was reachin' for me heart pills."

Peter saw the Woman in Black get into a waiting limousine.

"Travels first class, whoever she is." He caught the license plate number as the limo pulled away, jotted it down on the inside of his left wrist with a ballpoint pen.

Rosemay and Julia were watching Echo as she slit the envelope open.

"What is it, dear, an invitation?"

"Looks like one."

"Now, who's getting married this time?" Julia said. "Seems like you've been to half a dozen weddings already this year."

"No, it's—" Echo's throat seemed to close up on her. She sat down slowly on one of a pair of matched love seats.

"Good news or bad?" Peter said, adjusting the blinds over the window.

"My . . . God!"

"Echo!" Rosemay said, mildly alarmed by her expression.

"This is so . . . utterly . . . fantastic!"

Peter crossed the room and took the invitation from her.

"But why me?" Echo said.

"Part of your job, isn't it? Going to these shows? What's so special about this one?"

"Because it's John Leland Ransome. And it's the event of the year. You're invited."

"I see that. 'Guest.' Real personal. I'm overwhelmed. Let's play." He took out his cell phone. "After I run a plate."

Echo wasn't paying attention to him. She had taken the invitation back and was staring at it as if she were afraid the ink might disappear.

Stefan Konine's reaction was predictable when Echo showed him the invitation. He pouted.

"Not to disparage your good fortune but, yes, why you? If I wasn't aware of your high moral standards—"

Echo said serenely, "Don't say it, Stefan."

Stefan began to look over a contract that one of his assistants had silently slipped onto his desk. He picked up his pen.

"I confess that it took me literally *weeks* to finagle my way onto the guest list. And I'm not just anyone's old hand job in this town."

"I thought you didn't like Ransome. Something about art on a sailor's—"

Stefan slashed through an entire paragraph on the contract and looked up at Echo.

"I don't worship the man, but I adore the event. Don't you have work to do?"

"I'm not strong on the pre-Raphaelites, but I called around. There's a definite lack of viability in today's market."

"Call it what it is, an Arctic chill. Tell the appraiser for the Chandler estate that he might do better on one of those auction-junkie internet sites." Stefan performed strong-arm surgery on another page of the contract. "You will want to appear in something singularly ravishing for the Ransome do. All of us at Gilbard's can only benefit from your reflected glory."

"May I put the gown on my expense account?"

"Of course not."

Echo winced slightly.

"But perhaps," Stefan said, twiddling his gold pen, "we can do something about that raise you've been whining about for weeks."

FOUR

Cyrus Mellichamp's personal quarters took up the fourth floor of his gallery on East 58th Street. They were an example of what wealth and unerring taste could accomplish. So was Cy himself. He not only looked pampered by the best tailors, dieticians, physical therapists, and cosmeticians, he looked as if he truly deserved it.

John Ransome's fortune was to the tenth power of what Cy Mellichamp had managed to acquire as a kingpin of the New York art world, but on the night of the gala dedicated to himself and his new paintings, which he had no plans to attend, he was casually dressed. Tennis sweater, khakis, loafers. No socks. While the Mellichamp Gallery's guests were drinking Moët and Chandon below, Ransome sipped beer and watched the party on several TV monitors in Cy's study.

There was no sound, but thanks to the gallery owner's expensive surveillance system, it was possible, if he wanted, to tune in on nearly every conversation on the first two floors of the gallery, swarming with media—annointed superstars. Name a profession with glitter appeal, there was an icon, a living legend, or a superstar in attendance.

Cy Mellichamp had coaxed one of his very close friends, from a list that ran in the high hundreds, to prepare dinner for Ransome and his guests for the evening, both of whom were still unaware they'd been invited.

"John," Cy said, "Monsieur Rapaou wanted to know if there was a special dish you'd like added to his menu for the evening."

"Why don't we just scrap the menu and have cheeseburgers," Ransome said.

"Oh my God," Cy said, after a shocked intake of breath. "Scrap—? John, Monsieur Rapaou is one of the most honored chefs on four continents."

"Then he ought to be able to make a damn fine cheeseburger."

"Johnnn—"

"We're having dinner with a couple of kids. Basically. And I want them to be at ease, not worrying about what fork to use."

A dozen of the gallery's guests were being admitted at one time to the room in which the Ransome exhibition was mounted. To avoid damaged egos, the order in which they were being permitted to view the new Ransomes had been chosen impartially by lot. Except for Echo, Peter, and Stefan Konine, arbitrarily assigned to the second group. Ransome, for all of his indolence at his own party, was impatient to get on with his prime objective of the evening.

All of the new paintings featured the same model: a young black woman with nearly waist-length hair. She was, of course, smashing, with the beguiling quality that differentiates mere looks from classic beauty.

Two canvases, unframed, were wall-mounted. The other three, on easels, were only about three feet square. A hallmark of all Ransome's work were the wildly primeval, ominous or threatening landscapes in which his models existed aloofly.

Two minutes after they entered the room Peter began to fidget, glancing at Echo, who seemed lost in contemplation.

"I don't get it."

Echo said in a low firm tone, "Peter."

"What is it, like High Mass, I can't talk?"

"Just—keep it down, please."

"Five paintings?" Peter said, lowering his voice. "That's what all the glitz is about? The movie stars? Guy that plays James Bond is here, did you notice?"

"He only does five paintings at a time. Every three years."

"Slow, huh?"

"Painstaking." Peter could hear her breathing, a sigh of rapture. "The way he uses light."

"You've been staring at that one for—"

"Go away."

Peter shrugged and joined Stefan, who was less absorbed.

"Does Ransome get paid by the square yard?"

"The square inch, more likely. It takes seven figures just to buy into the playoff round. And I'm told there are already more than four hundred prospective buyers, the cachet-stricken."

"For five paintings? Echo, just keep painting. Forget about your day job."

Echo gave him a dire look for breaking her concentration. Peter grimaced and said to Stefan, "I think I've seen this model somewhere else. *Sports Illustrated*. Last year's swimsuit issue."

"Doubtful," Stefan said. "No one knows who Ransome's models are. None of them have appeared at the shows, or been publicized. Nor has the genius himself. He might be in our midst tonight, but I wouldn't recognize him. I've never seen a photo."

"You saying he's shy?"

"Or exceptionally shrewd."

Peter had been focusing on a nude study of the unknown black girl. Nothing left to the imagination. Raw sensual appeal. He looked around the small gallery, as if his powers of detection might reveal the artist to him. Instead who he saw was Taja, standing in a doorway, looking at him.

"Echo?"

She looked around at Peter with a frown, then saw Taja herself. When the Woman in Black had her attention she beckoned. Echo and Peter looked at each other.

"Maybe it's another special delivery," Peter said.

"I guess we ought to find out."

In the center of the gallery's atrium a small elevator in a glass shaft rose to Cy Mellichamp's penthouse suite. A good many people who considered themselves important watched Peter and Echo rise to the fourth floor with Taja. Stefan took in some bemused and outright envious speculation.

A super-socialite complained, "I've spent seventeen million with Cy, and *I've* never been invited to the penthouse. Who *are* they?"

"Does Ransome have children?"

"Who knows?"

A talk-show host with a sneaky leer and a hard-drive's capacity for gossip said, "The dark one, my dear, is John Ransome's mistress. He abuses her terribly. So I've been told."

"Or perhaps it's the other way around," Stefan said, feeling a flutter of distress in his stomach that had nothing to do with the quantity of hors d'oeuvres he'd put away. Something was up, obviously it involved Echo, and even more obviously it was none of his business. Yet his impression, as he watched Echo step off the elevator and vanish into Cy's sanctum, was of a lovely doe being deftly separated from a herd of deer.

Taja ushered Echo and Peter into Cy Mellichamp's presence and closed the door to the lush sitting room, a gallery in itself that was devoted largely to French Impressionists. A very large room with a high tray ceiling. French doors opened onto a small terrace where there was a candlelit table set for three and two full-dress butlers in attendance.

"Miss Halloran, Mr. O'Neill! I'm Cyrus Mellichamp. Wonderful that you could be here tonight. I hope you're enjoying yourselves."

He offered his hand to Echo, and a discreet kiss to one cheek, somewhere between businesslike and avuncular, Peter noted. He shook hands with the man and they were eye to eye, Cy with a pleasant smile but no curiosity.

"We're honored, Mr. Mellichamp," Echo said.

"May I call you Echo?"

"Yes, of course."

"What do you think of the new Ransomes, Echo?"

"Well, I think they're—magnificent. I've always loved his work."

"He will be very pleased to hear that."

"Why?" Peter said.

They both looked at him. Peter had, deliberately, his cop face on. Echo didn't appreciate that.

"This is a big night for Mr. Ransome. Isn't it? I'm surprised he's not here."

Cy said smoothly, "But he is here, Peter."

Pete spread his hands and smiled inquiringly as Echo's expression soured.

"It's only that John has never cared to be the center of attention. He wants the focus to be solely on his work. But let John tell you himself. He's wanted very much to meet you both."

"Why?" Peter said.

"*Peter*," Echo said grimly.

"Well, it's a fair question," Peter said, looking at Cy Mellichamp, who wore little gold tennis racket cuff links. A fair question, but not a lob. Straight down the alley, no time for footwork, spin on the return.

Cy blinked and his smile got bigger. "Of course it is. Would you mind coming with me? Just in the other room there, my study. Something we would like for you to see."

"You and Mr. Ransome," Peter said.

"Why, yes."

He offered Echo his arm. She gave Peter a swift dreadful look as she turned her back on him. Peter simmered for a couple of moments, took a breath and followed them.

The study was nearly dark. Peter was immediately interested in the array of security monitors, including three affording different angles on the small gallery where the newest Ransome paintings were on display. Where he had been with Echo a few minutes ago. The idea that they'd been watched from this room, maybe by Ransome himself, caused Peter to chew his lower lip. No reason Cy Mellichamp shouldn't have the best possible surveillance equipment to protect millions of dollars' worth of property. But so far none of this—Taja following Echo around town, the special invitations to Ransome's showing—added up, and Peter was more than ready to cut to the chase.

There was a draped, spotlighted easel to one side of Mellichamp's desk. The dealer walked Echo to it, smiling, and invited her to remove the drape.

"It's a work in progress, of course. John would be the first to say it doesn't do his subject justice."

Echo hesitated, then carefully uncovered the canvas, which revealed an incomplete study of—Echo Halloran.

Jesus, Peter thought, growing tense for no good reason. Even though what there was of her on the canvas looked great.

"Peter! Look at this!"

"I'm looking," Peter said, then turned, aware that someone had come into the room behind them.

"No, it doesn't do you justice," John Ransome said. "It's a beginning, that's all." He put out a hand to Peter. "Congratulations on your promotion to detective."

"Thanks," Peter said, testing Ransome's grip with no change of expression.

Ransome smiled slightly. "I understand your paternal grandfather was the third most-decorated officer in the history of the New York City police force."

"That's right." Cy Mellichamp had blue-ribbon charm and social graces and the inward chilliness of a shark cruising behind the glass of a seaquarium tank. John Ransome looked at Peter as if every detail of his face were important to recall at some later time. He held his grip longer than most men, but not too long. He was an inch taller than Peter, with a thick head of razor-cut hair silver over the ears, a square jawline softening with age, deep folds at the corners of a sensual mouth. He talked through his nose, yet the effect was sonorous, softly pleasing, as if his nose were lined with velvet. His dark eyes didn't veer from Peter's mildly contentious gaze. They were the eyes of a man who had fought battles, won only some of them. They wanted to tell you more than his heart could let go of. And that, Peter divined in a few moments of hand-to-hand contact with the man, was the major source of his appeal.

Having made Peter feel a little more at home Ransome turned his attention again to Echo.

"I had only some photographs," he said of the impressionistic portrait. "So much was missing. Until now. And now that I'm finally meeting you—I see how very much I've missed."

By candlelight and starlight they had cheeseburgers and fries on the terrace. And they *were* damn good cheeseburgers. So was the beer. Peter concentrated on the beer because he didn't like eating when something was eating him. Probably Echo's star-struck expression. As for John Leland Ransome—there was just something about aging yuppies (never mind the aura of the famous and reclusive artist) who didn't wear socks with their loafers that went against Peter's Irish grain.

Otherwise maybe it wasn't so hard to like the guy. Until it became obvious that Ransome or someone else had done a thorough job of prying into Echo's life and family relations. Now hold on, just a damn minute.

"Your name is given as Mary Catherine on your birth and baptismal certificates. Where did 'Echo' come from?"

"Oh—well—I was talking a blue streak at eighteen months. Repeated everything I heard. My father would look at me and say, 'Is there a little echo in here?'"

"Your father was a Jesuit, I understand."

"Yes. That was his—vocation, until he met my mother."

"Who was teaching medieval history at Fordham?"

"Yes, she was."

"Now retired because of her illness. Is she still working on her biography of Bernard of Clairvaux? I'd like to read it sometime. I'm a student of history myself."

Peter allowed his beer glass to be filled for a fourth time. Echo gave him a vexed look as if to say, *Are you here or are you not here?*

Ransome said, "I see the beer is to your liking. It's from an exceptional little brewery in Dortmund that's not widely known outside of Germany."

Peter said with an edge of hostility, "So you have it flown in by the keg, something like that?"

Ransome smiled. "Corner deli. Three bucks a pop."

Peter shifted in his seat. The lace collar of his tux was irritating his neck. "Mr. Ransome—mind if I ask you something?"

"If you'll call me John."

"Okay—John—what I'd like to know is, why all the detective work? I mean, you seem to know a h— a lot about Echo. Almost an invasion of her privacy, seems to me."

Echo looked as if she would gladly have kicked him, if her gown hadn't been so long. She smiled a tight apology to Ransome, but Peter had the feeling she was curious too, in spite of the hero-worship.

Ransome took the accusation seriously, with a hint of contrition in his downcast eyes.

"I understand how that must appear to you. It's the nature of detective work, of course, to interpret my curiosity about Echo as suspicious or possibly predatory behavior. But if Echo and I are going to spend a year together—"

"What?" Peter said, and Echo almost repeated him before pressing a napkin to her lips and clearing her throat.

Ransome nodded his point home with the confidence of those who are born and bred in the winner's circle; someone, Peter thought resentfully, who wouldn't break a sweat if his pants were on fire.

"—I find it helpful in my work as an artist," Ransome continued, "if there are other areas of compatibility with my subjects. I like good conversation. I've never had a subject who wasn't well read and articulate." He smiled graciously at Echo. "Although I'm afraid that I've tended to monopolize our table-talk tonight." He shifted his eyes to Peter. "And Echo is also a painter of promise. I find that attractive as well."

Echo said incredulously, "Excuse me, I fell off at that last turn."

"Did you?" Ransome said.

But he kept his gaze on Peter, who had the look of a man being cunningly outplayed in a game without a rule book.

With the party over, the gallery emptied and cleanup crews at work, John Ransome conducted a personal tour of his latest work while Cy Mellichamp entertained Stefan Konine and a restless Peter, who had spent the better part of the last hour obviously wishing he were somewhere else. With Echo.

"Who is she?" Echo asked of Ransome's most recent model. "Or is that privileged information?"

"I'll trust your discretion. Her name is Silkie. Oddly enough, my previous subjects have remained anonymous at their own request. To keep the curious at arm's length. I suppose that during the year of our relationships each of them absorbed some of my own passion for—letting my work speak for itself."

"The year of your relationships? You don't see them any more?"

"No."

"Is that at your request?"

"I don't want it to seem to you as if I've had affairs that all turned out badly. That's far from the truth."

With her lack of expression Echo kept a guarded but subtle emotional distance from him.

"Silkie. The name describes her perfectly. Where is she from?"

"South Africa. Taja discovered her, on a train from Durban to Capetown."

"And Taja discovered me? She does get around."

"She's found all of my recent subjects—by 'recent' I mean the last twenty years." He smiled a bit painfully, reminded of how quickly the years passed, and how slowly he worked. "I very much depend on Taja's eye and her intuition. I depend on her loyalty. She was an artist herself, but she won't paint any more. In spite of my efforts to—inspire her."

"Why can't she speak?"

"Her tongue was cut out by agents of one of those starkly repressive Cold War governments. She wouldn't reveal the whereabouts of dissident members of her family. She was just thirteen at the time."

"Oh God, that's so awful!"

"I'm afraid it's the least of what was done to Taja. But she has always been like a—for want of a better word, *talisman* for me."

"Where did you meet her?"

"She was a sidewalk artist in Budapest, living down an alley with whores and thieves. I first saw her during one of my too-frequent sabbaticals in those times when I wasn't painting well. Nor painting very much at all. It's still difficult for me, nearly all of the time."

"Is that why you want me to pose for—a year?"

"I work for a year with my subject. Take another year to fully realize what we've begun together. Then—I suppose I just agonize for several months before finally packing my pictures off to Cy. And finally—comes the inevitable night."

He made a weary, sweeping gesture around the "Ransome Room," then brightened.

"I let them go. But this is the first occasion when I've had the good fortune of knowing my next subject and collaborator before my last paintings are out of our hands."

"I'm overwhelmed, really. That you would even consider me. I'm sorry that I have to say—it's out of the question. I can't do it."

Echo glanced past at him, to the doorway where Peter was standing around with the other two men, trying not to appear anxious and irritable.

"He's a fine young man," Ransome said with a smile.

"It isn't just Peter, I mean, being away from him for so long. That would be hard. But there's my mother."

"I understand. I didn't expect to convince you at our first meeting. It's getting late, and I know you must be tired."

"Am I going to see you again?" Echo said.

"That's for you to decide. But I need you, Mary Catherine. I hope to have another chance to convince you of that."

Neither Echo nor Peter were the kind to be reticent about getting into it when there was an imagined slight or a disagreement to be settled. They were city kids who had grown up scrappy and contentious if the occasion called for it.

Before Echo had slipped out of the new shoes that had hurt her feet for most of the night she was in Peter's face. They were driving up Park. Too fast, in her opinion. She told him to slow down.

"Or put your flasher on. You just barely missed that cabbie."

"I can get suspended for that," Peter said.

"Why are you so *angry*?"

"Said I was angry?"

"It was a wonderful evening, and now you're spoiling it for me. *Slow down*."

"When a guy comes on to you like that Ransome—"

"Oh, please. Comes *on* to me? That is so—so—I don't want to say it."

"Go ahead. We say what is, remember?"

"Im-mature."

"Thank you. I'm immature because the guy is stuffing me in the face and I'm supposed to—"

"Peter, I never said I was going to do it! I've got my job to think about. My mom."

"So why did he say he hoped he'd be hearing from you soon? And you just smiled like, *sure*. I can hardly wait."

"You don't just blow somebody off who has gone out of his way to—"

"Why not?"

"Peter. Look. I was paid an incredible compliment tonight, by a painter who I think is—I mean, I can't be flattered? Come on."

Peter decided against racing a red light and settled back behind the wheel.

"You come on. You got something arranged with him?"

"For the last time, *no*." Her face was red, and she had chewed most of the gloss off her lower lip. In a softer tone she said, "You know it's not gonna happen, have some sense. The ball is over. Just let Cinderella enjoy her last moments, okay?—They're honking because the light is green, Petey."

Six blocks farther uptown Peter said, "Okay. I guess I—"

"Overreacted, what else is new? Sweetie, I love you."

"How much?"

"Infinity."

"Love you too. Oh God. Infinity."

Rosemay and Julia were asleep when Echo got home. She hung up the gown she'd worn to John Leland Ransome's show in her small closet, pulled on a sleep shirt and went to the bathroom to pee and brush her teeth. She spent an uncharacteristic amount of time studying her face in the mirror. It wasn't vanity; more as if she were doing an emotional self-portrait. She smiled wryly and shrugged and returned to her bedroom.

There she took down from a couple of shelves of cherished art books a slim oversized volume entitled *The Ransome Women*. She curled up against a bolster on her studio bed and turned on a reading lamp, spent an absorbed half hour looking over the thirty color plates and pages with areas of detail that illustrated aspects of the artist's technique.

She nodded off about three, then awoke with a start, the book sliding off her lap to the floor. Echo left it there, glanced at a landscape on her easel that she'd been working on for several weeks, wondering what John Ransome would think of it. Then she turned off the light and lay face-up in the dark, her rosary gripped unsaid in her fist. Thinking *what if, what if*.

But such a dramatic change in her life was solely in her imagination, or in a parallel universe. And *Cinderella* was a fairy tale.

FIVE

Peter O'Neill was working the day watch with his partner Ray Scalla, investigating a child-abuse complaint, when he was abruptly pulled off the job and told to report to the Commissioner's Office at One Police Plaza.

It was a breezy, unusually cool day in mid September. Pete's

lieutenant couldn't give him a reason for what was officially described as a "request."

"Downtown, huh?" Scalla said. "Lunch with your old man?"

"Jesus, don't ask me," Peter said, embarrassed and uncomfortable.

The offices of the Police Commissioner for the City of New York
were on the fourteenth floor. Peter walked into reception to find his
father also waiting there. Corin O'Neill was wearing his dress uniform, with the two stars of a borough commander. Pete would have
been slightly less surprised to see Elvis Presley.

"What's going on, pop?"

Corin O'Neill's smile was just a shade uneasy. "Beats me. Any
problems on the job, Petey?"

"I'd've told you first."

"That you would."

The commissioner's executive assistant came out of her office.
"Good morning, Peter. Glad you could make it."

As if he had a choice. Pete made an effort to look calm and
slightly unimpressed. Corin said, "Well, Lucille. Let's find out how
the wind's blowin' today."

"I just buzzed him. You can go right in, Commander."

But the commissioner opened his own door, greeting them
heartily. His name was Frank Mullane.

"Well, Corin! Pleasure, as always. How is Kate? You know we've
had a lot of concern."

"She's nearly a hundred percent now, and she'll be pleased you
were askin'."

Mullane looked past him at Peter, then gave the young detective
a partial embrace: handshake, bicep squeeze. "When's the last time I
saw you, Peter? Rackin' threes for Cardinal Hayes?"

"I think so, yes, sir."

Mullane kept a hand on Peter's arm. "Come in, come in. So are
you likin' the action in the 7–5?"

"That's what I wanted, sir."

As soon as they were inside the office, Lucille closing the door
behind them, Peter saw John Ransome, wearing a suit and a tie today. It had been more than a month since the artist's show at the
Mellichamp Gallery. Echo hadn't said another two words about Ransome; Peter had forgotten about him. Now he had a feeling that a
brick was sinking to the pit of his stomach.

"Peter," Mullane said, "you already know John Ransome." Pete's father gave him a quick look. "John, this is Corin O'Neill, Pete's father, one of the finest men I've had on my watch."

The older men shook hands. Peter just stared at Ransome.

"John's an artist, I suppose you know," Mullane said to Corin. "My brother owns one of his paintings. And John has been a big supporter of police charities since well before I came to the office. Now, he has a little request, and we're happy to oblige him." Mullane turned and winked at Peter. "Special assignment for you. John will explain."

"I'm sure he will," Peter said.

A chartered helicopter flew Peter and John Ransome to the White Plains airport, where a limousine picked them up. They traveled north through Westchester County on route 22 to Bedford. Estate country. They hadn't talked much on the helicopter, and on the drive through some of the most expensive real estate on the planet Ransome had phone calls to make. He was apologetic. Peter just nodded and looked out the window. Feeling that his time was being wasted. He was sure that, eventually, Ransome was going to bring up Echo. He hadn't forgotten about her, and in his own quiet way he was a determined guy.

Once Ransome was off the phone for good Peter decided to go on the offensive.

"You live up this way?"

"I was raised here," Ransome said. "Bedford Village."

"So that's where we're going, your house?"

"No. The house I grew up in is no longer there. I let go of all but a few acres after my parents died."

"Must've been worth a bundle."

"I didn't need the money."

"You were rich already, is that it?"

"Yes."

"So—this special assignment the commissioner was talking about? You need for somebody to handle a, what, situation for you? Somebody causing you a problem?"

"You're my only problem at the moment, Peter."

"Okay, well, maybe I guessed that. So this is going to be about Echo?"

Ransome smiled disarmingly. "Do you think I'm a rich guy out to steal your girl, Peter?"

"I'm not worried. Echo's not gonna be your—what do you call it, your 'subject?' You know that already."

"I think there is more of a personal dilemma than you're willing to admit. It affects both you and Echo."

Peter shrugged, but the back of his neck was heating up.

"I don't have any personal dilemmas, Mr. Ransome. That's for guys who have too much time and too much money on their hands. You know? So they try to amuse themselves messin' around in other people's lives, who would just as soon be left alone."

"Believe me. I have no intention of causing either of you the slightest—" He leaned forward and pointed out the window.

"This may interest you. One of my former subjects lives here."

They were passing an estate enclosed by what seemed to be a quarter mile of low stone walls. Peter glimpsed a manor house in a grove of trees, and a name on a stone gatepost. Van Lier.

"I understand she's quite happy. But we haven't been in touch since Anne finished sitting for me. That was many years ago."

"Looks to be plenty well-off," Peter said.

"I bought this property for her."

Peter looked at him with a skeptical turn to his lips.

"All of my former subjects have been well provided for—on the condition that they remain anonymous."

"Why?"

"Call it a quirk," Ransome said, with a smile that mocked Peter's skepticism. "Us rich guys have all these quirks." He turned his attention to the road ahead. "There used to be a fruit and vegetable stand along this road that had truly wonderul pears and apples at this season. I wonder—yes, there it is."

Peter was thirsty and the cider at the stand was well chilled. He walked around while Ransome was choosing apples. Among the afternoon's shoppers was a severely disabled young woman in a wheelchair that looked as if it cost almost as much as a sports car.

When Ransome returned to the limo he asked Peter, "Do you like it up here?"

"Fresh air's giving me a headache. Something is." He finished his cider. "How many have there been, Mr. Ransome? Your 'subjects,' I mean."

"Echo will be the eighth. If I'm able to persuade—"

"No *if*. You're wasting your time." Peter looked at the helpless young woman in the wheelchair as she was being power-lifted into a van.

"ALS is a devastating disease, Peter. How long before Echo's mother can no longer care for herself?"

"She's probably got two or three years."

"And after that?"

"No telling. She could live to be eighty. If you want to call it living."

"A terrible burden for Echo to have to bear. Let's be frank."

Peter stared at him, crushing his cup.

"Financially, neither of you will be able to handle the demands of Rosemay's illness. Not and have any sort of life for yourselves. But I can remove that burden."

Peter put the crushed paper cup in a trash can from twenty feet away, turning his back on Ransome.

"Did you fuck all of them?"

"You know I have no intention of answering a question like that, Peter. I will say this: there can never be any conflict, any—hidden tension between my subjects and myself that will adversely affect my work. The work is all that really matters."

Peter looked around at him as blandly as he could manage, but the sun was in his eyes and they smarted.

"Here's what matters to us. Echo and me are going to be married. We know there're problems. We've got it covered. We don't need your help. Was there anything else?"

"I'm happy that we've had this time to become acquainted. Would you mind one more stop before we head back to the city?"

"Take your time. I'm on the clock, pop said. So far it's easy money."

————

At the end of a winding uphill gravel drive bordered by stacked rock walls that obviously had been there for a century or longer, the limousine came to a pretty Cotswold-style stone cottage with slate roofs that overlooked a lake and a wildfowl sanctuary.

They parked on a cobblestone turnaround and got out. A caterer's van and a blue Land Rover stood near a separate garage.

"That's Connecticut a mile or so across the lake. In another month the view turns—well, as spectacular as a New England fall can be. In winter, of course, the lake is perfect for skating. Do you skate, Peter?"

"Street hockey," Peter said, taking a deep breath as he looked around. The sun was setting west of a small orchard behind the cottage; there was a good breeze across the hilltop. "So this is where you grew up?"

"No. The caretaker lived here. This cottage and about ten acres of woods and orchard are all that's left of the five hundred acres my family owned. All of it is now deeded public land. No one can build another house within three-quarters of a mile."

"Got it all to yourself? Well, this is definitely where I'd work if I were you. Plenty of peace and quiet."

"When I was much younger than you, just beginning to paint, the woods in all their form and color were like an appetite. Paraphrasing Wordsworth, a different kind of painter—poetry being the exotic pigment of language." He looked slowly around, eyes brimming with memory. "Almost six years since I was up here. Now I spend most of my time in Maine. But I recently had the cottage redecorated, and added an infinity pool on the lake side. Do you like it, Peter?"

"I'm impressed."

"Why don't you have a look around inside?"

"Looks like you've got company. Anyway, what's the point?"

"The point is, the cottage is yours, Peter. A wedding present for you and Echo."

Peter had hit a Trifecta two years ago at Aqueduct, which rewarded him with twenty-six hundred dollars. He'd been thrilled by the windfall. Now he was stunned. When his heartbeat was more or less under control he managed to say, "Wait a minute. You . . . can't do this."

"It's done, Peter. Echo is in the garden, I believe. Why don't you join her? I'll be along in a few minutes."

"Omigod, Peter, do you *believe* it?"

She was on the walk that separated garden and swimming pool, the breeze tugging her hair across her eyes. There were a lot of roses in the garden, he noticed. He felt, in spite of the joy he saw in Echo's face, a thorn in his heart. And it was a crushing effort for him just to breathe.

"Jesus, Echo—what've you done?"

"Peter—"

He walked through the garden toward her. Echo sat on a teak-wood bench, hands folded in her lap, her pleasure dimmed to a defensive smile because she knew what was coming. He could almost see her stubborn streak surfacing, like a shark's fin in bloodied waters. Peter made an effort to keep his tone reasonable.

"Wedding present? That's china and toasters and things. How do we rate something like this? Nobody in his right mind would give away—"

"I haven't done anything," Echo said. "And it isn't ours. Not yet."

"I'm usually in my right mind," John Ransome said pleasantly. Peter stopped, halfway between Echo and Ransome, who was in the doorway to the garden, the setting sun making of his face a study in sanguinity. He held a large thick envelope in one hand. "Escrow to the cottage and grounds will close in one year, when Mary Catherine has completed her obligation to me." He smiled. "I don't expect an invitation to the wedding. But I wish you both a lifetime of happiness. I'll leave this inside for you to read." Nobody said anything for a few moments. They heard a helicopter. Ransome glanced up. "My ride is here," he said. "Make yourselves at home for as long as you like, and enjoy the dinner I've had prepared for you. My driver will take you back to the city when you're ready to go."

The night turned unseasonably chilly for mid September, temperature dropping into the low fifties by nine o'clock. One of the caterers built a fire on the hearth in the garden room while Echo and Peter were served after-dinner brandies. They sipped and read the contract John Ransome had left for Echo to sign, Peter passing pages to her as he finished reading.

A caterer looked in on them to say, "We'll be leaving in a few minutes, when we've finished cleaning up the kitchen."

"Thank you," Echo said. Peter didn't look up or say a word until he'd read the last page of the contract. Wind rattled one of the stained-glass casement windows in the garden room. Peter poured more brandy for himself, half a snifter's worth, as if it were cherry Coke. He drank all of it, got up and paced while Echo read by firelight, pushing her reading glasses up the bridge of her nose with a forefinger when they slipped.

When she had put the twelve pages in order, Peter fell back into the upholstered chair opposite Echo. They looked at each other. The fire crackled and sparked.

"I can't go up there to see you? You can't come home, unless it's an emergency? He doesn't want to paint you, he wants to own you!"

They heard the caterer's van drive away. The limo chauffeur had enjoyed his meal in a small apartment above the garage.

"I understand his reasons," Echo said. "He doesn't want me to be distracted."

"Is that what I am? A distraction?"

"Peter, you don't have a creative mind, so I really don't expect you to get it." Echo frowned; she knew when she sounded conde-scending. "It's only for a year. I can *do* this. Then we're set." She looked around the garden room, a possessive light in her eyes. "My Lord, this place, I've never even dreamed of— I want mom to see it! Then, if she approves—"

"What about my approval?" Peter said with a glower, drinking again.

Echo got up and stretched. She shuddered. In spite of the fire it was a little chilly in the room. He watched the rise and fall of her breasts with blurred yearning.

"I want that too."

"And you want this house."

"Are you going to sulk the rest of the evening?"

"Who's sulking?"

She took the glass from his hand, sat down in his lap and cradled her head on a wide shoulder, closing her eyes.

"With real estate in the sky, best we could hope for is a small house in, you know, Yonkers or Port Chester. This is *Bedford*."

Peter cupped the back of her head with his hand.

"He's got you wanting, instead of thinking. He's damn good at it. And that's how he gets what *he* wants."

Echo slipped a hand over his heart. "So angry." She trembled. "I'm cold, Peter. Warm me up."

"Isn't what we've always planned good enough any more?"

"Oh, Peter. I love you and I'm going to marry you, and nothing will ever change that."

"Maybe we should get started home."

"But what if this *is* home, Peter? Our home." She slid off his lap, tugged nonchalantly at him with one hand. "C'mon. You haven't seen everything yet."

"What did I miss?" he said reluctantly.

"Bedroom. And there's a fireplace too."

She dealt soothingly with his resistance, his fears that he wasn't equal to the emotional cost that remained to be exacted for their prize. He wasn't steady on his feet. The brandy he had drunk was hitting him hard.

"Just think about it," Echo said, leading him. "How it could be. Imagine that a year has gone by—so fast—" Echo kissed him and opened the bedroom door. Inside there was a gas log fire on a corner hearth. "—and here we are." She framed his face lovingly with her hands. "What do you want to do now?" she said, looking solemnly into his eyes.

Peter swallowed the words he couldn't speak, glancing at the four-poster bed that dominated the room.

"I know what I want you to do," she said.

"Echo—"

She tugged him into the room and closed the door with her foot.

"It's all right," she said as he wavered. "Such a perfect place to spend our first night together. I want you to appreciate just how much I love you."

She left him and went to a corner of the room by the hearth where she undressed quickly, a quick-change artist down to the skin, slipping then beneath covers, to his fuming eyes a comely shadow.

"Peter?"

He touched his belt buckle; dropped his hands. He felt at the point of tears; ardor and longing were compromised by too much drink. His heartbeat was fueled by inchoate anger.

"Peter? What's wrong?"

He took a step toward her, stumbled, fell against a chair with a lyre back. Heavy, but he lifted it easily and slammed it against the wall. His unexpected rage had her cowering, his insulted hubris a raw wound she was too inexperienced to deal with. She hugged herself in shock and pain.

Peter opened the bedroom door.

"I'll wait in the fuckin' limo. You—you stay here if you want! Stay all night. Do whatever the hell you think you've got to do to make yourself happy, and just never mind what it'll do to us!"

SIX

The first day of fall, and a good day for riding in convertibles: un-clouded blue sky, temperatures on the East Coast in the sixties. The car John Ransome drove uptown and parked opposite Echo's build-ing was a Mercedes two-seater. Not a lot of room for luggage, but she'd packed frugally: the clothes she would need for wintering on a small island off the coast of Maine. And her paintbox.

He didn't get out of the car right away; cell phone call. Echo lin-gered an extra few moments at her bedroom windows hoping to see Peter's car. They'd talked briefly about one A.M., and he'd sounded okay, almost casual about her upcoming enforced absence from his life. Holidays included. He was trying a little too hard not to show a lack of faith in her. Neither of them mentioned John Ransome. As if he didn't exist, and she was leaving to study painting in Paris for a year.

Echo picked up her duffels from the bed and carried them out to the front hall. She left the door ajar and went into the front room where Julia was reading to Rosemay from the *National Enquirer*. Julia was a devotee of celebrity gossip.

Commenting on an actress who had been photographed trying to slip out of a California clinic after a makeover, Julia said, "Sure and she's at an age where she needs to give up plastic surgery and place her bets with a good taxidermist."

Rosemay smiled, her eyes on her daughter. Rosemay's lips trem-bled perceptibly; her skin was china-white, mimicking the tone of the bones within. Echo felt a strong pulse of fear; how frail her mother had become in just three months.

"Mom, I'm leaving my cell phone with you. It doesn't work on the island, John says. But there's a dish for Internet, no problem with e-mail."

"That's a blessing."

"Peter comin' to see you off?" Julia asked.

Echo glanced at her watch. "He wasn't sure. They were working a triple homicide last night."

"Do we have time for tea?" Rosemay asked, turning slowly away from her computer and looking up at Echo through her green eyeshade.

"John's here already, mom."

Then Echo, to her surprise and chagrin, just lost it, letting loose a flood of tears, sinking to her knees beside her mother, laying her head in Rosemay's lap as she had when she was a child. Rosemay stroked her with an unsteady hand, smiling.

Behind them John Ransome appeared in the hallway. Rosemay saw his reflection on a window pane. She turned her head slowly to acknowledge him. Julia, oblivious, was turning the pages of her gossip weekly.

The expression in Rosemay's eyes was more of a challenge than a welcome to Ransome. Her hands came together protectively over Echo. Then she prayerfully bowed her head.

Peter double-parked in the street and was running up the stairs of Echo's building when he met Julia coming down with her Save the Trees shopping bag.

"They're a half hour gone, Peter. I was just on my way to do the marketing."

Peter shook his head angrily. "I only got off a half hour ago! Why couldn't she wait for me, what was the big rush?"

"Would you mind sittin' with Rosemay while I'm out? Because it's goin' down hard for her, Peter."

He found Rosemay in the kitchen, a mug of cold tea between her hands. He put the kettle on again, fetched a mug for himself and sat down wearily with Rosemay. He took one of her hands in his.

"A year. A year until she's home again. Peter, I only let her do this because I was afraid—"

"It's okay. I'll be comin' around myself, two, three times a week, see how you are."

"—not afraid for myself," Rosemay said, finishing her thought. "Afraid of what my illness could do to you and Echo."

They looked at each other wordlessly until the kettle on the stove began whistling.

"Listen, we're gonna get through this," Peter said, grim around the mouth.

Rosemay's head drooped slowly, as if she hadn't the strength to hold it up any longer.

"He came, and took her away. Like the old days of lordship, you see. A privilege of those who ruled."

Echo didn't see much of Kincairn Island that night when they arrived. The seven-mile ferry trip left her so sick and sore from heaving she couldn't fully straighten up once they docked at the fishermen's quay. There were few lights in the clutter of a town occupying a small cove. A steady wind stung her ears on the short ride cross-island by Land Rover to the house facing two thousand miles of open ocean.

A sleeping pill knocked her out for eight hours.

At first light the cry of gulls and waves booming on the rocks a hundred feet below her bedroom windows woke her up. She had a hot shower in the recently updated bathroom. Some eyedrops got the red out. By then she thought she could handle a cup of black coffee. Outside her room she found a flight of stairs to the first-floor rear of the house. Kitchen noises below. John Ransome was an early riser; she heard him talking to someone.

The kitchen also had gone through a recent renovation. But the architect hadn't disturbed quaint and mostly charming old features: a hearth for baking in one corner, hand-hewn oak beams overhead.

"Good morning," John Ransome said. "Looks as if you got your color back."

"I think I owe you an apology," Echo mumbled.

"For getting sick on the ferry? Everybody does until they get used to it. The fumes from that old diesel banger are partly to blame. How about breakfast? Ciera just baked a batch of her cinnamon scones."

"Coffeecoffeecoffee," Echo pleaded.

Ciera was a woman in her sixties, olive-skinned, with tragic dark eyes. She brought the coffeepot to the table.

"Good morning," Echo said to her. "I'm Echo."

The woman cocked her head as if she hadn't heard correctly.

"It's just a—a nickname. I was baptized Mary Catherine."

"I like Mary Catherine," Ransome said. He was smiling. "So why don't we call you by your baptismal name while you're here."

"Okay," Echo said, with a glance at him. It wasn't a big thing; nicknames were childish anyway. But she felt a slight psychic disturbance. As if, in banishing "Echo," he had begun to invent the person whom he really wanted to paint, and to live within a relationship that he firmly controlled.

Foolish, Echo thought. *I know who I am*.

The rocky path to Kincairn light, where Ransome had his studio, took them three hundred yards through scruffy stunted hemlock and blueberry barrens, across lichen-gilded rock, thin earth and frost-heaves. At intervals the path wended close to the high-tide line. Too close for Echo's peace of mind, although she tried not to appear nervous. Kincairn Island, about eight and a half crooked miles by three miles wide with a high, forested spine, was only a granitic pebble confronting a mighty ocean, blue on this October morning beneath a lightly cobwebbed sky.

"The light is fantastic," she said to Ransome.

"That's why I'm here, in preference to Cascais or Corfu for instance. Clear winter mornings are the best. The town is on the lee side of the island facing Penobscot. There's a Catholic church, by the way, that the diocese will probably close soon, or Unitarian for those who prefer Religion Lite."

"Who else lives here?" Echo asked, blinking salt spume from her eyelashes. The tide was in, wind from the southeast.

"About a hundred forty permanent residents, average age fifty-five. The economy is lobsters. Period. At the turn of the century Kincairn was a lively summer community, but most of the old saltbox cottages are gone; the rest belong to locals."

"And you own the island?"

"The original deed was recorded in 1794. You doing okay, Mary Catherine?"

The ledge they were crossing was only about fifty feet above the breakers and a snaggle of rocks close to shore.

"I get a little nervous . . . this close."

"Don't you swim?"

"Only in pools. The ocean—I nearly drowned on a beach in New Jersey. I was five. The waves that morning were nothing, a couple of feet high. I had my back to the water, playing with my pail and shovel. All of a sudden there was a huge wave, out of nowhere, that caught everybody by surprise."

"Rogue wave. We get them too. My parents were sailing off the light, just beyond that nav buoy out there, when a big one capsized their boat. They never had a chance."

"Good Lord. When was this?"

"Twenty-eight years ago." The path took a turn uphill, and the lighthouse loomed in front of them. "I'm a strong swimmer. Very cold water doesn't seem to get to me as quickly as other people. When I was nineteen—and heavily under the influence of Lord Byron—I swam the Hellespont. So I've often wondered—" He paused and looked out to sea. "If I had been with my mother and father that day, could I have saved them?"

"You must miss them very much."

"No. I don't."

After a few moments he looked around at her, as if her gaze had made him uncomfortable.

"Is that a terrible thing to say?"

"I guess I— I don't understand it. Did you love your parents?"

"No. Is that unusual?"

"I don't think so. Were they abusive?"

"Physically? No. They just left me alone, most of the time. As if I didn't exist. I don't know if there's a name for that kind of pain."

His smile, a little dreary, suggested that they leave the topic alone. They walked on to the lighthouse, brilliantly white on the highest point of the headland. Ransome had remodeled it, to considerable outrage from purists, he'd said, installing a modern, airport-style beacon atop what was now his studio.

"I saw what it cost you," Ransome said, "to leave your mother—your life. I'd like to think that it wasn't only for the money."

"Least of all. I'm a painter. I came to learn from you."

He nodded, gratified, and touched her shoulder.

"Well. Shall we have a look at where we'll both be working, Mary Catherine?"

Peter didn't waste a lot of time taking on a load at the reception following his sister Siobhan's wedding to the software salesman from Valley Stream. Too much drinking gave him the mopes, followed by a tendency to take almost anything said to him the wrong way.

"What've you heard from Echo?" a first cousin named Fitz said to him.

Peter looked at Fitz and had another swallow of his Irish in lieu of making conversation. Fitz glanced at Peter's cousin Rob Flaherty, who said, "Six tickets to the Rangers tonight, Petey. Good seats."

Fitz said, "That's two for Rob and his girl, two for me and Colleen, and I was thinkin'—you remember Mary Mahan, don't you?"

Peter said ungraciously, "I don't feel like goin' to the Rangers, and you don't need to be fixin' me up, Fitz." His bow tie was hanging limp and there was fire on his forehead and cheekbones. A drop of sweat fell unnoticed from his chin into his glass. He raised the glass again.

Rob Flaherty said with a grin, "You remind me of a lovesick camel, Petey. What you're needin' is a mercy hump."

Peter grimaced hostilely. "What I need is another drink."

"Mary's had a thing for you, how long?"

"She's my mom's godchild, asshole."

Fitz let the belligerence slide. "Well, you know. It don't exactly count as a mortal sin."

"Leave it, Fitz."

"Sure. Okay. But that is exceptional pussy you're givin' your back to. I can testify."

Rob said impatiently, "Ah, let him sit here and get squashed. Echo must've tied a knot in his dick before she left town with her artist friend."

Peter was out of his chair with a cocked fist before Fitz could step between them. Rob had reach on Peter and jabbed him just hard enough in the mouth to send him backwards, falling against another of the tables ringing the dance floor, scarcely disturbing a mute couple like goggle-eyed blowfish, drunk on senescence. Pete's mom saw the altercation taking shape and left her partner on the dance floor. She took Peter gently by an elbow, smiled at the other boys, telling them with a motion of her elegantly coiffed head to move along. She dumped ice out of a glass onto a napkin.

"Dance with your old ma, Peter."

Somewhat shamefaced, he allowed himself to be led to the dance floor, holding ice knotted in the napkin to his lower lip.

"It's twice already this month I see you too much in drink."

"It's a wedding, ma." He put the napkin in a pocket of his tux jacket.

"I'm thinking it's time you get a grip on yourself," Kate said as they danced to a slow beat. "You don't hear from Echo?"

"Sure. Every day."

"Well, then? She's doing okay?"

"She says she is." Peter drew a couple of troubled breaths. "But it's e-mail. Not like actually—you know, hearin' her voice. People are all the time sayin' what they can't put into words, you just have to have an ear for it."

"So—maybe there's things she wants you to know, but can't talk about?"

"I don't know. We've never been apart more than a couple days since we met. Maybe Echo's found out—it wasn't such a great bargain after all." He had a tight grip on his mother's hand.

"Easy now. If you trust Echo, then you'll hold on. Any man can do that, Petey, for the woman he loves."

"I'll always love her," Peter said, his voice tight. He looked into Kate's eyes, a fine simmer of emotion in his own eyes. "But I don't trust a man nobody knows much about. He's got walls around him you wouldn't believe."

"A man who values his privacy. That kind of money, it's not surprising." Kate hesitated. "You been digging for something? Unofficially, I mean."

"Yeah."

"No beefs?"

"No beefs. The man's practically invisible where public records are concerned."

"Then let it alone."

"If I could see Echo, just for a little while. I'm half nuts all the time."

"God love you, Peter. Long as you have Sunday off, why don't the two of us go to visit Rosemay, take her for an outing? Been a while since I last saw her."

"I don't think I can, ma. I, uh—need to go up to Westchester, talk to somebody."

"Police business, is it?"

Peter shook his head.

"Her name's Van Lier. She posed for John Ransome once."

Seven

The Van Lier residence was a copy—an exact copy, according to a Web site devoted to descriptions of Westchester County's most spectacular homes—of a sixteenth-century English manor house. All Peter saw of the inside was a glimpse of slate floor and dark wainscoting through a partly opened front door.

He said to the houseman who had answered his ring, "I'd like to see Mrs. Van Lier."

The houseman was an elderly Negro with age spots on his caramel-colored face like the spots on a leopard.

"There's no *Mrs.* Van Lier at this residence."

Peter handed him his card.

"Anne Van Lier. I'm with the New York police department."

The houseman looked him over patiently, perhaps hoping if his appraisal took long enough Peter would simply vanish from their doorstep and he could go back to his nap.

"What is your business about, Detective? Miss Anne don't hardly care to see nobody."

"I'd like to ask her a few questions."

They played the waiting game until the houseman reluctantly took a Motorola TalkAbout from a pocket of the apron he wore over his Sunday suit and tried to raise her on a couple of different channels. He frowned.

"Reckon she's laid hers down and forgot about it," he said.

"Well, likely you'll find Miss Anne in the greenhouse this time of the day. But I don't expect she'll talk to you, police or no police."

"Where's the greenhouse?"

"Go 'round the back and walk toward the pond, you can't hardly miss it. When you see her, tell Miss Anne I did my best to raise her first, so she don't throw a fit my way."

Peter approached the greenhouse through a squall of copper beech leaves on a windy afternoon. The slant roofs of the long greenhouse reflected scudding clouds. Inside a woman he assumed was Anne Van Lier was visible through a mist from some overhead pipes. She wore gloves that covered half of her forearms and a gardening hat with a floppy brim that, along with the mist float above troughs of exotic plants, obscured most of her face. She was working at a potting bench in the diffused glimmer of sunlight.

"Miss Van Lier?"

She stiffened at the sound of an unfamiliar voice but didn't look around. She was slight-boned in dowdy tan coveralls.

"Yes? Who is it?" Her tone said that she didn't care to know. "You're trespassing."

"My name is Peter O'Neill. New York City police department."

Peter walked a few steps down a gravel path toward her. With a quick motion of her head she took him in and said, "Stay where you are. Police?"

"I'd like to show you some identification."

"What is this about?"

He held up his shield. "John Leland Ransome."

She dropped a three-pronged tool from her right hand onto the bench and leaned against it as if suddenly at a loss for breath. Her back was to Peter. A dry scuttle of leaves on the overhead glass cast a kaleidoscope of shadow in the greenhouse. He wiped mist from his forehead and continued toward her.

"You posed for Ransome."

"What of it? Who told you that?"

"He did."

She'd been rigidly still; now Anne Van Lier seemed pleasurably agitated.

"You *know* John? You've seen him?"

"Yes."

"When?"

"A couple of months ago." Peter had closed the distance between them. Anne darted another look his way, a gloved hand covering her profile as if she were a bashful child; but she no longer appeared to be concerned about him.

"How is John?" Her voice was suddenly rich with emotion. "Did he—mention me?"

"That he did," Peter said reassuringly, and dared to ask, "Are you still in love with Ransome?"

She shuddered, protecting herself with the glove as if he'd thrown a stone, seeming to cower.

"What did John say about me? *Please.*"

Knowing he'd touched a nerve, Peter said soothingly, "Told me the year he spent with you was one of the happiest of his life."

Still it bothered him when, after a few moments, she began softly to weep. He moved closer to Anne, put a hand on her arm.

"Don't," she pleaded. "Just go."

"How long since you seen him last, Anne?"

"Eighteen years," she said despondently.

"He also said—it was his understanding that you were very happy."

Anne Van Lier gasped. Then she began shaking with laughter, as if at the cruelest joke she'd ever heard. She turned suddenly to Peter, knocking his hand away from her, snatching off her gardening hat as she stared up at him.

The shock she gave him was like the electric jolt from a hard jab to the solar plexus.

Because her once-lovely face was a horror. She had been brutally, deeply slashed. Attempts had been made to correct the damage, but plastic surgeons could do only so much. Repairing damage to severed nerves was beyond any surgeon's skill. Her mouth drooped on one side. She had lost the sight of her left eye, filled now with a bloom of suffering.

"Who did this to you? Was it Ransome?"

Jarred by the blurted question, she backed away from Peter.

"What? *John?* How dare you think that!"

Gloved fingers prowled the deep disfiguring lines on her face.

"I never saw my attacker. It happened on a street in the East Village. He could have been a mugger. I didn't resist him, so why, *why?*"

"The police—".

"Never found him." She stared at Peter, and through him, at the past. "Or is that what you've come to tell me?"

"No. I don't know anything about the case. I'm sorry."

"Oh. Well." Her fate was dead weight on her mind. "So many years ago."

She put her gardening hat back on, adjusted the brim, gave Peter a vague look. She was in the past again.

"You can tell John—I won't always look like this. Just one more operation, they promised. I've had ten so far. Then I'll—finally be ready for John." She anticipated the question Peter wasn't about to ask. "To pose again!" A vaguely flirtatious smile came and went. "Otherwise I've kept myself up, you know. I do my exercises. Tell John—I bless him for his patience, but it won't be much longer."

In spite of the humidity and the drifting spray in the greenhouse Peter's throat was dry. His own attempt at a smile felt like hardening plaster on his face. He knew he had only glimpsed the depths of her psychosis. The decent thing to do now was to leave her with some assurance that her fantasy would be fulfilled.

"I'll tell him, Miss Van Lier. That's the news he's been waiting for."

The following Saturday night Peter was playing pool with his old man at the Knights of Columbus, and letting Corin win. The way he used to let him win at Horse when Corin was still spry enough for some basketball: *just a little off my game tonight*, Peter would always say, pretending annoyance. Corin bought the beers afterward and they relaxed in a booth at their favorite sports bar.

"Heard you was into the cold case files in the Ninth," Corin said, wiping some foam off his mustache. He looked at one of the big screens around the room. The Knicks were at the Heat, and tonight they couldn't throw one in the ocean.

"You hear everything, Pop," Pete said admiringly.

"In my borough. What's up?"

"Just something I got interested in, I had a little spare time." He explained about the Van Lier slashing.

"How many times was she cut?"

"Ten slashes, all on her face. He just kept cutting on her, even after she was down. That sound like all he wanted was a purse?"

"No. Leaves three possibilities. A psycho, hated women. Or an old boyfriend she gave the heave-ho to, his ego couldn't take it. But you said the vic didn't make him."

"No."

"Then somebody hired it done. Tell me again what your interest is in the vic?"

"Eighteen, nineteen years ago, she posed for John Ransome."

Corin rubbed a temple and managed to keep his disapproval muted. "Jeez Marie, Petey."

"My girl is up there in Maine with him, pop!"

"And you're lettin' your imagination— I see your mind workin'. But it's far-fetched, lad. Far-fetched."

"I suppose so," Peter mumbled in his beer.

"How many young women do you think have posed for him in his career?"

"Seven that anybody knows about. Not counting Echo."

Corin spread his hands.

"But nobody knows who they are, or where they are. Almost nobody, it's some kind of secret list. I'm tellin' you, pop, there is too much about him that don't add up."

"That's not cop sense, that's your emotions talkin'."

"Two damn months almost, I don't see her."

"That was his deal. His and hers, and there's good reasons why Echo did it."

"Didn't tell you this before. That woman friend of his, whore, whatever: she carries a knife and Echo saw her almost use it on a kid in the subway."

"Jeez Marie, where's this goin' to end with you?" Corin sat back in the booth and rapped the table once with the knuckles of his right fist. "Tell you where it ends. Right here, tonight. You know why? Too much money, Petey. That's what it's always about."

"Yeah, I know. I saw the commissioner's head up Ransome's ass."

"Remember that." He stared at Peter until exasperation softened into forgiveness. "Echo have any problems up there she's told you about?"

"No," Peter admitted. "Ransome's just doing a lot of sketches of her, and she has time to paint. I guess everything's okay."

"Give her credit for good sense, then. And do your part."

"Yeah, I know. Wait." His expression was pure naked longing

and remorse. "Two months. And you know what, Pop? It's like one of us died. Only I don't know which one, yet."

As she had done almost every day since arriving on Kincairn Echo took her breakfast in chilly isolation in a corner of the big kitchen, then walked to the lighthouse. Frequently she could only see a few feet along the path because of fog. But sometimes there was no fog; the air was sharp and windless as the rising sun cast upon the copper face of the sea a great peal of morning.

She'd learned early on that John Ransome was an insomniac who spent most of the deep night hours reading in his second-floor study or taking long walks by himself in the dark, with only a flashlight along island paths he'd been familiar with since he was a boy.

Sleep would come easier for him, Ransome assured her, as if apologizing, once he settled down to doing serious painting. But the unfinished portrait he'd begun in New York on a big rectangle of die board had remained untouched on his easel for nearly six weeks while he devoted himself to making postcard-size sketches of Echo, hundreds of them, or silently observing her own work take shape. Late at night he would leave Post-it notes of praise or criticism on her easel.

When they were together he was always cordial but preferred letting Echo carry the conversation. He seemed endlessly curious about her life. About her father, who had been a Jesuit until the age of fifty-one, when he met Rosemay, a Maryknoll nun. He never asked about Peter.

There were days when Echo didn't see him at all. She felt his absence from the island but had no idea of where he'd gone, or why. Not that it was any of her business. But it wasn't the working relationship she'd bargained for. His inability to resume painting made her uneasy. And it wasn't her nature to put up with being ignored, or feeling slighted, for long.

"Is it me?" she'd asked him at dinner the night before.

Her question, the mood of it, startled him.

"No. Of course not, Mary Catherine." He looked distressed, random gestures substituting for the words he couldn't find to reassure her. "Case of nerves, that's all. It always happens. I'm afraid I'll begin and—then I'll find myself drawing from a dry well." He paused to pour himself more wine. He'd been drinking more before and af-

ter dinner than was his custom; his aim was a little off and he grimaced. "Afraid that everything I do will be trite and awful."

Echo had sensed his vulnerability—all artists had it. But she
wasn't quite sure how to deal with his confession.

"You're a great painter."

Ransome shook his head, shying from the burden of her suggestion.

"If I ever believe that, then I will be finished." Echo got up,
pinched some salt from a silver bowl and spread it over the wine
stain on the fine linen tablecloth. She looked hesitantly at him.

"How can I help?"

He was looking at the salted stain. "Does that work?"

"Usually, if you do it right away."

"If human stains were so easy to remove," he said with sudden
vehemence.

"God's always listening," she said, then thought it was probably
too glib, patronizing and unsatisfactory. She felt God, but she also
felt there was little point in trying to explain Him to someone else.

After a silence the unexpected flood of his passion ebbed.

"I don't believe as easily as you, Mary Catherine," he said with a
tired smile that became tense. "But if we do have your God watching
us, then I think it likely that his revenge is to do nothing."

Ransome pushed his chair back and stood, looked at Echo, put
out a hand and lifted her head slightly with thumb and forefinger on
her chin. He said, studying her as if for the first time, "The light in
your eyes is the light from your heart."

"That's sweet," Echo said demurely, knowing what was coming
next. She'd been thinking about it, and how to handle it, for weeks.

He kissed her on the forehead, not the lips. As if bestowing a
blessing. That was sweet too. But the erotic content, enough to
cause her lips to part and put a charge in her heartbeat, took her by
surprise.

"I have to leave the island for a few days," he said then.

Ransome's studio had replaced the closetlike space that once had held
the Kincairn Light and reflecting mirror. It sat upon the spindle of the
lighthouse shaft like a flying saucer made mostly of glass that was
thirty feet in diameter. There was an elevator inside, another addition,

but Echo always used the circular stairs coming and going. Ciera was a very good cook and the daily climb helped Echo shed the pounds that had a tendency to creep aboard like hitchhikers on her hips.

She had decided, because the day was neither blustery enough to blow her off her Vespa nor bitterly cold, to pack up her paints and easel and go cross-island for an exercise in plein air painting on the cove and dock.

Approaching Kincairn village, Echo saw John Ransome at the end of the town dock unmooring a cabin cruiser that had been tied up alongside Wilkins' Marine and the mail/ferry boat slip. She stopped her puttering scooter in front of the cottage where a lone priest, elderly and in virtual exile in this most humble of parishes, lived with an equally old housekeeper. Echo had no reason for automatically keeping her distance from Ransome until she also saw Taja at the helm of the cruiser. Which wasn't much of a reason either. She hadn't seen the Woman in Black nor given her much thought since the night of the artist's show at Cy Mellichamp's. Ransome never mentioned her. Apparently she seldom visited the island.

Friend, business associate, confidante? Mistress, of course. But if she kept some distance between them now, perhaps that was in the past. Even if they were no longer lovers Echo assumed she might still be emotionally supportive, a rare welcome visitor to his isolato existence; his stiller doom, Echo thought with a certain poignancy, remembering a phrase of Charlotte Bronte's from Echo's favorite novel, *Jane Eyre*.

Watching Ransome jump into the bow of the cruiser, Echo felt frustrated for his sake. Obviously he was not going to be painting anytime soon. She also felt a dim sense of betrayal that made no sense to her. Yet it lingered like the spectral imprint of a kiss that had made her restless during a night of confused, otherworldly dreams; dreams of Ransome, dreams of being as naked in his studio as a snail on a thorn.

Echo watched Taja back the cruiser from the dock and turn it toward the mainland. Pour on the power. She decided to take a minute to go into the empty church. Was it time to ring the bell for a confession of her own? She couldn't make up her mind about that, and her heart was no help either.

Cy Mellichamp was using a phone at a gallery associate's desk in the second-floor office when Peter was brought in by a secretary. Mellichamp glanced at him with no hint of welcome. Two more associates, Mellichamp's morale-boosting term for salespeople, were working the phones and computers. In another large room behind the office paintings were being uncrated.

Mellichamp smiled grievously at something he was hearing and fidgeted until he had a chance to break in.

"Really, Allen, I think your affections are misplaced. There is neither accomplishment nor cachet in the accident of Roukema's success. And at six million—no, I don't want to have this conversation. *No.* The man should be doing frescoes in tombs. You wanted my opinion, which I freely give to you. Okay, please think it over and come to your senses."

Cy rang off and looked again at Peter, with the fixed smile of a man who wants you to understand he could be doing better things with his time.

"Why," he asked Peter, "do otherwise bright young people treat inherited fortunes the way rednecks treat junk cars?" He shrugged. "Mr. O'Neill! Delighted to see you again. How can I help you?"

"Have you heard anything from Mr. Ransome lately?"

"We had dinner two nights ago at the Four Seasons."

"Oh, he was in town?" Cy waited for a more sensible question. "His new paintings sell okay?"

"We did very, very well. And how is Echo?"

"I don't know. I'm not allowed to see her, I might be a distraction. I thought Ransome was supposed to be slaving away at his art up there in Maine."

Cy looked at his watch, looked at Peter again uncomprehendingly.

"I was hoping you could give me some information, Mr. Mellichamp."

"In regard to?"

"The other women Ransome has painted. I know where one of them lives. Anne Van Lier." The casual admission was calculated to provoke a reaction; Peter didn't miss the slight tightening of Cy Mellichamp's baby blue eyes. "Do you know how I can get in touch with the others?"

Cy said after a few moments, "Why should you want to?" with a muted suggestion in his gaze that Peter was up to no good.

"Do you know who and where those women are?"

An associate said to Cy, "Princess Steph on three."

Distracted, Cy looked over his shoulder. "Find out if she's on St. Barts. I'll get right back to her."

While Cy wasn't watching him Peter glanced at a computer on a nearby desk where nobody was working. But the person whose desk it was had carelessly left his user ID on the screen.

Cy looked around at Peter again. "I could not help you if I did know," he said curtly. "Their whereabouts are none of my business."

"Why is Ransome so secretive about those women?"

"That, of course, is John's prerogative. Now if you wouldn't mind—it *has* been one of those days—" He summoned a moment of the old charm. "I'm sorry."

"Thanks for taking the time to see me, Mr. Mellichamp."

"If there should be a next time, unless it happens to be official, you would do well to leave that gold shield in your pocket."

EIGHT

Peter got home from his watch at twenty past midnight. He fixed himself a sardine sandwich on sourdough with a smelly slice of gouda and some salsa dip he found in the fridge. He carried the sandwich and a bottle of Sam Adams up the creaky back stairs to the third floor he shared with his brother Casey. The rest of the house was quiet except for his father's distant whistling snore. But with no school for two days Case was still up with his iMac. Graphics were Casey's passion: his ambition was to design the cars of the future.

Peter changed into sweats. The third floor was drafty; a wind laced with the first fitful snow of the season was belting them.

There was an e-mail on the screen of his laptop that said only *missyoumissyoumissyou*. He smiled bleakly, took a couple of twenties from his wallet and walked through the bathroom he shared with Casey, pausing to kick a wadded towel off the floor in the direction of the hamper.

"Hi, Case."

Casey, mildly annoyed at the intrusion, didn't look around.

"That looks like the Batmobile," Peter said of the sleek racing machine Casey was refining with the help of some Mac software.

"It is the Batmobile."

Peter laid a twenty on the desk where Casey would see it out of the corner of his eye.

"What's that for?"

"For helping me out."

"Doing what?"

"See, I've got this user ID, but there's probably gonna be a log-on code too—"

"Hack a system?"

"I'm not stealing anything. Just want to look at some names, addresses."

"It's against the law."

Peter laid the second twenty on top of the first.

"Way I see it, it's kind of a gray area. There's something going on, maybe involves Echo, I need to know about. Right away."

Casey folded the twenties with his left hand and slid them under his mouse pad.

"If I get in any trouble," he said, "I'm givin' your ass up first."

After nearly a week of Ransome's absence, Echo was angry at him, fed up with being virtually alone on an island that every storm or squawl in the Atlantic seemed to make a pass at almost on a daily basis, and once again dealing with acute bouts of homesickness. Never mind that her bank account was automatically fattening twice a month, it seemed to be payment for emotional servitude, not the pleasant collaboration she'd anticipated. Only chatty e-mails from girl friends, from Rosemay and Stefan and even Kate O'Neill, plus Peter's maddeningly noncommittal daily communications (he was hopeless at putting feelings into words), provided balance and escape from depression through the long nights. They reminded her that the center of her world was a long way from Kincairn Island.

She had almost no one to talk to other than the village priest, who seemed hard-put to remember her name at each encounter, and Ransome's housekeeper. But Ciera's idea of a lively conversation was two sentences an hour. Much of the time, perhaps affected by the dismal weather that smote their rock or merely the oppression of passing time, Ciera's face looked as if Death had scrawled an "overdue" notice on it.

Echo had books and her music and DVDs of recent movies arrived regularly. She had no difficulty in passing the time when she wasn't working. But she hated the way she'd been painting lately, and missed the stealth insights from her employer and mentor. Day after day she labored at what she came to judge as stale, uninspired landscapes, taking a palette knife to them as soon as the light began to fade. She didn't know if it was the creeping ennui or a faltering sense of confidence in her talent.

November brought fewer hours of the crystal lambency she'd discovered on her first day there. Ransome's studio was equipped with full-spectrum artificial light, but she always preferred painting outdoors when it was calm enough, no tricky winds to snatch her easel and fling it out to sea.

The house of John Ransome, built to outlast centuries, was not a house in which she would ever feel at home, in spite of his library and collection of paintings that included some of his own, youthful work that would never be shown anywhere. These she studied with the avid eye of an archaeologist in a newly unearthed pyramid. The house was stone and stout enough but at night in a hard gale had its creepy, shadowy ways. Hurricane lamps had to be lit two or three times a week at about the same time her laptop lost satellite contact and the screen's void reflected her dwindled good cheer. Reading by lamplight hurt her eyes. Even with earplugs she couldn't fall asleep when the wind was keening a single drawn-out note or slapdash, grabbing at shutters, mewling under the eaves like a ghost in a well.

Nothing to do then but lie abed after her rosary and cry a little as her mood worsened. And hope John Ransome would return soon. His continuing absence a puzzle, an irritant; yet working sorcery on her heart. When she was able to fall asleep it was Ransome whom she dreamed about obsessively. While fitful and half awake she recalled every detail of a self portrait and the faces of his women. Had any of his subjects felt as she now did? Echo wondered about the depth of each relationship he'd had with his unknown beauties. One man, seven young women—had Ransome slept with any of them? Of course he had. But perhaps not every one.

His secret. Theirs. And what might other women to come, lying awake in this same room on a night as fierce as this one, adrift in loneliness and sensation of their own, imagine about Echo's involvement with John Leland Ransome?

Echo threw aside her down comforter and sat on the edge of the bed, nervous, heart-heavy. Except for hiking shoes she slept fully dressed, with a small flame in one of the tarnished lamp chimneys for company and a hammer on the floor for security, not knowing who in that island community might take a notion, no matter what the penalty. Ciera went home at night to be with her severely arthritic husband, and Echo was alone.

She rubbed down the lurid gooseflesh on her arms, feeling guilty in the sight of God for what raged in her mind. For sexual cravings like nettles in the blood. She put her hand on the Bible beside her bed but didn't open it. *Dear Lord, I'm only human*. She felt, honestly, that it was neither the lure of his flesh nor the power of his talent but the mystery of his torment that ineluctably drew her to Ransome.

A shutter she had tried to secure earlier was loose again to the incessant prying of the wind, admitting an almost continual flare of lightning centered in this storm. She picked up the hammer and a small eyebolt she'd found in a tool chest along with a coil of picture wire.

It was necessary to crank open one of the narrow lights of the mullioned window, getting a faceful of wind and spume in the process. As she reached for the shutter that had been flung open she saw by a run of lightning beneath boiling clouds a figure standing a little apart from the house on the boulders that formed a sea wall. A drenched white shirt ballooned in the wind around his torso. He faced the sea and the brawling waves that rose ponderously to foaming heights only a few feet below where he precariously stood. Waves that crashed down with what seemed enough force to swamp islands larger than Kincairn.

John Ransome had returned. Echo's lips parted to call to him, small-voiced in the tumult, her skin crawling coldly from fear, but the shutter slammed shut on her momentary view of the artist.

When she pushed it open again and leaned out slightly to see him, her eyelashes matting with salt spray, hair whipping around her face, Ransome had vanished.

Echo cranked the window shut and backed away, tingling in her hands, at the back of her neck. She took a few deep breaths, wiping at her eyes, then turned, grabbed a flashlight and went to the head of the stairs down the hall from her room, calling his name in the darkness, shining the beam of the light down the stairs, across the foyer to the front door, which was closed. There was no trace of water on the floor, as she would have expected if he'd come in out of the storm.

"ANSWER ME, JOHN! ARE YOU HERE?"

Silence, except for the wind.

She bolted down the stairs, grabbed a hooded slicker off the wall-mounted coat tree in the foyer and let herself out.

The three-cell flashlight could throw a brilliant beam for well over a hundred yards. She looked around with the light, shuddering in the cold, lashed in a gale that had to be more than fifty knots. She heard thunder rolling above the shriek of the wind. She was scared to the marrow. Because she knew she had to leave the relative shelter afforded by the house at her back and face the sea where she'd last seen him.

With her head low and an arm protecting her face, she made her way to the sea wall, the dash of waves terrifying in the beam of the flashlight. Her teeth were clenched so tight she was afraid of chipping them. Remembering the shock of being engulfed on what had been a calm day at the Jersey shore, pulled tumbling backwards and almost drowning in the sandy undertow.

But she kept going, mounted the seawall and crouched there, looking down at the monster waves. It was near to freezing. In spite of the hood and slicker she was already soaked and trembling so badly she was afraid of losing her grip on the flashlight as she crawled over boulders. Looking down into crevices where he might have fallen, to slowly drown at each long roll of a massive wave.

Thought she saw something—something alive like an animal caught in discarded plastic wrap. Then she realized it was a face she was looking at in the down-slant of the flashlight, and it wasn't plastic, it was Ransome's white shirt. He lay sprawled on his back a few feet below her, dazed but not unconscious. His eyelids squinched in the light cast on his face.

Echo got down from the boulder she was on, found some footing, got her hands under his arms and tugged.

One of his legs was awkwardly wedged between boulders. She couldn't tell if it was broken as she turned her efforts to pulling his foot free. Hurrying. Her strength ebbing fast. Battling him and the storm and sensing something behind her, still out to sea but coming her way with such size, unequaled in its dark momentum, that it would drown them both in one enormous downfall like a building toppling.

"MOVE!"

Echo had him free at last and pushed him frantically toward the top of the sea wall. She'd managed to lose her grip on the flashlight but it didn't matter, there was lightning around their heads and all of the deep weight of the sea coming straight at them. She couldn't make herself look back.

Whatever the condition of his leg, Ransome was able to hobble with her help. They staggered toward the house, whipsawed by the wind, until the rogue wave she'd anticipated burst over the seawall and sent them rolling helplessly a good fifty feet before its force was spent.

When she saw Ransome's face again beneath the flaring sky he was blue around the mouth but his eyes had opened. He tried to speak but his chattering teeth chopped off the words.

"WHAT?"

He managed to say what was on his mind between shudders and gasps.

"I'm n-n-not w-worth it, y-you know."

Hot showers, dry clothing. Soup and coffee when they met again in the kitchen. When she had Ransome seated on a stool she looked into his eyes for sign of a concussion, then examined the cut on his forehead, which was two inches long and deep enough so that it would probably scar. She pulled the edges of the cut together with butterfly bandages. He sipped his coffee with steady hands on the mug and regarded her with enough alertness so that she wasn't worried about that possible concussion.

"How did you learn to do this?" he asked, touching one of the bandages.

"I was a rough-and-tumble kid. My parents weren't always around, so I had to patch myself up."

He put an inquisitive fingertip on a small scar under her chin.

"Street hockey," she said. "And this one—"

Echo pulled her bulky fisherman's sweater high enough to reveal a larger scar on her lower rib cage.

"Stickball. I fell over a fire hydrant."

"Fortunately . . . nothing happened to your marvelous face."

"Thanks be to God." Echo repacked the first aid kit and ladled clam chowder into large bowls, straddled a stool next to him. "Ought to see my knees," she said, as an afterthought. She was ravenous, but before dipping the spoon into her chowder she said, "You need to eat."

"Maybe in a little while." He uncorked a bottle of brandy and poured an ounce into his coffee.

Echo bowed her head and prayed silently, crossed herself. She dug in. "And thanks be to God for saving our lives out there."

"I didn't see anyone else on those rocks. Only you."

Echo reached for a box of oyster crackers. "Do I make you uncomfortable?"

"How do you mean, Mary Catherine?"

"When I talk about God."

"I find that . . . endearing."

"But you don't believe in Him. Or do you?"

Ransome massaged a sore shoulder.

"I believe in two gods. The god who creates, and the god who destroys."

He leaned forward on the stool, folded his arms on the island counter, which was topped with butcher's block, rested his head on his arms. Eyes still open, looking at her as he smiled faintly.

"The last few days I've been keeping company with the god who destroys. You have a good appetite, Mary Catherine."

"Haven't been eating much. I don't like eating alone at night."

"I apologize for—being away for so long."

Echo glanced thoughtfully at him.

"Will you be all right now?"

He sat up, slipped off his stool, stood behind her and put a hand lightly on the back of her neck.

"I think the question is—after your experience tonight, will *you* be all right—with me?"

"John, were you trying to kill yourself?"

"I don't think so. But I don't remember what I was thinking out there. I'm also not sure how I happened to find myself sitting naked on the floor of the shower in my bathroom, scrubbed pink as a boiled lobster."

Echo put her spoon down. "Look, I cut off your clothes with scissors and sort of bullied you into the shower and loofah'd you to get your blood going. Nothing personal. Something I thought I'd better do, or else. I left clothes out for you then went upstairs and took a shower myself."

"You must have been as near freezing as I was. But you helped me first. You're a tough kid, all right."

"You were outside longer than me. How much longer I didn't know. But I knew hypothermia could kill you in a matter of minutes. You had all of the symptoms."

Echo resumed eating, changing hands with the spoon because she felt as if her right hand was about to cramp; it had been doing that for an hour.

She had cut off his clothes because she wanted him naked. Not out of prurience; she'd been scared and angry and needed to distance herself from his near-death folly and the hard reality of the impulse that had driven him outside in his shirt and bare feet to freeze or drown amid the rocks. Nude, barely conscious and semicoherent, the significance of *Ransome* was reduced in her mind and imagination; sitting on the floor of the shower and shuddering as the hot water drove into him, he was to her like an anonymous subject in a life class, to be viewed objectively without unreliable emotional investment. It gave her time to think about the situation. And decide. If it was only creative impotence there was still a chance she could be of use to him. Otherwise she might as well be aboard when the ferry left at sunrise.

"Mary Catherine?"

"Yes?"

"I've never loved a woman. Not one. Not ever. But I may be in love with you."

She thought that was too pat to take seriously. A compliment he felt he owed her. Not that she minded the mild pressure of his palm on her neck. It was soothing, and she had a headache.

Echo looked around at Ramsome. "You're bipolar, aren't you?"

He wasn't surprised by her diagnosis.

"That's the medical term. Probably all artists have a form of it. Soaring in the clouds or morbid in the depths, too blue and self-pitying to take a deep breath."

Echo let him hold her with his gaze. His fingers moved slowly along her jawline to her chin. She felt that, all right. Maybe it was going to become an issue. He had the knack of not blinking very often that could be mesmerizing in a certain context. She lifted her chin away from his hand.

"My father was manic-depressive," she said. "I learned to deal with it."

"I know that he didn't kill himself."

"Nope. Chain-smoking did the job for him."

"You were twelve?"

"Just twelve. He died on the same day that I got—my—when I—" She felt that she had blundered. *Way too personal, Echo; and shut up*.

"Became a woman. One of the most beautiful women I've been privileged to know. I feel that in a small way I may do your father honor by preserving that beauty for—who knows? Generations to come."

"Thank you," Echo said, still resonant from his touch, her brain on lull. Then she got what he was saying. She looked at Ransome again in astonishment and joy. He nodded.

"I feel it beginning to happen," he said. "I need to sleep for a few hours. Then I want to go back to that portrait of you I began in New York. I have several ideas." He smiled rather shyly. "About time, don't you think?"

NINE

After a few days of indecision, followed by an unwelcome intrusion that locked two seemingly unrelated incidents together in his mind, Cy Mellichamp made a phone call, then dropped around to the penthouse apartment John Ransome maintained at the Pierre Hotel. It was snowing in Manhattan. Thanksgiving had passed, and jingle bell season dominated Cy's social calendar. Business was brisk at the gallery.

The Woman in Black opened the door to Cy, admitting him to the large gloomy foyer. Where she left him standing, still wearing his alpaca overcoat, muffler, and cossack's hat. Cy swallowed his dislike and mistrust of Taja and pretended he wasn't being slighted by John Ransome's gypsy whore. And who knew what else she was to Ransome in what had the appearance, to Mellichamp, of a *folie à deux* relationship.

"We were hacked last night," he said. "Whoever it was now has the complete list of Ransome women. Including addresses, of course."

Taja cocked her head slightly, waiting, the low light of a nearby sconce repeated in her dark irises.

"The other, ah, visitation might not be germane, but I can't be sure. Peter O'Neill came to the gallery a few days ago. There was belligerence in his manner I didn't care for. Anyway, he claimed to know Anne Van Lier's whereabouts. Whether he'd visited her he didn't say. He wanted to know who the other women are. Pressing me for information. I said I couldn't help him. Then, last night as I've said, someone very resourceful somehow plucked that very information from our computer files." He gestured a little awkwardly, denying personal responsibility. There was no such thing as totally secure in a world managed by machines. "I thought John ought to know."

Taja's eyes were unwinking in her odd, scarily immobile face for a few moments longer. Then she abruptly quit the foyer, moving soundlessly on slippered feet, leaving the sharp scent of her perfume behind—perfume that didn't beguile, it mugged you. She disappeared down a hallway lined with a dozen hugely valuable portraits and drawings by Old Masters.

Mellichamp licked his lips and waited, hat in hand, feeling obscurely humiliated. He heard no sound other than the slight wheeze of his own breath within the apartment.

"I, I really must be going," he said to a bust of Hadrian and his own backup reflection in a framed mirror that once had flattered royalty in a Bavarian palace. But he waited another minute before opening one of the bronze doors and letting himself out into the elevator foyer.

Gypsy whore, he thought again, extracting some small satisfaction from this judgment. Fortunately he seldom had to deal with her. Just to lay eyes on the Woman in Black with her bilious temperament and air of closely held violence made him feel less secure in the world of social distinction that, beginning with John Ransome's money, he had established for himself: a magical, intoxicating, uniquely *New York* place where money was in the air always, like pixie dust further enchanting the blessed.

Money and prestige were both highly combustible, however. In circumstances such as a morbid scandal could arrange, disastrous events turned reputations to ash.

The elevator arrived.

Not that he was legally culpable, Cy assured himself while descending. It had become his mantra. On the snowy bright-eyed street he headed for his limo at the curb, taking full breaths of the heady winter air. Feeling psychologically exonerated as well, blamelessly distanced from the tragedy he now accepted must be played out for the innocent and guilty alike.

Peter O'Neill arrived in Las Vegas on an early flight and signed for his rental car in the cavernous baggage claim area of McCarran airport.

"Do you know how I can find a place called the King Rooster?"

The girl waiting on him hesitated, smiled ironically, looked up and said softly, "Now I wouldn't have thought you were the type."

"What's that mean?"

"First trip to Vegas?"

"Yeah."

She shrugged. "You didn't know that the King Rooster is, um, a brothel?"

"No kidding?"

"They're not legal in Las Vegas or Clark County." She looked thoughtfully at him. "If you don't mind my saying—you probably could do better for yourself. But it's none of my business, is it?" She had two impish dimples in her left cheek.

Next, Peter thought, she was going to tell him what time she got off from work. He smiled and showed his gold shield.

"I'm not on vacation."

"Ohhh. NYPD Blue, huh? I hated it when Jimmy Smits died." She turned around the book of maps the car company gave away and made notations on the top sheet with her pen. "When you leave the airport, take the Interstate south to exit thirty-three, that's Route 160 west? Blue Diamond Road. You want to go about forty miles past Blue Diamond to Nye County. When you get there you'll see this big mailbox on the left with a humungous, um, red cock—the crowing kind—on top of it. That's all, no sign or anything. Are you out here on a big case?"

"Too soon to tell," Peter said.

The whorehouse, when he got there, wasn't much to look at. The style right out of an old western movie: two square stories of cedar with a long deep balcony on three sides. In the yard that was dominated by a big cottonwood tree the kind of discards you might see at a flea market were scattered around. Old wagonwheels, an art-glass birdbath, a dusty carriage in the lean-to of a blacksmith's shed. There was a roofed wishing well beside the flagstone walk to the house. A chain-link fence that clashed with the rustic ambience surrounded the property. The gate was locked; he had to be buzzed in.

Inside it was cool and dim and New Orleans rococo, with paintings of reclining nudes that observed the civilities of *Fin de Siècle*. Nothing explicit to threaten a timid male; their pussies were as chaste as closed prayerbooks. A Hispanic maid showed Peter into a separate parlor. Drapes were drawn. The maid withdrew, closing pocket doors. Peter waited, turning the pages of an expensive-looking leather-bound book featuring porn etchings in a time of derbies and bustles. The maid returned with a silver tray, delicate china cups and coffee service.

She said, "You ask for Eileen. But she is indispose this morning. There is another girl she believe you will like, coming in just a—"

Peter flashed his shield and said, "Get Eileen in here. Now."

Ten more minutes passed. Peter opened the drapes and looked at sere mountains, the mid-range landscape pocked and rocky. A couple of wild burros were keeping each other company out there. He drank coffee. The doors opened again. He turned.

She was tall, a little taller than Peter in her high heels. She wore pale green silk lounging pajamas and a pale green harem mask that clung to the contours of her face but revealed only her eyes: they were dark, plummy, febrile in pockets of mascara. Tiny moons of sclera showed beneath the pupils.

"I'm Eileen."

"Peter O'Neill."

"Is there a problem?"

"What's with the mask, Eileen?"

"That's why you asked for me, isn't it? All part of the show you want."

"No. I didn't know about—. Mind taking the mask off?"

"But that's for upstairs," she protested, her tone demure. She began running her hands over her breasts, molding the almost sheer material of the draped pajamas around dark nipples. She cupped her breasts, making of them an offering.

"Listen, I didn't come here to fuck you. *Just take it off.* I have to see—what that bastard did to you, Eileen."

Her hands fell to her sides as she exhaled; the right hand twitched. Otherwise she didn't move.

"You *know*? After all these years I'm going to find out who did this to me?"

"I've got a good idea."

She made a sound deep in her throat of pain and sorrow, but didn't attempt to remove the mask. She shied when Peter impatiently put out a hand to her shrouded face.

"It's okay. You can trust me, Eileen." Inches from her body, feeling the heat of her, aware of a light perfume and arousing musk, he reached slowly behind her blond head and touched the little bow where her mask was tied as gently as if he were about to grasp a butterfly.

"I've only trusted one man in my life," she said dispiritedly. Then, unagressively but firmly, she snugged her groin against his, tamely laying her head on his shoulder so he could easily untie the mask.

He'd been expecting scars similar to those Anne Van Lier wore for life. But Eileen's were worse. Much of her face had burned, rendered almost to bone. The scar-gullies were slick and mahogany-colored, with glisters of purple. He could see a gleam of her back teeth on the left, most heavily-damaged side.

She flinched at his appalled examination, lowering her head, thrusting at him with her pelvis.

"All right," she said. "Now you're satisfied? Or are we just getting started?"

"I told you I didn't want to—"

"That's a lie. You're ready to explode in your pants." But she relented, stepping back from him, with a grin that was almost evil in the context of a ravaged face. "What's the matter? Your mommy told you to stay away from women like me? I'm clean. Cleaner than any little piece you're likely to pick up in a bar on Friday night. Huh? We're regulated in Nevada, in case you didn't know. The Board of Health dudes are here every week."

"I just want to talk. How did you get the face, Eileen?"

Her breath whistled painfully between her teeth.

"Fuck you mean? It's all in the case file."

"But I want to hear it from you."

Her face had little mobility, but her lovely eyes could sneer.

"Oh. Cops and their perversions. You all belong in a Dumpster. Give me back my mask."

She shied again when he tried to tie the mask on, then sighed, touching one of Peter's wrists, an exchange of intimacy.

"My face, my fortune," she said. "Would you believe how many men need a freakshow to get them up? God damn all of them. Present company excluded, I guess. You try to act tough but you've got a kind face." With the mask secure she felt bold enough to look him in the eye. "Your coffee must have cooled off by now," she said, suddenly the gracious hostess. "Would you like another cup?"

He nodded. She sat on the edge of a gilt and maroon-striped settee to pour coffee for them.

"So you want to hear it again. Why not?" She licked a sugar cube a couple of times before putting it into her cup. "I was alone in the lab, working on an experiment. Part of my Ph.D. requirement in O-chem." Peter sipped coffee from the cup she handed him as he remained standing close to the settee. Still encouraging the intimacy she seemed to crave. It wasn't just cop technique to get someone to spill their guts. He felt anguish for Eileen, as her eyes wandered in remembrance. "I, I was tired, you know, hadn't slept for thirty-six hours. Something like that. Didn't hear anyone come in. Didn't know he was there until he was breathing down my neck." She looked up. "Is this what turns you on?" she said, as if she'd lost track of who he was. Only another john to be entertained. She took Peter's free hand, raised it to her face, guided his ring finger beneath the mask and between her lips, touching it with the tip of her tongue. That was a new one on Peter, but the effect was disturbingly erotic.

"I started to turn on my stool," Eileen said, her voice close to a whisper as she looked up at Peter, lips caressing his captive finger, "and got a cup of H_2SO_4 in my face."

"But you didn't see—"

"All I saw was a gloved hand, an arm. Then—I was burning in hell." She bit down on his finger, at the base of the nail, laughed delightedly when he jerked his hand away.

"I can tell you who it was," Peter said angrily. "Because you're not the first woman who posed for John Ransome and got a face like yours."

He wasn't fully prepared for the ferocity with which she came at him, hissing like a feral cat, hands clawlike to ream out his eyes. He caught her wrists and forced her hands down.

"John Ransome? That's crazy! John loved me and I loved him!"

"Take it easy, Eileen! Did he come to see you after it happened?"

"No! So what? You think I wanted him to see me like this? Think I want anyone looking at me unless they're paying for it? Oh how I make them pay!"

"Eileen, I'm sorry." He had used as much force as he dared; she was strong in her fury and could inadvertently break a wrist struggling with him. When she was off balance Peter pushed her hard away from him. "I'm sorry, but I'm not wrong." He moved laterally away from her, not wanting some of his face to wind up under her fingernails. But she had choked on her outrage and was having trouble getting her breath.

"F-Fuck you! What are you cops . . . trying to *do* to John? Did one of the others say something against him? Tell me, I'll tear her fucking heart out!"

"Were you that much in love with him?"

"I'm not talking to you any more! Some things are still sacred to me!"

Eileen backed up a few steps and sat down heavily, her body in a bind as if she wore a straitjacket, harrowing sounds of grief in her throat.

"Whatever happened to that Ph.D.?" he asked calmly, though the skin of his forearms was prickling.

"That was someone else. Get out of here, before I have you thrown out. The sheriff and I are old friends. We paint each other's toenails. The chain-link fence? The goddamn desert? Forget about it. This is my *home*, no matter what you think. I *own* the Rooster. John paid for it."

Saying his name she quaked as if an old, unendurable torment was about to erupt. She leaned forward and, one arm moving jerkily like a string puppet's, she began smashing teacups on the tray with her fist. Shards flew. When she stopped her hand was bleeding profusely. She put it in her lap and let it bleed.

"On your way, bud," Eileen said to Peter. "Would you mind asking Lourdes to come in? I think it may be time for my meds."

While he was waiting at the Las Vegas airport for his flight to Houston, delayed an hour and a half because of a storm out of the Gulf of Mexico, Peter composed a long e-mail to Echo, concluding with:

> So far I can't prove anything. There's at least two more of them I need to see, so I'm on my way to Texas. But I want you to get off the island *now*. No good-byes, don't bother to pack. Go to my Uncle Charlie's in Brookline. 3074 East Mather. Wait for me there, I'll only be a couple of days.

By the time he boarded his flight to Houston, there still was no acknowledgment from Echo. It was six thirty-six P.M. in the east.

John Ransome was still working in his aerie studio and Echo was taking a shower when the Woman in Black walked into Echo's bedroom without a knock and had a look around. Art books heaped on the writing desk. The blouse and skirt and pearls she'd laid out for a leisurely dinner with Ransome. Her silver rosary, her Bible, her laptop. There was an e-mail message on the screen from Rosemay, apparently only half-read. Taja scrolled past it to another e-mail from a girl whom she knew had been Echo's college roommate. She skipped that one too and came to Peter O'Neill's most recent message.

This one Taja read carefully. Obviously Echo hadn't seen it, or she wouldn't have been humming so contentedly in the slow-running shower. Washing her hair.

Taja deleted the message. But of course if Peter didn't hear from Echo soon, he'd just send another, more urgent e-mail. The weather was decent for now, the wi-fi signal steady.

She figured she had four or five minutes, at least, to disable the laptop skillfully enough so that Echo wouldn't catch on that it had been sabotaged.

But Peter O'Neill was the real problem—just as she had suspected and conveyed to John Ransome in the beginning, when Ransome was considering Echo as his next subject.

No matter how he rated as a detective, he wasn't going to learn anything useful in Texas. Taja could be certain of that.

And she had a good idea of where he would show up during the next forty-eight hours.

TEN

"Eventually they would have reconstructed her face," the late Nan McLaren's aunt Elisa said to Peter. "The plastic surgery group is the best in Houston. World-renowned, in fact."

He was sitting with the aging socialite, who still retained a certain gleam that diet and exercise afforded septuagenerians, in the orangerie of a very large estate home in Sherwood Forest. There was a slow drip of rain from two big magnolias outside that were strung with tiny twinkling holiday lights. The woman had finished a brandy and soda and wanted another; she signaled the black houseboy tending bar. Peter declined another ginger ale.

"Of course Nan would never have looked the same. What was indefinable yet unique about her youthful beauty—gone forever. Her nose demolished; facial bones not just broken but shattered. Such unexpected cruelty, so deadly to the soul, destroyed her optimism, her innocent ecstasy and *joie de vivre*. If you're familiar with the portraits that John Ransome painted, you know the Nan I'm speaking of."

"I saw them on the Internet."

"I only wish the family owned one. I understand all of his work has increased tremendously in value in the past few years." Elisa sighed and shifted the weight of the bichon frisé dog on her lap. She stared at a recessed gas log fire in one angle of the octagonal garden room. "Who would have thought that a single, unexpected blow from a man's fist could do such terrible damage?"

"In New York they're called 'sly-rappers,'" Peter said. "Sometimes they use a brick, or wear brass knuckles. They come up behind their intended victims, usually on a crowded sidewalk, tap them on a shoulder. And when they turn, totally defenseless, to see who's there—"

"Is it always a woman?"

"In my experience. Young and beautiful, like Nan was."

"Dreadful."

"I understand Houston PD didn't get anywhere trying to find the perp."

"'Perp?' Yes, that's how they kept referring to him. But it happened so quickly; there were only a couple of witnesses, and he disappeared while Nan was bleeding there on the sidewalk." She reached up for the drink that the houseboy brought her. "Her skull was fractured when she fell. She didn't regain consciousness for more than a week." Elisa looked at Peter while the bichon frisé eagerly lapped at the brimming drink she held on one knee. "But you haven't explained why the New York police department is interested in Nan's case."

"I can't say at this time, I'm sorry. Could you tell me when Nan started doing heroin?"

"Between, I think, her third and fourth surgeries. What she really needed was therapy, but she stopped seeing her psychiatrist when she took up with a rather dubious young man. He, I'm sure, was the one who—what is the expression? Got her hooked."

"Calvin Cotrona. A few busts, petty stuff. Yeah, he was a user."

Elisa took her brandy and soda away from the white dog with the large ruff of head; he scolded her with a sharp bark. "Can't give him any more," she explained to Peter. "He becomes obstreperous, and pees on the Aubusson. Rather like my third husband, who couldn't hold his liquor either. Quiet down, Richelieu, or mommy will become deeply annoyed." She studied Peter again. "You seem to know so much about Nan's tragedy and how she died. What is it you hoped to learn from me, Detective?"

Peter rubbed tired eyes. "I wanted to know if Nan saw or heard from John Ransome once she'd finished posing for him."

"Not to my knowledge. After she returned to Houston she was quite blue and unsociable for many months. I suspected at the time she was infatuated with the man. But I never asked. Is it important?" Elisa raised her glass but didn't drink; her hand trembled. She looked startled. "But you can't mean—you can't be thinking—"

"Mrs. McLaren, I've talked to two other of Ransome's models in the past few weeks. Both were disfigured. A knife in one case, sulphuric acid in the other. In a day or two, with luck, I'll be talking to another of the Ransome women, Valerie Angelus. And I hope to God that nothing has happened to *her* face. Because that's stretching coincidence way too far. And already it's scaring the hell out of me."

In his room at a Motel Six near Houston's major airport, named for one of the U.S. presidents who had bloomed and thrived where a stink of corruption was part of the land, Peter called his uncle Charlie in Brookline, Massachusetts. Thirty-six hours had passed since he'd e-mailed her from Vegas, but Echo hadn't showed up there. He tried Rosemay in New York; she hadn't heard from Echo either. He sent another e-mail that didn't go through. In exasperation he tried leaving a message on her pager, but it was turned off.

Frustrated, he stretched out on the bed with a cold washcloth over his eyes. Traveling always gave him a queasy stomach and a headache. He chewed a Pepcid and tried to convince himself he had nothing to seriously worry about. The other Ransome women he knew of or had already interviewed had been attacked months after their commitments to the artist, and, presumably, their love affairs, were over.

Violent psychopaths had consistent profiles. Pete couldn't see the urbane Mr. Ransome as a part-time stalker and slasher, no matter what the full moon could do to potentially unstable psyches. But there was another breed, and not so rare according to his readings of case studies in psychopathology, who, insulated by wealth and position and perverse beyond human ken, would pay handsomely to have others gratify their sick, secret urges.

There was no label he could pin on John Ransome yet. But the notion that Ransome had spent several weeks already carefully and unhurriedly manipulating Echo, first to seduce and finally to destroy her, detonated the fast-food meal that had been sitting undigested in his stomach like a bomb. He went into the bathroom to throw up, afterward sat on the floor exhausting himself in a helpless rage. Feeling Echo on his skin, allure of a supple body, her creases and small breast buds and tempting, half-awake eyes. Thinking of her desire to make love to him at the cottage in Bedford and his stiff-necked refusal of her. A defining instance of false pride that might have sent his life careening off in a direction he'd never intended it to go.

He wanted Echo now, desperately. But while he was savagely getting himself off what he felt was a whore's welcome in silk, what he saw was the rancor in Eileen's dark eyes.

John Ransome didn't show up at the house until a quarter of ten, still wearing his work clothes that retained the pungency of the studio. Oil paints. To Echo the most intoxicating of odors. She caught a whiff of the oils before she saw him reflected in the glass of one of the bookcases in the first-floor library where she had passed the time with a sketchbook and her Prismacolor pencils, copying an early Ransome seascape. Painting the sea gave her a lot of trouble; it changed with the swiftness of a dream.

"I am so sorry, Mary Catherine." He had the look of a man wearied but satisfied after a fulfilling day.

"Don't worry, John. But I don't know about dinner."

"Ciera's used to my lateness. I need twenty minutes. You could select the wine. Chateau Petrus."

"John?"

Yes?"

"I was looking at your self-portrait again—"

"Oh, that. An exercise in monomania. But I was sick of staring at myself before I finished. I don't know how Courbet could have done *eight* self-studies. Needless to say he was better looking than I am. I ought to take that blunder down and shove it in the closet under the stairs."

"Don't you dare! John, really, it's magnificent."

"Well, then. If you like it so much, Mary Catherine, it's yours."

"What? No," she protested, laughing. "I only wanted to ask you about the girl—the one who's reflected in the mirror behind your chair? So mysterious. Who is she?"

He came into the library and stood beside her, rubbed a cheekbone where his skin, sensitive to paint-thinner, was inflamed.

"My cousin Brigid. She was the first Ransome girl."

"No, really?"

"Years before I began to dedicate myself to portraits, I did a nude study of Brigid. After we were both satisfied with the work, we burned it together. In fact, we toasted marshmallows over the fire."

Echo smiled in patient disbelief.

"If the painting was so good . . ."

"Oh, I think it was. But Brigid wasn't of age when she posed."

"And you were?"

"Nineteen." He shrugged and made a palms-up gesture. "She

was very mature for her years. But it would have been a scandal. Very hard on Brigid, although I didn't care what anyone would think."

"Did you ever paint her again?"

"No. She died not long after our little bonfire. Contracted septicemia at her boarding school in Davos." He took a step closer to the portrait as if to examine the mirror-cameo more closely. "She had been dead almost two years when I attempted this painting. I missed Brigid. I included her as a—I suppose your term would be guardian angel. I did feel her spirit around me at the time, her wonderful, free spirit. I was tortured. I suppose even angels can lose hope for those they try to protect."

"Tortured? Why?"

"I said that she died of septicemia. The results of a classmate's foolhardy try at aborting Brigid's four-month-old fetus. And, yes, the child was mine. Does that disgust you?"

After a couple of blinks Echo said, "Nothing human disgusts me."

"We made love after we ate our marshmallows, shedding little flakes of burnt canvas as we undressed each other. It was a warm summer night." His eyes had closed, not peacefully. "Warm night, star bright. I remember how sticky our lips were from the marshmallows. And how beautifully composed Brigid seemed to me, kneeling. On that first night of the one brief idyll of our lives."

"Did you know about the baby?"

"Brigid wrote to me. She sounded almost casual about her pregnancy. She said she would take care of it, I shouldn't worry." For an instant his eyes seemed to turn ashen from self-loathing. "Women have always given me the benefit of the doubt, it seems."

"You're not convincing either of us that you deserve to suffer. You were immature, that's all. Pardon me, but shit happens. There's still hope for all of us, on either side of heaven."

While she was looking for a bottle of the Chateau Petrus '82 that Ransome had suggested they have with their dinner, Echo heard Ciera talking to someone. She opened another door between the rock-walled wine storage pantry and the kitchen and saw Taja sitting at the counter with a mug of coffee in her hands. Echo smiled but Taja only stared before deliberately looking away.

"Oh, she comes and goes," Ransome said of Taja after Ciera had served their bisque and returned to the kitchen.

"Why doesn't she have dinner with us?" Echo said.

"It's late. I assume she's already eaten."

"Is she staying here tonight?"

"She prefers being aboard the boat if we're not in for a blow."

Echo sampled her soup. "She chose me for you—didn't she? But I don't think she likes me at all."

"It isn't what you're thinking."

"I don't know what I'm thinking. I get that way sometimes."

"I'll have her stay away from the house while you're—"

"No, please! Then I really am at fault somehow." Echo sat back in her chair, trailing a finger along the tablecloth crewelwork. "You've known her longer than all of the Ransome women. Did you ever paint Taja? Or did you toast marshmallows over those ashes too?"

"It would be like trying to paint a mask within a mask," Ransome said regretfully. "I can't paint such a depth of solitude. Sometimes . . . she's like a dark ghost to me, sealed in a world of night I'm at a loss to imagine. Taja has always known that I can't paint her." He had bowed his head, as if to conceal a play of emotion in his eyes. "She understands."

ELEVEN

The Knowles-Rembar Clinic, an upscale facility for the treatment of well-heeled patients with a variety of addictions or emotional traumas, was located in a Boston suburb not far from the campus of Wellesley College. Knowles-Rembar had its own campus of gracefully rolling lawns, brick-paved walks, great oaks and hollies and cedars and old rhododendrons that would be bountifully ablaze by late spring. In mid December they were crusted with ice and snow. At one-twenty in the afternoon the sun was barely there, a mild buzz of light in layered gray clouds that promised more snow.

The staff psychiatrist Peter had come to see was a height-disadvantaged man who greatly resembled Barney Rubble with thick glasses. His name was Mark Gosden. He liked to eat his lunch outdoors, weather permitting. Peter accommodated him. He drank vending machine coffee and shared one of the oatmeal cookies Gosden's mother had baked for him. Peter didn't ask if the psychiatrist still lived with her.

"This is a voluntary facility," Gosden explained. "Valerie's most recent stay was for five months. Although I felt it was contrary to her best interests, she left us three weeks ago."

"Who was paying her bills?"

"I only know that they went to an address in New York, and checks were remitted promptly."

"How many times has Valerie been here?"

"The last was her fourth visit."

Peter was aware of a young woman slipping up on them from behind. She gave Peter a glance, put a finger to her lips, then pointed at Gosden and smiled mischievously. Mittens attached to the cuffs of her parka dangled. She had a superb small face and jug-handle ears. In spite of the smile he saw in her eyes the blankness of a saintly disorder.

"And you don't think much of her chances of surviving on the outside," Peter said to the psychiatrist, who grimaced slightly.

"I couldn't discuss that with you, Detective."

"Do you know where I can find Valerie?"

Gosden brushed bread crumbs from his lap and drank some consommé from his lunchbox thermos. "Well, again. That's highly confidential without, of course, a court order."

When he put the thermos down the young woman, probably still a teenager, Peter thought, put her chilly hands over Gosden's eyes. He flinched, then forced a smile.

"I wonder who this could be? I know! Britney Spears."

The girl took her hands away. "Ta-da!" She pirouetted for them, mittens flopping, and looked speculatively at Peter.

"How about that?" Gosden said. "It's Sydney Nova!" He glanced at his watch and said with a show of dismay, "Sydney, wouldn't you know it, I'm running late. 'Fraid I don't have time for a song today." He closed his lunchbox and got up from the bench, glancing at Peter. "If you'll excuse me, I do have a seminar with our psych-tech trainees. I'm sorry I can't be of more help."

"Thanks for your time, doctor."

Sydney Nova leaned on the back of the bench as Gosden walked away, giving her hair a couple of tosses like a frisky colt.

"You don't have to run off, do you?" she said to Peter. "I heard what, I mean who, you and Goz were talking about."

"Did you know Valerie Angelus?"

Sydney held up two joined fingers, indicating the closeness of their relationship. "When she's around, I mean. Do you have a cigarette I can bum?"

"Don't smoke."

"Got a name?"

"Peter."

"Cop, huh? You're yummy for a cop, Pete."

"Thanks. I guess."

Sydney had a way of whistling softly as a space filler. She continued to look Peter over.

"Yeah, Val and I talk a lot when she's here. She trusts me. We tell each other our dirty little secrets. Did you know she was a famous model before she threw a wheel the first time?"

"Yeah. I knew that."

"Say, dude. Do you like your father?"

"Sure. I like him a lot."

Sydney whistled again a little mournfully. She cocked her head this way and that, as if she were watching rats racing around her mental attic.

"Magazine covers when she was sixteen. Totally demento at eighteen. I guess fame isn't all that it's cracked up to be." Sydney cocked her head again, making a wry mouth. "But nothing beats it for bringing in the money." Whistling. "I haven't had my fifteen minutes yet. But I will. Keep getting sidetracked." She looked around the Knowles-Rembar campus, tight-lipped.

"Tell me more about Valerie."

"More? Well, she got like resurrected by that artist guy, spent a whole year with him on some island. Talk about head cases."

"You mean John Ransome?"

"You got it, delicious dude."

"What did he do to Valerie?"

"Some secrets you don't tell! I'll eat rat poison first. Oh, I forgot. Been there, done that. Hey, do you like *The Sound of Music*? I know all the songs."

As if she'd been asked to audition, Sydney stood on the bench with her little hands spread wide and sang some of "Climb Ev'ry Mountain." Peter smiled admiringly. Sydney did have a good voice. She basked in his attention, muffed a lyric, and stopped singing. She looked down at him.

"I bet I know where Val is. Most of the time."

"You do?"

"Help me down, Pete?"

He put his hands on her small waist. She contrived to collapse into his arms. In spite of the bulky parka and her boots she seemed to weigh next to nothing. Her parted lips were an inch from his.

"Val has a thing for cemeteries," Sydney said. "She can spend the whole day—you know, like it's Disneyland for dead people."

Peter set her down on the brick walk. "Cemeteries. For instance?"

"Oh, like that big one in Watertown? Mount Auburn, I think it is. Okay, your turn."

"For what, Sydney?"

"Whatever Gosden said about *voluntary*, it's total bullshit. I'm in here like forever. But I could go with you. In the trunk of your car? Get me out of this place and I'll be real sweet to you."

"Sorry, Sydney."

She looked at him awhile longer, working on her lower lip with little fox teeth. Her gaze earthbound. She began to whistle plaintively.

"Thanks, Sydney. You were a big help."

She didn't look up as he walked away on the path.

"I put *my* father's eyes out," Peter heard her say. "So he couldn't find me in the dark any more."

Peter spent a half hour in Mount Auburn cemetery, driving slowly in his rental car between groupings of very old mausoleums resembling grim little villages, before he came to a station wagon parked alongside the drive, its tailgate down. A woman in a dark veil was lifting an armload of flowers from the back of the wagon. He couldn't tell much about her by winter light, but the veil was an unfortunate clue. He parked twenty feet away and got out. She glanced his way. He didn't approach her.

"Valerie? Valerie Angelus?"

"What is it? I still have sites to visit, and I'm late today."

There were more floral tributes in the station wagon. But even from where he was the flowers didn't appear to be fresh; some were obviously withered.

"My name is Peter O'Neill. Okay if I talk to you, Valerie?"

"Could we just skip that, I'm very busy."

"I could help you while we talk."

She had started uphill in a swirl of large snowflakes toward a mausoleum of rust-red marble with a Greek porch. She paused and shifted the brass container of wilted sprays of flowers that she held in both arms and looked around.

"Oh. That would be very nice of you. What is the nature of your business?"

"I'm a New York City detective." He walked past the station wagon. She was waiting for him. "Are you in the floral business, Valerie?"

"No." She turned again to the mausoleum on the knoll. Peter caught up to her as she was laying the memorial flowers at the vault's entrance.

"Is this your family—"

"No," she said, kneeling to position the brass pot just so in front of barred doors, fussing with the floral arrangement. She stepped back for a critical look at her work, then glanced at the inscription tablet above the doors. The letters and numerals were worn, nearly unreadable. "I don't know who they were," she said. "It's a very old mausoleum, as you can see. I suppose there aren't many descendants who remember, or care." She exhaled, the mourning veil fluttering. The veil did a decent job of disguising the fact that her facial features were distorted. If the veil had been any darker or more closely woven, probably she wouldn't be able to see where she was going. "But we'll all want to be remembered, won't we?"

"That's why you're doing this?"

"Yes." She turned and walked past him down the knoll, boots crunching through snow crust. "You're a detective? I thought you might be another insurance investigator." The cold wind teased her veil. "Well, come on. We're doing that one next." She pointed to another vault across the drive from where she'd left her station wagon.

Peter helped her pull a white fan-shaped latticework filled with hothouse flowers onto the tailgate. The weather was too brutal for her not to be wearing gloves, but with her arm extended an inch or so of wrist was exposed. The multiple scars there were reminders of more than one suicide attempt.

They carried the lattice to the next mausoleum, large enough to enclose a family tree of Biblical proportions. A squirrel nickered at them from a pediment.

"They wouldn't pay, you know," Valerie said. "They claimed that because of my . . . history, I disabled my own car. Now that's just silly. I don't know anything about cars. How the brakes are supposed to work."

"Your brakes failed?"

"We'll put it here," Valerie said, sweeping away leaves collected in a niche. When she was satisfied that the tribute was properly displayed she looked uneasily around. "Next we're going to that sort of ugly one with the little fountain. But we need to hurry. They make me leave, you know, they're very strict about that. I can't come back until seven-thirty in the morning. So I . . . must spend the night by myself. That's always the hard part, isn't it? Getting through the night."

She didn't talk much while they finished unloading the flowers and dressing up the neglected mausoleums. Once she appeared to be pleased with her afternoon's work and at peace with herself, Peter asked, as if all along they'd been having a conversation about Ransome, "Did John come to see you after your accident?"

Valerie paused to run a gloved hand over a damaged marble plinth.

"Seventeen sixty-two. Wasn't *that* a long time ago."

"Valerie—"

"I don't know why you're asking me questions," she said crossly. "I'm cold. I want to go to my car." She began walking away, then hesitated. "John is . . . all right, isn't he?"

"Was the last time I saw him. By the way, he sends his warmest regards."

"Ohhh. Well, there's good news. I mean that he's all right. And still painting?" Peter nodded. "He's a genius, you know."

"I'm not one to judge."

Her tone changed as they walked on. "Let's just skip it. Talking about John. I can't get Silkie to shut up about him. He was always so generous to me. I don't know why Silkie is afraid of him. John wouldn't hurt her."

"Who's Silkie?"

"My friend. I mean she comes around. Says she's my friend."

"What does she say about John?"

Valerie closed the tailgate of her wagon. She crossed her arms, shuddering in spite of the fur-lined greatcoat she wore.

"That John wanted to—destroy all of us. So that only his paintings live. How ridiculous. The one thing I was always sure of was John's love for me. And I loved him. I'm able to say it now. *Loved* him. I was going to have his baby."

Peter took a few unhappy moments to absorb that. "Did he know?"

"Uh-uh. I found out after I left the island. I tried and tried to get in touch with John, but—*they* wouldn't let me. So I—"

Valerie faced Peter. In the twilight he could see her staring at him through the mesh over her face. She drew a horizontal line with a finger where her abdomen would be beneath the greatcoat.

"—Did this. And then I—" She held up an arm, exposing another scarred wrist above the fur cuff of the coat sleeve. "—did this. I was so . . . angry." She let her arm drop. "I don't know why I'm telling you this. But Dr. Gosden says 'Don't keep the bad things hidden, Valerie.' And you *are* a friend of John's. I would never want him to think poorly of me, as my mother used to say. Skip my mother. I never talk about her. Would you let John know I'm okay now? The anger is gone. I'll be just fine, no matter what Goz thinks." She lifted her face to the darkened sky, snowflakes spangling her veil. She swallowed nervously. "Do you have the time, Peter?"

"Ten to five." He stamped his feet; his toes were freezing.

"Gates close at five in winter. We'd better go."

"Valerie, when did Silkie pose for Ransome?"

"Oh, that was over with a year ago. I've never been jealous of her."

"Has Silkie had any accidents you know of?"

"No," Valerie said, sounding mildly perplexed. "But I told you, obsessing about John John *John* all the time has her in a state. What I think, she's just having a hard time getting over him, so she makes up stuff about how he wants to hurt her. When it's the other way around. Goz would say she's having neurotic displacements. Anyway, she uses different names and doesn't have a home of her own. Picks up guys and stays with them a couple of nights, week at the most, then moves on."

"Then you don't know how I can get hold of her."

"Well—she left me a phone number. If I ever needed her, she said." Valerie turned the key in the ignition and the engine rumbled.

She looked back at Peter. "I can try to find the number for you, later." Her usually somber tone had lightened. "Why don't you come by, say, nine o'clock?"

"Where?"

"Four-fifteen West Churchill. I'm in six-A. I know I must seem old to you, Peter. Sometimes I feel—ancient. Like I'm living a whole lot of lives at the same time. Skip that. Truth is I'm only twenty-seven! You probably wouldn't have guessed. I'm not coming on to you or anything, but I could make dinner for us. Would you like that?"

"Very much. Thank you, Valerie."

"Call me Val, why don't you?" she said, and drove off.

Echo was rosy-fresh from a long hot soak, sitting at the foot of her bed with her hair bound up, frowning at the laptop computer she couldn't get to work. She looked up at a knock on her door; she was clearing her throat to speak when the door opened and John Ransome looked in.

"Oh, Mary Catherine. I'm sorry—"

"No, it's okay. I was about to get dressed. John, there's something wrong with my laptop, it isn't working at all."

He shook his head. "Wish I could help. I'm barely computer-literate; I've never even looked inside one of those things. There's a computer in my office you're welcome to use."

"Thank you."

He was closing the door when she said, "John?"

"Yes?"

It's going well for you, isn't it? Your painting. You know, you looked happy today—well, most of the time."

"Did I?" he smiled, almost reluctant to confirm this. "All I know is, the hours go by so quickly in good company. And the work—yes, I am pleased. I don't feel tired tonight. How about you? Posing doesn't seem to tire or bore you."

"Because I always have something interesting to think about or tell you. I try not to talk *too* much. I'm not tired either but I'm *star*ving."

"Then I'll see you downstairs." But he didn't leave or look away from her. He'd had his own bath. He wore corduroys and a thick sweater with a shawl collar. He had a glass of wine in his left hand. "Mary Catherine, I was thinking—but this really isn't the time, I'm intruding."

"What is it, John? You can come in, it's okay."

He smiled and opened the door wider. But he stayed in the doorway, drank some wine, looked fondly at her.

"I've been thinking of trying something new, for me. Painting you contrapposto, nothing else on the canvas, no background."

She nodded thoughtfully.

"Old dog, new tricks," he said with a shrug, still smiling.

"You'd want me to pose nude, then."

"Yes. Unless you have strong reservations. I'd understand. It's just an idea."

"But I think it's a good idea," she said quickly. "You know I'm in favor of whatever makes the work go more easily, inspires you. That's why I'm here."

"You don't have to decide impetuously," he cautioned. "There's plenty of time—"

Echo nodded again. "I'm fine with it, John. Believe me."

After a few moments she rose slowly from the bed, her lips lightly compressed, with a certain inwardness that distanced her from Ransome. She slowly and with pleasure let down her hair, arms held high, glistening by lamplight. She gave her abundant dark mane a full shakeout, then stared at the floor for a few seconds longer before turning away from him as she undid the towel.

Ransome's face was impassive as he stared at Echo, his creative eye absorbing motion, light, shadow, coloring, contour. In that part of his mind removed from her subtle eroticism there was a great cold weight of ocean, the tolling waves.

Having folded the towel and lain it on the counterpane, Echo was still, seeming not to breathe, a hand outstretched as if she were a nymph reaching toward her reflection on the surface of a pool.

When at last she faced him she was easeful in her beauty, strong in her trust of herself, her purpose, her value. Proud of what they were creating together.

"Will you excuse me now, John?" she said.

TWELVE

When Valerie finished dressing for her anticipated dinner date with Peter O'Neill, having selected a clingy rose cocktail dress she'd almost forgotten was in her closet and a veil from her drawerful of veils to match, she returned to the apartment kitchen to check on how dinner was coming along. They were having gingered braised pork with apple and winter squash kebobs. She'd marinated the pork and other ingredients for two hours. The skewers were ready to grill as soon as Peter arrived. There was a bowl of tossed salad in the refrigerator. For dessert—now what had she planned for dessert? Oh, yes. Lemon-mint frappes.

But as soon as she walked into the small neat kitchen Valerie saw that the glass dish on the counter was empty and clean. No pork cubes marinating in garlic, orange juice, allspice and olive oil. The unused metal skewers were to the left of the dish. The recipe book lay open.

She stared blankly at the untouched glass dish. Her scarred lips were pursed beneath her veil. She felt something let go in her mind and build momentum swiftly, like a roller-coaster on the downside of a bell curve with a 360-degree loop just ahead. She heard herself scream childishly on a distant day of fun and apprehension.

But I—

"There's nothing in the refrigerator either," she heard her mother say. "Just a carton of scummy old milk."

The roller-coaster plummeted into a pit of darkness. Valerie turned. Her mother was leaning in the kitchen doorway. The familiar sneer. Ida had compromised the ardor of numerous men (including Valerie's daddy), methodically breaking them on the wheel of her scorn. Now her once-lush body sagged; her potent beauty had turned, glistering like the scales of a dead fish.

"Hopeless. You're just hopeless, Valerie."

Valerie swallowed hurt feelings, knowing it was pointless to try to defend herself. She closed her eyes. The thunder of the roller-coaster had reached her heart. When she looked up again her mother was still hanging around with her wicked lip and punishing sarcasm. Giving it to little Val for possessing the beauty Ida had lost forever. Valerie could go deaf when she absolutely needed to. Now should she take a peek into the refrigerator? But she knew her mother had been right. Good intentions aside, Val accepted that she'd drifted off somewhere when she was supposed to be preparing a feast.

Okay, embarrassing. Skip all that.

Valerie returned to the dining nook where the table was set, the wine decanted, candles lit. Beautiful. At least she'd done that right. She was thirsty. She thought it would be okay if she had a glass of wine before John arrived.

No, wait—could he really be coming to see her after all this time? She glanced fearfully at her veiled reflection in the dark of the window behind the table. Then she picked up the carafe in both hands and managed to pour a glass nearly full without spilling a drop. As she drank the roller-coaster stopped its jolting spree, swooping from brains to heart and back again.

Her mother said, "You can't be in any more pageants if you're going to wet yourself onstage. We're all fed up, just fed up and disgusted with you, Val."

Valerie looked guiltily at the carpet between her feet where she was dripping urine. The roller-coaster gave a start-up lurch, pitching her sideways. And she wasn't securely locked in this time. She felt panic.

Her mother said, "For once have the guts to take what's coming to you."

Valerie said, "You're an evil bitch and I've always hated you."

Her mother said, "Fuck that. You hate yourself."

No use arguing with her when Ida was in high dander and fine acidic fettle. When she was death by a thousand tiny cuts.

Valerie felt the slow, heavy, ratcheting-up of the coaster toward the pinnacle that no longer seemed unobtainable to her. Her throat had swelled nearly closed from unshed tears.

She set her glass down and filled it again. Walked a little unsteadily with the motion of the roller-coaster inside her providing impetus through the furnished apartment that was bizarrely decorated with old putrid flowers she picked up for nickels and dimes at the wholesale market. She unlocked the door and walked out, leaving the door standing open.

When the elevator came she wasn't at all surprised to see John Ransome inside.

"Where're you going?" he asked her. "To the top this time?"

"Of course."

He pushed the button for the twentieth floor. Valerie sipped her wine and stared at him. He looked the same. The smile that went down like cream and had you purring in no time. But that was then.

"You did love me, didn't you?" she asked timidly, barely hearing herself for the racket the roller-coaster was making, all the screaming souls aboard.

"Don't make me deal with that now," he said, a hint of vexation souring his smile.

Valerie pushed the veil she'd been holding away from her face to the crown of her head, where it became tangled in her hair.

"You were always an insensitive selfish son of a bitch."

"Good for you, Valerie," her mother said. Coming from Ida it was like a benediction.

John Ransome acknowledged her human failings and with a ghostly nod forgave her.

"I believe this is your floor."

Valerie got off the elevator, kicked her shoes from her feet (no good for walking on walls) and proceeded to the steel door that led to the roof of her building. There she quailed.

"Isn't anyone coming with me?" she said.

When she turned around she saw that the elevator was empty, the doors silently closing.

Oh, well, Valerie thought. *Skip it.*

Peter arrived at four-fifteen West Churchill thirty seconds behind the fire department—a pumper truck and a paramedic bus—which had passed him on the way. Two police cars were just pulling up from different directions. Two couples with dogs on leashes were looking up at the roof of the high-rise building. The doorman apparently had just finished throwing up in shrubbery.

The night was windless. Snow fell straight down, thick as a theatre scrim. The dogs were agitated in the presence of death. The body lay on the walk about twenty feet outside the canopy at the building's entrance. Red dress contrasting with an icy, broken-off wing of an arbor vitae. Peter knew who it was, had to be, before he got out of the car.

He checked his watch automatically. Eight minutes to nine o'clock. His stomach churned from shock and rage as he walked across the street and stepped over a low snowbank, shield in hand.

One of the cops was taking a tarp and body bag out of the trunk of his unit. The other one was talking to the severely shaken doorman.

"She just missed me." He looked at the front of his coat as if afraid of finding traces of spattered gore. "Hit that tree first and bounced." He looked around, face white as snails. "Aw Jesus."

"Any idea who she is?"

"Well, the veil. She always wore veils, you know, she was in an accident, went head-first through the windshield. Valerie Angelus. Used to be a model. Big-time, I mean."

Peter kneeled beside Valerie's body, lying all wrong in its heaped brokenness. Twenty-one stories including the roof, a minimum of two hundred twenty feet. Her blood black on the recently cleared walk, absorbing snowflakes. The cop put his light on Valerie's head for a few seconds; fortunately not much of her face was showing. Peter told him to turn the flashlight off. He crossed himself and stood.

"Want I should check the roof?" the uniform asked him. "Before CSI gets here?"

Peter nodded. He was a couple of states outside of his jurisdiction and still on autopilot, trying to deal with another dead end of a long-running tragedy.

The paramedics had come over. Peter didn't want to explain his presence or interest in Valerie to the detectives who would be showing up along with CSI. Time to go.

When Peter turned away he saw a familiar face through the fall of snow. She was about a hundred feet away. She had stepped out of a Cadillac Escalade on the driver's side that was idling at an intersection. He knew her, but he couldn't place her.

She was tall, a black woman, well-dressed. Even at the distance an expression of horror was vivid on her face. He wondered how long she'd been there. He stared at her, but nothing clicked right away. Nevertheless he began walking briskly toward the woman.

His interest startled her. She slipped back into the Escalade.

Glimpsing her from a different angle, he remembered. She had been John Ransome's model before Echo. And as far as he could tell, although the snow obscured his vision, there was nothing wrong with her face.

Then she had to be Silkie, Valerie's friend. Who, Valerie had claimed, was afraid—very afraid—of John Ransome.

He began running toward the Escalade, shield in hand. But Silkie, after staring at him for a couple of moments through the windshield, looked back and threw the SUV into reverse. Hell-bent to get out of there. As if the shock of Valerie's death had been replaced by fear of being detained by cops and questioned.

Of all the Ransome women, she just might be the one who could help him nail John Ransome's ass. He ran. She couldn't drive backwards forever, even though she was pulling away from him.

At the next intersection she swerved around a car that had jammed on its brakes and slid to the curb. Obviously the Escalade was in four-wheel drive; no handling problems. She straightened out the SUV and gunned it. But Peter got a break as the headlights of the car she had nearly run up on the sidewalk shone on the license plate. Long enough for him to pick up most of the plate number. He stopped running and watched the SUV disappear down a divided street. He took out his ballpoint pen and jotted down the number of the Escalade. Missing a digit, probably, but that wouldn't be a problem.

He had Silkie. Unless, of course, the SUV was stolen.

The wind was high. Echo dreamed uneasily. She was naked in the cottage in Bedford. Going from room to room, desperate to talk to Peter. He wasn't there. None of the phones she tried were working. Forget about e-mail; her laptop was still down.

John Ransome was calling her. Angry that she'd left him before she finished posing. But she didn't want to be with him. His studio was filled with ugly birds. She'd never liked birds since a pigeon pecked her once while she was sitting on a bench at the Central Park Zoo. These were all black, like the Woman in Black. They screeched at her from their perches in the cage John had put her in. He painted her from outside the cage, using a long brush with a sable tip that stroked over her body like waves. She wasn't afraid of these waves, but she felt guilty because she liked it so much, trembling at the onset of that great rogue wave that was rolling erotically through her body. She tried to twist and turn away from the insidious strokes of his brush.

"No! What are you trying to do to us? You're not going anywhere!"

Echo sat straight up in bed, breathing hard at the crest of her sex dream. Then she sagged to one side, weak from vertigo. All but helpless. Her mouth and throat were dry. She lay quietly for a minute or so until her heartbeat subsided and strength crept back into her hands. Her reading lamp was on. She'd fallen asleep while reading *Villette*.

The wind outside moaned and that shutter was loose again. When she moved her body beneath the covers she could tell her sap had been running at the climax of her dream. She sighed and yawned, still spikey with nerves, turned to reach for a bottle of water on the night table and discovered John Ransome standing in the doorway of her bedroom.

He was unsteady on his feet, head nodding a little, eyes glass. Dead drunk, she thought, with a jolt of fear.

"John—"

His lips moved but he didn't make a sound.

"You can't be here," she said. "Please go away."

He leaned against the jamb momentarily, then walked as if he were wearing dungeon irons toward the bed.

"No, John," she said. Prepared to fight him off.

He gestured as if waving away her objection. "Couldn't stop her," he mumbled. "Hit me. Gone. This is—"

Three feet from Echo he lost what little control he had of his body, pitched forward onto the bed, held onto the comforter for a few moments, eyes rolling up meekly in his head; then he slowly crumpled to the floor.

Echo jumped off the bed to kneel beside him. She saw the swelling lump as large as her fist through the hair on the left side of his head. There was a little blood—in his hair, sprinkled on his shirt collar. Not a gusher. She didn't mind the sight of blood but she knew she might have lost it if he was critically injured. Didn't look so bad on the outside but the fragile brain had taken a beating. That was her biggest worry. There was no doctor on the island. Three men and a woman were certified as EMTs, but Echo didn't know who they were or where they lived.

She was able to lift him up onto the bed. Déjà vu all again, without the threat of hypothermia this time. He wasn't unconscious. She rolled him onto his stomach and turned his head aside so he would be less likely to aspirate his own vomit if he became nauseous. Ciera, she knew, sometimes got the vapors over a hot stove and kept ammonium carbonate on hand. Echo fled downstairs to the kitchen, found the smelling salts, twisted ice in a towel and ran back to her room.

She heard him snoring gently. It had to be a good sign. She carefully packed the swelling in ice.

What a crack on the head. Let him sleep or keep him awake? She wiped at tears that wouldn't stop. Go down the road and knock on doors until she found an EMT? But she was afraid to go out into freezing wind and dark, afraid of Taja.

Taja, she thought, as the shutter slammed and her backbone iced up to the roots of her hair. Couldn't stop her, John had said. *Gone.* But why had she done this to him, what were they fighting about?

Echo slid the hammer from under the bed. She went to the door. There was no lock. She put a straight-back chair against it, jammed under the doorknob, then climbed back onto her bed beside John Ransome.

She counted his pulse, wrote it down, noted the time. Every fifteen minutes. Keep doing it, all night. While watching over him. Until he woke up, or—but she refused to think about the alternative.

At dawn he stirred and opened his eyes. Looked at her without comprehension.

"Brigid?"

"I'm Ec—Mary Catherine, John."

"Oh." His eyes cleared a little. "Happened to me?"

"I think Taja hit you with something. No, don't touch that lump." She had him by the wrist.

"Wha? Never did that before." An expression close to terror crossed his face. "Where she?"

"I don't know, John."

"Bathroom."

"You're going to throw up?"

"No. Don't think so. Pee."

She helped him to her bathroom and waited outside in case he lost consciousness again and fell. She heard him splash water in his face, moaning softly. When he came out again he was steadier on his feet. He glanced at her.

"Did I call you Brigid?"

"Yes."

"Would've been like you, if she'd lived."

"Lie down again, John."

"Have to—"

"Do what?"

He shook his head, and regretted it. She guided him to her bed and he stretched out on his back, eyes closing.

"Stay with me?"

"I will, John." She touched her lips to his dry lips. Not exactly a kiss. And lay down beside him, staring at the first flush of sun through the window with the broken shutter. She felt anxious, a little demoralized, but immensely grateful that he seemed to be okay.

As for Taja, when he was ready they were going to have a serious talk. Because she understood now just how deeply afraid John Ransome was of the Woman in Black.

And his fear had become hers.

THIRTEEN

The SUV Silkie had been driving belonged to a thirty-two-year-old architect named Milgren who lived a few blocks from MIT in Cambridge. Peter called Milgren's firm and was told he was attending a friend's wedding in the Bahamas and would be away for a few days. Was there a Mrs. Milgren? No.

Eight inches of fresh snow had fallen overnight; the street in front of the building where Milgren lived was being plowed. Peter had a late breakfast, then returned. The address was a recently renovated older building with a gated drive on one side and tenant parking behind it. He left his rental car in the street behind a painter's van. The day was sharply blue, with a lot of ice-sparkle in the leafless trees. The snow had moved west.

The gate of the parking drive was opening for a Volvo wagon. He went in that way and around to the parking lot, found the Cadillac Escalade in its assigned space. Apartment 4-C.

Four apartments on the fourth floor, two at each end of a wide well-lit marble-floored hallway. There was a skylight above the central foyer: elevator on one side, staircase on the other.

The painter or painters had been working on the floor, but the scaffold that had been erected to make it easier to get at the fifteen-foot-high tray ceiling was unoccupied. On the scaffold a five-gallon can of paint was overturned. A pool of it like melted pistachio ice cream was spreading along the marble floor. The can still dripped.

Peter looked from the spilled paint to the door of 4-C, which stood open a couple of feet. There was a TV on inside, loudly showing a rerun of *Hollywood Squares*.

He walked to the door and looked in. An egg-crate set filled with decommissioned celebrities was on the LCD television screen at one end of a long living room. Peter edged the door half open. A man wearing a painter's cap occupied a recliner twenty feet from the TV. All Peter could see of him was the cap, and one hand gripping an arm of the chair as if he were about to be catapulted into space.

Peter rapped softly and spoke to him but the man didn't look around. There was a lull in the hilarity on TV as they went to commercials. Peter could hear the man breathing. Shallow, distressed breaths. Peter walked in and across the short hall, to the living room. Plantation-style shutters were closed. Only a couple of low-wattage bulbs glowed in widely separated wall sconces. All of the apartment was quite dark in contrast to the brilliant day outside.

"I'm looking for Silkie," he said to the man. "She's staying here, isn't she?"

No response. Peter paused a few feet to the left of the man in the leather recliner. His feet were up. His paint-stained coveralls had the look of impressionistic masterpieces. By TV light his jowly face looked sweaty. His chest rose and fell as he tried to drag more air into his lungs.

"You okay?"

The man rolled his eyes at Peter. The fingers of his left hand had left raw scratch marks all over the red leather armrest. His other hand was nearly buried in the pulpy mass above his belt. Peter smelled the blood.

"She—made me do it—talk to the lady—get her to—unlock the door. Help me. Can't move. Guts are—falling out. My daughter's coming home—for the holidays. Now I won't be here."

Peter's gun was in his hand before the man had said ten words. "Where are they?"

The painter had run out of time. He sagged a little as his life ebbed away. His eyes remained open. There was a burst of laughter from the TV.

"Jesus and Mary," Peter whispered, then raised his voice to a shout. "Silkie, you okay? It's the police!"

With his other hand he dug out his cell phone, dialed without looking, identified himself.

"Do you want police, fire, or medical emergency?"

"Cops. Paramedics. I've got a dying man here."

He began his sweep of the apartment while he was still on the phone.

"Please stay on the line, Detective," the dispatcher said. "Help is on the way."

"I may need both hands," Peter said, and dropped the cell phone back into his pocket.

He kicked open a door to what appeared to be the architect's study and workroom. Enough light coming in here to show him at a glance the room was empty.

"Silkie!"

The master bed- and sitting room was at the end of the hall. Double doors, one standing open. As he approached along one wall, Glock held high in both hands, he made out the shapes of furnishings because of a bathroom light shining beyond a four-poster bed draped with a gauzelike material.

Furniture was overturned in the sitting room. A fish tank had been shattered.

Peter edged around the foot of the Victorian bedstead and had a partial view of a seminude body face down on the tiles. Black girl. There was broken glass from a mirror and a ribbon of blood.

"Silkie, answer me, what happened here?"

He was almost to the bathroom door when Silkie stirred, looked around blank-eyed, then tried to push herself up with both hands as she flooded with terror. Blood dripped from a long cut that started below her right eye and ran almost to the jawline.

"Is she gone?" Silkie gasped.

Peter read the shock in her widening eyes but was a split second late turning as Taja came off the bed, where she'd been lying amid a pile of pillows he hadn't paid enough attention to, and slashed at him with her stiletto.

He turned his wrist just enough so veins weren't severed but lost his automatic. He backhanded her in the face with his other hand. Taja went down in a sprawl that she corrected almost instantly, cat-quick, and rushed him again with her knife ready to thrust, held close to her side. Her face looked as wooden as a ceremonial mask. She knew her business. He blocked an attempt she made to slash upward near his groin and across the femoral artery. She knew where he was most vulnerable and didn't try for the chest, where her blade could get hung up on the zipper of his leather jacket, or his throat, which was partially protected by a scarf. And she was in no hurry, she was between him and his only way out. Acrobatic in her moves, she feinted him in the direction she wanted him to go—which was back against the bed and into the mass of sheer drapery hanging there.

Peter heard Silkie scream but he was too busy to pay attention to her. The bed drapery clung to him like spiderweb as he struggled to free himself and avoid Taja. She slashed away methodically, the material beginning to glow red from his blood.

His gun fired. Deafening.

Taja flinched momentarily, then went into a crouch, turning away from Peter, finding Silkie. She was standing just inside the bathroom, Peter's Glock 9 in both hands.

"Bitch." She fired again, range about eight feet. Taja jerked to one side; hesitated a second, glanced at Peter, who had fought his way out of the drapery. Then she sprang to the bedroom doors and vanished.

Peter slipped a hand inside his jacket where his side stung from a long caress of Taja's stiletto. A lot of blood on the hand when he looked at it. Holy Jesus. He looked at Silkie, who hadn't budged from the threshold of the bathroom nor lowered his gun. When he moved toward her she gave him a deeply suspicious look. She was nude to well below her navel. Blood dripped from her chin. She had beautifully modeled features even Echo might have envied. Peter coughed, waited suspensefully, but no blood had come up. He saw that the cut on Silkie's face could've been a lot worse, the flesh laid open. Part of it was just a scratch down across the cheekbone. A little deeper in the soft flesh near her mouth.

He had to pry his gun from Silkie's hands. His own hands were so bloody he nearly dropped the Glock. He no longer considered going after Taja. Shock had him by the back of the neck. He heard sirens before a rising teakettle hiss in his ears shut out the sound. His face dripped perspiration, but his skin was turning cold. He had to lean against the jamb, his face a few inches from the tall girl's breasts. My God but they were something.

"What's your name?" he asked Silkie.

She had the hiccups. "Ma-MacKENzie."

"I'm Peter. Peter O'Neill. We're old friends, Silkie. We dated in New York. I came up here for a visit. Can you remember that?"

"Y-yes. P-P-PETEr O'Neill. From New York."

"And you don't know who attacked you. Never saw her before. Got that?"

He looked her in the eye, wondering if they had a chance in hell of selling it. She looked back at him with a slight twitch of her head.

"Why?"

"Because Valerie Angelus is dead and you came close and that, *that* he does not get away with, don't care how much money. I want John Ransome. Want his ass all to myself until I'm ready to hand him over."

"But Taja—"

"Taja's just been doing the devil's work. That's what I believe now. *Help me*, Silkie."

She touched a finger to her chin, wiped a drop of blood away. The wound had nearly stopped oozing.

"All right," she said, beginning to cry. "How bad am I?"

"Cut's not deep. You'll always be beautiful. Listen. Hear that? Medics. On the way up. Now I need to—" He began to slide to the floor at her feet. Shuddering. His tongue getting a little thick in his mouth. "Sit down before I uh pass out. Silkie, put something on. Now listen to me. Way you talk to cops is, keep it simple. Say it the same way every time. 'We met at a party. He's only a friend.' No details. It's details that trip you up if you're lying."

"You are—a friend," she said, kneeling, putting an arm around him for a few moments. Then she stood and reached for a robe hanging up behind the bathroom door.

"We'll get him, Silkie. You'll never be hurt again. Promise." Finding it hard to breathe now. He made himself smile at her. "We'll get the bastard."

———

When Echo woke up half the day was gone. So was John Ransome, from her bed.

She looked for him first in his own room. He'd been there, changed his clothes. She found Ciera in Ransome's study, straightening up after what appeared to have been a donnybrook. A lamp was broken. Dented metal shade; had Taja hit him with it? Ciera stared at Echo and shook her head worriedly.

"Do you know where John is?"

"No," Ciera said, talkative as ever.

The day had started clear but very cold; now thick clouds were moving in and the seas looked wild as Echo struggled to keep her balance on the long path to the lighthouse studio.

The shutters inside the studio were closed. Looking up as she drew closer, Echo couldn't tell if Ransome was up there.

She skipped the circular stairs and took the cabinet-size birdcage elevator that rose through a shaft of opaque glass to the studio seventy-five feet above ground level.

Inside some lights were on. John Ransome was leaning over his worktable, knotting twine on a wrapped canvas. Echo glanced at her portrait that remained unfinished on the large easel. How serene she looked. In contrast to the turmoil she was feeling now.

He'd heard the elevator. Knew she was there.

"John."

When he looked back he winced at the pain even that slow movement of his head caused him. The goose egg, what she could see of it, was a shocking violet color. She recognized raw anger in conjunction with his pain, although he didn't seem to be angry at her.

"Are you all right? Why didn't you wake me up?"

"You needed your sleep, Mary Catherine."

"What are you doing?" The teakettle on the hot plate had begun to wheeze. She took it off, looking at him, and prepared tea for both of them.

"Tying up some loose ends," he said. He cut twine with a pair of scissors. Then his hand lashed out as if the stifled anger had found a vent; a tall metal container of brushes was swept off his work table. She couldn't be sure he'd done it on purpose. His movements were haphazard, they mimicked drunkenness although she saw no evidence in the studio that he'd been drinking.

"John, why don't you—I've made tea—"

"No, I have to get this down to the dock, make sure it's on the late boat."

"All right. But there's time, and I could do that for you."

He backed into his stool, sat down uneasily. She put his tea within reach, then stooped to gather up the scattered brushes.

"Don't do that!" he said. "Don't pick up after me."

She straightened, a few brushes in hand, and looked at him, lower lip folded between her teeth.

"I'm afraid," he said tautly, "that I've reached the point of diminished returns. I won't be painting any more."

"We haven't finished!"

"And I want you to leave the island. Be on that boat too, Mary Catherine."

"Why? What have I— you can't mean that, John!"

He glanced at her with an intake hiss of breath that scared her. His eyes looked feverish. "Exactly that. Leave. For your safety."

"My—? What has Taja done? Why were you fighting with her last night? Why are you afraid of her?"

"Done? Why, she's spent the past few years hunting seven beautiful women after I had finished painting them."

"Hunting—?"

"Then she slashed, burned, maimed—*killed*, for all I know! And always she returned to me after the hunt, silently gloating. Now she's out there again, searching for Silkie MacKenzie."

"Dear *God*. Why?"

"Don't you understand? To make them pay, for all they've meant to me."

Echo had the odd feeling that she wasn't fully awake after all, that she just wanted to sink to the floor, curl up and go back to sleep. She couldn't look at his face another moment. She went hesitantly to a curved window, opened the shutters there and rested her cheek on insulated safety glass that could withstand hurricane winds. She stared at the brute pounding of the sea below, feeling the force of the waves in the shiver of glass, repeating the surge of her own heartbeats.

"How long have you known?"

"More than two years ago I became suspicious of what she might be doing during prolonged absences. I hired the Blackwelder Organization to investigate. What they came up with was horrifying, but still circumstantial."

"Did you really *want* proof?" Echo cried.

"Of course I did! And last night I finally received it, an e-mail from Australia. Where one of my former models—"

"Another victim?"

"Yes," Ransome said, his head down. "Her name is Aurora Leigh. She'd been in seclusion. But she was in adequate shape emotionally to identify Taja as her attacker from sketches I provided."

"Adequate shape emotionally," Echo repeated numbly. "Why did Taja hit you last night?"

"I confronted her with what I knew."

"Was she trying to kill you?"

"No. I don't think so. Just letting me know her business isn't finished yet."

"Oh Jesus and Mary! The police—did you call—"

"I called my lawyers this morning. They'll handle it. Taja will be stopped."

"But what if Taja's still here? You'll need—"

"Her boat's gone. She's not on the island."

"There are dozens of islands where she could be hiding!"

"I can take care of myself."

"Oh, *sure*," Echo said, bouncing the heel of her hand off her forehead as she began to pace.

"Don't be frightened. Just go back to New York. If there's even a remote possibility Taja will be free long enough to return to Kincairn—well then, Taja is, she's always been, my responsibility."

Echo paused, stared, caught her breath, alarmed by something ominous hanging around behind his words. "Why do you say that? You didn't make her what she is. That must have happened long before you met her, where—?"

"In Budapest."

"Doing what, mugging tourists?"

"When I first saw Taja," he said, his voice laboring, "she was drawing with chalk on the paving stones near the Karoly Kert gate. For what little money passersby were willing to throw her way." He raised his head slowly. "I don't know how old she was then; I don't know her age now. As I told you once, terrible things had been done

to her. She was barefoot, her hair wild, her dress shabby." He smiled
faintly at Echo. His lips were nearly bloodless. "Yes, I should have
walked on by. But I was astounded by her talent. She drew wonderful, suffering, religious faces. They burned with fevers, the hungers
of martyrdom. All of the faces washing away each time it rained, or
scuffed underfoot by the heedless. But every day she would draw
them again. Her knees, her elbows were scabbed. For hours she
barely paused to look up from her work. Yet she knew I was there.
And after a while it was my face she sought, my approval. Then, late
one afternoon when it didn't rain, I—I followed her. Sensing that she
was dangerous. But I've never wanted a tame affair. It's immolation I
always seem to be after."

His smile showed a slightly crooked eye tooth Echo was more or
less enamored with, a sly imperfection.

"Just how dangerous she was at that time became a matter of no
great importance. You see, we may all be dangerous, Mary Catherine,
depending on what is done to us."

"Oh, was the sex that good?" Echo said harshly, her face flaming.

"Sometimes sex isn't the necessary thing, depending on the nature of one's obsession."

Echo began, furiously, to sob. She turned again to the horizon,
the darkening sea.

After a couple of minutes he said, "Mary Catherine—"

"You know I'm not going! I won't let you give up painting because of what Taja did! You're not going to send me away, John, you
need me!"

"It's not in your power to get me to paint again."

"Oh, isn't it?" She wiped her leaky nose on the sleeve of her fisherman's sweater; hadn't done that in quite a few years. Then she
pulled off the sweater, gave her head a shake, swirling her abundant
hair. Ransome smiled cautiously when she looked at him again, began to stare him down. A look as old, as eternal as the sea below.

"We have to complete what we've started," Echo said reasonably. She moved closer to him, the better for him to see the fierce-
ness of eye, the high flame of her own obsession. She swept a hand
in the direction of her portrait on his easel. "Look, John. And look
again! I'm not just a face on a sidewalk. I *matter*!"

She seized and kissed him, knowing that the pain in his sore head made it not particularly enjoyable; but that wasn't her reason just then for doing it.

"Okay?" she said mildly and took a step back, clasping hands at her waist. The pupil. The teacher. Who was who awaited clarification, perhaps the tumult and desperation of an affair now investing the air they breathed with the power of a blood oath.

"Oh, Mary Catherine—" he said despairingly.

"I asked you, *is it okay*? Do we go on from here? Where? When? What do we do now, John?"

He sighed, nodded slightly. That hurt too. He put a hand lightly to the bump on his head.

"You're a tough, wonderful kid. Your heart . . . is just so different than mine. That's what makes you valuable to me, Mary Catherine." He gravely touched her shoulder, tapping it twice, dropped his hand. "And now you've been warned."

She liked the touch, ignored his warning. "Shall I pick up the rest of those brushes that were spilled?"

After a long silence Ransome said, "I've always found salvation in my work. As you must know. I wonder, could that be why your god sent you to me?"

"We'll find out," Echo said.

Peter heard one of the detectives ask, "How close did she come to his liver?"

A woman, probably the ER doc who had been stitching him up, replied, "Too close to measure."

The other detective on the team, who had the flattened Southie nasal tone, said, "Irish luck. Okay if we talk to him now?"

"He's awake. The Demerol has him groggy."

They came into Peter's cubicle. The older detective, probably nudging retirement, had a paunch and an archaic crook of nose like an old Roman in marble. The young one, but not that young—close to forty, Peter guessed—had red hair in cheerful disarray and hard-ass good looks the women probably went for like a guilty pleasure. Cynicism was a fixture in his face, like the indentations from long-ago acne.

He grinned at Peter. "How you doin', you lucky baastud?"

"Okay, I guess."

"Frank Tillery, Cambridge PD. This here is my Fathah Superior, Sal Tranca."

"Hiya."

"Hiya."

Peter wasn't taken in by their show of camaraderie. They didn't like what they had seen in the architect's apartment and they didn't like what they'd heard so far from Silkie. They didn't like him, either.

"Find the perp yet?" he said, taking the initiative.

Sal said, "Hasn't turned up. Found her blade in a can of paint. Seven inches, thin, what they call a stiletto in the old country."

Tillery leaned against a wall with folded arms and a lemon twist of a grin and said, "Pete, you mind tellin' us why you was trackin' a homicidal maniac in our town without so much as a courtesy call to us?"

"I'm not on the job. I was—looking for Silkie MacKenzie. Walked right into the play."

"What did you want with MacKenzie? I mean, if I'm not bein' too subtle here."

"Met her—in New York." His ribs were taped, and it was hard for him to breathe. "Like I told you at the scene, had some time off so I thought I'd look her up."

"Apparently she was already shacked up with one guy, owns the apartment," Sal said. "Airline ticket in your coat pocket tells us you flew in from Houston yesterday morning."

Peter said, "I got friends all over. On vacation, just hangin' out."

"Hell of a note," Tillery said. "Lookin' to chill, relax with some good-lookin' pussy, next thing you know you're in Mass General with eighty-four stitches."

"She was real good with that, what'a'ya call it, stiletto?"

Sal said, "So, Pete. Want to do your statement now, or later we come around after your nap? As a courtesy to a fellow shield. Who seems to be goddamn well connected where he comes from." Sal looked around as if for a place to spit.

"I'll come to you. How's Silkie?"

"Plastic surgeon looked at her already. There's gonna be some scarring they can clean up easy."

"She say she knew the perp?"

Tillery and Tranca exchanged jaundiced glances. "About as well as you did," Sal said.

"Well, you enjoy that dark meat," Tillery said. He was on the way out when something occurred to him to ask. He turned to Peter with his cynical grin.

"How long you had your gold, Pete?"

"Nine months."

"Hey, congrats. Sal here, he's got twenty-one years on the job. Me, I got eleven."

"Yeah?" Peter said, closing his eyes.

"What Frank is gettin' at," Sal said dourly, "we can smell a crock of shit when it's right under our noses."

FOURTEEN

Echo was putting her clothes back on inside the privacy cubicle in John Ransome's studio when she heard the door close, heard him locking her in.

"John!"

The door was thick tempered glass. He looked back at her tiredly as she emerged holding the sweater to her bare breasts and tugged at the door handle, not believing this.

"I'm sorry," he said. His voice was muffled by the thickness of the door. "When it's done—if it's done tonight—I'll be back for you."

"No! Let me out *now*!"

He shook his head slightly, then clattered down the iron staircase like a man in search of a nervous breakdown while Echo battled the door; still unwilling to believe that she was locked up until Ransome decided otherwise.

She glanced at the nude study he had begun, only a free-flowing sketch at this point but unmistakably Echo. She then demonstrated, at the top of her voice, how many obscene street oaths she'd picked up over the years.

But the harsh wind off a tumbled sea that caused her glass jail to shimmy on its high perch wailed louder than she could hope to.

Peter woke up with a start when Silkie MacKenzie put a hand on his shoulder. He felt sharp pain, then nausea before he could focus on her.

"Hello, Peter. It's Silkie."

He swallowed his distress, attempted a smile. The right side of her face was neatly bandaged. "How you doin'?"

"I'll be all right."

"What time is it, Silkie?"

She looked at her gold Piaget. "Twenty past three."

"Oh, Jesus." He licked dry lips. There was an IV hookup in the back of his left hand for fluids and antibiotics. But his mouth was parched. With his heavily-wrapped right hand—how many times had Taja cut him?—he motioned for Silkie to lean her face close to his. "Talk to you," he whispered. "Not here. They may have left a device. Couldn't watch both of them all the time."

"Isn't that illegal?"

"Wouldn't be admissable in a courtroom. But they don't trust either of us, so they could be fishing—for an angle to use during an interrogation. Walk me to the bathroom."

She got him out of bed and supported him, rolling the IV pole with her other hand. He had Silkie come inside the bathroom with him. All the fluids they'd dripped into Peter had him desperate to pee. Silkie continued to hold his elbow for support and looked at a wall.

"Today wasn't the first time Taja came after you," Peter said.

"No. Five months ago I was in Los Angeles. I had a commercial, the first work my agent was able to get for me after I'd finished my assignment with John. But John didn't want me working, you see. My face all over telly. That would have destroyed the—the allure, the fascination, the mystery he works so hard to create and maintain."

"So keep the paintings, destroy the model. I've seen Anne Van Lier and Eileen Wendkos."

Silkie looked around at him; she was close enough for Peter to feel the tremor that ran through her body.

"Then I had a glimpse of Taja, at a restaurant opposite Sunset Plaza. She pretended not to notice me. But I—all of my life I've had premonitions. There was suddenly the darkest, angriest cloud I'd ever seen pressing down on Sunset Boulevard. So I ran for my life. Later I hired private detectives. I was very curious to know what had happened to my—my predecessors? I found out, as you did. And once I talked to Valerie, I understood what my sixth sense had always told me about John. I believe he may be insane."

"We have to get out of here. Now. I have a rental car if Cambridge PD didn't impound it. But I'm not sure how much driving I can do." He bumped her as he turned in their small space; weakness followed pain, and it worried him. "Silkie, help me pull this IV out of my hand, then bring the rest of my clothes to me."

"Where are we going?"

"The nearest airport to Kincairn Island is in Bangor, Maine."

"I don't think the weather is good up there."

"Then the sooner we leave, the better. Get my wallet and watch from the lockbox. Use my credit card to reserve two seats on the next flight Boston to Bangor."

"I'm not so sure I want to do that. I mean, go back there. I'm afraid, Peter."

"Please, Silkie! You gotta help me. My girl's on that island with that sick son of a bitch Ransome!"

The owner and chief pilot of Lola's Flying Service at Bangor airport was going over accounts in her office when Peter and Silkie walked in at ten minutes to eight. Snow particles were flying outside the hangar, and they had felt sharp enough to etch glass.

Lola was a large cockeyed jalopy of a woman, salty as Lot's wife. Peter explained his needs.

"Chopper the two a ya's down to Kincairn in this freakin' weather? Not if I hope to achieve my average life expectancy."

Peter produced his shield. Lola greeted that show of authority with a lopsided smile.

"I'm Born Again, honeybunch; and I surely would hate to miss the Rapture. Otherwise what's Born Again good for?"

Silkie said, "Please listen to me. We must get there. Something very bad is going to happen on the island tonight. I have a premonition."

Lola, looking vastly amused, said, "Bullshit."

"Her premonitions are very accurate," Peter said.

Lola looked them over again. The bandages and bruises.

"I had my tea leaves read once. They said I shouldn't get involved with people who show up looking like the losers in a domestic disturbance competition." She picked up the remains of a ham on whole wheat from a takeout carton and polished it off in two bites.

Silkie patiently opened her tote and took out a very large roll of bills, half of which, she made it plain to Lola, were hundreds.

"On the other hand," Lola said, "you have any premonitions about what this little jaunt is gonna cost you?"

"Name your price," Silkie said calmly, and she began laying C-notes in the carton on top of a wilted lettuce leaf.

Echo's immediate needs were met by a chemical toilet; a small refrigerator that contained milk, a wedge of Jarlsburg, bottled water and white wine; and an electric heater that dispelled the worst of the cold after sundown. There was also a large sheepskin throw to wrap up in while she rocked herself in the only chair in John Ransome's studio. Physically she was fine. She had drunk the rest of an already-opened bottle of Cabernet Sauvignon, ordinarily enough wine to put her soundly to sleep. But the wind that was hitting forty knots according to the gauge outside and her circumstances kept her alert and sober, with an aching heart and a sense of impending tragedy.

If it's done tonight, Ransome had said forebodingly. What did he know about Taja, and what was he planning?

Every few minutes, between decades of the rosary that went everywhere with her, Echo jumped up restlessly to pace the inner circumference of the studio, then stop to peer through the shutters in the direction of the stone house three hundred yards away. She could make out only blurred lights through horizontal lashings of snow. She'd seen nothing of Ransome since his head had disappeared down the circular lighthouse stairs. She hadn't seen anyone except Ciera, who had left the house early, perhaps dismissed by Ransome. In twilight, on her way across the island, Ciera's path had brought her within two hundred feet of the Kincairn light. Echo had pounded on the glass, screamed at her, but Ciera never looked up.

She'd turned off the studio lights. After the wine she had a lingering headache, more from stress than from drinking. The light hurt her eyes and made it more difficult to see anything outside. At full dark she relied on the glow from the heater and the red warning strobe atop the studio for illumination.

When she tired of walking in circles and trying to see through the fulminating storm, she slumped in the rocking chair with her feet tucked under her. She was past sulking, brooding, and prayer. It was time to get tough with herself. *You have a little problem, Mary C.? Solve it.*

That was when the pulse of the strobe overhead gave her an idea of how to begin.

On the way down from Bangor in the three-passenger Eurocopter that had become surplus when Manuel Noriega fell out of favor with the CIA, Peter had plenty of time to reflect on the reasons why he'd never taken up flying as a hobby.

It was a strange night, clearing up in places on the coast but still with force eight winds. The sea from twelve hundred feet was visible to the horizon; beneath them it was a scumble of whitecaps going every which way. The sky overhead was tarnished silver in the light from the moon. Lola, dealing with the complexities of flying through the gauntlet of a gale that had the chopper rattling and vibrating, looked unperturbed, confident of her skills, although she was having a hard chew on the wad of grape-flavored gum in her right cheek.

"Should've calmed down some by now," she groused. "That's why we waited."

Silkie had become sick to her stomach two minutes after they lifted off at twelve-thirty in the morning, and she'd stayed sick and moaning all the way. Peter, whose father and uncles had always owned boats, was a competent sailor himself and used to rough weather, although this was something special even for him. The knife wounds Taja had inflicted were throbbing; at each jolt they took he hoped the stitches would hold.

Lola and Peter wore headphones. Silkie had taken hers off to get a better grip on her head with both hands.

"Where are we now?" Peter asked Lola.

"Over Blue Hill Bay. See that light down to our left?"

"Uh-huh," he said, his teeth clicking together.

"That's Bass Harbor head. Uh-oh. That's a Coast Guard cutter down there, steaming southwest. Somebody's got trouble. Take a dip in those waters tonight, you've got about twelve minutes. Okay, southwest is where we're heading now; right two-four-zero and closer to the deck. It's gonna get rougher, kids."

Peter checked the action of the old Colt Pocket Nine he'd borrowed from his uncle Charlie in Brookline before heading up to Maine. Then he looked at islands appearing below. A lot of islands, some just specks on the IR.

"How are you going to find—"

"I know Kincairn by its light. Problem is, I don't think anyone's tried to land a helicopter there. Not a level spot on the island. Wind shear around a rock pile like Kincairn, conditions are just about perfect for an SOL funeral."

"SOL?" Silkie said. She'd put her headphones back on.

"Shit outa luck," Lola said, and laughed uproariously.

From a window of his study John Ransome observed through binoculars the lights in the studio flashing. A familiar sequence. Morse Code distress signal. Mary Catherine's ingenuity made him smile. Of course he wouldn't have expected less of her. She was the last and the best of the Ransome women.

When he looked at the base of the Kincairn light, then down the road to the town, he saw one of the two Land Rovers he kept on the island coming up from the cove. When it stopped near the lighthouse, he wasn't surprised to see Taja get out.

Mary Catherine's face appeared behind salt-bleared glass, then vanished quickly, as if she'd seen Taja.

When the Woman in Black started toward the lighthouse, she walked slowly and stiffly, head lowered against the blasts of wind. She held her right side as if she'd been thrown around and injured while bringing the boat in through rough seas. Watching her, Ransome felt neither pity not regret. She was just a blight on his soul, as he had tried to explain to Mary Catherine. The time had come to remove it.

He put the binoculars down on his desk and unlocked a drawer. He kept an S & W police model .38 there. Hadn't fired the revolver in years but the bore was clean when he checked it.

Afterward a couple of phone calls and everything would be taken care of for him. As it always was. No messy publicity.

He felt deep empathy for Mary Catherine. It was unfortunate she had to be a part of the cleansing. But he would take care of her afterward, as he had all of the Ransome women. He had never used his genius as an excuse for poor behavior. When her own god failed her—as He would tonight—John Ransome would provide.

He was putting on his coat when he heard, above the wind, a helicopter fly low over the house.

"Peter, it's Taja!" Silkie yelled.

He saw the Woman in Black, looking up at the helicopter a hundred yards away. She had opened the door at the base of the lighthouse.

The studio lights were blinking again. Then Echo rushed to the windows, frantically signaling the helicopter.

"Who is that?" Silkie said.

"It's Echo," Peter said happily. Then, as Taja entered the lighthouse his momentary elation vanished. "Put us down!" he said to Lola.

"Not here! Maybe in the cove, on the dock!"

"How far's that?"

"Three miles south, I think."

"No! Can you drop me off here? Next to the lighthouse?"

"What are you doing?" Silkie asked anxiously.

"I can't maintain a hover more than three-four seconds," Lola advised him. "And not closer than ten feet off the ground!"

"Close enough!" Peter said. "Silkie! Go back with Lola. There's an APB out on Taja. Call the state cops, tell them she's on Kincairn!"

He opened the door on his side, looked at the rocks below in the undercarriage floodlight. The danger of it chilled him more than the wind in his face. If he landed wrong, a ten-foot jump onto frozen stony ground was going to feel like fifty.

In John Ransome's studio, Echo saw Taja get off the small elevator outside. They looked at each other for a few moments until Echo turned to the windows, seeing the helicopter fly away.

When she turned again Taja had unlocked the glass door and walked inside.

With the door open Echo's only thought was to get the hell out of there. But she couldn't get past Taja, who was quick and strong. An image of the PR boy in the subway repeated in Echo's mind as she was caught by one arm and pushed back. All the way to the easel that still held Ransome's beginning nude study of her. The portrait seemed to distract Taja as Echo struggled in her grip, swearing, swinging a wild left hand at the Woman in Black.

Taja's free hand came away from her side. The glove was sticky with blood. She groped behind her on the worktable. Her fingers closed on the handle of the knife that Ransome honed daily before trimming his brushes.

And Echo screamed.

Peter was halfway up the circular iron stairs, hobbling on a sprained ankle, when he heard the scream. Knew what it meant. But he was too slow and far from Echo to do her any good.

Taja struck once at Echo, slashing her across the heel of the hand Echo flung up to protect her face.

Then, instead of a lethal follow-up, Taja took the time to drive the knife into the canvas on the easel, ripping it in a gesture of fury.

Taja's body was momentarily at an angle to Echo, and vulnerable. Echo braced herself against the worktable and drove a knee high to the rib cage where Silkie had shot her in the Cambridge apartment.

Taja went down with a hoarse scream, dropped the knife. She was groping for it when Peter barreled into the studio and lunged at her.

"No, goddamn it, no!"

He grabbed her knife hand as she tried to come up off the floor at him. His free hand went to Taja's face, street-fighter style. He missed her eyes, tried to get a grip as she jerked her head aside.

Part of her flesh seemed to come loose in his hand. But it was only latex.

The face beneath her second skin was pocked with random, circular scars, as if from a dozen cigarette burns.

They were both hurt but Peter couldn't hold her. He knew the knife was coming. Then Echo got an armlock on Taja's neck and pulled her back; Peter stepped in with a short hook to Taja's jaw that dropped her instantly. He wrenched the knife away and pulled her back onto her feet. She wasn't unconscious but her eyes were crossing, no fight left in her.

"Let her go, Peter," John Ransome said behind them. "It's finished."

Peter shot a look behind him. "Not yet!" He looked again into Taja's eyes. "Tell me one thing! Was it Ransome? Did he send you after those women? Tell me!"

"Peter, she can't talk!" Echo said.

Taja still wasn't focusing. There was a trickle of blood at one corner of her mouth.

"Find a way to talk to me! I want to know!"

"Peter," John Ransome said, "please let her go." His tone weary. "It's up to me to deal with Taja. She's my—"

"Was it Ransome!" Peter screamed in Taja's face, as she blinked, stared at him.

She nodded. Her eyes closed. A second later Ransome shot her. Blood and bits of bone from the hole in her forehead splattered Peter's face. She hung in his grip as Echo screamed. Still holding Taja up, Peter turned to Ransome, speechless with rage.

Ransome lowered his .38, taking a deep breath. "My responsibility. Sorry. Now will you put her down?"

Peter let Taja fall and went for his own gun, brought it up in both hands inches from Ransome's face.

"Drop your piece! So help me God I'll cap you right here!"

"Peter, no—!"

Ransome took another breath, his gun hand moving slowly toward the worktable, his finger off the trigger. "It's all right." He sounded eerily calm. "I'm putting the gun down. Just don't let your emotions get the best of you. No accidents, Peter." The .38 was on the table. He lifted his hand slowly away from it, looked at Taja's body between them. Peter moved him at gunpoint back from the table.

"You're under arrest for murder! You have the right to remain silent. You have the right to be represented by an attorney. Anything you say can and will be used against you in a court of law. Do you understand what I've just said to you?"

Ransome nodded. "Peter, it was self-defense."

"Shut up, damn you! You don't get away with that!"

"You're out of your jurisdiction here. One more thing. I *own* this island."

"On your knees, hands behind your head."

"I think we need to talk when you're in a more rational—"

Peter took his finger off the trigger of the 9mm Colt and bounced it off the top of Ransome's head. Ransome staggered and dropped to one knee. He slowly raised his hands.

Peter glanced at Echo, who had pulled the sleeve of her sweater down over the hand that Taja had slashed. She'd made a fist to try to stop the bleeding. She shook from fear.

"Oh Peter, oh God! What are you going to do?"

"You own the island?" Peter said to Ransome. "Who cares? This is where we get off."

FIFTEEN

The boat Taja had used getting back and forth was a twenty-eight-foot Rockport-built island cruiser. Peter had John Ransome in the wheelhouse attached to a safety line with his hands lashed together in front of him. Echo was trying to hold the muzzle of the Colt 9mm on him while Peter battled wind gusts up to fifty knots and heavy seas once they left the shelter of Kincairn cove. In addition to the safety lines they all wore life vests. They were bucked all over the place. Peter found he could get only about eighteen knots from the Volvo diesel, and that it was nearly impossible to keep the wind on his stern unless he wanted to sail to Portugal. The wind chill was near zero. They were shipping a lot of water with a temperature of only a few degrees above freezing. The pounding went on without letup. Under reasonably good conditions it was thirty minutes to the mainland. Peter wasn't at all sure he had half an hour before hypothermia rendered him helpless.

John Ransome knew it. Watching Peter try to steer with one good hand, seeing Echo shaking with vomit on the front of her life vest, he said, "We won't make it. Breathe through your nose, Mary Catherine, or you'll freeze your lungs. You know I don't want you to die like this! Talk sense to Peter! Best of times it's like threading a needle through all the little islands. In a blow you can lose your boat on the rocks."

"Peter's s-sailed b-boats all his life!"

Ransome shook his head. "Not under these conditions."

A vicious gust heeled them to port; the bow was buried in a cornering wave. Water cascaded off the back of the overhead as the cruiser righted itself sluggishly.

"Peter!"

"We're okay!" he yelled, leaning on the helm.

Ransome smiled in sympathy with Echo's terror.

"We're not okay." He turned to Peter. "There is a way out of this dilemma, Peter! If you'd only give me a chance to make things right for all of us! But you must turn back *now*!"

"I told you, I don't have dilemmas! Echo, keep that gun on him!"

Ransome said, his eyes on the shivering girl, "I don't think Peter knows you as well as I've come to know you, Mary Catherine! You couldn't shoot me. No matter what you think I've done."

Echo, her eyes red from salt, raised the muzzle of the Colt unsteadily as she tried to keep from slipping off the bench opposite Ransome.

"Which one—are you tonight?" she said bitterly. "The g-god who creates, or the god who destroys?"

They were taking on water faster than the pump could empty the boat. The cruiser wallowed, nearly directionless.

"Remember the rogue wave, Mary Catherine? You saved me then. Am I worth saving now?"

"Don't listen to him!" Peter rubbed his eyes, trying to focus through the spume on the wheelhouse window. What he saw momentarily and some distance away were the running lights of a large yacht or even a cutter. Because of the cold he had only limited use of his left hand. His wrist had begun bleeding again during his fight with Taja at the lighthouse. With numbed fingers he was able to open a locker in front of him. "Echo, this guy has fucked up every life he ever touched!"

"There's no truth in that! It was Taja, no matter what she wanted you to believe. Her revenge on me. And I was the only one who ever cared about her! Mary Catherine, last night I tried to stop her from going after Silkie MacKenzie! You know what happened. But the story of Taja and myself is not easy to explain. You understand, though, don't you?"

"You should have seen what I've seen the last forty-eight hours, Echo! The faces of Ransome's women. Slashed, burned, broken! Two that I know of are dead! Nan McLaren O.D.'d, Ransome—you hear about that?"

"Yes. Poor Nan—but I—"

"Last night Valerie Angelus went off the roof of her building! You set her up for that, you son of a bitch!"

Ransome lifted his head.

"But you could've stopped her. A year, two years ago, it wouldn't have been too late for Valerie! You didn't want her. Don't talk about caring, it makes me sick!"

Ransome lunged off his bench toward Echo and easily took the automatic from her half-frozen hands. He turned toward Peter with it but lost his footing. Peter abandoned the helm, kicked the Colt into the stern of the boat, then pointed a Kilgore flare pistol, loaded with a twenty-thousand-candlepower parachute flare, at Ransome's head.

"I think the Coast Guard's out there to starboard," Peter said. "If you make a big enough bonfire they'll see it."

"The flare will only destroy my face," Ransome said calmly. "I suppose you would consider that to be justice." On his knees, Ransome held up his bound hands suppliantly. "We could have settled this among ourselves. Now it's too late." He looked at Echo. "*Is it too late, Mary Catherine?*"

She was sitting in a foot of water on the deck, exhausted, just trying to hold on as the boat rolled violently. She looked at him, and looked away. "Oh God, John."

Ransome struggled to his feet. "Take the helm, Peter, or she'll roll over! And the two of you may still have a life together."

"Just shut up, Ransome!"

He smiled. "You're both very young. Some day I hope you will learn that the greater part of wisdom is . . . forgiveness."

He unclipped his safety line from the vest as the bow of the cruiser rose, letting the motion carry him backwards to the transom railing. Where he threw himself overboard, vanishing into the pitch-dark water.

Echo cried out, a wail of despair, then sobbed. Peter felt nothing other than a cold indifference to the fate the artist had chosen. He raised the flare pistol and fired it, then returned to the helm as the flare shed its light upon the water, bringing nearby islands into jagged relief. A few moments later they heard a siren through the low scream of wind; a searchlight probed the darkness and found them. Peter closed his eyes in the glare and leaned against the helm with Echo laid against his back, arms around him.

Below decks of the Coast Guard cutter as it returned to the station on Mount Desert Island with the cruiser in tow, a change in pitch in the cutter's engine and a shudder that ran through the vessel caused Echo to wake up in a cocoon of blankets. She jerked violently.

"Easy," Peter said. He was sitting beside her on the sick bay rack, holding her hand.

"Where are we?"

"Coming in, I guess. You okay?"

She licked her chapped lips. "I think so. Peter, are we in trouble?"

"No. I mean, there's gonna be a hell of an inquiry. We'll take what comes and say what is. Want coffee?"

"No. Just want to sleep."

"Echo, I have to know—"

"Can't talk now," she protested wanly.

"Maybe we should. Get it out of the way, you know? Just say what is. Either way, I promise I can deal with it."

She blinked, looked at him with ghostly eyes, raised her other hand to gently touch his face.

"I posed for him—well, you saw the work Taja took a knife to."

"Yeah."

She took a deep breath. Peter was like stone.

"I didn't sleep with him, Peter."

After a few moments he shrugged. "Okay."

"But—no—I want to tell you all of it. Peter, I was getting ready to. Another couple of days, a week—it would've happened."

"Oh, Jesus."

"I just needed to be with him. But I didn't love him. It's something I—I don't think I'll ever understand about myself. I'm sorry."

Peter shook his head, perplexed, dismayed. She waited tensely for the anger. Instead he put his arms around her.

"You don't have to be sorry. I know what he was. And I know what I saw—in the eyes of those other women. I don't see it in your eyes." He kissed her. "He's gone. And that's all I care about."

A second kiss, and her glum face lost its anxiety, she began to lighten up.

"I do love you. Infinity."

"Infinity," he repeated solemnly. "Echo?"

"Yes?"

"I looked at a sublet before I left the city a few days ago. Fully furnished loft in Williamsburg. Probably still available. Fifteen hundred a month. We can move in by Christmas."

"Hey. Fifteen? We can swing that." She smiled slightly, teasing. "Live in sin for a little while, that what you mean?"

"Just live," he said.

On a Sunday in mid April, four weeks before their wedding, Peter and Echo, enjoying each other's company and one of life's minor enchantments, which was to laze with no purpose, heard the elevator in their building start up.

"Company?" Peter said. He was watching the Knicks on TV.

"Mom and Julia aren't coming until four," Echo said. She was doing tai chi exercises on a floor mat, barefoot, wearing only gym shorts. The weather in Brooklyn was unseasonably warm.

"Then it's nobody," Peter said. "But maybe you should pull on a top anyhow."

He walked across the painted floor of the loft they shared and watched the elevator rising toward them. In the dimness of the shaft he couldn't make out anyone in the cage.

When it stopped he pulled up the gate and looked inside. A wrapped package leaned against one side of the elevator. About three feet by five. Brown paper, tape, twine.

"Hey, Echo?"

She wriggled into a halter top and came over to look. Her lips parted in astonishment.

"It's a painting. Omigod!"

"What?"

"Get it! Open it!"

Peter lugged the wrapped painting, which seemed to be framed, to the table in their kitchen. Echo followed with scissors and cut the twine.

"But it can't be! There's no way—! No, be careful, let me do this!"

She removed the thick paper and laid the painting flat on the table.

"Oh no," Peter groaned. "I don't believe this. He's back."

The painting was John Ransome's self-portrait that had been hanging in the artist's library on Kincairn when Echo had last seen it.

Echo turned it over. On the back Ransome had inscribed, "Given to Mary Catherine Halloran as a remembrance of our friendship." It was signed and dated two days before Ransome's disappearance.

She turned suddenly, shoving Peter aside, and ran to the loft windows that overlooked a cobbled mews and afforded a partial view of the Brooklyn Bridge, with lower Manhattan beyond.

"Peterrrr!"

He caught up to her, looked over her shoulder and down at the mews. There were kids playing, a couple of women with strollers. And a man in a black topcoat getting into a cab on the corner where the fruit and vegetable stand was doing brisk business. The man had shoulder-length gray hair and wore dark glasses. That was all they could see of him.

Peter looked at Echo as the cab drove away. Touched her shoulder until she focused on him, on the here and now.

"He drowned, Echo."

She turned with a broad gesture in the direction of the portrait. "But—"

"Maybe his body never turned up, but the water—we nearly froze ourselves on the boat. His hands were tied. Telling you, no way he survived."

"John told me he swam the Hellespont once. The Dardanelles Strait. That's at least a couple miles across. And hypothermia—everybody's tolerance of cold is different. Sailors have survived for hours in seas that probably would kill you or me in fifteen minutes." She gestured again, excited. "Peter—who else?"

"Maybe it was somebody works for Cy Mellichamp. That slick son of a bitch. Just having his little joke. Listen, I don't want the damn picture in our house. I don't want to be reminded, Echo. How you got short-changed on your contract. None of it." He waited. "Do you?"

"Well—" She looked around their loft. Shrugged. "I guess it wouldn't be, uh, appropriate. But obviously—it was meant as a wedding gift." She smiled strangely. "All I did was say how much I admired his self-portrait. John told me all about it. There's quite a story goes with it, which would make the painting especially valuable to a collector. It's unique in the Ransome canon."

"Yeah? How valuable?"

"Hard to say. I know a Ransome was knocked down recently at Christie's for just under five million dollars."

Peter didn't say anything.

"The fact that his body hasn't been recovered complicated matters for his estate. But," Echo said judiciously, "as Stefan put it, 'it certainly has done no harm to the value of his art.'"

"You want a beer?"

"I would love a beer."

Echo remained by the windows looking out while Peter went to the refrigerator. While he was popping tops he said, "So—figure we just put the portrait away in a closet a couple years, then it could be worth a shitload?"

"Oh baby," Echo replied.

"Then, also in a couple years," Peter said, coming back to her and carefully fitting a can of Heineken into her hand, "when Ransome's estate gets settled, that cottage in Bedford, which looks like a pretty nice investment, will go on the market?"

"Might." Echo took a long drink of the beer and began laughing softly, ironically, to herself.

"All this could depend on, you know, he doesn't turn up." Peter looked out the window. "Again."

The last Ransome woman was silent. Wondering, lost in a private rapture.

Peter said, "You want to order in Chinese for Rosemay and Julia tonight? I've still got a few bucks left on my MasterCard."

"Yeah," Echo said, and leaned her head on his shoulder. "Chinese. Sounds good."